MOJANG
MINECRAFT™
THE SHIPWRECK

MOJANG
MINECRAFT™
THE SHIPWRECK

C. B. LEE

1 3 5 7 9 10 8 6 4 2

Del Rey
20 Vauxhall Bridge Road
London SW1V 2SA

Del Rey is part of the Penguin Random House group of companies whose
addresses can be found at global.penguinrandomhouse.com.

Penguin
Random House
UK

Minecraft: The Shipwreck is a work of fiction. Names, places and incidents either
are products of the author's imagination or are used fictitiously. Any resemblance to
actual events, places, locales, or persons, living or dead, is entirely coincidental.

First published in the United States by Penguin Random House in 2020
First published in the UK by Del Rey in 2020
This edition published by Del Rey in 2021

www.penguin.co.uk

A CIP catalogue record for this book is available from the British Library.

ISBN 9781529101416

Book design by Elizabeth A. D. Eno

Printed and bound in Great Britain by Clays Ltd, Eclograf S.p.A.

The authorised representative in the EEA is Penguin Random House Ireland,
Morrison Chambers, 32 Nassau Street, Dublin DO2 YH68.

Penguin Random House is committed to a sustainable future
for our business, our readers and our planet. This book is made
from Forest Stewardship Council® certified paper.

For anyone who's ever wanted to build something
new, in themselves and in the world

MOJANG

MINECRAFT™

THE SHIPWRECK

CHAPTER ONE

JAKE

"Here we are, home sweet home!"

Jake steps out of the truck and shuts the door. The tar on the street almost seems to sink under his feet as he stands. It's fresh, still soft from the hot sun, marked with crisp, clean, recently painted lines of white.

Dad whistles, the sun hitting the top of his balding head just right. He puts his hands on his hips, nodding to himself.

Jake follows Dad's proud gaze and looks across the street at the gray building situated on the corner of a tree-lined street. A wide swath of grass separates it from the sidewalk. The apartment complex seems just as drab and dull as the rest of the buildings on this street. It's a far cry from the beachside paradise Dad had been gloating about on their three-state road trip. The neighborhood has seen better days: rows and rows of mismatched apartment buildings and peeling paint, yellowing lawns and trash-lined streets. Jake sighs and shakes his head as Dad turns back to flash him a grin.

"This is the place you're tearing down?" Jake eyes the ancient apartment complex.

"Yup. Already did one of the buildings in this complex, the one we're moving into. Oh, you're gonna love it. Everything is brand new and perfect, eh?"

Three towers of apartments are clustered behind the first building. One is clearly new; gleaming white, shining glass windows reflecting the pale blue sky, almost as if the tower is trying to be a part of the sky itself. The other two are built from the same dull gray concrete as the first, occasionally spotted with bricks flecked with color for a bit of artistic flair. Jake can't help but smile, thinking about lines of ore in Minecraft. He imagines destroying the entire complex, one row of blocks at a time, gathering the jewels, coal, and different types of rock from the building's sides. He sees two, maybe three different building materials. They look a lot more sturdy than whatever the new building is made out of, although the glass is pretty neat. It'd be interesting, mining a tower like this, but simple enough, just craft a few ladders and get to the top and make your way down —

Jake's in the middle of his daydream when he realizes Dad's still waxing poetic about the project.

"It's going to be a long haul — my company is doing this complex and two more down the street for a fancy new design firm. There's a lot of work in Los Angeles. Aren't you excited? All this great California sunshine, and we can go to the beach whenever we want!"

"Sure, Dad." The sun feels like any other sun Jake's ever felt; then again, it is the same sun. He would hope so.

Dad gives him a small smile full of promise, one that Jake

wants to believe means they'll actually go to the beach together. Every new state, every new city in the past three years has been full of the same promises: *We'll go to the country fair. I'll take you to a ball game. We're going to go camping.* But Dad said it was because he was still building up his company's reputation, and now everything is going to change, apparently.

Jake will believe it when he sees it. Chicago, San Antonio, Seattle—each of these places Dad said would be home, and each of them just turned out to be a stopping point.

"Isn't it beautiful? I tell you, the architect who dreamed up the renovation, she's a genius." Dad grabs a box from the back of the truck and sighs happily, still admiring the view.

Jake makes a noncommittal grunt in reply. It's just another picture-perfect condo, filled with the same uncomfortable furniture and nondescript landscape paintings. There's a moving van parked outside that isn't theirs, and for a moment Jake wonders what it's like to actually have comfortable furniture that you'd haul across the country, knickknacks and little odds and ends that make a home.

They don't actually own furniture anymore. They haven't really, not since they packed up their old house in Maryland and everything went into storage. Jake tries not to think about the boxes of photo albums, the yellowing Perfect Attendance certificates Mom kept from first through third grade, the perfect ratty couch he loved. All of it is slowly gathering dust on the other side of the country.

Now every place they move into comes with furniture, usually leftovers from model homes or staging, weird pieces thrown together that never really feel intentional, much less like a home. He goes to the back of the truck and grabs his backpack and a box of his stuff and follows Dad across the street, up to their new place.

"The stuff I ordered got here yesterday, so we should be all set! Are you ready?"

Jake shrugs.

They pass by a young couple laughing as they heave a squashy couch up the steps. It looks worn in and perfect and Jake glances away, almost colliding with a small boy who completely doesn't notice as he scoots a toy truck across the sidewalk.

"See, people are moving in already. What did I tell you? These new condos are spectacular, if I do say so myself, and we really got here at the perfect time. This neighborhood is going to skyrocket in price." Dad proudly tugs his own box closer to himself as he hums the first chords of a cheerful tune.

Jake hasn't been too impressed since arriving in California. He was asleep for most of the drive, and since waking up he hasn't seen a single palm tree or celebrity or even a pool. So far this neighborhood on the outskirts of Los Angeles looks like every other town, with its strip malls and stoplights and sidewalks, and this street looks like any other street in any other city. Jake's seen so many of them now that it doesn't mean anything anymore.

Dad's struck up a conversation with the couple as he helps them through the main glass double doors of the first building. Up close, the place looks even more unappealing: a dusty lobby with another set of glass doors on the other side, open to a court-yard of some sort. The new building stands out even more now, a polished monstrosity of off-white slabs and gleaming glass. It looks jarringly strange next to its neighboring towers.

Jake closes his eyes and takes a deep breath. He opens them again, imagining the street transformed, brick by brick. The build-ing is just another set of resources, ready for him to reconstruct and rebuild in his own design, and—

"Come on, buddy, let's go check it out!" Dad's voice jolts him back to reality and all its disheartening glory.

Jake follows him up the steps to where Dad has the heavy-looking door propped open with his foot.

"Look, I know you're upset, but this time I promise it's gonna be the last move. We're gonna stick around Los Angeles. This is a really lengthy renovation project and I've got more coming soon."

"Did you design this one?"

Dad looks down at his feet quickly and then back up at Jake. "Just project managing. But we have three more buildings to ren-ovate, and it's a project that's going to take years, maybe." He gives Jake a small smile. "You're starting high school. I figured it was time to stop moving around."

Jake nods but doesn't reply. He's used to the moves by now, always being the new kid. It's tough, trying to make new friends, especially when he doesn't know how long he's going to stay.

The lobby is empty and dark, the only light emanating from the two sets of double doors that flank each side of the wide room. It's weirdly big for an apartment building, and as Jake walks through he can see why. The lobby opens up into a huge room with dingy and dust-covered furniture, and doors that look like they haven't been opened in a decade.

PACIFIC CREST COMMUNITY CENTER
AND APARTMENTS

The words are mounted on a faded sign above a huge painted mural. The sign is cracked and falling apart, but the wall itself is still bright and cheerful. The buildings are painted a deep aqua-marine here, and different scenes show laughing people walking through a park, swimming in pools, working in a computer lab. In the center of the mural, a cartoon sun wearing sunglasses grins down at the building, and an ocean sparkles behind it, a wave cresting in a swooping painted arc. The rest of that wall is covered in blue waves, a colorful contrast to the rest of the room: gray bricks stacked tediously on top of one another, and fake ficus trees, the kind you see in office buildings attempting to feel more homey. The trees have a thick layer of dust on them, and the open space is filled with empty tables, empty chairs, and a broken pool table in the corner. There's a mostly bare bulletin board with a single sheet of paper that reads ACTIVITY SIGN-UP. It's blank.

"Yeah, cheesy, I know. Don't worry, all of this is gonna be completely rehauled. I mean, a 'technology room'?" Dad shakes his head. "Talk about outdated, even for my time. No one's even stepped foot in this activity center for ages. I don't blame them; there's nothing here."

A laminated poster is propped on an easel with a mock-up of the completed complex: all shining glass and slabular architecture. In the graphic, the three buildings dwarf a manicured park with strange steel-and-glass sculptures. The community center facing the sidewalk is replaced with a sleek set of coffee shops and fancy-looking boutiques. "Now, that's what I'm talking about! Isn't it beautiful?" Dad says, nodding at the poster.

"Sure, Dad," Jake says, clutching his backpack strap tighter.

Through the lobby of the abandoned community center and the next set of glass doors, they're met with an overgrown mess of shrubberies and trees and wilting flowers. The complex on the inside is just as unimaginative and dull as the outside, not at all like the lush park Dad was talking about where he could play sports and make friends. Jake rolls his eyes as he takes it all in. He turns around and considers walking back out, but there's nowhere to go. He sighs, looking at a dingy plate that reads MANAGER on the door of a single apartment attached to the first building.

Must suck to live there, so close to the street and the doors where everyone goes in and out, Jake thinks. *At least we don't have that unit.*

"Let's go!" Dad says, leading the way to the brand-new tower.

They walk past a sign that reads POOL, even though Jake can't see anything except an overgrown fence and in the distance, some sort of playground structure amid the scraggly trees and weeds.

"This timing is great. You'll get a head start on making new friends before school, huh?" Dad says cheerfully.

Jake looks around the empty courtyard and sighs. Yup. The perfect place to make new friends.

At least they'll have Wi-Fi.

The new building still smells like fresh paint and something sharp, like the metal of the bare support columns inside. After fumbling for the elevator, they arrive on the second floor with their boxes. Jake eyes the courtyard from the outdoor corridor that links the doors of all the apartments, wondering if it's going to be noisy.

"Here we go!" Dad wobbles and nearly drops the box labeled KITCHEN trying to get the keys out of his pocket. He balances the box on his hip and unlocks the door.

"Our new place! Executed perfectly by my team," Dad says. "I'll get the rest of the stuff from the truck. You need anything?"

"Nah," Jake says, setting his box down. "Internet?"

"Looks like someone will be coming in tomorrow," Dad says. *Great.*

Jake's room is a blank square, like so many blank squares before. It's already got a brand-new mattress in it, still wrapped in plastic. Jake sets his box and backpack down and walks over to the thing, giving it a shove. It flops over, revealing an unassembled bed frame behind it. Jake sighs and yanks a sheet out of his box. It's not the right one, but he doesn't care right now. He drags it over the mattress and flops on top with his laptop; the plastic crinkles underneath him. He can make the bed later for real once it's sunk in that he's somehow both in Los Angeles and not anywhere near the ocean or Disneyland or anything cool at all, really.

There's also no Internet.

Jake sighs and checks the time. It's probably dinnertime over in Maryland, not that Danny has been logging in to the Minecraft server they share recently anyway. They used to be best friends back when they lived in the same neighborhood, and stayed in touch when Jake moved to Chicago. But that was three moves ago and now they barely see each other, even in Minecraft. Usually Jake will build something funny for him to find or vice versa, but it's a far cry from the days when they used to plan epic missions to look for strongholds together.

Hopefully they'll get connection soon. Jake can play offline, but he definitely will want to work on his most recent build in their server at some point. Jake's put in too much work mining quartz to build a replica of the Roman Colosseum to let it go unfinished.

Jake lies on his stomach and starts Minecraft. The familiar music cues up, a trilling welcome, a call to anticipation, discovery, and excitement. Jake selects Singleplayer and scans through his older worlds. He could open up any one of these and have a good time—there's the one with the half-finished Eiffel Tower, the one where he's gotten super into enchanting and all the best weapons and armor, the one where he's mapped out entire continents and discovered monuments and strongholds. Each of these worlds is special. No matter where he is in the real world, what city he's in, what school he's going to with new rules and new people and new cliques to figure out, he can always count on Minecraft.

Here the rules are steady: A log always yields four planks, four planks always make a crafting table, and you can always deconstruct something to its bare building essentials. Here, Jake is in control. He decides what stays, what goes, where he travels to, and what the places he spends time in will look like.

Jake taps on Create New World and smiles. He's home.

Jake spawns in a forest biome, filled with pixelated flowers and trees. He wastes no time getting what he needs to survive his first night. He's done this so many times before, but it never fails to amuse him, how adept he is at gathering resources; it's old hat now, and by the time night falls in the game, he's built a shelter and is safe from the zombies prowling about. He waits for the sun to rise and keeps moving.

Jake's tempted to explore until he finds a picturesque spot to build a base, but it'll be smarter to gather what resources he can rather than just wandering around and making no progress. He builds a temporary hideout close to a mountain that turns out to be a reliable source of coal, returning to the hideout each night with his day's worth of supplies. Slowly but surely he builds his fort up, even though he's not quite sure he wants to stay here permanently yet, but it's worth having a steady supply of food from the small wheat farm he's started. He'll need iron and other ores soon if he wants to craft better armor, but randomly striking into the mountain hasn't yielded anything.

It's by chance that he finds the cave system.

Jake's running away from a creeper when it explodes, catching Jake in the center of the impact. He groans; he'd just been on a successful mining run and was carrying a good amount of coal. He respawns back in his base. Jake crafts a few more pickaxes and makes loaves of bread for the journey before he heads off again, determined to pick up his items before they despawn.

Starting over in Minecraft is easy to Jake; he knows exactly what he needs to do and how to succeed. He tries to remember where exactly he met the creeper, trusting his gut and going east. Things look familiar—there's that mountaintop that looks like a wolf's head, there's that lava flow careening down into a lake. The trees around it are slowly catching fire, and Jake takes care to avoid the inferno. He skirts around the lava, reassured when he sees a swath of floating treetops leftover from his search for lumber.

Yesterday's crater is easy to spot in the next morning's light. The explosion's exposed a mass of rock, and Jake spots the opening as he gathers his things.

"Ooh, nice," Jake says. He cracks his pickaxe into the small dark window, enlarging it by several blocks. Torches to mark his place and to light his way. Inside, Jake spots the beginnings of a promising cavern, with twists and turns and even water in the distance. He builds a chest and stashes most of the coal in case he doesn't survive this particular adventure, then drops into the cave.

Here in the dark, without the cycle of night and day, Jake loses track of time. At some point Dad tells him he's going to a work thing, and Jake grunts out a reply, lost in the game. He finds veins of coal and a good source of iron, and puts up a good fight against the skeletons he encounters, even though he eventually loses. He respawns back at the hideout and takes the time to craft more weapons and torches and plenty of bread to help him heal after attacks, and travels back to the cavern. With a steady supply of iron a short journey away the hideout becomes a real base in just a few days, well-stocked with food and iron ore ready to be crafted into even better armor and weapons. Jake is fortifying a new perimeter wall when his stomach grumbles.

He blinks, and the starkness of the physical world hits him. The bare white walls, the emptiness of the floors, the single box and backpack he's dragged in here sitting forlornly in the corner. It's dark now, everything cast in a strange, sinister shadow. The only colors are the rich greens of the fields and forests beyond and the bright reds and blues and yellows of flower fields bursting with vibrancy from his laptop screen.

Staring at the computer, Jake supposes he should refuel his physical body before coming back to this. In the game, he makes sure he's behind the perimeter wall at his base before he saves and quits so he'll come back in a safe spot. He stretches. His reflection in the window stretches with him, a mousy brown-haired boy, pale and sickly-looking. Jake frowns and shakes his head, preferring the armored hero he sees when he plays. He pads to the window and yanks it open with some difficulty; someone had painted the window into the windowsill, almost fully sealing it shut.

Night air blows inside, fresher and cooler than the stuffy heat that's built up in his room. Jake takes in a deep breath. He kind of wishes they were on a higher floor for a better view, but it isn't bad. He can see the skyscrapers huddling together—downtown, he guesses. Their lights sparkle, and a trail of red and white lights blink steadily in a flowing river of cars traveling to and from where they are.

From up here the courtyard seems even more like an overgrown forest, hacked at to keep it in line. A play structure with swings lies in the center, and an empty concrete pool sits in the far west corner, filled with leaves and branches and trash. Jake shakes his head.

The living room is filled with boxes labeled carefully with things like ELECTRONICS and JAKE SCHOOL SUPPLIES and OFFICE. There's an older box with neat, printed handwriting with large rounded letters that reads BASEBALL. Jake traces the way Mom made her A's, his fingers lingering on the box. He doesn't open it.

The apartment is a blank canvas, all gray modern furniture sitting in the hot, dry heat. His dad's drafting desk is sitting unconstructed in pieces, leaning against the wall of the hallway to his office. Inside, the room is mostly set up, the plain desk already cluttered with blueprints and folders and a half-finished cup of coffee.

Dad's bedroom isn't set up; his mattress is standing up against the wall, empty bedframe and an empty suitcase sitting next to it. Clothes and jackets are scattered across the floor, like Dad got dressed in a hurry. Must have been a last-minute business meeting or something. Jake always tells Dad to just pack his lucky suit separately so he won't have to look for it, but he never remembers. Jake snorts to himself as he gathers the clothes and shoves them into an empty dresser.

The hard gray couch is still wrapped in plastic, and on the dining table is a twenty-dollar bill and a note.

For pizza. Will be back late. Have a great first night!

Love,
Dad

Jake pockets the cash and opens the refrigerator, finding it empty. He sighs, wondering if it's worth it to walk around and find a grocery store.

Shouts and laughter echo from the kitchen window. Jake struggles to open this one as well, making a note to tell Dad that his painters haven't been doing a good job. He manages to get it a few inches open, and fresh air starts to stream in.

From this window he can see the park area more clearly, the early evening bustling with activity. Cars honk and people chatter and somewhere there's a TV playing a telenovela. On the swings are two boys—eight or nine, he guesses. Babies, practically. Jake is fourteen and about to start high school, too old to be playing on a swing set, but something about it looks fun. Maybe he could see if there's anything to do around the community center. He watches the two boys jump off the swings, grinning at each other and throwing up their arms in excitement. They run to the monkey bars, laughing as they goad each other on to climb higher and higher. Must be nice, having a best friend like that, someone who gets you and can make any time turn into a great time.

"It's Tank! Run!" The shrieks draw him back to the window, where Jake watches the two boys flee as a shadow approaches. A new boy, older than Jake, probably—he looks tough and mean. His dark hair is slicked back and he wears a thick denim jacket despite the heat. He shakes his head as the kids empty the playground, and then takes a seat on the swing, pushing himself slowly. "That's right, run," he says, scoffing as he squares his shoulders.

Footsteps echo behind him, and a little girl with pigtails approaches. She has the same forehead and wide eyes as the boy, Tank. "Push me, Thanh-anh," she says, and Jake watches the boy's shoulders soften as he gives the girl a small, secret smile while she gets on the swing. He pushes her gently, laughing as she laughs and reaches for the sky.

CHAPTER TWO

TANK

Tank sets the boxes down with a heavy clunk. He stretches and shakes out his arms, catching his breath. He wipes the sweat off his forehead and grins.

"Is that all, Mr. Mishra?"

Mr. Mishra counts out change for the customer, a tall woman in a business suit. She takes her packs of gum and looks up at Tank, her eyes widening with distrust as she takes a step back.

Tank hunches down, trying to look as unintimidating as possible, but reflected in the glass of the milk-and-soda cooler, he sees what she sees: the way he towers over her, the way his reflection is so big his shoulders spill into the next door with the lunch meats.

He thinks about the assembly that all the seventh graders had to go to, the one he'd slept through and then heard all the jokes about later, about bodies and how they changed. He knew, in a vague sense, that of course kids get taller and stuff, but no one told him it could happen all at once, that suddenly none of his clothes would fit, and his throat would hurt, and people would look at him differently. Like they were scared of him now.

Shark says it's a good thing, that people know he's tough — it means no one is going to mess with him, which Tank appreciates. Shark is smart about things like that. Before he met Shark, Tank ate lunch alone and talked to no one, and now he has friends. Friends who look out for him, friends who he can hang out with.

Tank had drifted through seventh and most of eighth grade just on his own, invisible, and then one day after spring break a lunch tray clattered down next to his and he'd looked up and saw Shark grinning at him.

"You should hang out with us," Shark said, even though he had never spoken to him before.

"Yeah?" He'd been nervous all day, barely fitting into the T-shirt and jeans he took out of Ba's closet because none of his own clothes fit him anymore.

"You ever been to Fortress Park?"

He had not. Kids from school hung out there all the time, whether it was buying the soda and pretzels and hot dogs from the Snack Shack or playing mini golf or racing one another on the go-karts. He had only seen the place on his way home from school, a long wall of fake stone and painted turrets rising over the strip malls by the freeway. It was the kind of place that would only be fun with friends, and no one had ever asked him to go. He'd figured he wasn't missing much, probably just a bunch of cheesy games and kids from school he was too shy to talk to.

But that day Shark invited him, and after school they'd gone to

Fortress Park with AJ and Gus, and by the end of it the guys were clapping him on the shoulder and calling him Tank.

And that had been that.

Suddenly other kids recognized him in the hallways, made room for him to pass, gave him things like chips or soda from the vending machines or extra tickets for the Fortress Park games. People were always giving Shark things, and being Shark's friend made Tank part of all of it. He has a name people can pronounce now, a name people say with respect.

He can't help it if people find him scary. It happens more and more every day, and Tank takes comfort in knowing that no one in this neighborhood is going to bother him or Viv because he's tough-looking.

But sometimes, it hurts when people assume he's a bad guy.

Tank shakes off the feeling; the woman is long gone, the sound of her heels disappearing in the distance.

"Thank you, Thanh," Mr. Mishra says. "You did great. I really appreciate it."

"Anything else I can do?"

Mr. Mishra shakes his head. "Thank you for all the help. Sorry I don't have more hours for you today."

"Can I come tomorrow?"

"What about Thursday? That's when the soda shipments come in, and my back's not the same as it once was."

"Sure thing, Mr. Mishra."

Mr. Mishra smiles at him, soft and kind. Tank bets he smiles at his own kids like that, even brighter. *He's a good dad*, Tank thinks. Sometimes he sees the Mishra family in the little park in the complex, Mr. Mishra smiling with his wife, his daughters chasing each other in a game of tag. Tank kind of wishes sometimes that Viv was still that age; it was easier when she was easily entertained.

Now she's a little too lost in her own world, and it's hard for her to make friends. The Mishra twins are too young for Viv to take any interest, but they're some of the few kids who don't run away at the sight of him now, and Tank appreciates that.

"See you Thursday, Thanh." Mr. Mishra counts out cash from the register and hands it to Tank.

Tank shoves all of it into his pocket without looking at it. He nods at the man and leaves the convenience store, a little heavy-hearted. Mr. Mishra offered to hire him for real, but that would require job permits and all of that legal stuff where you have to be sixteen and Tank doesn't know how to explain that he's only fourteen.

The walk back to Pacific Crest Apartments is a short few blocks, and Tank's grateful he doesn't run into Shark or anyone he knows right now. He slips through the crack in the iron gate by the recycling bins, and pushes his way through a row of shrubberies before emerging in the courtyard.

He brushes leaves off himself before cutting through the park to the looming gray tower of apartments, getting more and more nervous, the money seemingly growing heavier in his pocket. He passes by the brand-new apartment tower and shakes his head. What an ugly building. Most of the people in the original building ended up moving out during the renovation because it was such a hassle. Mr. Mishra had hated it the whole time because he and his family had to stay at a hotel for the three months while the construction company was working on that building.

Tank doesn't know if his family will stay either, when the time comes for their tower to be renovated. He guesses the company would make them the same offer as the Mishras, the discount on the hotel, but he doesn't really want to move.

He opens the door to the West Tower and ignores the clunky

old elevator for the stairwell in the corner, taking the stairs two at a time until he gets to his floor. He slows his pace, approaching the apartment quietly so his footsteps don't echo. Unlocking the door, slipping inside, and shutting it behind him without making any noise is just part of his routine.

He counts the money and exhales. It's not a lot, but it'll help. Ma is in the bedroom, still asleep. She'll wake up soon for her night shift, but for now she's resting. Tank delicately walks over to the nightstand where her purse is sitting, being as quiet as possible. He pulls out her slim wallet, sliding half the cash inside before padding softly out of the bedroom. In the kitchen, he finds the envelope taped behind the second utensil drawer and stashes all but one of the twenties in there for safekeeping. Maybe he can ask Ma if they can run the new air conditioning this week; it's been almost unbearable.

Tank collapses on the couch and closes his eyes. It's not quiet—outside, he can still hear cars and footsteps and people talking, doors slamming shut as someone moves through the building.

His own apartment door opens and closes in a familiar rhythm, joined by a clunk of keys and shoes being kicked off.

"Hey, Thanh, did you just get back from work? Do you have any money for groceries?"

Tank opens his eyes. Ba is looking at him but not quite looking at him. His father is more looking at the floor, a grease stain on his mechanic's shirt and a resigned set to his shoulders.

Tank sighs, thinking of the twenty in his pocket. He was hoping to save up this summer for brand-new sneakers—Shark says he could get the coolest ones for cheap, but even half of the mall price is too much for him. The gleaming white sneakers, Shark says, would make him undoubtedly cool, untouchable. Tank wants that, something for himself, something he's worked toward.

"We didn't get any customers today so I left work early," Ba says, shifting uncomfortably from one foot to the other.

Great. So instead of just sticking it out at the auto shop and maybe helping some actual paying customers, he came home to try to be "useful" instead, which Ma hates, because he usually ends up tinkering with something that didn't need to be tinkered with, trying to save them money somehow. But it always backfires, and then Mrs. Jenkins crossly informs them they'll need to pay extra for damaging the electric system and that it's actually illegal to split your neighbor's Wi-Fi cable.

"Auntie Phuong made a whole bunch of food yesterday, I think we're still good," Tank offers.

Ba grins, a familiar inventive gleam in his eye. "Yeah, but we could do something nice. How about this, I'm going to make dinner and when Ma gets home we can all eat, like a happy family, okay?"

"Ma has work tonight. She won't be home until six." Tank sighs.

"Then we can eat breakfast like a happy family."

"At six in the morning? Ba, we don't have school. I'm not waking up at six."

"Fine, then I'll eat with you kids and save some for Ma in the morning." Ba frowns. "Where's Vivian?"

"She's in her room studying. Don't bother her."

"Thought you said you don't have school."

"She's smart. She's studying to get ahead for next year."

Ba shuffles like he's going to Vivian's room to talk to her, and Tank finds himself reaching into his pocket. He's going to regret this later, but Viv deserves to have time to herself. She doesn't need Ba asking her to hold his tools while he tries something new with the electricity or teaching her how to change oil again, because he keeps forgetting what he has and hasn't taught them. Viv's more patient than Tank is, and she'd just play along.

"Here, go get some groceries," Tank says, handing him the twenty. A mess in the kitchen is better than a mess of their wiring. "Don't mess with the electricity. We're still in trouble for what you did to the air-conditioning last month."

Ba shrugs, because he's like that, careless. He doesn't think about how Tank had to try to find a job fast to help pay for the extra repairs, how Mom and Auntie Phuong don't leave their work early because they felt like it, and how Viv is just a baby who shouldn't have to be thinking about all of this. Ba shuffles out the door, money in hand.

Tank pours himself a glass of water and drinks it, pressing the cool glass to his forehead as he shifts through the apartment. Viv is in the other bedroom, her headphones on, her head bobbing as she sways to the music. Her back is to the door, and she hasn't noticed him yet, completely immersed in the world of Minecraft. Tank smiles to himself, watching her enjoy the game. She's back at the base, in one of the elaborately constructed houses she's built, doing something intricate with redstone Tank doesn't quite understand. Viv sticks her tongue out in concentration before leaning back to admire her latest construction. Despite their clunky outdated design, the two monitors and computer tower look good; clean, well maintained, and functional. The tower is glowing with bright blue LEDs that Tank installed for Viv last week, so she could get the cool gamer effect.

Tank thinks of kids' rooms in TV shows, how they're filled with soft toys and knickknacks and color. This bedroom, aside from the computer, is the same as it was five years ago, ten years ago, before Viv was born and when he was the one sharing the bedroom. It had been Uncle Tho then, before he got married and moved out. Now it's Auntie Phuong, her twin bed done up in a faded quilted bedspread matching Viv's. A flimsy folding screen divides the space, and every available inch is maximized; for storage, for clothes, for things they've never bothered to get rid of in case they could find a use for it again.

"You gonna come in or become part of the door?"

Tank laughs, shuffling forward through the narrow aisle between Auntie Phuong's dresser and Viv's bed to join her at her desk, a sturdy folding table he'd picked up off the street. Tank peers at her screen. Her avatar is standing in a stone tunnel, part of it excavated to reveal some chests and a line of redstone circuitry, repeaters and other stuff that's all pretty much magic to Tank.

"Looks cool. Subway station, right? I thought you were finished."

"No," Viv groans. "I mean, the tunnel took forever, but I finished that yesterday. I've been working on the minecart dispenser all day, but it keeps breaking. I think it's the ticket system. Right now it only works without it."

She smashes up one of the lines of redstones and repeaters, picking everything up before setting stone down back on top. "Come on, check it out."

Viv's avatar approaches the minecart track, bouncing up and down before Tank leans over her shoulder to watch. Viv steps on a pressure plate, and a hopper above them drops a minecart onto the track. Her glittery avatar jumps into it, and Tank watches as she speeds on a harrowing journey through an elaborate stone tunnel. He's impressed, especially with the expansive glass wall in one section that opens up to caverns with streaming pools of lava.

"The tunnel looks great, Viv."

"I added some sightseeing windows to the cool stuff I found while digging it out," Viv says proudly.

The cart comes to a sudden stop and then Viv is standing on the stone platform.

"Where'd the cart go?" Tank asks.

"The cactus block breaks it, so you automatically dismount. Cool, huh?"

"Very. Definitely an upgrade from last week."

"Yeah, we figured why stop at building an efficient subway system between the main base and this new one?" Viv steps into a water elevator that shoots her upward. She emerges in a stone square plaza with a fountain streaming merrily in the center. "Ugh, I don't know what I'm doing wrong. I've been working on this all day. Mina and Rocky can't figure it out, either. Rocky says we can just bring our own carts but that's just not the point of having an automated system."

"I'm sure you'll figure it out. You already made it work without the ticket system, and the minecarts dropping automatically is super cool."

"Wanna join us?"

"Eh." Tank shrugs. He's always happy to play Minecraft with his little sister, but he can't quite follow what she and her friends get up to in their server. He first joined with her to make sure everyone was being nice, but then fell far behind. His own simple farmhouse and flower orchard in the shared home base looks very much the same as when they started the server a year ago. Viv and the other players quickly built elaborate houses and greenhouses and intricately decorated mansions with multiple floors and secret rooms and hallways. They've explored the outer reaches of the world, built incredible things and new bases with themes, and even automated travel between them now.

Tank doesn't quite understand them most of the time; Mina is on the East Coast somewhere and Rocky lives in Japan and Tank can't keep track of any of the newer players. Once the server opened up to more people, it got too complicated with the money system and the shops and the constant change in guidelines and the new games Rocky's always starting, some sort of complicated quest RPG thing Tank can't follow. They've all got an easy friendship with Vivian, and though Tank can't quite keep up, he's glad Vivian's having fun.

He's tired but it's still bright outside; maybe he could try to nap, but he'll just end up waking up when Auntie Phuong gets home and then when Ma leaves for work. And then inevitably whenever Ba gets home as well. His creaky too-small twin bed is right next to the front door, and despite the bedsheet Ma put up for him for a bit of privacy, it doesn't stop sound or the way the wall shakes when the door opens and shuts. Tank's weighing whether catching a few hours and waking up groggy is better than nothing when Viv elbows him in the stomach.

"What?" Tank yawns.

"I said, I can disconnect and we can play in the world we started last week," Vivian says.

"Nah, you're hanging out with your friends. I can go do something else—"

"It's all right, we're just redesigning some stuff. Rocky's figured out a way to automatically turn on and off this Nether portal, but they want to put one right outside of town and Cogs hates the idea of it and everyone's arguing about how best to design the water flow for the switches and I don't need the drama." Viv disconnects and swivels in her chair, spinning around and around with glee. It's times like these Tank remembers just what a baby she is, even if she talks like she's swallowed a programming book most of the time.

"Ready?"

Tank ruffles her hair and heads to the closet where he stores his stuff and pulls out his laptop. It's an older model but Viv deserves a nicer computer, especially since she's the one who's going to make it out of here.

Viv loads their world onto her computer, and the familiar bright flowers of the gardens Tank's laid out greet them on her screen. Viv hums to herself as she walks around the main house, a beautiful construction with floor-to-ceiling glass walls, shaded with bamboo. The bamboo was Tank's idea; it makes him feel happy and content to see so much green and color flourishing in the little safe world they've created together.

"I'm going to go make an automatic wheat farm."

"Uh—"

"Don't worry, I'll do it away from the main house so it won't ruin the aesthetic of your fields and gardens." She sticks her tongue out at him.

Tank snorts and shakes his head. "Thanks."

She's already wandered off before his laptop has booted up, and by the time he connects to the world her avatar is off in the distance, a clunky-looking glass monstrosity rising up around new green stalks of wheat on a dirt platform.

He takes a moment to stop and watch her build, a bubble of pride growing bigger and bigger in his chest. It's really cool how into the redstone stuff she is, from learning how to make contraptions like the automated farms to really creative ideas like the ticketed subway lines and remote-controlled alarm systems and secret passageways. She's an absolute nerd, but she's his nerd, and he'll never admit it but his little sister is pretty cool.

Tank settles into the farm he's started, a design alternating wheat, pumpkins, beetroot, and carrots. It's relaxing and methodical, going through the fields and harvesting crops. He doesn't mind spending the time, even though he knows building an automated farm is faster. Tank likes the repetition of it, plus the fields look great with the pops of color bounded by water. Some more variation in height would look good, though. Sugar cane, that's what he wants. Tank empties his bucket into the trench he's dug alongside where he'll plant the sugar cane, and watches the water flow. Now the whole farm is optimized so every plant can get as much water as it needs.

Tank stores his harvest away and organizes it carefully in the farmhouse he's built. He's quite proud of this one, with its cheerful red tapestries and large windows. Furnaces, crafting tables, a bed, everything he needs. On the far wall are his rows of meticulously organized chests, each below its own label. Tank takes note of how much of everything he has, and shakes his head when he sees that amongst his seeds and flowers are random things like granite and feathers. Vivian must have gone through here and just dumped everything in her inventory into the nearest chest. She's always doing this, never reading any of Tank's labels.

He puts everything back in its rightful place, and then wanders around the farm. Maybe he can redecorate the south side a bit. He leans back to admire the tableau of different flowering bushes, a lovely display of colors.

Tending the plants on their farm is peaceful, and he works on it for a while until Viv wants to go exploring and fighting monsters. He tags along until he dies and respawns back at the base.

He plans and lays out the foundation for a new hedge maze and then gets to organizing and reorganizing his flower collection, every now and then looking up to watch Viv continue to mine and explore on her screen. It's an easy companionship, and Tank settles in, going to check on the animals in their pens.

"You're no fun," Viv complains. "You just want to farm and make the base nice. And this looks exactly like the last farm you made. Why not make something new?"

Tank shrugs. He likes neat rows of crops and flowers and tending to his trees.

"You know there's so much to explore?"

"You can do it, I don't really care about the monsters," Tank says.

"Want to download a new world and explore it with me? Look at all these cool mods we can use. The other day I found one that turns all squids into *giant* squids, imagine—"

"Sure. Whatever you want."

"But what do *you* want?"

Tank gestures at his wall of chests inside his farmhouse. The flowers are all organized by color so designing a new garden is easy. He is running a little low on some colors that he'll need for his new maze, though. "I guess we can go look for more plants. I think there are some peonies in the forest I saw beyond that swamp we were at yesterday."

"Flowers, again?" Viv sighs and gives him a long-suffering look.

Tank snorts. "Look, you can do whatever you want. Go build something new in Creative."

"I guess," Viv says. "I don't want to spend all summer picking flowers with you."

"Shut up," Tank says, but there's no heat in it. "No one asked you to pick flowers. I can find them on my own."

"Nah, I haven't explored that area in a while. Oh wait, I think I saw some blue orchids over where I'm at, want to meet me here?"

"Sure."

"Wait, let me craft you some more armor, do you have feathers for arrows?"

They're going to end up fighting monsters. Tank shakes his head. "I'll come fight monsters with you. Just tell me where you are."

She always gets her way. What a brat. Viv grins and sends him the coordinates, and Tank follows.

CHAPTER THREE

JAKE

Jake's new world is coming along nicely. He's got a secure home base, iron armor, cleared out the cavern and started a brand-new mine all the way down to the bedrock to look for diamonds. He's starting to think about expanding and maybe building something cool, but it'd be a lot easier to design something epic with the right tools and resources, even though he's had fun starting from scratch in this new world.

Danny 8:32 A.M.
Hey! Sorry it took me forever to respond. Soccer practice has been a lot, haha! But I built you a giant sheep statue in the server, you should go find it :)

Jake starts to tap out a long reply, starting with how boring the new apartment is, lots of questions about how Danny's summer is going, and how he can't wait to find the statue. He sighs and erases the paragraph. Too chatty. Sounds desperate. Ugh.

Jake 8:39 A.M.
Haha thanks! I'll check it out once we get Internet. How's your summer going?

Jake shoves his phone in his pocket so he doesn't dwell on it. "Dad! Did the Wi-Fi get fixed yet?"

Dad pauses on his way out, a bagel dangling from his mouth. He takes a bite out of it and tries to hold it in his armful of rolled-up blueprints and his briefcase. "I thought they came yesterday?"

"No one showed up all day." Jake's sure of that. It'd just been him and his offline game all day. The complex has been pretty quiet, despite the fact that it's summer and he thought there'd be kids hanging out everywhere. Sometimes he would hear people outside, but it's all shadows and footsteps and faded conversations. Everyone either bustles off to work or keeps to their own apartments, Jake guesses. He doesn't blame them. The overgrown park with its empty and disgusting pool and dilapidated play structure doesn't really inspire him, either.

"I'll call the cable company and make sure they stop by. Did you plug the router in and everything?"

Jake gives Dad a blank stare. "Having the tools and the right equipment doesn't mean anything if we're not connected to the power."

Dad chuckles. "Got it in one, buddy. I'll see you tonight. I'll make dinner, and there's groceries in the fridge."

Jake opens the fridge, nodding as he looks over the contents. Nice. Mozzarella sticks, yogurt, slices of cheese and deli meats. There's even bread and a couple boxes of Jake's favorite cereal on the counter, too. He pulls out a gallon of milk that actually isn't expired and cracks it open. "Thanks, Dad," he says, a hopeful feeling growing in his chest. It usually starts out this way—new place, new attitude—but maybe Dad will keep it up this time. He rustles around in the half-unpacked box on the counter and finds his cereal bowl.

"You should make some friends! There's a bunch of other families with kids in the building." Dad beams at Jake, a broad, sunny smile that inspires as much confidence as the faded fake plants in the lobby.

Jake makes a *mhm* noise as he opens the cereal box and pours himself a generous amount of crunchy oaty fruity sugary goodness.

"You could check out that community center, looks like there were games and stuff? Of course, that's all going to be torn down during the renovations soon, so now's your chance to take a look. I'm actually going to go meet with the architect now. She's got big plans for that place!"

"Uh huh," Jake mumbles, pouring milk into his cereal.

"You should go outside today," Dad says. He rebalances his armload, placing his bagel carefully on top of his paperwork. "Hand me that coffee and grab the door, will you?"

Jake gives his cereal a quick stir to distribute the milk just so, then grabs the travel mug. He secures the lid tightly before handing it to Dad and opens the door. Bright sunshine streams into the otherwise dimly lit apartment, making Jake wince.

"Oh wow, look at all this amazing California sunshine! If we were in Seattle, you'd be begging me to go out and play. Why waste a day like this?" Dad chuckles.

Jake lets his eyes adjust and regrets it. The light is bouncing off all the white walls and the shining counters and bombarding his eyes with too much brightness. He squints, ignoring Dad's teasing.

"Don't you have to be at work?"

"Yeah, yeah, I'm going. Oh hey, there're some kids your age at that park. Maybe they'll go to your school? Why don't you go say hi?"

Jake shrugs and shuts the door, waving Dad off before returning the apartment to its optimal dimly lit state. He finishes his cereal and contemplates starting another new world. Or he could just keep building and making the next step in technological improvements, but what he really wants is to see what Danny left for him and work the builds he had in that server. It's annoying starting over when he's already made so much progress; mining just isn't the same or as efficient when he doesn't have his diamond tools.

Laughter echoes from the courtyard.

Jake peers through the blinds, spotting the boys from the other day playing tag with a few other kids, racing around the play structure, screaming and laughing with one another.

Jake rinses his bowl and stretches, imagining Dad's voice about how lucky he is to have this Summer of Possibility. That's what he's been calling it, like it's going to Mean Something. Dad has this idea about every day as a teen leading to some magical, profound adventure or something.

There's a whole wide world out there, and you can do anything, Dad would say. Never mind the fact that Jake would always be stuck far away from anything interesting, with no money, no easy way to get there, and the whole "you can do anything" idea is so limitless that it's daunting.

Jake's always been up for trying his best—it's how he survived being the new kid three times. He wouldn't have made any friends at all if he didn't take that first step, but he hasn't seen anyone around the complex so far except these little kids.

Jake peers out the window. The kids playing tag have scattered from the playground area, and he can see clearly why. There are three boys leaning against the dull gray brick of the courtyard's inner walls, talking to one another. They look older, tougher, meaner, and part of him instinctively says he should stay inside, that he shouldn't meet these boys at any cost.

The tallest of the boys laughs as he pulls a golden-colored bottle out of his pocket and pours generous amounts onto rags. The other two snicker as they start wiping the playground equipment. It's cooking oil, Jake realizes with horror.

Jake's phone buzzes on the kitchen counter. It's probably Dad; there isn't any one else in his address book aside from Danny and pizza delivery places for towns he no longer lives in.

Dad 9:23 A.M.
Have a great day!

Dad 9:24 A.M.
Remember to keep an eye out for the cable company. They might not be able to get into the building and the buzzers don't work.

Jake sighs and brings his laptop to the living room so he can watch the window. He goes back to yesterday's game and refortifies the wall around his base, fingers itching to make progress on his other projects. Danny doesn't text back, but then again, Jake doesn't expect him to. He's probably busy with his soccer friends.

Movement out of the corner of his eye startles him; there's a guy in a polo shirt and official-looking hat holding a clipboard and peering through the back gate behind the building.

The cable company! Wi-Fi!

Jake scrambles off his seat and races out of the apartment, bounding down the stairs two at a time. He sprints through the courtyard, trying to remember where he saw the cable guy—Left? No, right. Jake turns and darts for the corner, nearly tripping on his unlaced shoes as he throws himself around the corner.

FLOMP.

Jake crashes into something—someone—solid, and falls backward, and several soft things bounce off him. He blinks, startled for a moment, and his first thought is *sheep?*

"Hey!"

It's the boy from yesterday—Tank. Up close, he's even bigger and more intimidating, a broad-shouldered Asian boy with slicked-back hair and a leather jacket. He's built like a linebacker, taking up all the space in the narrow alley between the two towers.

Tank scowls and reaches for the fallen objects: rolls of paper towels, not sheep, now that Jake can see them clearly.

"Sorry, so sorry," Jake mumbles. With relief, he spots the cable guy still puzzling at the intercom, and hastily grabs one of the rolls and offers it back to Tank, who balances it atop his laden armful, his mouth hardening into a thin line.

Jake awkwardly pretends not to run as he makes his way to the back gate, but he sees the guy turn around to leave and he's got to—

Yes!

Jake flings open the gate. "Hi," he says breathlessly. "Wi-Fi?"

The man blinks at him. "Oh. No, delivery for B-three-oh-seven. That you?" He holds aloft a bulky cardboard box.

Jake shakes his head.

"Which one of these towers is it, do you think? I can never figure out this complex. Like, is this the front door or the back door, and there're like three different addresses inside, it's all a mess, and this intercom never works, and if I have to call that scary lady again I'm just gonna leave these at the post office."

Jake squints at the address on the box. "Uh, the shiny new one is A. B and C are the older towers, so uh, one of them?" He shrugs.

"Thanks for the door, kid." The delivery man shakes his head and makes his way into the courtyard before heading for the West Tower.

Jake closes and latches the gate, shuffling back inside to the courtyard. The sun is out in full force now, and he winces at the heat. At least the air conditioning is working in the apartment.

He walks back toward his own tower, distracted by his disappointment until it's too late.

The low-pitched laughter sends the hair on the back of his neck straight up, and Jake realizes with horror he's walked right into the midst of the older boys by the vending machine. They're leaning against the wall, staring at him, the tallest of them wearing a beanie and a smirk on his face. They must have seen him run through the courtyard like an idiot.

Great. Well, now they've already spotted him, so Jake has to just pretend he came here on purpose. He has to walk past them to get to his tower, and he tries to make it as quick as possible, even as he feels their eyes bearing down on him. In the distance, he spots Tank over by the playground, hiding the paper towels in the shrubberies. Huh. Must be some sort of weird game. Tank's eyes widen when he catches Jake's gaze, and he dashes away out of view.

"What are you looking at?" Tall and skinny grins at Jake. One of his teeth is crooked, a sharp incisor that juts out like a fang. The way the smile stretches is slow and terrifying, one Jake's come to associate with boys like these who find humor in other people's pain. "Who are you supposed to be?"

"Uh . . . I'm Jake."

"Going to get yourself a soda?"

Jake shrugs as if to say *obviously*.

It's the wrong move, of course.

The grin widens. "I'm Shark. This is Gus and AJ."

"Do you live here?" Jake tilts his head, thinking about the long list of rules that he found on the kitchen counter when they moved in that lists COMMUNITY GUIDELINES. He's pretty sure he saw something about only residents and their guests.

"Oh. Yeah. We're friends of Tank." Shark glances at Gus. "He text back? He said he'd meet us here at noon."

Gus shrugs.

AJ steps forward, closer to Jake. "I think you should buy us all a soda. Shark here likes the root beer."

Jake doesn't have any money on him. He doesn't even have his keys, he thinks. He just ran out without thinking. He takes a step backward, his head spinning, wondering if these guys will end up going to his school. He thinks about Dad shaking his head in disappointment when he learned that Jake had been giving his lunch money every week to a menacing boy with a bad haircut who scared him, and that the school counselor had said it was important to set boundaries and he—he—

"Hey, Shark." Tank appears out of nowhere, his hands stuffed into his pockets.

The three whirl around just as Tank jerks his head in a way that Jake has come to recognize as some sort of secret boy code he doesn't know.

What is Jake supposed to do? Smile? Wave? Nod back? He

doesn't even know how to do that head thing; it's more of a shake than a nod—

"Thought we were going to Fortress Park," Tank says casually. "You said you wanted a rematch on the go-kart race, remember?"

Wait, no, this is a *distraction*—

Jake stumbles backward before catching his balance, scurrying across the open courtyard. He ducks into the first door he sees.

"Hello?"

Jake lets his eyes adjust to the dark; the scant afternoon sunlight barely filters through the glass doors, as grimy as they are. He's in one of those big empty lobbies at the front of the main entry building. He wipes his hands on his jeans, looking around. Oh. Right. This is the community center his dad was talking about, the one his company is going to renovate.

Might as well look around. Shark and those guys are still out there, and there isn't another way back to his tower without walking past them again. He takes another step inside the dimly lit room, exhaling with relief. He's far from the bullies and he's got something to explore. He smiles in spite of himself, imagining he's found a cavern and he's safe from the mobs outside.

Jake crosses the empty lobby to the set of wooden doors propped open with a broken milk crate. The doors could have been handsome once, carved with intricate details of leaves and letters to form the words PACIFIC CREST COMMUNITY CENTER. The space for the rest seems to linger with sadness. Jake brushes his fingers over the carvings, wondering how long it took to craft this dedication to this space.

He crosses the threshold into the area he only gave a passing glance when they first moved in, taking it all in. There's a pool table but no pool cues, and three lonely-looking balls are sitting on the faded green felt. On the far wall there's a television that's seen better days, an archaic-looking model that more resembles a refrigerator than television. Jake jabs a few buttons experimentally and gets nothing but static. There are some DVDs on the shelf below it, nothing of interest, just some movies made for toddlers and boring documentaries. On the bookshelf next to the TV are a bunch of yellowing romance novels and Westerns, a few faded board games, and several tattered decks of cards. Jake pokes at the boxes half-heartedly; it looks like everything is broken or missing pieces.

He sighs. So much for amenities. At least when Dad's company is done with this project it'll be nicer. It's not like they'd be able to stick around to enjoy it, though. Dad's just gonna get another project and they'll move again.

Jake glances at the stained couch and decides not to sit on it.

There are three more doors to try.

The first is locked, and because the door is smaller Jake assumes it's probably a closet. The second door is also locked, but has a window to see inside. It doesn't look like much: a mishmash of broken furniture, desks and tables and chairs heaped together, all covered by a thick helping of dust. Jake pushes against the third door experimentally; it's unlocked and creaks open with a solemn groan. It's heavier than he expected. Jake throws his shoulder against the door and presses it open in its entirety.

The next room is equally dusty, and completely dark. He amuses himself by imagining he's going deeper into the unknown cave, looking for treasure and fighting monsters, going by touch. The wall is cold and bits of paint flake off onto his fingers as he fumbles along the wall. Finally he finds a light switch.

Click.

The room is bathed in ugly fluorescent lights flickering onto the rows of blocky computers. It's a mess of electronic debris, desktops and towers and dust-covered machines. There's one row at the front of the room that is fully set up, like someone started to build a computer lab ten years ago and then couldn't be bothered to finish. The rest of the room is a cluster of old computers and keyboards and boards of circuits and wires all jumbled together. There's at least a decade's worth of different kinds of machines, models Jake didn't even know existed, with tiny monitors and heavy-looking plastic and slots for strangely shaped disks. Jake passes by one that he thinks might even be from before his Dad's time. Whoa. How could someone even type on this?

"Wow," Jake mutters, pulling up a chair in the first row. There isn't dust on this table, which probably means it's functional. Three monitors and towers sit on the cracked tabletop, and the one closest to the door has a keyboard that looks well worn. The A key is faded out entirely, and the tower is covered with glittery seashell stickers.

Jake taps it experimentally, imagining who played on this well-loved computer. It takes him a moment to find the power button on the tower, but he's rewarded by the familiar sound of it starting up.

A sign on the wall reads COMPUTER USE LIMITED TO TWO HOURS WHEN LAB IS OPEN. A faded clipboard reads SIGN-UP FOR INTERNET TIME.

Huh. Internet?

Jake peers more closely at the row of set-up desktops and spots a familiar bright yellow cord. He follows it and finds it plugged into a phone jack in the wall.

"Internet!" Jake says, scooting under the table while the computer is still starting up. If these are connected to a LAN, he could get online —

All the wires are zip-tied together and behind some sort of wire framework built right into the underside of the desk. There's not even enough room for Jake to pry it open. He'd need a screwdriver or something. There's no way to pull the Ethernet cable free so he can hook his laptop up to it.

Jake pulls himself back up onto the chair and stares at the welcome screen with the Pacific Crest logo. There're a few basic programs installed: browsers, Word, solitaire, and then he sees it: the Minecraft launcher.

"No way," Jake says.

Someone else in this complex must have installed it!

He logs in to his account, so excited he misspells his name and password twice before he gets in. He wonders who else in this complex plays Minecraft, if they—

No. It's too much to think about, to hope that another kid would want a friend like Jake.

But he could look around and see if there is anyone. Just to see.

"What if . . ."

Jake tries looking in singleplayer first. There are a bunch of worlds here; it looks like someone has been busy. Some of them have silly names, likely named after the people who made them or in-jokes they have with their friends. Jake laughs as he scrolls past the movie references he understands and many he doesn't. Throughout the list Jake sees the same name pop up over and over again: Bella.

The names and numbering patterns vary; the creator must have been going between numbering versions, finalizing one, then starting over again. Bella's World Final. Bella's World FINAL final. Bella ACTUAL FINAL ACTUALLY. Bella Beta Test. Some of the dates on these worlds go back to when he was younger, from right when Minecraft was first made.

Whoever was creating all of these worlds was trying to perfect something. But what?

Jake switches over to multiplayer. After a few seconds of the program searching for local games, a single server pops up: Bella Beta 7. The thumbnail is a simple seashell icon, and it looks heavily modded, but Jake's up to checking out whatever that person was working on so hard and testing out in singleplayer.

He spawns on a rocky shore of what seems to be an endless ocean. Stretches of sand and sugar cane line the shore, and a forest sprawls behind him. In the distance, strange buildings rise over the horizon. Excitement starts to thrum in his veins. A whole new world with things to discover.

Jake cracks his knuckles together before starting to explore. He travels light, gathering the basics and getting a sense of this world. The first set of buildings he comes across is a village, clearly fortified by a player against attack. There's a perimeter wall with some golems strutting around. In the center of town, there's a beautiful gazebo lined with blue flowers, and in the center are several signs.

Riddle the Seventeenth

Look westward to the sky and don't think twice
Add the number of shells left in the cave of ice.

Maybe the last players had some sort of ongoing game or something, leaving one another puzzles to solve. Jake takes a screenshot of the riddle and wanders around the village. It seems pretty standard, a blacksmith and a butcher and a few other basic occupations. The villagers grunt at him in their monosyllabic AI speak, and Jake feels the hair on his neck stand up. He turns back to read the riddle again. This sign. The perimeter wall around the village. The one house with a full chest of supplies, including coal and iron armor and feathers for fletching arrows.

< MCExplorerJake > hello?

There's no response.

It feels strange, like there's a ghost here. Jake can clearly see this is more than a village that someone left some of their effects in as they passed through. It's as if it was designed to be a natural stopping point, like an inn in an epic high fantasy where you re-fuel before going on your main quest, to rest and get some supplies or trade with the villagers here.

The whole village looks and feels more like someone's pretty little seaside town. Someone took time to decorate the wall and some of the houses with a similar motif. Blue tiles dot the perimeter wall in a repeating pattern, paintings of shells and kelp and boats are framed in each house.

Jake looks in each house and finds more questions than answers. In the grandest house, under a hidden trapdoor behind a painting, he finds a pretty library. "Cute," Jake says to himself, looking around at the bookshelves lining the walls and the way stairs and slabs and pistons have been arranged to look like chairs and tables. An enchanting table sits in the center of the room, which Jake is pleased to note. There's also a chest in the corner of the room that has a single Potion of Leaping in it. Jake pockets it and then looks around, like he's expecting another player to enter the room.

This village definitely isn't random, with the abundance of supplies and resources and eye for detail here. Usually in villagers' chests there's some food or books or random ores and things, but Jake's never come across potions before.

Satisfied he's seen everything in the village, he cuts wood from the nearby forest, thick and lush with oaks and saplings. As darkness falls, he watches zombies and skeletons roam the well-stocked fields from the safety of one of the houses. He wonders about the village. Who built it, and why? What does *Riddle the Seventeenth* mean? Are there sixteen that came before it?

Jake crafts some more tools, listening to the zombies groan before sleeping in the bed. Daylight comes quickly. He considers taking the bed with him, but decides to leave it when he notices that the dyed-blue bedspread matches the paintings and tiles in the wall.

Jake takes some wool instead.

He doesn't see another village or come across any more signs for hundreds of blocks. He's not sure what he's looking for. He's been in servers before, joined public ones just to try, and he's wandered around in other worlds with Danny, seen entire cities built by other people. He never really warmed to it, all the different mods and rules people came up with. It's cool to look at but he'd rather be in control of his world. The idea of new rules, new mobs, adding and changing things, it's just . . . it's not what he wants. He didn't want to learn how to handle the complicated new things that people were coming up with all the time. He likes his Minecraft exactly as it is. He knows all the rules and always has a good time, and is in control of what he builds and why.

This server is different, though. Someone else is in control here, and they left behind an intricately designed village with a riddle in the middle of it.

It must be a part of something bigger.

Jake traverses hundreds of blocks, drifting through the world before deciding to go back to see the riddle again. Maybe he missed something. He tries to head back the direction he came, but gets lost in the forest. He curses; he didn't mark the coordinates or anything. He's probably not going to find it again.

Disappointed, he decides to keep going and see if he can find anything else. He covers more ground by boat, swiftly following a river through jungles and plains until it peters out to a dead end. Jake emerges in a sandy desert.

Wait, what's that?

There's something strange on the horizon.

Jake runs, watching trees and mountain crags materialize as he gets closer. There's another village, and even more structures. Buildings. Signs.

Possibly more of the riddles.

He walks toward the village; he's still got a bit of time before dark, and he's well-armed enough to fight off a zombie or two.

Something blue glimmers in the distance.

The ocean?

Jake turns, striding forward toward the expanse of blue. It actually is the ocean, and not just the misty blue haze that surrounds the horizon, a mirage of water that disappears once the details of the world fill in when you get close. He steps onto the shore. It's just a little detour. He can still make it to that village before dark.

There's no tide here, just calm, smooth waters, the sun a perfect block. Fish swim in schools, and a turtle slowly makes its way across the sand. Soft, calming music starts to play, gentle chimes and a soothing melody, as if to say, *Hello. Enjoy the view. You're here.*

Jake's never seen the Pacific Ocean, and he shakes his head remembering Dad's promises to go to the beach together now that they're here. Well, until that happens, he can enjoy this and get to cool places and experience things all on his own.

Maybe he'll cross this ocean tomorrow. For now, he just dives into the water, enjoying the serenity of the kelp forests and the schools of fish playfully swimming by. He's careful to watch his health, coming back up for air periodically. The shoreline is dotted with cliffs and rocky slopes, so he swims alongside it, making a good pace. He watches the forest on the edge change from tall trees to the open plains of rocky desert, and there's an inset bay dotted with sugar cane that looks fairly promising. The sun is setting now, the sky a brilliant orange-yellow-gold over the horizon. He shouldn't be wasting time, but there's something about sunsets that makes him stop to look. He's definitely too far from the village to make it by dark now, and he has precious minutes to get to land and set up a camp for the night, but Jake stays where he is, treading water and taking in the peaceful way the square sun is sinking behind the horizon.

With the last light of the setting sun, Jake turns around to head back toward land when he spots something underwater. It's a huge, hulking shape, looming dark just beyond the kelp forest.

Jake should go. He won't be able to get very far if he's in the water in the dark.

But his curiosity is calling him and he dives.

The ocean is murky and ominous, but Jake can still kind of see. He swims down, down, watching his oxygen level carefully. As he swims past dolphins and fish and through the kelp forest, the thing starts to take shape: a tall mast, the clear and obvious bow of a ship. It's broken in half, resting on an outcrop of rock like it tried to survive a tempest and failed. Jake's running out of air and swims directly up, surfacing and taking a deep breath.

It's all dark now, but in the depths Jake can see an eerie green glow emitting from the wreck.

Jake dives again.

With the shipwreck directly underneath him, it's easy enough to find his way back. He lands on the deck of the ship, looking around for the source of the light. It's coming from the inside of the ship. He smashes through some empty chests, clearing the deck until he spots it. A trapdoor.

Once inside, he can see the source of the light: an underwater torch mounted on the wall, casting its blue-green light over everything. Someone went to the trouble of lighting this place, like a beacon.

Or a trap.

There's a single chest in the center of the room, and another trapdoor leading downward.

Jake opens it carefully.

There's a smattering of treasure inside—gold bars, some emeralds, and a piece of paper.

Jake takes everything and heads back to the surface. A crescent moon is just starting to rise, and stars blink overhead. Treading water, he takes a closer look at what he got.

Jake's heart pounds with excitement. A treasure map?

Wait. There was another door.

Jake dives back down to the wreck, past the first room, and makes for the second door. Outside, movement catches his eye—something too big to be a fish, not the right shape to be a dolphin. He's too deep for squid.

He jerks away from the door and stares out the gaping maw of the broken ship. Bubbles and kelp drift slowly in rhythm, and then it moves again.

Wait, could that be—

A mermaid?

Jake swims outside and he can see the shadow of a tail.

"Come back!"

He swims after the mermaid, not watching his health until—

`MCExplorerJake drowned`

Great.

Jake respawns in the dark. It takes him a few seconds to remember where he is: the last place he set up camp, a basic box in the middle of nowhere, built quickly as night fell.

Clink. Clink. Clink.

Just awesome—skeletons nearby.

Groan.

And zombies.

Jake punches the ground furiously to get enough dirt to close the box, but he built the walls out of stone and it's taking too long for him to break it without a pickaxe. He lost everything when he drowned, and he has no tools, no torch to light his way, no crafting table to work on making items to use his time at night wisely. He doesn't even have a bed where he can pass the time with sleep.

Worst of all, he's lost the treasure map.

He's not that far from the coast; he would only have to retrace the day's travel. He just has to get back in less than five minutes before they disappear forever. Minecraft mechanics. Jakes loves them and hates them sometimes. Like now. He can't just wait out the rest of the night. He curses himself for not saving the coordinates of the shipwreck. He's sure he can find it again—just head west and follow the river and go north up the coast until he reaches that bay, right? He punches his way out of the hideout again and starts heading in that direction.

Stars glimmer in the sky, and a zombie approaches. Ugh. Jake breaks into a run; maybe he'll be able to make it if he runs fast.

Another zombie groans. Panic sets in, and Jake scurries back to the hideout, setting blocks down to close it back up, but he can't see much and he missteps more than once, and he doesn't have enough—

Creak.

The door to the computer lab opens and shuts, and Jake looks up in surprise.

A girl breezes in, typing furiously on her phone, biting her lip in concentration. She hasn't noticed Jake, just walks to his row and takes the computer on the end, booting it up as if on autopilot while still typing away, her fingers flying across her phone. She's cute—too cute, like the kind of girl who'd never even talk to Jake back at his old school, with dark skin, soft-looking wavy brown hair curling softly down to her shoulders, and a heart-shaped face.

A zombie groans, startling Jake out of his reverie and interrupting the dusty silence of the computer lab. He'd forgotten the speakers were on, and sometimes there's a lull of no music. Jake catches the time; he's been here for hours. He looks up to see the girl blinking at him, looking genuinely startled.

Jake backs away from the zombie, punching ineffectively at it with his bare fists. He can't believe this. He looks totally inept, but he can't go down without a fight. Not that this girl would be impressed anyway, but he's got standards. He's torn between just disconnecting and minimizing everything, but he doesn't want to risk losing the map.

She glances at his screen and watches him die from the zombie attack; a look of surprise crosses her face for a brief moment before it's replaced with bored annoyance. She glances at her phone and scowls.

"Great," she says, standing up with an aggravated huff.

"Uh, hi. I'm Jake—I just moved here." He glances back at the screen and at the clock on the desktop menu; with a sinking feeling, he realizes his stuff is gone now. He disconnects from the game and sighs, leaning back in his chair, kicking up another round of dust. He looks at the girl and gives her a shy smile. He might as well try to make a friend, right?

She gives him a cursory glance, and suddenly Jake feels very aware of the spaghetti stain on his faded T-shirt. She's shorter than he is, and has to be about his age, but is exuding a confidence Jake has never had. With one look she somehow radiates both judgment and annoyance.

It's just in your head, Jake tells himself. *You think everyone is out to get you.*

His nervousness jumps to his throat and before Jake can stop himself, he's babbling. "From Maryland actually, but I've lived all over in the last year. I've never been to California, though. My dad keeps saying we can go to the beach now that we're close."

She snorts. "Close. Yeah, right," she says, drawling out the last word.

"So what's there to do for fun around here?"

"Here? You've pretty much seen it all, the best Pacific Crest has to offer." She gestures broadly to the computer lab and the open rec room through the doorway.

"Yeah," Jake agrees. "This computer lab isn't bad, though." He shrugs. "I don't have Wi-Fi working in my apartment yet."

"Shame." She stands up and smooths her dress, shaking out her hair.

Jake doesn't mean to stare, but it's like he's frozen and he can't do anything but watch the curls bounce effortlessly, making this dusty old room suddenly the most beautiful place in the world.

"What?"

"You know, when someone introduces themselves, it's nice to, like, introduce yourself back. Like I'm Jake, and you are . . . ?"

"Leaving," she says, rolling her eyes. She strolls out the door without a second glance, her curls catching the scant afternoon light streaming through the windows as she goes.

Right.

And that's why Jake shouldn't even bother trying.

CHAPTER FOUR

EMILY

Of course they're late. *We'll pick you up at 4pm*, the text said. It's 4:33 and Emily feels like a fool just waiting by the curb outside the fancy Glen Oaks Apartments two blocks away from home. She always waits here whenever Pattie picks her up, but usually Pattie isn't quite so late. Emily sighs and, pretends to be busy on her phone so people passing her by won't find her suspicious. She's already annoyed at wasting an hour. Emily was ready to go by three, after all, since originally Pattie said she'd pick her up at three-thirty. So she had already left her apartment when she got the four P.M. text, and it wasn't like she could just go back in after she'd negotiated a later curfew with her parents. So she'd gone to the old computer lab to wait a bit before walking over to Glen Oaks instead, but there was already someone *there*, and she had no choice but to leave early.

She shifts, tucking a stray curl behind her ear, fidgeting and trying to put the annoyance behind her, but she was in the middle of an epic construction and was on a roll. She could have been adding a new floor to that new watchtower for the village she just fortified. Emily snorts and shakes her head.

If you had them pick you up at your actual apartment you could have played for another half hour, a small voice inside her says. It's a logical one, a practical one, so of course, Emily ignores it.

She checks her nails, hoping that the gold-green color she'd mixed together to go with this outfit will be met with approval. Emily had been proud of it an hour ago, admiring the glint in the safety of her bedroom, imagining Pattie and Nita's reaction to the bold statement, but now she's starting to second guess. It doesn't quite match, though that was the point. But what if they don't get it?

Emily spots Pattie's mom's flashy Lexus rounding the corner just as her phone buzzes with a new text. Probably Pattie telling her she's outside, even though she's all the way at the end of the block. Pattie hates waiting, never mind that Emily's been here on the sidewalk forever.

The gleaming black car slows to a stop in front of Emily. Nita waves excitedly out the window; Pattie doesn't look up from her phone in the front seat. Emily bites back the scathing comment she had prepared and instead goes for flippancy. "We going to absolutely crush this sale or what?"

Nita giggles as she opens the back door for Emily. "Or what!"

Emily hops into the car, returning Nita's hug with equal fervor.

"We're going to do H&M, Forever, and then Orange Julius, but only because I've got this coupon, but it's buy one get one free, but that's fine because I'm only going to have half. Emily, you can share with me because Nita doesn't like chocolate malt." Pattie hardly breathes as she says this, but she glances over her shoulder, her lips quirking up in a smile as she gives Emily a once-over from the front seat. "Your nails look great. Nice color," she says, quirking her eyebrow at Emily's outfit. "Goes well with your shoes. Not quite matching is totally in right now."

"Heh, I thought it would be cute," Emily says, basking in the approval.

"I love it!" Nita grabs her hands and coos over her nails. "Do you still have this color? Paint mine next!"

"Seat belt, Emily," chides Pattie's mom in the front seat. She's glamorous and beautiful and works as a producer in television, and today has her hair in a sleek updo, offsetting an effortless pantsuit.

"Sorry, Mrs. Anderson," Emily says sheepishly, buckling herself in.

"Darling, call me Rose," Mrs. Anderson says smoothly.

Emily shakes her head and smiles as they glide out of the neighborhood and onto the freeway, leaving the sad gray mediocrity of their not-quite-suburb behind.

After spending more than two hours browsing stores at the mall, Emily hasn't spent any money, so she counts the trip as a success so far. She claimed she forgot her purse, and Nita still owed her for yesterday's ice cream so with that and Pattie's coupon, she still got to have the chocolate malt at Orange Julius and hang out with her friends. It's going to take a while with her very minimal allowance to make up for even half of last week's shopping trip, but Emily's sure she can make it work. Now Pattie wants to take pictures by the fountain, and it seems like they've been here forever trying to catch the perfect light dancing through the water in the background of her shots. Finally Pattie is satisfied, and offers generously to take a photo for Emily as well. Emily can't say no; Pattie takes amazing photos, and if she posts it on her feed then Emily will have confirmation of what she has been unsure of the whole summer: that Pattie sees her as a friend, an equal.

Click.

Emily shakes her hair out of her eyes, pouts a little, and stares beyond Pattie's shoulder.

Click.

"Hmm," Pattie says, looking down at her phone.

Emily looks over Pattie's shoulder and sees herself and the result of two hours of getting ready and then waiting for the perfect lighting—artfully blown-out hair, subtle-looking makeup, long lashes, a casual-but-artsy outfit—reflected in Pattie's hands. She can see her flaws immediately, though: the clumsiness of the contour, how her brows are uneven, and that expression. What was she even thinking? Pattie said she should look like she's thinking of a secret, a good one, and that this would definitely get Toby— and other boys—to notice her. And Emily couldn't think of a good secret except that she was afraid, afraid Pattie didn't really like her, that all of this would end, and the alliances she'd been building all year would disappear like smoke.

"Cute," Nita coos, bouncing up and down beside her.

Pattie doesn't say anything, just turns the phone toward Emily so she can see herself.

"What do you think?" Emily finally asks, because she needs to know.

"Re-gloss," Pattie demands, waving her hands at Nita.

Nita promptly offers the lip gloss tube. Emily plucks it out of Nita's manicured fingers, and pretends she's annoyed instead of afraid. They've been at this for what seems like an eternity. The sun is almost setting, but Pattie insisted that they catch the "golden hour" for these Instagram shots. Emily's heart starts to pound faster as the sun dips lower, sinking fast, too fast behind the apartment complexes and strip malls of East L.A. She bounces on her feet, anxiety starting to spike. In Minecraft, it means danger: zombies and skeletons and worse. Emily's fingers twitch, her autopilot already on—*How far am I from my home base? Do I have a safe house nearby? Am I too far? Build a shelter, quick, before the monsters come—*

"Come on, we don't have all day," Pattie snaps.

Emily is tired. Spending time with Pattie and Nita is fun, and she loves hanging out with her friends—picking out outfits and catching movies or enjoying a pretzel at the mall together—but sometimes it's tedious—taking pictures for Instagram, helping Pattie shoot her videos, planning and plotting how to get even more followers and likes for their channels.

She thinks about the boy in the computer lab, the animated way he'd leaned forward when he was fighting that zombie, the weird little grin on his face when he introduced himself. Part of her wanted to ask how long he'd been playing Minecraft, to check out his builds, but he looked her age, and more likely than not would be going to the same school. Better not to risk making friends with anyone who could hold her back from the social status she'd worked for.

Emily reapplies the lip gloss, smacking it with more force than necessary, which makes Nita giggle.

Pattie and Nita are her two best friends in the whole world. Pattie was the most popular girl at their middle school, and Emily's come a long way from being that invisible girl that everyone picked on. People notice her when she's with Pattie and Nita.

She's made a name for herself through hard work and time, agonizing over the perfect Instagram captions and comments. It took a month of carefully crafted run-ins with Pattie at the mall and then one lucky invitation to a sleepover before Emily was even considered for part of Pattie's inner circle. It's been two years—seventh and eighth grade—working toward that social safety, and Emily's spent too much time this summer to not have Pattie and Nita by her side when she starts high school. She can't risk them branding her as uncool.

Emily pouts again for the camera, and lets Pattie take photos until there's one that's acceptable. Emily posts it with Pattie's caption, hugs her friends goodbye, and lets Pattie's mom drop her off two blocks from her apartment building.

Emily waves and ducks into the courtyard of the beautiful Glen Oaks complex, and waits there until the Andersons' Lexus pulls away. When the coast is clear, she leaves and walks down the street. Dry grass rustles in the median, and trash rolls across the street as she walks briskly down the few blocks. It's funny how quickly neighborhoods change, and East Los Angeles is no different. As she walks over the pedestrian bridge across the storm channel that pretends to be a river, the manicured lawns and well-kept buildings give way to rusted and torn chain-link fences and older apartment complexes, and finally Emily sees the familiar drab gray sign that reads PACIFIC CREST COMMUNITY CENTER AND APARTMENTS. The font isn't even retro, she thinks. It's just old.

The thick square key sticks in the lock as it always does, and Emily gives it a shove, eyeing the moving van blocking the entrance to the parking lot. Someone else moving into the brand-new building, she guesses.

Emily trudges up the dimly lit stairwell to the West Tower, yanking off her false eyelashes as she goes.

High school. It's starting in only a few months, and Emily isn't . . . she isn't ready. She only just figured out middle school, the right clothes to wear, the best way to laugh even when she didn't find something funny, how to do her hair and her nails, and how to cultivate an air of *I don't care* for Pattie to call her her best friend, to not be that mousy, invisible girl no one thought anything about. People notice Emily now; they stop when she walks through the halls, smile at her, offer her compliments, but every day it's fleeting, every day is a new struggle, and if her purse doesn't match, if her gloss isn't perfect, if so-and-so commented on her Instagram. She could be better, thinner, prettier, shinier . . .

Emily takes off her makeup and flops into her comfy computer chair. She doesn't have any new comments and only two likes on her latest haul video, and notices that Pattie has gotten several hundred new hits on *her* latest video. Emily watches Pattie smile at the camera, thinking about how long it took to shoot these videos, how much work they put into it. She sighs, clicking on her notifications.

The two likes are from Pattie and Nita.

This whole YouTube thing is so hard. Pattie's had her channel since sixth grade and her mom works in television so she's always had professional lighting and cameras and everything. She says being a YouTuber is fun, but so far it's just been a lot of work. Emily isn't quite sure how to bring up that filming makeup tutorials isn't exactly how she likes to spend her time. Pattie loves everything to do with editing and the ins and outs of making a video cool; Emily just likes watching them.

She switches accounts and smiles as her feed changes from haul videos and makeup tutorials to everything Minecraft: playthroughs, news, joke videos, all of her favorite things. Emily goes through her subscriptions and catches up with her favorite You-Tubers, the pranks they're playing on one another, their newest constructions and mods. She watches a video about treasure maps, taking careful notes about the best way to proceed. She's at a good point in her current game—maybe she'll go look for treasure today.

Emily sits up a little straighter at the notification alert in her in-box. She gets so few likes and views on her videos that any sort of interaction is surprising. Emily at first thought it would be cool to show off her redstone constructions, so last summer she put up a video, but it's hard when you're not already famous. Maybe she should change her username.

No, she chose it because she *is* a rock star, and she's going to be. Fake it until you make it, and just keep learning, keep trying.

Oh, she's gotten a new comment!

PacificViv: thank you for the subscribe! I like what you're doing with pressure plates here, very cool design!

Oh, nice. This is someone Emily found a while ago who looks like an amateur YouTuber like herself, with a bunch of simple recordings right from the game. PacificViv never appears on-screen, unlike so many other players, who are eager to talk and laugh and joke with one another. It's frustrating, trying to make a name for yourself; not everyone can afford to have cool equipment to record themselves and green-screen themselves into the game. It's a whole new world with rules and people who are already best friends with each other, one that Emily hasn't quite figured out yet. She can't really imagine herself doing it, either. No, the kind of videos she should make are like Pattie's—cute outfits and fun makeup tips. It's not like she can really keep up doing both haul videos *and* redstone constructions—that's not going to work in the long run.

Emily quickly types out a response to the message, and then goes and likes a few more of their videos for good measure, leaving comments on each one. Her notification pings again with a reply. PacificViv must be online, replying to her comments in real time.

> **RoxXStarRedStone:** great video! I always thought this was super complicated but you make it sound super simple
>
> **PacificViv:** thank you! It's really fun, it took me a while to figure out but I really like it, it's just like another language you just gotta get fluent in it!
>
> **RoxXStarRedStone:** haha yeah I thought it would be my favorite part but I'm still figuring it out. My redstone constructions are still pretty basic
>
> **PacificViv:** not at all! I thought what you did with the trapdoor was really cool! And you're a redstone ROCK STAR, clearly

Emily hesitates before taking a chance and sending PacificViv her server name and asking if they want to play together. She waits anxiously and then a moment later, an excited *YESSSS!* beams across her screen.

Which world should she show PacificViv first? The one with the labyrinth? What about the one with the automated bee farm in the shape of a bee? Yeah, that would be impressive and cool. Emily fluffs the pillow on her chair and puts on her headphones, letting the soft notes of the opening music waft over her. She pauses, looking over each of her worlds, smiling at the memories built into each one. It's easy to lose herself, and she loves spending time catching up on her builds, designing a new structure, creating trapdoors and hallways. She could spend hours exploring and adventuring, and she's been trying to learn more about construction and all the possibilities of redstone. There are just endless things to do, to explore, to learn how to make.

PacificViv has joined the game.

PacificViv's avatar is a girl wearing leather armor, modded with pink hair done in pigtails. She waves excitedly at Emily.

< PacificViv > what do you want to do first?
< PacificViv > this is so cool!!! want to show me around?
< PacificViv > do you like to explore? any cool places you want to check out?
< RoxXStarRedStone > i love exploring
< PacificViv > awesome!! sometimes i play with my brother but all he wants to do is stay in one spot, its sooooo boring

Emily laughs as the conversation flows as quick as water; no need to double or triple check what she's saying, calculate the maximum social impact, determine who knows what and who likes who, who wore what last week. It's fun in an entirely new way. Is this what it's like to share something you love with your friends? She can't imagine playing Minecraft with Pattie and Nita at all.

< RoxXStarRedStone > there's a cavern a ways from my base that's covered in lava— i always die trying to get to the mine
< PacificViv > have you tried redirecting the flow?

< RoxXStarRedStone > i told you I keep dying

< PacificViv > hm lets go see and figure out how to get past it!

Emily leads the way with a new thrill of excitement for her new friend.

They build a base together. It starts to be really fun when she discovers that PacificViv has the same attitude toward adventure — which is to say, rushing headlong into it. Emily finds herself relaxing and laughing, pausing in surprise when text flashes across her screen.

< PacificViv > call me Viv

< PacificViv > what's your name? do you wanna voicechat easier than typin esp when we're fighting

A rush of pleased warmth floods through Emily, and she shyly types out her own name and downloads the app Viv suggests. She's never done voicechat on Minecraft — only ventured into multiplayer once and was too intimidated by the other players — but this, this feels just as easy as saying hello to a new friend on the playground and asking if they want to play tag. It was so much easier back then, before things got complicated with followers and likes and what everyone looked like.

Viv sounds like she's her age, but Emily isn't quite sure — she uses a lot of big words that make her sound older sometimes, but she's right, it is easier.

"To the left, to the left!" Viv shouts.

"Yaaaagh!" Emily backs up frantically, trying to get a better shot, arrows flying wildly at the skeleton.

"One more!"

"Got it!" Emily grins in triumph, taking a moment to breathe as they enjoy a brief respite in the cavern they're exploring. Her heart pounds with excitement, Viv's excited shrieks as she dives headfirst into a throng of skeletons echoing in her ear.

This is fun. Having a new friend to play Minecraft with.

"Hey, I gotta go soon but this has been awesome!"

"Yeah. You wanna play again tomorrow?"

"That's what summer is *for!*" Viv says brightly.

Viv logs out of the voicechat but stays in the game, leading the way back to their new base.

< PacificViv > yessss all the iron love it!

< RoxXStarRedStone > we did good

< PacificViv > hey

< PacificViv > do you want to join another server with me and my friends? there're a lot of fun projects there I think you'd like!

< RoxXStarRedStone > how many people are in your server?

< PacificViv > haha a lot

< PacificViv > 17 active right now, and in our district only five

< PacificViv > we're the original, haha, and then we invited more people

< PacificViv > there isn't really room in this area to build in the original township, but there's a great plot in the water district if you like!

< PacificViv > or we can go find and make a whole new
district!
< PacificViv > i know mina was excited to settle a new area...
< PacificViv > omg this is going to be so amazing!!! pls come
it'll be so much fun

Emily hesitates as she and Viv put away their loot. Viv seems nice, and one-on-one Emily can hold a conversation, and it's fun. With more people, she's worried it'll be harder, a level of social interaction she isn't prepared for. With a group, she'd have to figure out the rules in order to stay in, and she isn't sure she wants to do that right now.

Her phone buzzes. It's Pattie, asking for outfit opinions.

"Mija, can you go get the mail?" Mama calls from downstairs.

"Yeah! In a minute!" Emily calls back. She sighs.

< RoxXStarRedStone > maybe
< RoxXStarRedStone > ttyl

Emily saves and quits before pulling up Instagram, flopping back on her bed. Helping Pattie isn't that much different from her earlier venture with the skeletons and the cave; a bit of puzzling out what would work best where, remembering Pattie's accessories and when she last wore what and giving a prompt suggestion. It's a different kind of problem-solving, and she's good at it. Being popular is like a job, she thinks, as she scrolls through her feed and likes her friends' posts, staying up-to-date on what everyone is doing. Emily finally posts a selfie after changing the filter three times and crafting the perfect caption to direct people to her new YouTube video. Pattie likes it right away and comments with a bunch of heart emojis and *yes! Great video!*

Pattie was the one who encouraged her to start her own video channel. "You've got the talent and you just need the confidence. Come on, I believe in you," she said. Emily didn't have the heart to tell her she already had one where she posted her Minecraft constructions. And she loves putting together outfits, loves sharing that with Pattie, but sometimes she wonders if they would be friends if they didn't have that in common, if Pattie would even enjoy hanging out with her if Emily didn't have a sharp eye for fashion and a knack for finding sales.

Emily puts the walls back up between her two passions. It wouldn't do, to be fully herself. She has to separate everything; Viv would probably find her love for clothes silly, and Pattie would find Minecraft boring and nerdy. Just like how RoxX-StarRedStone and her haul account are two different people with two different interests. Cute clothes and videogames don't go together, right?

It's important, who you're seen with and what other people think of you. It's something that new kid, Jake, is going to learn very quickly. Emily sighs. She hopes he isn't going to be in the computer lab all the time. That was her spot, the one place she could guarantee no would ever see her, where she didn't have to pretend to feel anything she wasn't feeling, to put on a face for the world. Now it's just another public place, where she has to worry about being seen, how she looks, and what she's wearing.

He had been playing Minecraft, though. Emily caught a glimpse of his player name before she left.

Part of her feels guilty for being kind of a jerk, but it's expected. If he lives here, he's probably going to end up going to the same high school and it's not like they could be friends. Pattie and Nita would have a fit, and the cool kids she's worked so hard to fit in with—well, they'd throw her right back to the loser aisle where she knows she belongs. She can see her classmates now, making fun of this boy and his awkward little smile.

If things were different, Emily would have stopped to talk, if she had Viv's confidence and easygoing warmth, she could have—she could have made a friend. Maybe they could have played together.

Emily finds herself googling "how to make new friends" before lying back down in defeat. She doesn't know how to do this outside the rules of engagement at school. PacificViv was a fluke. Plus, she reached out to Emily, and it just happened to work.

Step one. Be authentic.

Emily closes the article and groans.

"No way."

The difference between her air-conditioned apartment and the bleak hallway outside is immediate; heat pools and collects here, sinking into the concrete. Down, down, down the stairwell, the temperature dropping a few wonderful degrees as Emily exits the West Tower. Outside isn't much better, but at least there's a breeze.

She wades through the weeds of the overgrown courtyard, walking quickly; sometimes those so-called tough guys hang out here, and she takes care to avoid them. They like to scare the younger kids in the complex. She definitely doesn't like the tallest of the boys—the skinny fish-named guy who made clicking noises at her back when he thought she couldn't hear.

She doesn't see those guys from her school lingering by the vending machine or any of their usual spots, so she cuts through the empty playground on her way to the mailboxes.

Oh. One of those guys *is* here. It's the big broad-shouldered one who looks like he's in high school, but Emily's seen him at school. He was in eighth grade, just like she was, drifting through the corridors and grunting back at the teachers. Tank, Emily remembers. She remembers in seventh grade a guy called him Frankenstein because of the lurching way he happened to walk and an unfortunate sweater choice in the first week of school, and it stuck for a whole year. She always felt sorry for him, but he started hanging out with those guys in eighth grade, so they must have made up or something.

Tank pulls an armful of paper towels out of some bushes, looking shifty as he makes his way to the play set.

Emily keeps quiet, lurking in the shadows of the shrubberies. What is he doing?

Tank sighs, picking something up off the ground and tossing it into the trash can. He glances around before ripping off a long roll of towel, then proceeds to wipe down the swing set chains.

He does the same for all the swings, and then wipes down the monkey bars before throwing the paper towels away and slouching off to the North Tower.

Emily steps out of the shrubberies and pads over to the trash can. Inside, on top of the other trash, is an empty plastic bottle of vegetable oil and the paper towels Tank had used.

Weird.

CHAPTER FIVE

JAKE

At first Jake thinks she's somebody's grandmother. She's wearing a faded sweater set that could have been floral once upon a time and sitting on one of the benches in the outside play area, her eyes closed and her head tilted back. Her face is long and sad. She's worrying something in her hands, a colorful frayed beanie. It looks clumsily knitted, nearly unraveled and topped with a pom-pom barely hanging on by a thread.

Jake approaches her, a little hesitant. She looks sweet, and he wonders if he could make her smile. His nana used to get forgetful, going for walks to buy milk and not remembering what she was doing or why. She was the only grandparent he knew, and his memories of her are hazy, just brief glimpses of his parents smiling at each other, with Christmas lights reflected in his dad's glasses, the crinkling of wrapping paper in the background. Mom and Dad held hands and Nana would pat him on the head, and it's almost like another life. Jake didn't know then, but it was after Nana died when everything started changing, too much, too fast. Mom got sick and then she was gone, too, and then Dad just— the job, the moves—

He likes grandparents. Whoever's grandma this is, they probably miss her.

"Are you okay?" Jake asks, gently.

The woman's eyes snap open and they immediately focus on Jake. "What are you doing here?" she practically snarls. "The playground is closed after five."

The cold tone takes Jake by surprise. The sharp way her eyebrows draw together and how her whole face just goes tight like a teacher about to give him detention makes him feel defensive.

Jake automatically responds like he does with strict teachers, by shrugging in a way he knows is annoying and snorting with amusement. "It's like, only ten minutes after. Plus, it's still bright. I think it's okay. My dad knows I'm out here."

She glares at Jake, shuffling her coat around herself tighter. "Does he know you're breaking the rules?"

"Geez, it's not a big deal."

The woman draws herself upright. "It most certainly is," she huffs. "What unit do you live in?"

"A-two-oh-four."

She tsks. "Right. You're Nigel Thomas's kid." She gives Jake another glare. "Tell your father he still needs to sign the community guidelines agreement. And that there are fines for children in the playground after hours."

"Right," Jake says, drawing out the word sarcastically. She gets up from the bench, doesn't take the hand Jake offers, and toddles off, mumbling to herself.

Wow. Guess she doesn't want to be friends.

The community center is quiet again, much to Jake's relief. After a few days, he feels like he's gotten to know the rhythms of the complex. In the morning there are a few waves of people leaving for work, adjusting their ties as they hustle to the bus stop at the end of the block, briskly walking down the stairs to the parking lot, with kids in tow for summer schools and camps, overladen with backpacks and soccer gear. In the afternoons when it starts to cool down, some younger kids will play in the courtyard, shrieking laughter on the swings or the jungle gym.

Jake's almost given up on the Wi-Fi. He could call the cable company himself, but he doesn't want to risk going through the ever-growing pile on his dad's desk to find the bills and information. Plus, Dad's been weirdly cheerful, showing up every night and making dinner and asking Jake about his day. He doesn't want to get into trouble for messing with Dad's stuff, not when he's in such a good mood.

Jake doesn't know how to explain that he's found something. A mystery all his own, and he's on the cusp of discovering something huge. He tells his dad he's been walking to the local library and checking out comic books, which seems to distract him from the friend questions for now.

But every day once it gets quiet, once the full force of the sun beams down on the harsh edges of the three towers, gleaming rays bouncing off every surface, growing hotter and hotter as the sun reaches its apex, Jake will steal downstairs. He knows to wait for when the clock slowly approaches eleven and the complex settles into empty echoes and groans, the occasional footfall, stairwell doors creaking closed.

By then, muffled conversations from the courtyard die down. From the window, Jake can see if Shark and his goons are lingering by the vending machines; sometimes they're waiting for Tank, and all of them disappear out the double doors, probably to cause trouble elsewhere. But Jake's learned he can walk the perimeter of the inner balcony and go down a stairwell that leads right to the community center.

To the computer lab. To his mystery.

Jake's managed to find the seaside village again, and he's turned the biggest house into a home base of sorts. He's taken an excessive number of screenshots, documenting all the anomalies and his questions. Now with decent armor and access to the brewing stand and enchanting table in the village, he can craft items that can help him uncover the mysteries of this server. He'll need more Potions of Water Breathing before he can go back to the shipwreck, but he isn't quite strong enough to brave the Nether for the nether wart he'll need. Biding his time, Jake wanders near and far, trying to make sense of this world.

He wishes there were a way to check the log to see if anyone's been here since he last checked in. He's left signs in the village, saying things like *Who are you? Why did you build this?* But there hasn't been any response.

Jake stands in the center of the gazebo, studying the riddle one more time.

"Look to the sky," he says to himself. "Ice cave."

To the east of the village is jungle, overgrown with bamboo and tall trees. To the north, plains; mountains rise to the west, and south is the ocean where Jake discovered the shipwreck.

"I'll be back," Jake mutters at the sun winking in the distance.

He climbs the mountain, figuring there must be something that he missed. He climbed it yesterday, throwing blocks of dirt so he could hop up the sheer cliffside, but at the top he found nothing but a snow-covered peak. There aren't any caves anywhere on that mountain, not close enough to still see the village. It has to be within sight; why else would the riddle point him this way?

Jake reaches the first stretch of ice and pauses. Wait a minute. He's found plenty of caverns by just mining directly into the ground, going as deep as possible. What's to stop him from axing right into the mountain?

The first patch of ice only yields stone beneath it, but the second reveals an expanse of darkness.

"Woohoo! Take that, Riddle the Seventeenth!" Jake places a torch at the cave's edge, making his way cautiously inside.

Placing torches every few blocks to light his way, Jake is prepared to venture deep into the unknown, but finds the end of the cave after only a few minutes. He attempts to smash through the wall, to see if there's something hidden inside, but his pickaxe breaks immediately.

He turns back to the dead end of the cave, pacing back and forth. The icy wall won't budge, and it's not like there are shells anywhere on the floor—

Wait.

What if it's about looking westward and *then* to the sky?

Jake looks up.

Embedded in the ceiling are paintings of shells and signs under them with a series of numbers. "Add the numbers," Jake mutters. "Okay."

He gets 108, 5, and 1,072.

Coordinates?

Jake gasps. That must be it. He's sure that he's cracked it. *Buzz buzz.*

Dad 6:02 P.M.
Where are you?
Dinner's ready

"What's this?"

"Chicken parmesan," Dad says with a pleased grin. He pushes a plate toward Jake. A breaded and fried chicken cutlet, melted cheese oozing gently onto the noodles underneath, sits in the center, a pile of broccoli adding a pop of color to the plate. "And I roasted the broccoli, so I can proudly say it even tastes good."

Jake spears a floret of broccoli and chews it thoughtfully. It's actually pretty nice, but he's not going to comment on it. What would be next, a whole dinner made out of broccoli? He takes another bite, and then cuts himself a piece of the chicken. It's juicy and savory, and Jake dips it into his noodles and sauce to get more of the flavor. "Are you like, taking a class or something?"

"Watched a few YouTube videos. Did you know you can learn just about anything online?" Dad shakes his head, digging into his own plate.

That makes three home-cooked meals this week, after Dad's attempt at cauliflower rice and Tuesday's tacos. The number of meals itself isn't that unusual; Dad usually makes a bunch of dishes throughout the week when he has time. Jake will discover them in the fridge in various containers, Dad's loopy handwriting labeling (and sometimes mislabeling) the contents. It never varies far from Dad's staples of mashed potatoes or rice, boiled veggies, and a rotisserie chicken from the supermarket deli. Sometimes he'll make chili or a cheesy casserole that'll last for a while until Jake gets tired of eating it every day, but they have a routine with Dad's odd hours. Jake is usually alone, left to assemble and eat whatever out of the random things in the fridge. He usually ends up eating cereal.

He's not quite sure what to make of Dad's sudden interest in trying new things. Or the fact that Dad is actually home at night and not networking or whatever with the local design industry.

Dad pushes some sort of outdoor goods catalog at him, the pages flipped open to a spread with some photogenic family sparkling and playing catch. "Looks like a cool sale! Check it out. Do you need a new glove? I think that old bat is probably still good. Where did we unpack all the baseball stuff? We could go play catch or something. What about a Dodgers game?"

Jake's heart gives a strange leaping lurch at each of Dad's questions. He should be used to it, the grand ideas, the energy Dad has for hanging out and doing stuff together whenever they move. The logical side of him says he shouldn't hope anymore, shouldn't believe in it because it always ends up with him being disappointed. And yet there's a part of him that wants all of these things, the time and the baseball games and everything Dad is proposing. "Sounds cool. When?" Jake can't help the sarcastic bite to the question, but Dad usually doesn't notice.

"Hm. I can't do this Saturday, but I'll take a look at the schedule and tickets and such."

Jake's stomach sinks. Right. He should have known. "Okay, whatever. Just let me know when you want to do stuff. 'Cause, you know. I've got stuff going on." He's itching to go back to the computer lab and see where those coordinates take him. How many more riddles would there be? And where do they lead?

"You can't say you're too busy, you haven't started school yet!" He laughs and ruffles Jake's hair. "Did you make some new friends? Meet anyone in the building?"

"I've met people," Jake says, rolling his eyes. Technically he has. They don't like him, but that won't matter. He's going to be moving away in a few months anyway and no one will remember. These little interactions won't matter at all.

"Have you been playing Minecraft?"

"Well, yeah. It's my favorite game."

"Thought you needed the Internet for that."

Jake shrugs. "I can play offline. I mean, I can't connect to the epic project I was working on in the server I share with Danny, but I can still play." He doesn't mention the other server. It's his mystery, and he doesn't think his dad would appreciate or understand it. He does want Wi-Fi at some point, though. "Can we please get it fixed as soon as possible?"

Dad nods. "Yeah, I'll call the cable company again. Hey, are you still making buildings and things?" He chuckles at his own joke. "Take after your old man with the designing and the construction, huh? You know, if you ever want some pointers, I'd love to see what you're working on."

"Uh . . . maybe." Jake blanches at the idea of showing Dad any of his builds. Even if he's asking to see, it feels weird, especially after last time.

Jake remembers it clearly. He was eleven and he can still feel the plush blue carpet in the hallway of their Chicago apartment. It was the first move, after Mom died. They'd been there a few weeks already, not quite settled but Dad had jumped headfirst into the project. Jake had discovered Minecraft for the first time, finding solace in the bricks and the endless possibilities. He'd spend hours and hours after school playing, going on adventures and taking the time to build intricate worlds, replicas of places from history, real places he loved. He'd spent a week rebuilding their old house in Maryland, right down to the staircase and the ivy-covered brick chimney.

He wasn't sure if Dad would want to see that; after all, Dad had boxed up all the family photos and Mom's things and they were gathering dust at Nana's old house somewhere. They'd moved with very little, and Jake didn't know how to talk to Dad. They didn't have time, anyway; Dad had just gotten promoted and was taking on even more responsibility, and it was all very well and important and made Jake feel small and insignificant. Sometimes, when he was a kid, he'd go with Dad to the construction sites, and Dad would show him the blueprints and how everything would come together. They'd go get ice cream afterward; Dad always got a plain scoop of vanilla but would steal bites out of Jake's rocky road. They'd walk around the city, Dad pointing out cool buildings and how design can change everything: the flow of people, how they interact with one another — adding a little curve could inspire conversation, turn strangers into friends.

It was a stupid idea, trying to share his Minecraft build with Dad back then, Jake thinks now of his eleven-year-old self longing for times that would never come back. Everything had changed and he had been too naïve to understand it. Despite the Chicago cold, he still wanted that ice cream. Or that site visit. Or even just to talk. Jake hadn't even known where Dad's new project site was: He'd stumble out the door, all bundled up and cursing the weather. The snow in Chicago was nothing like it had been in Maryland, the constant storms and the way the apartment never got quite warm enough despite the soft-looking carpet and the fancy new heater. Maybe it was the space, the cold, hard lines of the furniture or the bareness of the walls.

Jake had found Dad's blueprints and the mock-up photos for the project he was working on back then, an apartment complex. It was completely different from the big plazas and art museums and gardens Dad used to do: big open spaces with lots of meandering paths. "It's all about the flow," Dad would say, smiling at Mom as she would wander the expansive gardens.

Jake built the whole complex in Creative, making it bigger and even adding a little park and a maze filled with roses, just like Dad used to do. He kept building, taking immense care in getting every detail right: the pastel color palette, the little cutouts on the balconies, the trees in the courtyard surrounding the fountain. He'd been most proud of the fountain, getting the water to flow just right, even replicating the sculpture in the center of it, some modern-looking curve that had taken forever to build. Circles aren't really a thing in Minecraft, but Jake was really proud of the result.

Jake remembers the careful way he'd brought his laptop into Dad's office and turned it around for him to explore. "Hey, Dad, I made your current project in Minecraft." He'd pushed the computer across the desk, nervous and hopeful all at once. It was snowing again, the sky outside an endless storm of gray-and-white flurries, but the sun was shining and maybe they could walk around like they used to. Dad was looking at his computer, nodding away with his earpiece in, like he was listening to music or something, so Jake didn't know it wasn't a good time.

"Dad? Wanna see? I even added a rose garden."

"Not now, Jake, I'm on the phone," Dad mouthed at him, waving him off.

Jake adopted a bright smile. "Okay. Sure. You can look at it later! I'm almost done, and it'll be like a 3-D model. Maybe you could use it to show your clients! Wouldn't it be cool if they could walk through it like this?"

Jake had been so excited, he'd just sat down in his dad's office next to him, working on the sculpture and perfecting it.

"Sorry, Johnston, there's background"—Dad glared at Jake—"Turn that off, will you? Or go play outside."

"Sorry," Jake said sheepishly. He muted the game and waited patiently, adding flowers here and there, and making sure all the doors matched.

He even started to figure out how to build a working elevator when Dad finally got off the phone.

"Listen, Jake, you can't just barge in here when I'm working," Dad said, shaking his head.

"I just wanted you to see—"

"I don't have time for your silly game right now. I just need to get this project done! Don't you understand?"

Shocked, Jake just nodded and took his laptop back to his room. He never bothered Dad with any of his ideas after that.

CHAPTER SIX

TANK

"Hey, Tank, where ya goin'?"

"Family stuff," Tank says, staring resolutely at a shrubbery behind Shark's shoulder. He remembers a documentary about wild animals, how some species see direct eye contact as a sign of aggression, challenge. Shark likes to be in charge, likes to come up with ideas for what to do. Tank's supposed to be helping Mr. Mishra at the store today, and the idea of Shark there makes him really uncomfortable. The last time they were at Fortress Park, Tank saw him tuck bags of chips and gum into his jacket. AJ and Gus did the same, and they had all been looking at Tank, who didn't know what to do. They were his friends, and yeah, the place definitely overcharges for chips, but the stick of gum he slipped into his pocket seemed to burn for the rest of the afternoon.

"Sounds boring. Wanna ditch and race go-karts? I bet the fake ride tickets my brother made will still work." Shark waggles his eyebrows at him.

"Can't," Tank says. "See you later. Maybe tomorrow?"

AJ slaps him on the back; Gus jerks his head at him in a slight nod without looking up from his phone. Shark narrows his eyes but doesn't say anything.

"You know," Shark says, in a too-casual way that puts Tank immediately on edge, "I think we need to teach that punk in your building a lesson."

"Who? The kid in the brand-new tower?" Tank thought he was kind of thick, the way he'd just stared at them with his mouth open before having the good sense to run.

"Yeah. Saw him talking to you the other day. He give you any trouble?"

Oh. So Shark saw that.

Tank had been on his way back from work, about to open the door to trudge up the stairs. It opened unexpectedly, Jake on the other side. They stared at each other for a long moment before Tank narrowed his eyes and hardened his scowl. It was a habit now. Shark always said making sure the other kids knew they were the toughest guys in school was important. Reputation was everything.

"Oh. Hi. Tank, right?"

Tank ignored him, pushing past to make his way up the stairs. He was tired and didn't have time for this, but Jake kept talking. It was bad enough that Tank remembered his name.

"Thanks. For the other day. You know." Jake shrugged, and then smiled, like a hapless puppy.

"Whatever."

Tank had forgotten about it immediately, but apparently Shark is now making it a thing.

It feels like a test.

Tank doesn't like it.

"Nah. He just ran off at the sight of me," Tank says, flexing his arm.

Shark laughs, and something sharp and metallic glints in his mouth.

AJ notices, too. "Whoa, what's that, boss?"

Shark almost looks embarrassed, but he glares at them all, as if daring them to say anything. "Braces. My parents—my parents want to fix my crooked tooth. Can you believe?"

AJ and Gus both hum sympathetically, and Tank hopes his nod conveys solidarity, but he can't help thinking of the way Ma cried when the dentist told her how much filling Viv's cavities would cost. They'd made sure to brush carefully from then on. Braces? That was out of the question.

"Sucks, man," Tank offers. "I gotta go. See you later."

"Hey!" Shark says. "I've seen that kid slinking in and out of that abandoned room with all that old stuff. Wouldn't it be funny if he got stuck in there? What if we jammed a chair under the door?"

Tank blinks. "Why would that be funny?"

Shark guffaws. "You're a riot, Tank. See you later."

Tank yawns, mentally counting how much money he still needs before he can afford those sneakers. He'd had to pop back up to his apartment before leaving for Mr. Mishra's and then Ba was attempting to rewire their ancient speaker system and Tank had to talk him out of it, so he'd gotten to work late and missed out on an hour. He's gonna need to work all summer to be able to afford those shoes, but it'll be worth it. Especially now that the money he's given to Ma so far has caught them up on what they need for repairs. He stretches as he gets back to the complex, and he's about to take his usual shortcut through the side door, but he sees a light on in the front building.

The key sticks in the lock; Tank hardly ever comes through the main entryway. No one does—who wants to go through two extra sets of doors when you can exit directly to the street faster? Plus there's a bunch of old furniture and stuff that Mrs. Jenkins keeps saying she'll get rid of but it just keeps collecting dust. Tank's got allergies, man. He's got no time to be sneezing.

Tank pauses, Shark's comment floating to the forefront of his mind. He pushes open the heavy glass doors. The creak intensifies in the empty lobby. Yellow streetlight filters through the windows, leaving long streaks across the dusty linoleum. A dissonant white light shines from under the door of the computer lab— which, sure enough, has a chair wedged under the door handle.

Tank grabs the chair and scoots it aside with little difficulty. He pulls the door open.

Inside, Jake looks up from the first computer row, his eyes widening. He doesn't move, like a rabbit freezing right before it's about to run.

Tank's running through his head whether *hey* or *are you all right* would be better, when Jake suddenly moves, leaping up from his chair. Tank jumps back on autopilot, the loud clatter from the fallen chair startling him, and before he knows it Jake is running right past him.

The second set of doors clangs shut, and Tank grimaces, thinking about the fear in the other boy's eyes. He must think that Tank is the one who locked him in.

It's a good thing, he reminds himself. That everyone knows their place. That being big means being tough, and being tough means other kids are going to be scared of him. That's just the way the world works.

Tank recognizes the music from the computer Jake left on — Minecraft?

He steps inside.

He almost forgot there was a computer lab here. It's all clutter and junk, at least a decade old. A few computers work, Tank remembers — he used some last summer to browse the Internet when their Wi-Fi was down.

One lone lit monitor is indeed paused on the loading screen, chimes whirling and rising in the background. Oh. Jake was logged in.

Tank doesn't know how many people use this center, but he knows how he would feel if someone snuck into one of his open games and messed with any of his farms or builds. He carefully logs Jake out and turns off the computer, before trudging back out to head home.

CHAPTER SEVEN

EMILY

"Emily, dinner's ready!"

"A minute!" Emily calls, not tearing her eyes away from the screen, clicking furiously. She's surrounded by skeletons and in the distance she can see a spider ambling toward her as well. She slashes furiously at them, her health dropping as she charges forward.

Clang.

Great, that's the third sword she's gone through today. She quickly grabs another sword from her inventory, making a note to craft some more later, and fights her way out of the mob. Emily barely escapes, hobbling away as she stuffs her mouth with bread. There are still a few scattered skeletons chasing her, and Emily ducks behind a tree to avoid their arrows.

"Emily Rosario Quesada, don't you dare make us wait for you!"

Emily winces at the full name and disconnects. She brushes back her hair, straightens her skirt, and reapplies her lip gloss.

In the kitchen, the twins are already a mess, faces covered in sauce. Emily pats Ricky and then Minnie on the head affectionately and smooches her abuela on the cheek before sitting down. Her older sister Carmen is scrolling on her phone and unsuccessfully aiming a spoonful of soup toward her mouth, holding it suspended in midair.

"Mama, can I go to the mall tomorrow with Pattie and Nita?"

"The mall? You just went yesterday!" Mama frowns, her forehead wrinkling in distaste.

"I'm not going to buy anything, we're just going to hang out."

Mama clicks her tongue. "You know what I said about wasting money on things you don't need."

"I can't just wear what I wore in middle school to high school!"

"Why not? Carmen did."

Emily glares at her older sister, who is wearing what she always wears: a black T-shirt with some awful band logo, ripped black jeans that have seen better days, and way too much eyeliner. "We can't all just roll out of bed looking like we don't care!"

"At least I don't pander to society's expectations," Carmen says, rolling her eyes before going back to her phone.

"You don't know *anything* about—"

"Oye, both of you. We're not doing this again. You both have your own beautiful style," she says, pressing a loud and wet kiss to Carmen's cheek, and then Emily's.

"Mama!" Emily scowls, more out of habit than anything, smiling despite her annoyance.

Mama clucks her tongue. "But you know, when we give you kids money, we expect you to be responsible. You know your father and I work really hard to make sure you all have enough, a roof over your head, enough to eat. That money you should be grateful for." Mom shakes her head, disappointment creasing her forehead. "You should be more like your sister. She didn't need to go back-to-school shopping."

Carmen gives her a smug look.

"That's fine for her!" Emily bites her lip. "Look, *I* need new clothes, okay?"

"You need something, you let me know, and I'll find a good deal for you," Mama says fondly, patting Emily on the arm.

"Ma*ma*! The stuff you pick out is like, so old-looking!"

"I don't understand you. We gave you money for clothes last week. If you just want to spend time with your friends why don't you invite them to play here?"

Emily balks at the word *play*, like they're babies. "Ma—"

"There's a whole game room and stuff downstairs, right? You don't have to be going out all the time, spending money on pretzels and things. I can make you food, you can save money."

Emily can't even picture Pattie and Nita showing up here. They don't even know where she lives, for good reason. Emily always has them pick her up in front of that nice apartment complex a few blocks down. Imagine, the two most popular girls in school knowing she lives in this dump? Emily can see it now, Pattie and Nita gingerly stepping over the broken furniture, coughing at the dust, and laughing at the pitiful options in the game room. There would be absolutely nothing to do. The computers in that old lab can barely get Internet.

Papa enters the room with a grim expression, holding a shopping bag from Lemon Russo, the store Emily was at yesterday with Pattie and Nita. "Emily."

Emily's stomach drops. She knew that big shopping trip last

week was probably too much, but there was a summer sale, and buy-one-get-one-fifty-percent-off, and of course she had to get things to match, and Pattie had found that super cute top that went with those jeans, and they did say she could pick out clothes for going back to school.

Papa hands the receipt to Mama, and Emily freezes. Mama doesn't say anything, but her face gets tighter and tighter as she gets to the bottom of the receipt.

"Ba, ba, ba," Minnie says, reaching for the piece of paper.

Mama yanks it away, and the silence is deafening as the evidence of Emily's purchases lies on the table.

Carmen peers closer and lets out a low whistle.

Papa shushes her and turns his calculating gaze at Emily. She squirms in her chair, wishing she could disappear. Any argument she would make starts to die in her throat. She knows she shouldn't have done it, but Pattie had spent twice as much and she didn't want to look like she couldn't afford it in front of her friends. But now in the face of the thick tension in the air, she has nothing to say.

Emily looks down at her plate awkwardly. She had hidden the bags in the recycling bin, and had kept all the tags for the clothes—she was going to return like, half of it, and then they'd never know.

"I'm very disappointed in you," Papa says. "We trusted you with the credit card because you said you needed it for school, and you went and took advantage of us."

Mama folds her arms as she shakes her head. "I cannot believe this. Look at this. For three shirts and a pair of pants."

Emily wishes the floor below her would swallow her up, that she could punch the ground and just keep going and disappear.

"This is unacceptable," Papa says. "You're grounded. You're going to return all of these things, and Mama will do the rest of your shopping for what you need for school."

Emily gasps. "No! That's not fair! At least let me pick out—"

"No. You lost the right to pick when you betrayed our trust. And no laptop, no phone, no Internet."

"But—but—" That means no Instagram, no *Minecraft*—

"That's final," Papa says, and his voice is serious.

Emily leans back in her chair, shocked. Not having to do any social media is actually somewhat of a relief, and it'll be hard catching up on a week's worth of posts and gossip, but doable. Nita's definitely been grounded before and Pattie's gone on vacation with her parents and didn't have reception; it's understandable to be inactive for a while.

But a week without Minecraft is going to be the *worst*.

CHAPTER EIGHT

JAKE

The sound of high-pitched laughter sounds from the living room, and then Dad's embarrassed snort. Jake pauses in the hallway, listening to see if he can tell who it is. It's a game he sometimes plays, even if he doesn't know the names of all the people Dad works with. There's the High-Pitched Realtor, the Contractor Who's Always Late, the Guy with the Tile, and his personal favorite, the Toilet Man. No matter what city they're in, Dad always seems to know someone who knows someone else who can get the job done. It's what makes his company successful, Jake guesses.

The voice is impressed. It's a new one Jake doesn't recognize. Probably someone from Los Angeles for this project.

"Nigel, this construction plan is amazing. I can't believe how quick your team is at setting all of this up."

"I am the best project manager in the business." Dad sounds ridiculously proud.

"Would you be interested in another project of mine down in Long Beach?"

"Eh, maybe. I usually go where the best work is."

Jake snorts. More like where the best paycheck is.

"These plans are amazing. Have you been working in urban planning and design long?" Dad's in full work-flattery mode, adopting the super bright tone Jake recognizes immediately.

Jake enters the kitchen quietly, hoping he can sneak out without having to meet the new work friend or whatever. He hates how awkward it is, how adults always seem to ask the weirdest questions, like what he wants to do or if he's enjoying school. He catches a glimpse of a woman in the living room and wide outstretched arms holding large sheets of colorful paper.

"Jake! Come take a look at the Pacific Crest of the future." Dad beams at Jake, waving at him excitedly from the living room.

Great.

Jake mumbles a hello and waves awkwardly as he steps into the living room.

"This is Isabella Reyes. She's the one who brought me and the company out here to renovate this building." Dad grins, pointing at the new plans. "It's going to be spectacular."

"Hey there." Isabella nods at him. She's a tall woman with dark skin and slicked-back hair in a severe bun, dressed in a three-piece skirt suit and big clunky jewelry. "Isn't it amazing? We're going to turn this sad place into a state-of-the-art building where people can work, play, and live. Imagine being able to go to the grocery store, shop, and more without having to leave this beautiful central location!"

"Uh, I don't really do any of those things," Jake says, wondering why she's giving him what Dad calls "the pitch." Jake already never leaves "this beautiful central location."

Isabella laughs. "Such a great sense of humor!"

Right. That's what adults always say when they don't really understand what you say.

"This complex is getting a major upgrade. Lush gardens and walking paths, a brand-new pool and fitness center for residents, and of course this whole street-facing entry building is going to be completely transformed. Small businesses or restaurants or anything, the possibilities are endless!" Isabella points at the plans and claps her hands together in excitement.

Jake can see from the models that it'll likely be a lot of work. Maybe Dad might actually stick around for the whole thing, who knows?

"It's going to be amazing for families, for young couples, for singles, for people looking to work and live—"

Dad laughs, clapping Jake on the shoulder. "You don't need to do the sales pitch. He thinks it's cool, right?"

"It's cool," Jake mumbles. He runs his fingers over the new computer lab and center. Looks pretty neat. "When are you planning to do this? Next year?"

After they move, probably, Jake realizes. Dad's company does this all the time, swoops in, lets Dad charm everyone and set up the entire construction project and get all the contracts in place. Jake guesses Dad could stay and see the whole thing through, but he's always ended up hiring another person to oversee the project. In Maryland, Dad always found plenty of interesting things to do, but they've moved three times since they left. It's like Dad can't stay still, he needs to flounce off to a new city, a new state, bringing Jake with him, before they've even spent a full year in one place. Just enough time to feel like they've settled in before his whole world is uprooted again.

"We'll be starting construction next week," Dad says proudly. "And then I'll be overseeing the renovation of the next two towers."

"Wait, we're actually—" They're staying? Is Dad for real?

"What did I say?" Dad ruffles Jake's head. "You're starting high school at the end of the summer, and you're always telling me you can't make any friends. I figured I owed it to my son to invest my time and energy in staying in one spot."

"You're serious?"

"Yeah, I am." Dad almost looks nervous, looking at Jake for approval.

Jake knows all he ever wanted was to stay in one spot, but suddenly now that it's confirmed, he's terrified. He doesn't actually know how to do this. He's acted like an idiot in front of a cute girl, and a scary-looking guy probably hates him, and they're both going to go to his school and he's going to be here forever now? For years? And he's ruined his chances at a good first impression?

And construction begins in a week? Jake thought—he thought he had more time to figure out the mystery of the server, and the mermaids, and—

This can't be happening now!

"I—I gotta go."

Dad looks at him, his mouth falling open in surprise. "I made meatloaf for dinner—"

"Cool, cool, I just remembered, I had a, a thing, I'm uh, I'm meeting, uh, Tank—" The name is the first thing out of Jake's head, and he regrets it as soon as he says it because Dad just lights up.

"Oh, that's great, you made a friend, buddy! I knew you would. All right, don't stay out too late and your friends are welcome here, too, I made plenty!"

Jake exhales as he scoots backward and out the door.

Jake closes the door to the computer lab, exhaling heavily. They're going to be renovating this whole place? What will that mean for the center? Are they going to start tearing it up right away?

He catches his breath, trying to steady his thoughts. No, no, the mystery—he has to finish the game, and now that he's solved one of the riddles he needs to see it through! How many riddles are there? What is at the end?

He has to know.

Jake boots up the computer he's come to think of as his, heart pounding with every second it takes to get from startup to the login screen to loading Bella's world. He's made great progress, but he only discovered the server a few days ago, and he needs time, and the Riddle the Eighteenth he found at those last coordinates implies navigating an underwater maze but Jake is nowhere near ready. He'll need to put in so much more work to even get to the Nether and survive harvesting all the nether wart he'll need for potions!

Jake sighs and gets to work.

CHAPTER NINE

EMILY

The summer inland heat rises, settling in the buildings; heat pools in the concrete of the sidewalk, and the old air conditioning unit barely works in the apartment. Emily lies on the cool kitchen tile, listening to Mama clicking away from her home office, occasionally taking a call. There's some toddlers' show on the TV, and Minnie is babbling away.

This sucks. Emily can't even bother Carmen; she's hanging out with her goth friends somewhere. With no phone and no computer and no Internet, Emily's left with absolutely nothing to do, and a whole summer full of plans ruined.

She's grounded, so she can't exactly leave the complex, and her parents would know immediately if she was with Pattie or Nita. Embarrassment of all embarrassments, Mama talked to Pattie's mom, who agreed that Emily needed to learn responsibility and that they wouldn't be picking her up.

Mama allows her one phone call with Pattie once Emily argues that she needs to be able to tell her friends what's going on.

"Ugh, parents are the worst," Pattie says. "So, how long?"

"Uh. Not sure. Might be the whole summer." Emily's a little surprised how easy that was. She thought Pattie would be upset about losing her main camera person for her videos.

"No way! Ugh, you won't get to wear any cute summer dresses, and then school will start and we'll have to start planning for crisp fall outfits." Pattie sighs. "Is it just no phone and no Internet and no going out? I can like, come over and we can hang out at your place?"

Emily finds herself smiling, and then realizes with a start Pattie thinks she lives in a beautiful apartment two blocks away. "Oh no, no, I can't have friends over, either," she lies.

Pattie clicks her tongue. "Sucks. Well, maybe you can work on taking some photos with that old camera of yours. The vintage look is totally in, and those Polaroids would look great on your Instagram."

A helpful suggestion. Mama reminds her to be careful with her camera, but she approves of it as an activity, so Emily sets off, the old Polaroid heavy against her hip, the strap solid against her shoulder as she walks down the stairs. She looks real cute today, too, in a romper with her hair in a fishtailed braid.

Emily takes a few photos of herself in the reflection of her window before she remembers the big glass double doors of the community center.

Bounding downstairs, she can feel the temperature drop ever so slightly, and a breeze ruffles her hair. Emily takes photo after photo: the stark look of the new tower against the older buildings, clouds scuttling across the sky, a flower blooming in a crack in the sidewalk.

There was a pool at Pacific Crest once; now it's an overgrown excuse, filled with scummy water and plants growing wild in the empty shallows. Emily sits on the concrete edge, dangling her feet in the air as she takes a shot of the sun dipping behind the rising expanse of the weeds. The little park is empty today, and Emily traipses through the overgrown shrubberies to the base of an oak tree, capturing the sunlight filtering through the leaves.

Her friends would definitely appreciate these pictures, although she wonders how long it would take Pattie to figure out the perfect hashtags for the caption, and if she would stop and take a moment to appreciate the soft warm breeze ruffling her hair or enjoy the light tumbling through the branches. Emily thinks about all the cool things people have built in Minecraft, wonders how long it would take to re-create this tree and what blocks she could use, if there would be a way to automate leaves flowing down, if Pattie would like that, too; she likes pretty things —

Emily shakes herself, standing up and brushing leaves off her hair. No, she can't invite her friends here, and Pattie doesn't play Minecraft.

Viv would probably know, but then again, Viv is most interested in making efficient inventions and fighting.

Emily sighs, shaking her finished photos and tucking them inside her messenger bag before walking through the playground to the glass double doors for her shoot.

Huh. That's new.

The entire community center has been fenced off. A brand-new chain-link fence wraps around the whole entry building, a big DETOUR sign pointing toward the other exits.

Emily presses closer.

She knows they were always planning to fix it after old Jenkins finally sold the place; that poster with the 3-D model of the renovated design complex had been sitting in the lobby forever—the project description promising an entire update of all facilities, tower by tower. New pool and a whole bunch of stuff that Emily doesn't quite remember, but the renovation of the North Tower took a year. It was a whole mess, people moving out and having to get temporary housing or just not renewing their leases. A bunch of people complained, so it sounded like the other two tower renovations would either not happen' or might take years. Emily thought she'd be off at college before the big change actually became a thing.

The squat gray building now is surrounded by a fence with a sign that reads REYES DESIGN AND CONSTRUCTION, COMING SOON.

"Boo!"

Emily jumps backward in surprise at the sudden noise.

Her photos fall out of her open bag, tumbling onto the concrete. Ugh. It's that guy who calls himself Shark and thinks he's so tough.

Emily bites back the curse she wants to shout and scowls instead. She starts picking up the photos, one by one. They've scattered everywhere, a few of them caught by the wind right up to the chain-link fence.

"What are these supposed to be?"

Emily whirls around. Shark's crouched a few steps away from her, grabbing at the photos on the ground. He grins at her, showing off a disturbing amount of metal crammed in his mouth as he stands up. His blond hair is slicked back with an abundance of hair gel, just like all those guys he hangs out with.

Emily's heart pounds with nervousness as he dangles the photos in front of her, including the best one she got of the towers rising against the sunset reflected in the glass double doors of the community center this afternoon. "Give those back," Emily demands.

Shark laughs and then in one swift move, chucks the handful entirely over the fence. "Have fun!" he taunts before skipping off.

Emily stares in shock as her photos fly into the construction site. Ugh. She hates that guy and all the mean pranks he plays on people.

"Hey, it's dinnertime!"

Emily looks up from the courtyard and spots Carmen leaning over the balcony in the West Tower, waving crossly at her.

"I'm coming!" Emily says. She'll have to come back after dinner to get the photos.

Emily grips the camera strap and walks off without looking back.

CHAPTER TEN

TANK

"Thanh, hand me those pliers, yeah?"

Tank eyes the pair of legs sticking out from under the kitchen sink. "Ba, what are you doing?"

"Fixing the sink, what does it look like?"

"Don't you have work?" Tank sighs and drops into a crouch to see what's going on. He shines his phone's light under the sink and wishes he hadn't: His father's face is scrunched up in concentration as he wrenches away at the large pipe, and there's an alarming amount of duct tape on the lower half of the pipe — he doesn't even want to know what's happening there.

"Eh, going in late today. This bolt won't move and I just need to see what's going on —"

The clogged sink is full of suds and soapy dishes, and Tank

instinctively takes a step back as Ba gives the wrench a particularly hard jerk.

Dirty water splurts from the pipe, and Ba curses as it hits him in the face.

"Aaaugh! Thanh, the wrench!"

"What's going on here?" Auntie Phuong emerges from the hallway, crossing her arms.

"Ba's fixing the sink," Tank says.

Auntie Phuong shakes her head and sighs. "Again? We can't keep doing this, I'm calling a plumber—Thanh, make sure he doesn't—"

Tank obliges, pocketing the wrench, taking the whole toolbox with him, and placing it back underneath the bathroom sink.

She's still lecturing Ba when Tank heads back to the living room and flops onto the couch. He closes his eyes. He'll probably have to help clean up the mess later, talk to Auntie Phuong and calm her down, and talk to Ba and make sure he's got something to do.

Tank closes his eyes and leans back.

"Hey, Thanh-anh?"

Tank grunts.

"I found you some more of the lilacs you were looking for. Wanna decorate your garden?"

Tank raises his eyebrow at Viv, surprised. "You don't want me to come adventuring with you?"

Viv laughs. "Well, I was gonna ask after we decorated your plot in the server. But we also don't have to go in there if you don't want to— Oh, and I made something you might like—it's like a musical wind chime! Wanna put it in your world?"

Tank finds himself smiling and lets Viv tug him and his laptop into her room so he can set up next to her.

He's surprised but pleased when Viv boots up his favorite world instead of connecting to the server with her friends. It's in Creative, which she only uses when she's figuring out something; she prefers survival mode and the challenge of making all the technological advancements.

Tank feels a sense of peace and calm wash over him, the worry about the mess in the kitchen, about Ba and his family, about taking care of Viv, about Shark's persistence on how he needs to prove himself—it all fades away as his world comes into view.

He smiles, flying above the intricate maze he's created in his garden. Tank loves planning and making mazes. A spiral for the center, multiple pinwheels and bubbling brooks of water, fun little sculptures for visitors to discover. Viv's avatar with her bubblegum pink hair leads the way, navigating through it with only a few wrong turns.

It's easy to lose track of time in the game, and they end up playing well into the night, taking a quick break so Tank can make sure Ma eats something before she goes to work, and then they're back. Vivian's sure she found a stronghold somewhere, and they're traipsing all over the world, traversing thousands of blocks to find it until Tank's tired. "Come on, Viv, what are we looking for?"

"I know it was here! I wrote it down!"

Tank eyes the notepad next to Viv's computer, filled with coordinates and notes like "Safehouse 3" and "Weird jungle" and "Cool rock formation" and even more in Viv's practically undecipherable scrawl. "You wrote it down on this or you wrote it down somewhere else?"

Viv ducks her head sheepishly. "Uh, maybe I wasn't at home."

Tank immediately seizes up with a flash of worry. "You know you're not supposed to leave the complex, Viv!"

"I know, I know! I was here! The Wi-Fi shorted out last week while I was working on this world so I went downstairs to see if the computer lab had anything, and you know some of those old computers have Minecraft installed on them?"

"The game's been around for a while, Viv. It's not that weird."

"Yeah, but anyways, I played on one of those computers for a while and made good progress and I swear I totally found that stronghold. I must have left my notebook downstairs in the lab."

"Don't go out alone, Viv." Tank frowns at her, trying to let her know how serious he is, but she just laughs.

"Other kids do it all the time. Look, I'm eleven years old, I'm not a baby."

"Yes, you are. You shouldn't be going out by yourself." Tank's heart pounds nervously, and he can't stop thinking about what might happen, if anything—Ma and Auntie Phuong are always working and Ba's checked out in Ba-land, and he's the only one looking after her.

"Why can't I have other friends like normal kids? You're so boring. All you want is for me to stay at home, and you're not any fun to go exploring with in Minecraft and—"

"Mean! I'll go get your coordinates, just . . . just stay here. I'll be right back."

"You better!"

Tank sighs, thinking about summer and how everyone at school was excited, bubbling over with plans, going to the beach or Disneyland or barbecuing with their family or whatever. School's a lot of work but at least it's a good chunk of time he doesn't have to worry about Viv, and he doesn't quite have enough time or ideas to occupy her. Minecraft and YouTube are good, but she gets antsy, wants something more. She's started doing a lot of redstone construction and is learning more about programming, but Tank can't keep up with that. There are some books she's been wanting, but that'll take time to save up money for. Still he hopes once she gets them she'll be so busy she won't even remember she's stuck in this apartment complex, just like he is.

CHAPTER ELEVEN

JAKE

Jake pulls the chain-link fence aside where it's loose and slips inside the construction site. He carefully pushes the fence back into place and squeezes past the overgrown shrubberies. The past week has been busy; tractor loaders are now parked in front of the community center and rows of construction materials have been stacked carefully. The entire front entrance is closed, with signs redirecting residents to use the west and south doors.

REYES CONSTRUCTION AND DESIGN
THANKS YOU FOR YOUR PATIENCE

Jake ducks under the yellow caution tape hastily draped between two tractors and walks toward the community center. The power has been working this week, but he doesn't know how much longer it will be on. Judging from the rate of the equipment stacking up, the power will probably be shut off soon.

Too soon.

The Wi-Fi finally works in the apartment, but his old projects can't compare to the mystery of Bella's world, which is only hosted on the local area network in the computer lab. Jake's been spending all his time on the server, when he can sneak downstairs and away, but there's been a new development since bags and bags of concrete arrived: a security guard.

The first time Jake saw the man, he'd pretended he was going to get the mail. GRANT, his name tag read, a round-faced guy with a ring of keys jangling on his belt. After a few days Jake's figured out his schedule: Grant shows up at ten o'clock at night, and Jake once saw him leaving at six in the morning.

During the day, they deliver items, and Dad is usually on-site as well, talking with Isabella and people wearing hard hats. Jake's found a routine: He hangs out at home, unpacking and reading his comic books or surfing the Web. The crew usually leaves around four o'clock, and Dad generally has to stop by the design office for stuff, so Jake can sneak in a bit of time before he has to eat dinner with Dad. Sometimes after dinner he'll try to get some time in before Grant gets there but it's been tricky to navigate the timing. Jake's used to being on his own for most of the week, but now Dad's been making dinner and asking questions about his day, and keeps badgering him about when he wants to go see a Dodgers game.

It's weird. But nice.

But also, Jake's got a mystery to solve.

He has to know the answer. Who put the riddles there? What does it mean? He's only solved one of the clues so far, and he's stuck trying to prepare for the next one. The whole thing has to lead to something big, something amazing. He knows he saw a mermaid, he's sure of it. He hasn't seen any others since then, but what if there are more?

There was one huge mural in one of the villages he came across that was interesting. The designer took painstaking effort to build an incredible wall made out of different blocks of all colors and textures. Up close, it was just a cluster of color. But after trekking across the valley next to the village and climbing up a mountain, he can see the whole picture. From a distance, it almost looked like a painting. An entire city underwater, towers and monuments and mermaids, all under the shifting forest of kelp, bright sunshine shimmering through the water, chests filled with golden treasure, and gems glimmering everywhere.

Jake remembers how he felt, standing on that mountaintop looking at the image of the underwater city, filled with awe. That's the treasure at the end, he just knows it. Jake feels like an explorer in the old days, itching for adventure and treasure. He only just started here and he can't lose the one interesting thing he has going on. No community center, no computer lab, no mysterious Minecraft server filled with mysteries. He can't lose the secret of the server, not just yet. It doesn't exist anywhere without the LAN and once that's gone, who knows if he'll ever find it again? This place, this refuge, the world of Minecraft—he has to solve the puzzle.

Jake checks his watch; it's already nine thirty. He wanted to get away earlier, but Dad really got into dinner and making it together—they baked a pizza, which actually turned out pretty good. Jake had a lot of fun picking out toppings and customizing his own pie, and making fun of Dad and his olives.

Finally, once Dad was in his office again, Jake slipped away.

He doesn't have much time, but he can make good progress.

Jake pads across the empty space toward the community center.

In the distance, he sees the glow of a light.

Jake freezes.

No one else should be here. Grant isn't on shift yet.

A door opens from the other side and there's the scuffle of shoes on the dusty concrete pavement. Jake tries to shift and hide behind the tractor, but his foot gets caught in the tread and he slips. His phone falls out of his pocket, clattering loudly against the ground.

"Shark, is that you?"

Jake squints and in the darkness he can make out a face and slicked-back hair. "Tank?" he asks in disbelief.

He stands up awkwardly, relieved it's not the security guard.

Tank frowns at him. "What are you doing here?"

"What are *you* doing here?"

Tank blinks, looking at his feet and then back at Jake before speaking slowly. "None of your business. Meeting up with my friends." He glances outside. "I, uh—there's a hill that's supposedly haunted and we were going to check it out. Something a scaredy-cat like you would hate." Tank folds his arms together. He looks menacing in the dark.

"What kind of name is Shark?"

"What kind of name is Jake?" Tank tosses back at him. "What are *you* doing, anyways?"

"Nothing," Jake says. *Don't look at the community center, don't look at the community center, shoot—*

Tank follows his gaze. "No one's supposed to be here."

"Just—just forget you ever saw me. You didn't see me, okay?" Jake wants to yell in frustration. Is Tank going to wait here all night? He can't go play Minecraft now. He guesses he could just go home. Maybe he could pretend to leave and watch and wait until Tank leaves?

Tank grins at him. In the dark, all Jake can see are his teeth gleaming.

"It's gonna cost you."

"No way, I don't have any money!"

Footsteps.

Jake's heart leaps into his throat and he ducks behind the tractor, sinking into the dark. He squeezes in on himself, trying to make himself as small as possible.

Tank glances behind himself and curses, turning around quickly, like he's looking for an exit and thinking fast. Something falls out of his pocket and clatters to the floor with a loud metallic clank.

To Jake's horror, Tank heads right for him and his hiding spot. In the distant streetlight streaming through the community center, Jake can see the metal tool lying on the floor.

"Why do you have a *wrench*?" Jake whispers in horror. "What were you going to do?"

The footsteps get louder.

"Nothing, I was just holding it," Tank grunt-whispers. "Move over."

"No way, find somewhere else!"

Tank's already crouching down and Jake scoots over. If Tank gets caught, Jake won't be far behind.

The chain-link fence creaks like someone is pushing it aside to climb through. Jake would have thought the caution tape and the fence would have deterred people from using the fastest shortcut from the inside building through the courtyard to the side street, but he guesses not.

From his hiding spot Jake can see a pair of teal sneakers tiptoe past the tractor, stop, and then a pair of hands with blue nail polish reach down and hastily grab something off the ground.

The shuffling pauses.

"Hello?"

Jake peers over the tractor seat. In the scant light from the courtyard, he can just make out the face: the girl from the computer lab. What's she doing here?

Tank grabs his arm and squeezes in a warning.

"Is someone here? Whoever you are, I just want you to know that I know krav maga!" She shifts, taking a fighting stance as she scans the room. She looks right past Tank and Jake's hiding place, and Jake ducks out of view just in time. His heart pounds so loudly he's afraid she can hear it.

The community center doors facing the street open and close, and then a shot of cold white light flickers from inside the dark building. The beam flashes through the glass doors facing them and through the chain-link fence, and the girl freezes in her tracks.

"Oh no—"

She's not supposed to be here, either. Wait, where is she—

Jake realizes too late that the only hiding place is where he and Tank are already sitting in shadow behind the tractor. The light shifts again—it's the unforgiving beam of a heavy-duty flashlight. Jake knows it well; his dad has quite a few of them. They're only carried by construction people, security guards, and cops. None of these are good right now.

Keys jingle. Boots clomp.

Her face flickers with panic and then she's there, wide-eyed as she stares at Jake and Tank.

"Hey, what are you doing in there? This place is off-limits!" Grant pushes his way through the fence, shining his light directly at her, still frozen.

Everything stills for one moment: Jake frozen in his hiding place, Tank's eyes widening with fear, the girl standing there in shock. It's like they've paused the game right when a powerful monster is attacking in the middle of a battle they know they're going to lose. The world is at a standstill, and then abruptly starts again. The flashlight darts from her to the tractor and then wiggles around and lands on Jake's feet, and he knows he's spotted.

The security guard, Grant, stomps over. His mustachioed face is barely visible as the flashlight swivels up and around. The metal on his buckle and buttons gleams as he shakes the light at the three of them.

"Uh, hello," Jake says, as if he's answering the phone, slipping into the polite script he automatically defaults to whenever someone invariably calls the landline his Dad installs in all their apartments. "How can I help you?"

Tank elbows Jake and glares at him.

Grant stares at them in disbelief, his mustache twitching. "You kids are in so much trouble."

CHAPTER TWELVE

TANK

Tank considers running for it. He can probably make it. Grant isn't very fast. Tank's seen him this week just standing against the wall and not watching the construction site at all, his face illuminated by his phone. All he has to do is make a clean break when the guy isn't looking.

The only problem is Grant is standing right in front of them, and he's already got his phone out and is chattering away.

"Yeah, it's three kids, I think they live here, definitely seen one of them skulking around." Grant glares at Tank, and Tank hunches his shoulders, trying to appear smaller.

Yep. Grant remembers him.

It hadn't really been funny, and Tank didn't really want to get involved, but Shark had made a game of it on Wednesday night, sneaking behind Grant and stealing his keys off his belt.

Grant huffed and puffed as he chased them around the complex and then halfway down the block, as the four of them laughed and tossed the keys back and forth to one another. Shark eventually got bored and tossed the keys into an empty parking lot before heading over to Fortress Park, laughing as Grant cursed at them.

Tank found the keys later and left them by the counter in the lobby, hoping Grant would just forget about the whole thing and that Shark would move on, find another game.

Grant has definitely not forgotten.

Tank shifts awkwardly now with the full force of Grant's stare on him. He always thought hanging out with tough guys like Shark was good for his reputation, that it meant no one would mess with him or Viv, but right now he doesn't like how Grant's looking at him. Like he's a monster, an awful person.

Tank looks down at his feet.

He can't help it if Grant hates him — some adults just do.

"Yeah. Uh huh. Yeah, it's one of those boys, the ones always causing trouble. And two other kids. From the complex, yeah, I think so." Grant's listening very intently to whoever is on the other end of the phone now. He puffs out his chest as he preens. Tank can barely hear the man on the other line but he can tell the other voice is annoyed and curt. "Yeah, I can do that for you. I'll make sure they don't go anywhere." He glares at the three of them where they're all standing in front of the tractor now, awaiting whatever punishment is to come.

Great. Just great.

Tank thinks he could make it if he gets back in the community center and goes through the stairwell that connects to the West Tower, but the girl from school and that mousy Jake kid are between him and that route. He could dart around the tractor to his right—the whole community center and construction site is fenced in, but it's just chain-link. Tank could climb that easily.

Grant continues to stare at the three of them as he makes another call. The shrill voice on the other end is familiar—it's Old Woman Jenkins, the mean lady who owns the complex. Grant hangs up the phone and takes a step toward Tank and the others.

Instinctively Tank finds himself stepping in front of the others. They're smaller than he is, and something about the way the girl's lip wobbled when the flashlight was on her reminds him of Vivian.

Emily. That's her name. She looks up at Tank, her eyes widening with fear. She glances to her left—the escape route Tank was eyeing—and looks back at Tank. Oh, she's thinking about running, too. Good. Tank vaguely remembers her from school—she's one of the pretty girls who hangs out with the crowd Shark always sneers at, think they're too good for everyone and are stuck-up. Tank remembers seeing her during PE, flying around the track as they did laps for the fitness test. She's fast. She could make it.

She meets Tank's gaze and gives him the slightest of nods. Tank grunts back at her, the barest of acknowledgments. He doesn't know her. He doesn't really know anyone outside of Shark's friends, and even then he can't say he knows them, either. But if they're going to run, they're going to need to do it now.

This Jake kid, though. Tank doesn't know about him. The kid is frozen, staring up at Grant. Whatever, Tank doesn't have time for this. He can stay here and be punished—

Great. Jake *is* blocking the way. He's standing right between Tank and Emily and the path to freedom. Tank could shove past him, but he doesn't really like the idea much at all. It's a Shark move, and he doesn't want people to be really afraid of him. Maybe he's gonna have to—

No. He'll go the other way.

Tank catches Emily's eye and then looks quickly to his right, as if to say, *I'm going that way. You can follow if you want, but you're on your own if you get caught.*

He takes a step to the right.

"Don't even think about it, buddy." Grant shines the light directly on him and takes a step forward, blocking his path. "I've already called Ellen and the project manager and they're on the way."

Jake pales. "Wait, no—"

A door opens and shuts nearby—the apartment unit next to the community center. Ellen Jenkins appears, shuffling forward in her slippers and a mold-colored bathrobe. Her flyaway salt-and-pepper hair is done up in curlers.

She fixes her beady eyes on the three kids, her cold gaze all-knowing as she takes them in. "Thank you, Grant, for letting me know."

"Just doing my job, ma'am. Do you want me to call the cops? I already called Mr. Thomas." Grant grins vindictively at Tank. "Actions have consequences. I know your type. You're always breaking the rules, always ignoring the curfew, walking on the grass, lurking in the courtyard. Now you're going to have to face the music." His voice is so cold that Tank swears the temperature drops a few degrees.

"I don't think that's necessary," Mrs. Jenkins says. "This is my building—"

"Mr. Thomas is my boss, he said to wait for him before I take any action, but it sounded like he wanted to press charges."

"You called Mr. Thomas *first?*" Mrs. Jenkins asks, her eyebrows knitting together.

"Ye-es?" Grant looks down at his feet.

"How *dare you*. I am still in charge of this building, I'm the one giving you a paycheck—"

"Technically he hired me for this job to watch the site at night, and uh, you cut back my hours last month because you said you didn't need a doorman, so right now he's the one paying me, and this construction site is his, of course I called him first—"

Tank sprints to his right, trying to take advantage of the argument to get away. He feels the cold concrete beneath his feet, pushing off and picking up speed as he darts around the tractor, his pulse racing in his ears. He sees the fence ahead and the sweet taste of freedom behind it. He grabs the chain links, the metal digging into his fingers. He pulls himself up and tries to wedge his shoe into a fence link, but it's one of those cheap fences that wobbles and it's not stable enough for him to get a good foothold. Great, he'll have to go around—there, a gap. Tank wrenches his foot out from the fence and runs.

Behind him, he can hear quick exhales and footsteps. Emily must have followed him.

Tank turns back just to see—both she and Jake are running. Fine, whatever, Tank's not responsible for them, he just needs to get away. He can't be caught; Shark's told him so many stories about juvie and he thinks about records and he can't lose time, he has work and has to help Ma and—

FLOMP.

Tank's collided with something solid—no, someone.

He falls backward, wincing as he lands on the cold concrete, sending up sawdust and bits of drywall everywhere. He coughs, looking up, and freezes.

"Hold up there. Where do you think you're going?"

A middle-aged balding man wearing a crisp blue shirt buttoned up the wrong way stares down at him. Despite the dress

shirt and slacks, he's got the look of someone who's used to working with his hands, with broad shoulders and a calculating stare.
He offers Tank a callused hand. It feels like a trap but Tank would
rather not be on the ground when everyone else is standing.

He takes the hand, and the man pulls him to his feet with a
viselike grip.

"Now, what's all this I hear about vandalizing the construction
site?"

"It's these three, Mr. Thomas," Grant says, huffing as he
catches up to them. Mrs. Jenkins isn't far behind, shuffling after
them, her bathrobe trailing behind her like a cape.

The man—Mr. Thomas—looks Tank over with a scrutinizing
eye, and then he spots Emily behind him, and then his gaze settles on Jake.

"Jake?"

Jake offers an awkward small wave. "Hi, Dad."

Oh.

Tank freezes. This is bad, right? This is awful. He doesn't want
to see this. If it was *his* dad—

Mrs. Jenkins wheezes as she catches up to them.

"You see these troublemakers? Caught them red-handed, I
did. We've got evidence, too." Grant holds up the wrench and
waves it at Mr. Thomas.

"I had nothing to do with this!" Emily says, stomping her foot.
"I was just here!"

"Trespassing!" Grant snarls at her. "This whole site is off-
limits!" He glares at Mr. Thomas. "I can call the authorities now,
sir, and you can press charges."

Mr. Thomas is still gaping at Jake.

"Ahem." Mrs. Jenkins taps her cane on the ground. "There's
no need to be rash."

"Punishment! Consequences!" Grant says, eyes darting wildly between Mr. Thomas and Mrs. Jenkins. "I believe juvenile detention would certainly make these kids think twice about messing with anyone's personal property ever again."

Mrs. Jenkins flicks a switch on a heavy-duty construction light standing behind her. The site is flooded with a bright, stark fluorescent light, casting each of them in harsh shadow. She looks directly at Tank, her gaze locking him in. He freezes, like she's cast some sort of immobilizing spell and he can't move.

"Now, these youths you say were causing trouble," Mrs. Jenkins says, giving Grant a keen eye.

"I found this wrench here on the ground," Grant says quickly.

"And how do you know it didn't belong to the construction crew? Mr. Thomas, I cannot believe the blatant disregard for health and safety." Mrs. Jenkins clucks her tongue.

"That doesn't change that the kids were here trespassing," Grant says.

"I was just looking for my photos," Emily says quietly. "I dropped my Polaroids here earlier."

"I was helping," Jake says.

"Me too," Tank adds.

Grant casts a suspicious look at him. "Mr. Thomas, don't tell me you believe them!"

Mr. Thomas sighs. "Look, it's normal for kids to be curious. I know I did my fair share of sneaking around into places I shouldn't have been when I was your age. Now, I do believe breaking the rules warrants a punishment. Jake, you're grounded. And I'll call your friends' parents as well and let them know the severity of the situation."

"I'll say. You know that wrench doesn't belong to any of the crew. No one leaves their tools lying around," Grant mutters.

"I have a proposal," Mrs. Jenkins says. "Nigel, you gave me three weeks while you got your supplies delivered to clean out all my personal effects in the community center. And I know I've been taking my time—sorting through everything is quite difficult, as you know, with my back, and I requested more time . . ."

"What are you suggesting, Ellen?" Mr. Thomas asks, tilting his head.

"Community service. It's typical of what a judge would offer for this sort of light mischief." Mrs. Jenkins folds her arms, looking at the dilapidated building behind them. "Now, we don't need to do any of those official charges and consequences and stuff. I believe the children deserve a second chance."

"What, like picking up trash and stuff?" Tank's done that before at school. He's gotten into trouble a lot, and usually during detention they make all the kids walk the campus and pick up trash and scrape gum. He used to be humiliated, having to be seen doing that in front of the whole school, but he learned from Shark to wear it like a badge of honor. That he was one of the tough kids. That his reputation was etched in stone as someone not to be messed with.

Mrs. Jenkins nods. "A little more focused than that, but I like where your mind is going, Tank. Now, with three pairs of hands helping me, I'm sure I could get the whole place cleaned up and ready for you by the date you specified." Mrs. Jenkins smiles at Mr. Thomas, and Tank could swear her eyes are twinkling.

It's a little weird. He's never seen Mrs. Jenkins like this; she's always been stern or sad or some sort of combination of both.

"Vuong, isn't it?" She pulls a pad of paper out of her pocket and licks her forefinger before flipping to a new page. "V-U-O-N-G. Vuong, B-three-eleven." She glances at Emily. "You're one of the Quesada girls, huh. Carmen?"

Emily stays silent.

"No, you're wearing too much color. You're the other one. Emily," Mrs. Jenkins clucks to herself. "Quesada, C-two-fourteen." She marks it down on her pad and then she turns to Jake. "Thomas. A-two-oh-four." Her pen's scratching sounds echo in the construction site as she scribbles quickly, making flourishes as she writes.

"Here's a proposal. Is that sufficient for you? And I can call these two's parents right now."

Mr. Thomas takes the handwritten sheet, blinking at it owlishly. "This sounds agreeable. Thank you for your time, Ellen, and for the suggestion."

Tank watches as Mrs. Jenkins pulls out her phone. She jerks her head at Grant, who fumbles for his keys and unlocks the giant lock on the chain wrapped around the fence gate and pushes it open.

Emily follows him, her head held down, and Jake and Mr. Thomas step through as well. Mrs. Jenkins is calling someone, jabbing at her phone keypad with a tense ferocity. She huffs, hanging up, and then dials another number. The response is immediate, and Mrs. Jenkins speaks in urgent, quick Spanish. Tank doesn't understand, but he watches Emily's eyes widening as the woman on the other end of the call responds, the tone rapid-fire and angry.

Mrs. Jenkins gives Emily a satisfied smile. "Your parents are on their way down."

Tank bristles when Ellen turns to face him.

"And no one answered at your house."

Tank clenches and unclenches his fists. Ma's at work. Auntie Phuong is probably asleep. Viv would have her headphones in, playing Minecraft. He hopes the phone call to the landline just rang and rang and no one heard it, no one knows that he's gotten in trouble.

Doors open and shut from the direction of the West Tower. That must be Emily's parents on their way over.

Emily's lip wobbles. "I'm already grounded, though!"

Jake and his dad are having some sort of silent conversation that's making Tank incredibly uncomfortable. His dad isn't yelling or even saying anything, just looking at Jake with this weird, sad face.

Tank follows everyone out into the courtyard and watches Grant lock the gate back up, unsure of what to do.

Emily's parents are now here, a couple who look exhausted and disappointed. Emily looks like her parents, with her mom's brown curls and her dad's wide forehead and expressive eyebrows. She hangs her head as they speak to her in hushed disappointment. Her mom takes Emily by the elbow and leads her away after speaking with Mrs. Jenkins.

She's now talking to Mr. Thomas, and Tank can pick out "nine o'clock" and "about four or five hours a day should be sufficient" but he can't focus right now. Can he leave? Does Mrs. Jenkins expect his parents to show up? What happens when she realizes no one is going to pick up the phone?

Jake looks at Tank as his dad takes him by the shoulder. He offers up his hand—it's not quite a wave.

Tank shakes his head. He doesn't want anything to do with this kid; he just wanted to find Viv's notebook and because he heard a noise and stopped to talk to Jake, it's landed them all in trouble.

The Thomases disappear into the foyer of the North Tower, the brand-new one. He guesses it makes sense, if Mr. Thomas's company is the one doing the renovation. Tank doesn't know many people aside from the Mishras who live in that tower—most of them are new tenants. Most of the old ones couldn't afford to stay.

"Your parents work late, right?" Mrs. Jenkins turns her sharp eye on Tank.

He nods.

"I'll see you bright and early here tomorrow at nine, then," Mrs. Jenkins says. It's not a question. She looks up at Tank, her eyes glinting as hard as steel, and even though she's a tiny old woman, Tank is more than a little daunted.

"Okay," he offers, nodding at her.

Mrs. Jenkins gives him one last look before striding across the courtyard to return to her tower, her bathrobe flowing behind her regally.

Tank is now alone with Grant. The security guard has already settled, standing in front of the fence, looking at his phone, scrolling with the same boredom Tank's come to recognize as his daily routine. He wonders how much Grant makes to watch this place, if it's more than Tank makes helping Mr. Mishra with his boxes.

Tank can feel Grant's eyes on him as he tries to walk back to his own tower, and he hunches his shoulders instinctively, trying to make himself smaller, less threatening. He pauses, wondering, wanting to say something, but he doesn't know where to start.

"What, you want to laugh at me some more? You don't get enough of it with your friends?"

"I—" Tank stares at his feet. His shoes are scuffed and worn, and his socks are poking out of the sneakers' top. Grant's shoes are equally as shabby-looking, old boots that have seen better days. The *I'm sorry* sticks in his throat but he tries to say it anyway, and it comes out like a small mumble instead. Tank tries again. "Your keys. I'm—I'm sorry."

"Yeah? You're sorry for making my job harder? You know if I lose that set of keys the replacement cost will come out of my paycheck?"

Tank doesn't say anything. He thinks of how Shark laughed at Grant.

"Whatever, kid. Go home. You're lucky you got this deal."

Tank exhales. He doesn't feel lucky. Lucky would have meant avoiding this whole situation in the first place. But Viv had wanted her notebook with the coordinates, and they were in that computer lab somewhere, and he definitely can't get them now with Grant watching him with a careful eye.

Tank sticks his hands into his pockets and looks carefully away. He walks back to his tower alone. He glances up at the sky; the moon is a sliver, hiding behind the clouds. The courtyard is shrouded in shadow now that Mrs. Jenkins turned off the bright construction light, and it's back to the eerie strangeness of the middle of the night.

The door to the stairwell echoes with a loud metallic clang; Tank has always been used to it, the abandoned staircase that no one uses in the far west section of the tower. He walks up to the third floor, dreading every step that takes him closer to home.

He approaches his apartment door and pauses. His hand trembles as he tries to fit the key into the lock. He closes his eyes and presses his forehead against the door. The metal is cold against his skin, growing clammy with sweat. The longer he stays out here, the more time he has before anybody inside could know that he's failed everyone. He could stay out here forever.

The door opens without warning. Tank slips forward but catches himself before losing his balance.

Viv blinks up at him owlishly behind her round frames, cast in shadow. The streetlight from the courtyard barely enters the dim apartment, lighting only the knees of Viv's dinosaur pajamas.

"What are you doing, dummy?" Viv rolls her eyes at him. "Just standing outside forever?"

"Yeah. That's me. I'm a dummy. I just like leaning against the door and you ruined all that." Tank rolls his eyes and pretends to be annoyed, but he can't help but smile. She must have noticed he wasn't home and waited for him. It's nice, knowing that she cares about where he is.

"I heard shouting from the courtyard. Was that Old Woman Jenkins?"

"Yeah."

"What were you doing? Hanging out with Shark again? You know he's mean, right?"

Tank shrugs as he steps inside, feeling the weight of the world on his shoulders. He shuts the door behind him and makes his way through the dark of the living room. The kitchen is softly lit, a programming book flipped open and the single fluorescent lamp lighting it. Viv must have been hanging out here, waiting for him.

Tank sighs, making his way through the living room, his pathway memorized as he avoids the furniture on his way to the bathroom.

Footsteps pad behind him, and the hallway light flickers on. "I saw you. Being yelled at. There were a bunch of people downstairs by the community center."

Tank turns around and sighs. "I was trying to get your coordinates," he mutters. "Got caught up in some other kid's prank."

Viv's frown deepens, her forehead wrinkling with concern. "I made you a peanut butter and jelly sandwich." She offers the sandwich to him. It's made the way she likes it, cut diagonally across the middle, with a generous heaping of jelly oozing onto the plate. "Are you in trouble?"

"Yeah. Did you hear the phone ring earlier?"

Viv nods and points to the receiver where a blinking red 01 indicates a new voicemail.

Tank deletes the message. "I'll deal with it. No one has to know. We don't need to worry Ma."

"What are you going to do?"

Tank doesn't know. The only thing he does know is that he's going to show up at the community center tomorrow and do exactly what he needs to do to fix this.

CHAPTER THIRTEEN

EMILY

Emily wasn't sure what kind of work they'd be doing, which sucked because she couldn't plan an outfit appropriately. Would they be doing stuff in the garden? Would she need long pants? It's too hot for jeans, but she wears her oldest pair anyway, with a cute T-shirt she'd stopped wearing because she spilled soy sauce on it once. The stain was impossible to get out, but she couldn't give up on the shirt and the cute butterfly print and lacy cap sleeves.

Jake is already there, sitting morosely on a bench in the courtyard and staring at the community center. The caution tape wafts in the morning's scant winds, and Emily wonders if she should have brought a light sweater. Well, it's going to be sweltering later, so she should just stick it out, especially if they're outside.

"Hey," Jake says, smiling and waving at her.

Emily ignores him. If she hadn't stopped to see who was there, she wouldn't have gotten caught. Sure, she'd still be grounded, but at least she'd be grounded by herself. Being bored with no Internet is way better than being stuck with these guys.

Emily leans against one of the planters with faded silk flowers, ignoring Jake's offer of the seat next to him. She wishes she could check her Instagram feed, something, anything to keep her occupied for the next few moments of waiting so she doesn't have to talk to the boy who ruined her summer. Her parents gave her phone back but made sure that she didn't have access to any of her social media accounts, which is even more annoying.

"Look, I'm sorry you got caught up in this, but it's not my fault you're here."

"Sure it is. You were the one messing with the construction stuff. I was just retrieving my lost property."

"You were sneaking through an area that was clearly marked NO ENTRY!"

"Yeah, but if you two hadn't been there, I wouldn't have been caught." Emily snorts.

"I wasn't messing with anything! I just—I needed to do something in the computer lab."

"Like what?"

Jake looks at his feet. "You wouldn't understand."

He looks so sad and forlorn for a moment that Emily feels guilty for the way she snubbed him the first time they met. It's too late now to indulge the idea of inviting him to play Minecraft with her—it was just a fleeting thought, anyway.

"Try me," Emily says, defaulting to her usual sarcastic bite. Ouch. That sounded kind of harsh, though. Maybe she should say it again . . . more softly? How do people do this?

No, she's already said it, it's already done. Just wait. Relax. It's okay.

Jake takes a deep breath and looks her in the eye, like he's debating whether it's worth it, to have this conversation with her. It makes Emily prickle, the way she *does* want him to decide she's worth his time. Does he think she's an empty airhead? Would he dismiss her like so many of the other people at school?

It's one thing to play a part and another thing to have done it so well that no one ever truly knows you and they can only see the mask you put on.

"Hi. Have we started yet? What are we doing?" A new voice joins them—Tank. He's wearing ill-fitting jeans and a T-shirt three sizes too big, the same sort of tough-guy outfit she's always seen him in at school.

"Hey, Tank," Jake says, too brightly for someone who doesn't quite understand that talking to someone like Tank at school is like a death sentence. Then again, he just straight up introduced himself to Emily. Maybe he just has no fear.

Tank just rolls his eyes and leans against the planter opposite Emily. "So we just wait around? For what? It's past nine already."

Jake looks at his phone. "Hm. You think she forgot? It looks like the site is still locked up."

Tank shrugs.

Emily pushes herself off the planter and dusts herself off. "Well, I'm not going to sit around here for nothing. Come on, Mrs. Jenkins lives right over there." She strides off, not bothering to see if the boys are following her.

She skirts around the fence along the apartment unit attached to the community center and raps quickly on the door with the faded brass plate reading MANAGER.

"Mrs. Jenkins? Hello?"

No answer.

"Guess that means community service isn't happening," Emily says sweetly. Great. Now she can go home and take photos all day.

"Are you sure?" Jake frowns.

Emily shrugs. No one can say she didn't show up. She twirls around and walks right back through the courtyard toward the West Tower, Jake and Tank on her heels. Don't they live in different buildings? What are they following her for?

"There you are!" Mrs. Jenkins's hoarse voice echoes from the right. "Thought you could skip out, did you?"

"No, no, we were just looking for you," Jake says immediately. Suck up.

He gives Emily a look before breaking into a jog—wow. He's really running up to her, panting like he's scared he's going to be late.

Mrs. Jenkins doesn't look impressed as she unlocks the gate and beckons to Emily and Tank.

Inside the main lobby, cleaning supplies and a number of cardboard boxes have been assembled: disinfectant sprays, rags, brooms, and mops.

Mrs. Jenkins looks down her nose at them. "Now, I believe a good strong work ethic is the solution to any sort of mischief. Builds character. You're going to help me clear out all my personal things. You'll need to sort through all the items and my personal effects—sort them into these boxes. Like with like. Photos, files, memorabilia. Large furniture items you can leave in place—I'll have the movers come and get those to bring to the donation center."

"And the computers?" Jake asks.

Mrs. Jenkins frowns. "You can do that last. I'll have to sort out which machines to keep and which to recycle. Start with the other two rooms and the main office, and if you need more boxes come get me."

"You aren't going to stay?" Emily asks, brightening. If they aren't being supervised, what's to stop her from going home?

"I'm going to trust that the three of you are going to work together. If one of you isn't working, then I can just let Mr. Thomas know I changed my mind about pressing charges. I'm sure a judge would say a minimum of two hundred hours community service for trespassing and vandalism." Mrs. Jenkins shrugs.

"Two hundred—" Tank splutters. "That would be like, the whole summer!"

"Ten weeks, five hours a day, Monday through Friday," Mrs. Jenkins says, nodding.

No way. Emily's only grounded for two weeks.

Mrs. Jenkins holds out a clunky old key on a ring. "I don't want you bothering me every day to let you in. I trust you'd be responsible enough to manage your own time." She dangles the key out at them. "I've only got one of these, so someone take it."

Emily looks at Tank, who shrugs.

Jake finally pockets the key.

Mrs. Jenkins hands Emily a mop, Tank a broom, and Jake a bucket full of rags. "Or you can just work here until it's done. I don't care when you're here during the day or how often you come—figure it out amongst yourselves. The sooner you start, the sooner you finish."

Emily grips the mop, holding it like she would a staff. Great. All she has to do is finish this stupid cleaning project, and she can get back to her life.

CHAPTER FOURTEEN

TANK

Tank wishes he'd brought headphones.

Emily disappeared immediately with several boxes and rags, claiming the office. Tank thought it was a good plan, divide and conquer, so he followed suit, grabbing a few empty boxes and a bunch of cleaning rags before heading into the storage room. Figured that would be a cue for Jake to take the other storage room or the computer room, but the kid just followed Tank right inside, dusting noisily behind him.

Tank ignores him, starting with a shelf full of weird sculptures. Everything is caked with a thick, dark sheath of dust, and every move releases even more dust into the air. He coughs, spluttering.

"Oh, here—I brought these for everyone. Emily said it clashed with her outfit earlier, so she didn't want it, but I thought you might—I mean, they're good for like, air pollution and stuff in general, and I figured we might need them for here."

The kid is babbling again, and he pulls something out of his pocket, a crumpled piece of cloth. It looks like the masks that everyone wore back in his grandparents' town in Vietnam, when people were bustling about on motorcycles and scooters and cars and the air was filled with thick clouds of smoke. He kind of misses those long wet summers, weeks spent at his grandparents'. It's been two years since his last visit, but Tank knows they have to save money to send home.

He coughs again. Great. Dusting with allergies is so much fun, and it's only going to get worse.

Tank nods at Jake and takes the mask, shuffling it onto his face. Jake grins and bobs at him, looking more pleased than he ought to, like a puppy who's successfully retrieved a ball. Tank shakes his head and continues dusting.

The silence only lasts for a few minutes.

"Do you think she'll want the photos to stay in the frames? There are a lot of them here. What do you think, she'll want them organized by date?" Jake holds a stack of photo frames, standing in front of the bare wall. The wallpaper looks comical without the photos, spots of light yellow standing out against the darker color.

"Sure."

"Look at these weird haircuts!"

Tank peers over Jake's shoulder. A yellowing photograph sits in a wooden frame. "Pacific Crest Community Youth Council," reads the caption. Twenty or so grinning kids with old-fashioned haircuts, and Mrs. Jenkins beaming in the center. The date scrawled in the corner is from before Tank was born. "Guess kids used to really hang out here."

"Yeah," Jake says, whistling. He opens a folder filled with newspaper clippings. "Local Youth Council Cleans Up Beach," he reads. "Ellen Jenkins, founder of a local nonprofit community center, leads youths in community service. The state-of-the-art center provides children and teens a place to spend their time, learning new skills and making new friends."

"Cool," Tank says, squinting at a photo of a bunch of teens laughing in a park, wearing matching T-shirts and gloves as they dig holes for new tree saplings and flowerbeds. Planting in real life? That does look like fun. "I wonder why they stopped doing it. I've never seen this place like that." The community center in the photos looks well-loved, filled with kids and adults and a much younger Mrs. Jenkins.

Jake sifts through the newspaper clippings—they go from loose sheets to carefully laminated ones as they go back through the years, like some of these were framed and put on the walls. "Local Apartment Manager Wins City-Wide Grant for Innovative Youth Program," Jake reads. "This is the first one, I think." He whistles. "Ellen Jenkins, thirty-two—wow. This is like, thirty years ago. Look at the date."

In the photo, Mrs. Jenkins stands next to a handsome man with broad shoulders and warm brown skin. One of his arms is looped around her shoulders, a proud smile on his face, and between them is a young girl in pigtails.

Ellen Jenkins, Christopher Reyes, and their daughter at the groundbreaking ceremony of the Pacific Crest Community Center.

Tank eyes where Jake has now spread out all the clippings and is reading them slowly. "You know, you can just put them away and it takes less time. Mrs. Jenkins didn't say we had to be here on a specific schedule. It's up to us. So once this is all clean and organized we can go home." And Tank can go back to his summer — helping Mr. Mishra, taking care of Viv, saving up for those shoes, impressing Shark.

"Oh." Jake looks sheepish. "Sorry. I just thought it was interesting." He offers Tank a small smile. "Um, the other day in the computer lab, I was looking for Wi-Fi and hanging out in the lab, and I got up to go stretch but the door was jammed. For like . . . an hour until I saw you."

Tank was right. Jake totally did think he locked him in there.

"I never said thank you, for opening it. I'm sorry if I, like, ran away, I was just freaked out at first and I thought it might have been Shark and those other guys back to mess with me. I thought maybe you . . ." Jake smiles. "And then I remembered you distracted Shark and those guys last week, too. At the vending machine? So. Thanks."

"I don't know what you're talking about," Tank says gruffly, swiping his dust rag harder than necessary.

"Okay," Jake says, smiling at Tank. "It can be a secret."

Tank goes back to his shelf, moving all the knickknacks into a box. They're clumsy little sculptures, all painted gaudy colors. He wonders if it was one of the programs here. Tank shakes his head. He doesn't care about the arts and crafts that some kids made here more than a decade ago. He doesn't care about the stories about this place; he doesn't care that he sees it now, that he can't stop seeing it as he cleans, the laughter and life that used to flow in here.

He grabs a new dust rag and keeps cleaning. It's meditative, like planting rows and rows of plants, one after another, and Tank settles into the silence thankfully.

Bright sunlight streams in through the window, and Tank smiles at the clear view outside. He can see the dusty lot in front of the center that leads to the street, looking even more shabby now that it's surrounded by a chain-link fence.

"Nice job. We did good work so far," Jake says proudly.

"Yeah," Tank says.

"Aw, yeah! That was a smile! Give me five." Jake grins and raises his hand at Tank, like he has the overeager answer to a question in class.

Tank stares blankly at him.

"Oh. I thought, maybe now that we're friends—"

"We're not friends," Tank says, his voice stiff with annoyance. Is this Jake kid going to follow him around everywhere now like a shadow he can't shake? All summer? And then at school? Tank can't be seen with him. What even is he wearing, a collared shirt?

Jake's smile falters, but he doesn't lower his hand. "I just wanted a high five, dude. Like to say congrats on a good job?"

"I don't high-five." Tank glares at the open outstretched palm in the air. He steps forward with his most intimidating dark glare.

Jake just nods and lets his arm fall. "Good to know. You know, my cousin Aimee doesn't like people touching her, so no hugs or high fives, so it's, like, good to know what people like and don't like—"

"Anyone ever tell you you talk too much?" Tank shoulders past Jake and goes back to work, swabbing at the dusty shelves aggressively with his rag.

Jake laughs sheepishly. "Sorry, I tend to ramble when I get nervous. My dad told me I need to be friendly in order to make friends, which I always try to do when we move, but it's hard, you know?"

Tank doesn't know what to say to that, because he certainly knows what it's like not to have friends. But he has Shark and AJ and Gus now, and Shark's already made his feelings on where Jake belongs clear. The door opens and Emily flounces through. "Office is all sorted. What are you all doing in here?"

"Dusting. Boxing up this stuff." Tank jerks his head at the myriad of shelves still filled with mementos.

Emily nods and puts her headphones on. Finally, someone with some sense.

Tank goes back to work.

He can hear Emily's music through her headphones on the other side of the room. She's got some sort of complicated dance thing going on and she's just kind of lightly swabbing at surfaces without picking up things. That side of the room Tank was saving for later because the shelves are these huge, heavy-duty things that are holding crates and crates filled with who knows what and it'll likely take forever. He figured they'd need to open each crate and sort each thing slowly, but Emily's just dragging a rag along the shelf.

"Have you *never* dusted before?" Tank asks, shuffling in next to her and picking up a crate. "Let's put this stuff in the pile of stuff we have to go through. We gotta make sure all the shelves are clean."

"Of course I have. What's the point, though?" Emily says, rolling her eyes. "Why do we have to clean it if it's just going in the trash?"

"It's not trash. She said the furniture movers are taking everything to be donated," Jake says, too helpfully and eagerly, popping in out of nowhere. Tank is somewhat pleased to note that Jake's shelves are dusted properly and there is a sizeable growing pile of stuff he's added to the proper "to sort" pile, and the photo frames and newspaper clippings are stacked neatly in a box. Good that someone understands organization.

Tank flips an empty crate over and sits on it, enjoying the break. His phone says they've been here for only an hour. He sighs. This is going to take forever.

"Hey, man," Jake says, flipping over another crate and sitting down next to him. "Break time? Want a snack?"

He pulls out a squashed chocolate bar from his pocket.

Tank takes it, but not because they're friends. It's because he likes chocolate.

"Want some?"

Emily takes the bar he offers her warily, peeling it open and leaning back against the wall. "This doesn't mean I like you," she says.

"Noted," Jake says around a mouthful of chocolate.

Emily pulls out her phone, scrolling through it and leaning casually against the wall, throwing up a fresh cloud of dust. She startles and immediately starts dusting off her clothes.

Tank chuckles, watching her jump up in surprise like a startled squirrel.

"Do you know each other?" Jake asks. Emily shrugs and gives Tank an askance look, which Tank returns with a sideways glance of his own and a shrug, the look of acknowledgment where they recognize each other from school but definitely aren't friends.

"We went to the same middle school," Emily says.

Tank waits for her to call him Frankenstein like the kids used to, and is pleasantly surprised when she doesn't. He's glad that stupid nickname disappeared once Shark started calling him Tank. In the first week of seventh grade he came to school with a sweater that Ma had stitched together from two old sweaters that were slightly different colors. He'd been proud of the sweater, that it was a unique style that Ma had made—right up until he realized it wasn't cool at all, to wear this homemade thing covered in patches.

He was made fun of for a whole year until Shark came along, and even though he doesn't like some of the stuff they do, it's worth it, to be one of the guys that no one messes with.

"You hang out with . . ." Emily trails off, making a vague gesture with her hands. "Don't remember his name."

"Shark, yeah," Tank says.

"He is so mean. Why are you friends?"

Why is he friends with Shark, if he could call that friendship? A tenuous allyship is all he can hope for in this stupid game of survival, of who's who at school, and it's all about perception and what people think of you and what they can expect from you.

Tank shrugs, not wanting to explain. "He gets me," he finally says. "Why are you friends with those girls?"

Emily snorts. "Because I like them. I'm not sure that Shark likes anything except the sound of his own voice, but you do you."

Jake laughs. "What? I've met the guy. I feel like that's pretty accurate."

"And how did that go for you?" Emily asks, raising her eyebrow at him.

"He tried to get me to buy him a soda. Not sure that's the beginnings of a great friendship. But doing community service together might be." He grins at Tank and then at Emily.

Tank blinks at him and sighs. "We're just cleaning things together. We don't have to even talk."

Jake shrugs. "I've moved a lot in the past few years. I figure I might as well be nice to people. There's no harm in it. Even if people aren't nice to me. I mean, I get it, I'm a new kid, you don't know me. But you could. I think I'm pretty nice." He shuffles away, the line of his back looking sad, and for a second Tank feels guilty, before he shoves that feeling into a box.

Emily stares after him, a contemplative look on her face be-

fore a mask of indifference falls back over her features. She rolls
her eyes at Tank. "What are you looking at?"

"Nothing."

Emily goes back to her phone, her face ghostly lit by the
screen. She's wholly engrossed.

The storage room door opens and shuts, and in the hallway
Tank can hear another door open and close.

Might as well be nice to people, Jake's voice echoes in his ear.

The old computer lab is eerie, the square blocks of machines letting out a faint electronic hum.

Jake is in the first row, his face illuminated by the faint blue
glow of the machine. He shifts, his entire body flinching as he
dodges something, and he presses the keys harder. "No, you don't,
creeper!" he whisper-yells, his eyes gleaming with delight.

Tank shuffles over with interest. "You playing Minecraft?"

"Yeah," Jake says. "Do you play?"

"My little sister does," Tank says, grabbing a chair and spinning it around so he can sit in it backward. He watches Jake play,
his avatar roaming the world as he mines and fights monsters.
Tank feigns casualness, getting more and more annoyed when
Jake finally approaches what apparently is his home base. It's a
mess, scores and scores of wasted potential everywhere. Why is
there wheat mixed with potatoes? You can't harvest like that without knocking something over. Random pools of water? What even
is going on here?

Finally it bothers him so much he can't help but speak up.
"What's up with your farm?"

CHAPTER FIFTEEN

JAKE

"What do you mean, what's up with my farm?" Jake pulls away from Tank. "What's wrong with it?" He takes a second look at his crops; it's a bit chaotic, but he's been busy trying to solve riddles, so he doesn't have time to maximize crop efficiency or make fancy hoppers or automated things. He just needs the bare minimum.

He does take offense at Tank's tone, though.

"I thought you didn't play," Jake accuses.

Tank shrugs. "You know that those plants are failing because they aren't close enough to the water, right?"

"I'm just trying to grow some wheat, man, it doesn't have to be pretty," Jake says.

Jake wanted to use this break to play for a bit, and maybe over the coming weeks he could actually solve the mystery before the whole cleaning service project is over. He didn't mind Tank watching him play, but the criticism is not what he signed up for.

"You think you can do better?"

"Oh, I know I can."

Tank boots up the computer next to Jake, turning to watch him more closely as he waits.

Jake trudges around his perimeter wall and gathers more wheat before stopping to make bread for his next journey, and now feels more than a bit self-conscious because this basic cobblestone-and-dirt house and starter farm isn't representative of his best work at all. This isn't actually his base, just a waypoint on his way to solve the next riddle in this strange, mysterious server. If Tank plays Minecraft, maybe he'd be interested in it, too.

Would it be weird to ask if he wants to join him? Tank already said he wasn't interested in talking, just doing the community service as is. Jake's trying to figure out the best way to ask if he wants to play together and check out the server, but Tank's already pulling up one of his own worlds from some other server.

Tank cracks his knuckles. "I'll show you a farm."

The screen expands into a lush green paradise. Neat rows of pumpkins cheerfully line plots of carrots, wheat rustles gently in the wind, walkways and waterways line the paths in tidy little plots that go as far as the eye can see. Potatoes, beets, tall stalks of sugar cane—Jake isn't even sure what kind of vegetable that is over there. And are those . . . beehives?

Beyond a lake surrounded by bamboo and sugar cane, there are fields and fields of color. Jake can see a gentle path curving through a blue field of cornflowers, and behind it, lilacs and rose bushes and other colorful splashes of flowers.

"Wow," Jake says.

"Don't look at my flowers," Tank says. "Here, just know that water only reaches four blocks, so as long as you line the bed with—"

"Oh, I knew that," Jake says breezily. "I mean, this was just a temporary setup. See, I was in the middle of this epic puzzle—"

The door creaks open.

"What are you two doing?"

"Farming," Tank says. He jerks his head at Jake's screen. "Farming badly."

"Hey!"

Emily grabs a chair and pulls it up to them, leaning backward and sitting on it precariously, balancing all of her weight on the back two legs. "Minecraft?"

"Yeah," Jake says. "Do you wanna play?"

"Sure. More fun than cleaning, anyways. Scoot over, Tank."

Tank raises an eyebrow but shifts aside to make room for Emily and her chair at the last computer. She boots that up as well, and then whistles at Tank's farm. "Pretty. You do a whole Wizard of Oz reference there?"

"I just like flowers," Tank says, a tinge of red surging on his cheeks.

"Let's start a new game so we're all on the same level," Emily says cheerfully. She glances at Jake and his rudimentary weapons. "Not that you've progressed super far. How long have you been in this world?"

"You play Minecraft, too?" Jake asks. He's in shock. Now he feels really dumb for getting killed by a zombie in front of her. He absolutely doesn't want to admit he's been here doing a few hours every day for the past two weeks. He just started mining diamonds but he doesn't have them here on this rudimentary base out in the middle of nowhere. He's been trying to buff his character up and get what he thinks he'll need to solve Riddle the Eighteenth.

Emily doesn't answer his question, just logs in to her account and pulls up the multiplayer screen, looking at him expectantly. "So. New world?"

Jake looks back at his level twelve character and the progress he's made solving the mystery. "Um. That sounds fun, but uh, this server I found on the local network—it's actually really cool. The person who made it left these riddles I've been trying to solve—"

"Hmm." Emily's computer was already listing the servers. "Which one?"

"Bella Beta 7. It's a game on the local network. You should be able to see it."

"Huh. Sounds kind of familiar. Wait, I'll be right back." Emily heads out of the room and returns with a dusty notebook. "This was in that office room. Thought it was some weird coded journal, but it makes more sense now." She flips it open to show them pages full of cramped, tiny handwriting.

"It must have belonged to whoever made this server," Jake says. "Oh wow. They made a ton of versions." Each page is headed with a date, and it's clear to see that the creator worked on the server for *years*. He takes the notebook and scans through it quickly. A few phrases jump out at him, like *debug avatar skin scales* and *recalibrate Leviathan sequence* and *music cues*, but most of the notes don't make sense to him, they're all referencing some programming language. "That's neat. They must have lived in this apartment complex. The server is really cool, though, the creator added all these riddles and things, and it's, like, all a piece of a bigger puzzle. Wanna check it out?"

"Sounds cool." Emily spawns on the same rocky shore that Jake did when he first started and immediately starts heading into the forest.

"I'm over here." Jake writes down his coordinates and hands them to Emily.

"Oh, that's not too far. I think I can make it over to you in a few days in-game," Tank says. A quick glance at his screen shows Tank's already hard at work chopping wood and getting first-time essentials.

"Oooh, I found a cave. I'm gonna check this out," Emily says. "Hey, Tank. Nice avatar."

"My sister designed it," Tank says. "She's the smart one."

Jake bites back a chuckle. From Emily's screen it looks like Tank is some kind of anime character with blue hair and glasses. She leaves him quickly behind as Tank starts gathering supplies, and Jake turns back to his own screen to focus.

"We can meet up in the middle. I'll come back toward you two and I can show you the riddles and stuff and what I'm working on." Jake starts gathering all the supplies he'll need for the days' worth of travel, his heart pounding with excitement.

This is new.

This is terrifying.

This is going to be awesome.

First nights in Minecraft in a new world are special. Jake has a plan, he has a system on how to be as efficient as possible: gather wood, build tools, create a shelter before night falls.

This? *This* is madness.

"What *are* you doing?" Jake says, aghast.

Emily isn't gathering any supplies or building anything—well, no, she's got a sword already, which means she had enough wood to do that, but why not a pickaxe or a shovel? Her avatar runs right into the cave Jake passed on his first day, where he carefully noted its location as something to explore once he's prepared. She's just—she's charging ahead, grinning wildly without any fear of the mobs inside, no protection, no armor, nothing.

"Cave," Emily says cheerfully. She points to her screen as if it's obvious.

Caves are good. Caves have coal, which is necessary eventually, but on the first night one doesn't really need coal; it's better in Jake's opinion to be safe and wait for the next day. "I think I have a stash of coal and stuff nearby there. Go east a bit and you should be able to find it."

"Nah, I'm good."

"The sun's already setting!"

"Oh. Yeah. No worries," Emily says. "In a cave."

Tank glances over at her screen with a cursory nod of approval as Emily starts throwing bricks of dirt to block the cave entrance, closing it to the outside.

"What about the creatures on the inside?"

Emily keeps putting bricks of dirt up until she's completely closed herself in the dark.

"You don't even have a bed!" Jake always tries to get the essentials first: wood, for a crafting table and for basic tools, then sheep, so he can at least pass the time between pockets of safety.

"Don't need it. First night, still got plenty of health." Emily grins. "Gotta mine, get ore for armor." She jerks her head at Jake's screen. "What are *you* doing?" she scoffs.

"Waiting for sunrise!" Jake glances back at his screen, where he expects it to have skipped to the next morning, but nothing's happening. His avatar's blocky feet are just lying in bed, and he's still there.

Tank, next to him, shakes his head. "It won't skip if other players are still awake."

"Yeah, I'm going to be here awhile." Emily slaps a torch on a wall and whistles as she delves deeper into the cave.

Jake's nerves jump to attention as soon as he hears the familiar *plink plink* of arrows. Emily's taking a lot of damage, her health dropping dangerously low, but she just heads right for the skeleton, stabbing mercilessly until it disappears. "Sweet, got a good vein of coal and a whole bunch of other stuff here if you wanna come over. Could be a good place to build a base."

"Absolutely not," Jake says. He'd taken one look at the deep chasm and the river below and the fissures that dotted the cave and knew that it'd be a prime place for mobs to form. He doesn't want spiders or anything spawning near his home base. "Just come toward me, I already have a nice spot started. If you want to make something new we should find like a nice grassy field or some plains, someplace near sheep and cows, something flat so we don't have to terraform it."

"Welcome to the Iron Age, baby!" Emily croons, wielding a new iron pickaxe.

"Nice," Tank says. Over on his screen, Jake can see the beginnings of a wheat farm already, neat little plots of seedlings next to water sources and tall stalks of sugar cane. There's a decent little dirt house with a door, too. Tank's busy outside, chopping trees even as it starts to get dark outside the ring of torches he's set up outside his house.

"Why are you planting wheat? I thought you were coming toward me."

"You said you were coming back this way."

"I said we could meet halfway," Jake says, shaking his head. "Never mind, you already did it. Having more hideouts is always good, I guess."

The moan of zombies gets closer, and Jake shudders. This is the scariest part, he doesn't want to admit it, but it's why he prioritizes finding sheep so he can make a bed. Passing the night without one is terrifying, when the mobs come and you can just hear them right outside your hideout.

Jake realizes with a start that the zombie is actually coming from Tank's screen.

"Tank, watch out!"

Tank moves quickly, running into the house and shutting the door just in time. Outside, the zombie groans, plodding mindlessly into the door.

"Thanks, man," Tank says, and it sounds sincere.

The inside of the house is simple enough, but it's got a lot of good stuff already. Tank's been busy. There's a crafting table and two chests.

Jake watches Tank sort through his inventory for a few minutes as he meticulously organizes seeds, wood, and other supplies into neat rows by block type. "Oh, neat. You've got some wool, you can make a bed."

"Good idea." Tank crafts a bed and throws it in a corner and hops into it immediately.

Jake exhales a sigh of relief. "Nice. Emily, if you disconnect we can skip to morning—"

"No way, I'm finding way too much good stuff here! You two can sleep if you want to." Emily's picking away at a vein of iron, humming to herself.

To Jake's horror, Tank isn't even sleeping anymore but back outside his house, creating a perimeter wall around his farm.

Jake scowls. "Forget this." He's not going to just sit here and watch other people play. He can do that on YouTube anytime. Tank's coordinates look close enough. He sits back down in the dusty seat, wakes his avatar up, and gathers his supplies. He punches a hole into the dirt hideout and leaps into the night.

Tank's new base isn't too far from Jake, but it's a terrifying run as he speeds through the landscape. A blocky crescent moon slowly makes its way across the sky, and stars illuminate the forest as he runs. He's faster than the zombie pursuing him, but only by so much, and he can't keep this up forever. In the distance, something tall and spindly lurks—an enderman, Jake realizes with fear, and he quickly looks away, hoping it didn't lock on to him. The groans multiply. Great. A whole slew of zombies, perfect. He's going to die here and lose all his stuff and respawn super far away and what kind of people don't build a *bed* the first night? Granted, you can't always find sheep but at least you should hide. Finally he spots the gleam of torches in the distance, a bright beacon against the night. That must be Tank's camp. Jake takes a hard left, the zombies in hot pursuit. He presses on his keyboard harder, angling forward as he speeds toward the light.

"Aaah, open the door, open the door!"

"Where are you? I don't have a door in the perimeter wall yet, just—"

Jake punches the dirt wall out of panic and keeps running.

"Okay, don't step on the plants, dude—"

Jake barrels right through the wheat field and jumps into the house, slamming the door shut on the mob of zombies. "That was close."

"Euuurgghh." The zombies plod uselessly against the door.

"I said don't step on the plants," Tank says, turning around to glare at him. "What'd you do that for?"

"In case you didn't notice, I was running for my life!"

"*And* you broke my wall."

"I'll fix it tomorrow," Jake grumbles. "Wait, where are you going? We should sleep!"

"Why are you so obsessed with sleep?" Emily says, tossing her hair over her shoulder. A quick glance at her screen shows her deep in her mine, plinking away at a vein of gold ore.

"Because it's nighttime! It's not safe!"

"Got things to do," Tank says. He crafts a new pickaxe and roots around in a chest before heading down a hallway at the back of the dirt house.

"Where are you going?"

"Can't go outside now that you brought a ton of zombies here. Might as well go down. Come on, we can explore. I started a mine here earlier. Didn't get too far, but it seemed promising."

Tank's already disappearing from Jake's sight.

Jake's fingers twitch. He's not going to just sit here and wait. "All right, I'm coming," he says. He takes a quick moment to drop all the extra items he was hoarding in one of Tank's chests: seeds, pumpkins, feathers—stuff he'll want later.

He scurries to catch up; the hallway leads down, down, down into the depths of the earth. Tank's blue-haired avatar is already disappearing out of view. "One of these levels has a lot of iron in it," Tank says. "Hm, I think it was—yep, this one!"

"Emily, what are your coordinates again?"

Jake does some quick math. "Oh, I wonder if this will connect. Tank, let's head east."

Tank's level opens up into a cavern, and it's got plenty of ore veins as he said. Jake gets to work, mining when he sees iron or coal, plinking away when he hears Tank suddenly yelp.

"Gahh! Spider!" Tank slashes at it with his wooden sword. "No, no, I'm gonna—"

"I got you!" Jake shoots an arrow directly at the charging spider, whose beady red eyes are now focused on Jake. "C'mon, let's go!" He slays the spider easily and picks up the silk string it drops. "You okay? Want some food?"

"Yeah, thanks." Tank shudders. "I hate spiders."

"The worst. Come on, let's go this way. I think we're close to Emily, she's got a lot of cool stuff near her."

"All right," Tank says.

He sounds a little nervous, which is weird considering how big and intimidating he actually is.

"I've got an iron sword for you, here." Jake hands him the extra weapons. "Here, take my armor, too. I've got more health than you."

Tank follows close behind, and Jake feels a strange new surge of confidence as the two of them fight their way through the cavern together. Time stretches and collapses as they collect iron ore and coal, and finally he can see Emily's avatar—a sixties-style aviator pilot—wave at them from a cliffside chasm next to a steaming pool of lava. Jake is impressed and terrified by the deft way she's building a one-block bridge across the dangerous substance.

This whole cavern is spectacular. Jake would never have gone this deep on his own.

Rivulets of lava flow into a quick-moving river. Above Emily, the night sky is barely visible through the gorge, and the interior of the cavern is open to what look like endless caves and chasms, an eternity of exploration.

"What are you waiting for? Let's go!" Emily calls out, bouncing impatiently up and down.

He takes out his sword and follows his friends into the unknown.

CHAPTER SIXTEEN

EMILY

Emily whistles to herself as she slays skeleton after skeleton, watching her experience go up. Ugh, the beginning is always so slow. She'll need more levels if she wants to enchant, and she's so tired of these basic weapons and armor.

Her pickaxe breaks with an annoying *plink* and Emily sighs. "Anyone have sticks on them?"

Jake tosses a pile of logs at her. "How are you going through so many tools so fast?"

"Gotta mine, gotta buff up," Emily says simply. She crafts a new set of tools quickly and gets back to work.

"Okay, not that this isn't a good find—nice work, Emily—"

Emily finds herself grinning. This is kind of nice, she realizes. Playing with Viv was really fun—they had similar styles of exploration—but Jake's never-ending commentary and Tank's taciturn one-word answers or confused questions is kind of hilarious. Not that she'd admit it.

"—now that we're all together, I can show you this cool thing. There's, like, a whole seaside village that was, like—"

"Cool, we can trade with the villagers, where is it?"

"No, I mean—yeah, it would be useful but, like, the village itself. This whole world. Someone built it!" Jake's voice rises with excitement.

"Oh, like they left their old buildings and bases here? I mean, we are playing in someone else's server. What'd they make?" Tank asks.

"No, not like—not like someone was *playing* here. Someone built this server as a game for someone else to play. There's, like, all these riddles and things."

Emily utterly destroys the last skeleton, looks at her achingly slow experience gain and tries not to sigh. This is going to take forever. She glances at Jake, who, sitting in the lab, seems to be twitching with excitement. "This why you were sneaking into the lab?"

"Yeah," Jake admits. "It's really cool. I mean, we're really close to where I first saw that shipwreck, I think. There were mermaids and I found this riddle that led me to these coordinates with a new riddle to solve."

"Mermaids?" Emily asks. "That's not a thing."

"I know!" Jake says. "That's what I've been trying to tell you. This server is special. Someone programmed and modded all these things and I've been trying to figure it out."

Hm. That does sound interesting. "All right, let's see this shipwreck," Emily says.

Jake breaks into a smile so wide Emily's kind of concerned for his face. It's a good look for him, though, transforming him from the meek kid she thought he was into a delighted ball of energy.

They follow Jake out of the cavern, and Jake leads them through forests and plains and doubles back several times before Emily starts to get annoyed.

"It was here, I know it was," Jake mutters. "Come on!"

He leads Emily and Tank down the mountain, carefully placing blocks or digging footholds to make his way down.

Emily leaps from block to block without fear, taking fall damage. It's an easy way to level up in acrobatics at least.

"Hey, watch out!" Tank calls out as Emily tumbles down the slope, bouncing as she goes.

"Got plenty of health, don't worry!" Emily munches on some steak, watching her health go back up after she maxes her hunger meter.

"Not for long you won't," Tank says, following Jake at a safe pace. "So, are you sure you even saw mermaids?"

"Absolutely."

Tank turns to Emily. "Mermaids aren't a part of any new updates or anything, right?"

Next to him, Emily shakes her head. "It must be a mod."

"Yeah. This whole world—whoever built it, all of these structures and the signs—I think it's part of something they were planning." Jake forges ahead toward the sparkling shoreline, avoiding a squid playfully dipping after him as he goes. "Yeah. You know, all of those versions in that notebook, there were a few versions of this on the computer I'm using. The creator must have been working forever on making this perfect, and this multiplayer server is the latest version. Bella Beta 7."

"Hm," Emily says. A beta version of someone's special project, huh. Could be interesting.

"Maybe it's around the other hill? No, that patch of cut sugar cane looks familiar. We're definitely going the right way. Come on!"

Emily spots the rooftops of a few buildings in the distance, but Jake doesn't lead them there. Instead he keeps going, running past the village along the shoreline, looking carefully for something.

Jake takes off from the shore, swimming farther out toward the horizon.

He dives.

The water gets darker the deeper they go, and Emily's health is slowly declining.

She pauses to go back up for air. Sea turtles. If they could make helmets out of turtleshells, that would help. Or a Potion of Water Breathing. How far down is this place anyway?

"There! The shipwreck!"

Emily can just see the bulk of it far below them, but the outline is too rigidly defined to be anything natural. The mast of the ship, the bow, and the stern are clearly visible in the depths.

"You see it?"

"It's neat," Emily says. "I don't know why you're all worked up about these mermaids, though—could it be you just saw a fish?" She doesn't see anything, but a shipwreck isn't new at all to her.

"No, it was definitely the size of a person, except with a tail—"

Tank shrugs. "Shipwrecks do happen—"

Something swims past her.

Emily startles. "What was that?"

It's a dark shadow, swimming around the shipwreck amidst the schools of fish. Emily dives closer, trying to get another look. Fishes swim away, but the large shape is farther down, deeper by the shipwreck, gliding through the water almost in a teasing, playful manner—

"I'm gonna die, guys, I'm going back up," Tank says.

Emily presses on, closer to the shipwreck, and then she sees it—the mermaid.

Jake was right.

She can't believe it.

The mermaid is swimming around the ship. Her body is covered in green and gold scales, her unmistakable tail swishing back and forth as she swims. This is so new and strange and completely out of the realm of what she's used to that she can't help staring.

```
RoxXStarRedStone drowned
MCExplorerJake drowned
```

Jake jabs his keyboard in frustration.

Tank groans. "Come on, really? I don't have room for all of your stuff."

"Keep the ore, toss that, toss that, Tank, why are you holding on to so many flowers?" Emily almost laughs.

"It's really hard to find the blue ones, okay?" Tank mumbles. "But fine. Where did you respawn?"

Emily's back at the start point. It looks like Jake's in a basic dirt shack with a bed and nothing else.

"It's okay, let's regroup. Tank, where's your camp at?"

New coordinates light up the screen.

"I hope it was worth it," Tank says. "You both owe me a stack of cornflowers."

"It was," Jake says, pausing the game to minimize the screen. "I got a screengrab. Look!"

He throws up the frozen image, and there it is.

Undeniable proof that what they saw was real. The mermaid is real.

"Whoa," Tank breathes.

Up until now Emily had thought this was just a random world that Jake had seen some remnants of other players' builds in, but seeing the mermaid swim around like that is clear evidence of advanced programming, that this isn't just a vanilla Minecraft server.

She'd started playing because she figured it would be more fun than cleaning, but now to her surprise she wants to keep playing to figure out why the mermaids are here.

"Do you think it's like a friendly mob?" she asks. "Do you think they'd attack us?"

"Hm. There were more, I think. We could brew some underwater breathing potions and go back."

Emily shakes her head. They're going to have to work a lot harder to get everything they'll need to get down there and find out. The challenge sparks something inside of her: a new determination to see this quest through.

"They might be guarding something," Emily says. "I think there was a sign with stuff written on it on the shipwreck. You said there was a treasure map?"

"Yeah."

Something creaks outside.

The three of them swivel their heads toward the door, and Emily realizes that they've been playing Minecraft for almost two hours. She stands up hastily, her legs prickling with the fuzzy pins and needles that come with sitting for too long. The computers are facing the door so it's fine, it's fine —

"Quick! Look busy!" She gestures frantically.

Jake freezes. Tank grabs a dust rag and starts mopping at a random monitor. Emily hops into the second row and shuffles some old keyboards into a box.

"Hello?" Mrs. Jenkins opens the door. "How are you all doing?"

She gives a sweeping look at the cluttered computer lab and narrows her eyes. "Looks like you've been hard at work. You know, the point of character-building through work is that it doesn't get done if the work isn't being done."

"Oh, we're doing work," Jake says quickly. "I mean, we made really good progress in the other room! Why don't you take a look?"

Jake leads Mrs. Jenkins out the door before mouthing *turn it off* at them.

Emily saves and quits, does the same for Jake. She follows Tank out of the computer lab and listens in on Jake and Mrs. Jenkins's conversation.

"Not bad for your first day," Mrs. Jenkins says.

"The community center looks like it was really cool back in the day," Jake says. "How come you don't do activities and stuff like that anymore?"

Mrs. Jenkins's mouth hardens. "Things change, young man."

"Oh, okay," Jake says in a small voice.

"We have a few boxes all done and sorted, where do you want them, Mrs. J?" Tank asks.

"You can bring them to my apartment at the end of the week," she says gruffly.

"Oh, we can start moving them earlier if you want," Emily says. She grabs the first full box she sees. It's heavier than it looks; the photo frames inside it slide forward, and she loses her balance. The file folder on top of the frames falls flat to the floor, scattering news article clippings everywhere in a grayscale flutter.

A shadow falls over Mrs. Jenkins's face. "That's just trash. You can take that to the curb. The rest of the stuff you can bring to me on Friday."

She sweeps out of the door without another look at the rest of them.

Emily picks up a scrap of paper from the floor, carefully placing it back in the file. "Come on, help me."

"She just said it was trash?" Tank looks confused, but starts helping her anyway.

Emily shakes her head. After picking apart social cues and body language forever, she knows that this stuff is important from the way Mrs. Jenkins's eyes widened when she saw the box, the sad shadow that came over her. "Listen, Pattie took this quiz once that defines, like, your color palette, and she was convinced for a hot second that she was a Spring and not a Summer. So she was going to throw out all her pastels, even though she loved this specific pink sundress. And she was all ready to throw it out, and said she hated all pastel colors, but I knew that dress was her favorite, and that she didn't want to throw it out. She just thought she did."

Jake picks up the last newspaper clipping and places it in the folder solemnly. "You're right, I think it's important, too. Let's hang on to it."

Tank rearranges the photo frames in the box, stacking them neatly by size. "Here." He takes the folder and closes the box, taping it shut. "We'll put this here for now." He hefts the box and shifts it to the corner. He looks down at Emily and smiles, a soft and easy one, a little shy.

There's something unspoken in the air among the three of them now, something shared with this secret, with the mermaids and the mysterious server and the way they're holding on to this box of memories for an old lady who pretends that they aren't important. It feels like the start of something new. Something different.

Emily smiles back at the two of them. "I'll see you both tomorrow."

CHAPTER SEVENTEEN

TANK

Tank finds Shark waiting for him at the bottom of the stairwell on his way to the community center the next day.

"You haven't texted me back," Shark accuses. "AJ and Gus are terrible at mini golf. Come on, you expect me to hang out just with those losers?"

"I can't today," Tank says.

"Okay, well, when can you hang out? My older brother is gonna go check out the hill that all of his dumb friends swear is haunted if you wanna come. He said this time the spirits or ghosts or whatever will definitely show up, move things around and stuff."

"Sounds cool," Tank says. It definitely does not sound cool. He doesn't like haunted things or the idea of ghosts at all. "I got in trouble and I have to do this community service thing. Every day. So I probably can't for a while."

"Oh man," Shark says, his eyes widening. "What'd you do?"

Tank shrugs.

"Strong and silent, man, that's what I like about you." Shark claps Tank on the shoulder. "I'll tell them you got juvie." He winks. "Will help with your rep."

"Thanks." Tank isn't sure how that would help, but if Shark says so, then it must. He walks across the courtyard and pretends to go back to the West Tower, and waits until he sees Shark walking down the street, away from his building, before he returns to the community center.

Jake and Emily are already at work. Emily's wearing the mask Jake brought for her—a patterned floral one that matches the one in Tank's pocket. She matched her T-shirt and sneakers to the mask as well, and Tank is pleased to see she's actually dusting properly, picking up the knickknacks and setting them aside before wiping down the shelf.

"I brought a speaker," Jake says. "What kind of music do you like?"

"Electronic," Tank says.

Emily folds her arms. "Rock."

"Uh, okay, well, I like folk music but I listen to everything. Wanna switch off with playlists?"

"Sounds good," Emily says. "I think we can finish this room today."

They start with one of Jake's playlists, which mixes pop and some interesting acoustic guitar sounds and is actually really nice and relaxing. Meditative. Tank isn't sure they would have enough work to last a week, actually.

"So, what's up with the riddles in that server?"

Jake brightens, like he's been waiting for Tank to ask this all morning.

"So, the first one I found was in the middle of this village and the sign said Riddle the Seventeenth, and then when I solved it, it led me to another one. I think there's, like, a whole hidden underwater city at the end."

Emily pauses. "That's so cool."

"Have you ever gone to the End? Of the game?" Tank and Viv have before, in one of their older games. It had taken them forever to build up to it and be able to defeat the ender dragon. Viv had planned it for months.

"Got there, but I kept dying. That dragon is gnarly," Emily says.

"It's not really something you're supposed to do by yourself," Jake says. "I mean, I've tried, but I've never succeeded, either."

Emily shrugs. "Well, everyone knows what it looks like. I want to see something I've never seen before. There's treasure, right?"

"Yeah. There's this huge mural I found that shows what I think is at the end of this game."

Emily tosses her dusting rag into an empty bucket, whooping when it lands squarely inside. "Great. I'm tired of dusting already anyways. Let's go!"

"We've only been working for ten minutes," Tank says. "But I guess we did make a lot of progress yesterday. Before we started playing."

Jake grins at him. "That's the spirit!"

Tank coughs as he follows Jake and Emily into the computer lab. "Can we at least finish dusting the stuff in this room before we play, though? I've got allergies."

"Sure. We do have to clean it anyways."

Tank's glad Jake and Emily agree, and they get to work. Tank starts unplugging and taking apart the other rows, and spots a folded sheet of notebook paper on the floor. Oh! Viv's coordinates. The whole reason why he got caught in the first place.

He pockets it to give to her later.

It takes only about an hour to sort all the electronic clutter into boxes. They leave the three working computers set up and push all the boxes into a clean corner. Once they've organized everything, the place looks and feels completely different. Tank even opens the window, letting fresh air flow in. The trees from the courtyard flutter gently in the breeze, and the patch of green is a nice respite from the faded gray wallpaper.

Minecraft's soothing music welcomes them back to the world, and Tank finds himself grinning, his heart pounding faster with anticipation. He'd always found Viv's endless energy for quests rather tiring, but he did it because she liked to and he liked spending time with her. He'd much rather spend time building more hedge mazes and epic gardens, and find new ways to create greenhouses.

This mystery of the mermaids feels completely different, like a puzzle to solve. And Tank loves puzzles.

"This way to the mural," Jake says, minimizing a Word document.

"What else do you know about this server?" Tank asks.

Jake opens up a folder on his computer and shows them a series of screenshots: stunning vistas, a seaside village with a square, an icy cave. A treasure map. A shipwreck. A document filled with coordinates and notes.

"It's some sort of game. I feel like by riddle number seventeen the designer expected the players to be more advanced already, there's some stuff that has been difficult, but I wanna show you what I found so far."

Jake leads them west. "Here's a blank map. Let's fill in this corner of the world while we're at it."

Tank gingerly places the map in his other hand, watching the color fill in as they cross mountains and grassy plains.

"Hey, wait up!" Tank can barely see Emily and Jake ahead through the thickness of the brush. The open plains have given way to dense jungle, and he can barely move without crashing into overgrown vines. He keeps getting trapped in thick leaves and he can barely keep up. "How are you moving so fast?"

"I'm just hacking my way through," Emily says.

"Hold up," Jake says. "We gotta stick together."

Tank exhales in relief—he can see Emily ahead, her armor a quick flash of gray against the thick green jungle. He can see the path now, if you could call it that. Leaves float above, vines trail down and disappear where Emily's blazed through the jungle in a winding, almost zigzag fashion, leaving blocks in her wake. Tank collects the wood—jungle logs, he notes with interest—carefully. One can always use building materials.

"Wouldn't it be more efficient to just go in a straight line?" Jake calls.

"I'm just following the path of least resistance," Emily says. She nods at Tank now that he's caught up, and dashes ahead until she's just a gray shimmer amongst the green.

Tank picks up the pace, running after her; it's easier now that he can just follow behind her without having to guess where to go, and they're making good time. He glances at the map in his hand; it's filling up in quick bursts of green, and Tank's pleased to see how much they've covered so far.

He looks back up and realizes he can't see Jake or Emily anywhere.

"Where are you?"

"Oh, I'm on top of the trees. See me?"

"How are you—" Tank shakes his head. He spots movement in the treetops—Jake jumping up and down. "Do you see Emily?"

"Yeah. You coming up?"

He might as well. Climbing the tree takes some effort and throwing blocks of dirt underneath him, but Tank makes it to the top of the jungle canopy, where Jake's waiting patiently for him. From here, the treetops stretch out endlessly in a lush, verdant expanse. In the distance, lava streams from a cavern just visible in the high cliffs of a mountain.

"It's easier than cutting your way through—I think jungle's the best for this. Forests aren't usually grown in thick enough, and it's easy to fall."

It makes Tank nervous, walking across the treetops—a single misstep and he could fall and lose precious health at this early stage of the game, but he watches Jake and follows his path.

Finally they catch up to Emily just as the sun is starting to set. Torches light a simple dirt building. "Ready? I know Jake here is scared of the dark."

"I am not," Jake mutters. "It's just smarter to wait out the night."

"You could say thank you for building you a hideout," Emily says, snorting.

Tank is the last to enter, and he stacks dirt carefully behind him to prevent any wayward mobs from coming in.

"Thank you," he says, grinning over at Emily.

"And now we wait," Jake says. "Anyone bring a bed?"

"Nope," Emily says.

Tank has a bed but figures it would be pointless to say, so he keeps quiet. He leans back and stretches, wondering if they should go back to cleaning for a bit. His stomach growls, and Tank remembers he brought a snack. He gets up and grabs the pack of instant ramen from his backpack, popping it open. He tears open the bag of seasoning and sprinkles it inside the pack before crushing it and shaking it. He opens it back up and pops the crunchy dry noodles in his mouth, chewing noisily.

Jake blinks at him.

"You want some?" Tank offers him the bag.

Jake pulls a chunk of noodle out and crunches it thoughtfully. "That's actually pretty good," he says.

Tank tilts the bag at Emily, who takes a piece without looking away from her screen, where she's categorizing her inventory. "Nice. You ever put butter on it and put it in the toaster oven?"

"Huh. That sounds good," Tank says. "We don't have one anymore after my dad messed it up. I think he was trying to repair the TV."

"With the toaster oven?" Emily asks, raising an eyebrow.

"He likes to fix things," Tank says, with a sigh. "I think there was a wire he needed or something. Sometimes what he comes up with is pretty cool, and sometimes it's more trouble than it's worth."

"That sucks," Emily says. "My older sister once ruined the sink with her hair dye and I had purple hands for days. Days! It was the worst."

"I always thought having siblings would be fun," Jake says wistfully.

Emily gives him an incredulous look. "Fun? It's never quiet and everyone's always touching my stuff."

"I have a little sister," Tank says. "She can be annoying sometimes because she thinks she knows everything."

Emily laughs. "I'm right in the middle. I bet that'll be fun once the twins get older." She shakes her head. "You don't know how lucky you are," she says to Jake.

Jake shrugs, opening his mouth and then closing it again.

"Right," Tank says, suddenly feeling awkward. He never talks about his family. Shark and AJ and Gus never wanted to talk about anything except shoes and what to do at Fortress Park.

He focuses on the game and smashes through the dirt hideout wall to see how much time has passed—it's already midmorning, judging from the sun's position. Clouds flutter across the bright blue sky, and they've wasted precious time.

"All right, got all the torches? Let's go." Jake leads the way, stopping every now and then to make sure Tank is right behind him.

The mural becomes visible quickly; it's a huge swath of wall, made out of thousands of blocks, outside a village. Up close, it's hard to tell what it depicts, but Tank can see the sheer amount of work that went into creating this huge, elaborate mosaic. From across the valley, they climb a mountain to see the mural as it was meant to be seen—from afar.

It's breathtaking.

Tiers and tiers of pyramidlike buildings. Platforms and bridges suspended across streets and alleyways dripping with seaweed. Chests filled with sparkling gems. Mermaids swimming back and forth in the sparkling sunlight filtering through the water.

"An underwater city," Emily breathes.

"Incredible, right? I think for what's next we would need potions and enchanted armor to get farther, and I'm nowhere near—"

"We need to get to work then!" Emily says with a brusque confidence Tank wishes he had. He likes building things in Creative and designing things, but when he played with Viv she usually gave him items she'd already worked on. She did still complain about him being too slow or not having the drive to just fight mobs and go exploring with her enough. What if Emily and Jake find that he isn't fun to play with, either?

"Sounds like a good plan. We'll need to buff up to get enchantments and to brew potions, need paper for books—I've got a good place started a little east of here."

They follow Jake to his base, and though Tank is still skeptical about Jake's farming skills, he has to admit this place has much more potential than the one he saw Jake in yesterday.

"Tank, you like organizing and building, right? Can you make the farm at the base super efficient? Emily and I can go look for diamonds."

"Yes! Mining!" Emily whoops. "We're gonna need the best armor and weapons to go into the Nether for the nether wart we'll need."

With the tasks set and a plan to level up, Tank has to admit he likes that Jake has identified what he's good at. He would be terrible at the mines. It would be good to get experience, but he doesn't want to if he doesn't have to. Instead, he's glad to be useful in this way.

Tank whistles as he seeds a new line of wheat, admiring the rows and how efficient they are. The new pumpkin patch is coming along quite nicely now that he's organized Jake's previously chaotic mess. Tank harvests a new batch of sugar cane before planting more along the shore of the lake he's dug out inside the perimeter of the base. There. That's great. Now the sugar cane looks healthy and happy. Maybe it would be fun to make a little design with the water. What about a moat?

"Hey, this looks great," Jake says when he and Emily get back from their next mining run. It's been a nice way to spend the time, getting to be creative and decorate while Jake and Emily focus on fighting monsters and mining. Jake and Emily came back a few times to drop off loot and to refresh their supplies, and then Jake spent some time working on the south end of their base on something as Emily went back on her own.

"Ooh, super efficient. I like how you've organized all the inventory," Emily says with approval as she digs up the ground in front of each of the carefully labeled chests, placing crafting tables in a neat row in front of them. "Never got this specific before, but I like how you can find everything easily. Stone, wood, weapons, seeds, food . . ."

"Thanks," Tank says, proud of his process.

"You know, there's a redstone thing you can build that sorts all of this stuff for you. I can put one together if you like," Emily says.

"Oh, that would be great!" Tank beams.

Emily closes the last chest at the end of the row. "Yeah, it's no problem, I like figuring stuff out like that. Huh, you have so many flowers collected. For potions and stuff?"

"Yeah. I mean, I also just like to decorate with them. I, uh, I like it when things are colorful," Tank says, watching for their reactions, waiting for the judgment or laughter or teasing.

"That's cool," Jake says. "Yeah, I really liked how you set up your farm in the world you showed me yesterday. You know, there's a field here, next to where we put the cows—"

"Oh yeah!" Emily walks over to the empty area, which was exactly where Tank was considering building something decorative, but he wasn't sure with a shared base if the others would like it.

"A hedge maze would look great," Jake muses.

"Oh, okay, sure," Tank says, unable to keep the pleased note out of his voice. "I know decorating isn't like finding treasure or fighting monsters, or even the point of the game—"

Jake shakes his head. "Everyone has their own way of playing and having fun. This is great! Come on, let me show you what I've been working on."

"Brewing stand is complete, and an enchanting table," Jake says. There's a new corner of the house, decked out in bookshelves. Tank walks inside, pleased with the ambiance. It feels like a magical library, with all the books stacked up on shelves and the miasma of purple dust floating over the enchanting table in the center.

The base is hustling with activity. Tank's never quite fit in with Viv's friends on her server—they were leagues ahead of him, always building epic constructions and designing things that he could barely comprehend. When he and his sister play together, it's a specific kind of partnership that has evolved over time.

This feels good, being a part of a team.

CHAPTER EIGHTEEN

JAKE

"What in the—" Jake stumbles backward as he watches his health drop. "Who put a campfire in the middle of the hallway?"

"Oh, I needed to cook some food," Emily says.

"Why didn't you use a furnace?" Jake scowls as he retreats to a safe, fire-free section of the hallway. Who puts a fire right in the middle of the main hallway of the house, anyway? He quickly eats a few loaves of bread before grabbing a pickaxe to get rid of the hazard.

"Eh, didn't have all the materials on hand," she responds.

"There's a room I set aside for a kitchen," Tank says. "There are furnaces in there."

Jake enters the room next to the main room, admiring the way Tank's used staircases and trapdoors to mock up chairs and tables.

There're even potted plants in front of glass windows. Furnaces line a wall, giving it a stove-and-cabinets effect with how the chests are embedded in the wall. He cooks a stack of raw beef, watching them cook into steaks one by one.

Jake's stomach growls; sometimes he forgets he has a body when he's so absorbed in the game. The kitchen reminds him that there's actually a kitchen in this community center. There was a microwave, too.

"Do you all want lasagna? My dad forgets that we're only, like, two people, and he made a ton. If you don't help me eat it we're gonna have it for dinner for the next few nights, and I'd really rather not."

"Uh, sure. Yeah, I could use a lunch break."

Tank blinks at him. "Do you need help?"

"Nah, I'm good."

Jake runs back up to his apartment and grabs the half-full lasagna and three plates and forks, then carefully walks it all back to the community center.

The microwave in the center's kitchen is old but is still working, and Jake can hear Tank and Emily in the computer lab as it heats up.

"Tank, where are you?"

"Expanding the farm. Do you need me?"

"Yeah, I need cover! Mining this obsidian takes forever and I can't get it with all these skeletons. Come on!"

"All right, all right." There's a long pause before he says, "Do you need anything?"

"Did Jake get any more diamonds? This pickaxe is about to break."

"I put some in the chest earlier!" Jake calls out.

"Found it. On my way," Tank says.

Jake watches the microwave count down and listens to the soft electronic hum of it heating up and the sounds of Tank and Emily from the other room with a smile.

"Lunch is ready!" Jake calls.

"Where even are you?" Emily's voice echoes from the hall.

"The kitchen."

"There's a kitchen?" Tank asks, incredulous.

"Go through the lobby and past the game area."

Emily opens the door, peering inside curiously. "Whoa, I never even knew this was here. You think they used to have like events and stuff?"

"Yeah. According to the articles, there were cooking classes and all sorts of stuff. Mrs. Jenkins had a lot of programming." Jake hands them each a plate.

"Thanks," Emily says. "I can bring food next time, if you want."

"That sounds good."

They eat in silence for a bit, the dusty room echoing the sounds of chewing. It's awkward now that they aren't playing Minecraft or busy cleaning. Eating together is—it's a thing you do with people you like.

"So did you all get in trouble with your parents for this? I mean, I was already grounded before and at first I thought they might double down on the punishment, but my parents gave me back my phone because I'm doing the work here." Emily smiles, pleased with herself.

"My parents don't know and I'm going to keep it that way," Tank says. "My mom has enough to worry about."

"What about you?" Emily turns to Jake. "What's the level of strictness here? Your dad is in charge of the construction site, huh? That must have really hurt."

"He thinks the community service is good," Jake says carefully. He shrugs. "Dad's never really been the strict one."

"Your mom, then? She must have had a fit." Emily nods as she pulls a forkful of lasagna toward herself, admiring the cheese dripping from the utensil. "It's always my mom who comes down much harder. Papa at least can be convinced if I promise not to do it again."

"My mom died three years ago," Jake says quietly.

Tank pauses, his fork halfway to his mouth.

"Oh," Emily says. "That sucks."

And that's it. Just a simple statement of truth, no fake apologies or pretending to understand. Right after it happened, Jake had hated it—how the school made him talk to a counselor, her saccharine smile, the way other kids had treated him, like they didn't know how to talk to him.

He suddenly appreciates Emily's bluntness.

"My ông nội—my grandfather—he died last year," Tank says. "It was a lot. I still miss him. He had the best jokes, and he taught me how to play cards."

"He sounds cool," Jake says wistfully. "Yeah, Mom was the best."

They eat in silence for a while, and then Tank takes their empty dishes to the sink, rinsing them off.

"Thanks for the lunch," Emily says, squeezing Jake's shoulder. "I can bring tamales sometime if you like. My family makes a whole bunch of them every Christmas and we always have some in the freezer."

"Sounds good," Jake says.

"I can bring food the next day. We can switch? Or go out, there's a good pizza place down the street." Tank smiles, and for once he actually looks his age instead of the intimidating line-backer Jake thought he was.

"Ooh yeah, or tacos! The best stand in town is only like a ten-minute walk." Emily grins, bouncing up and down on her toes. "Tell your dad the lasagna was amazing."

Jake smiles and shakes his head. "I won't, it'll go to his head. He's been trying a lot of new things lately, and if I say one of my friends likes something he'll just keep making this forever. Not that it's a bad thing, but some variety is nice."

Emily just tosses her hair back as she laughs.

Tank chuckles. "My dad is a disaster in the kitchen. Drives my mom wild because he makes a mess if he attempts to cook. He can make, like, one thing pretty much, it's like a braised pork dish with marinated eggs." He looks at his plate, an embarrassed flush starting on his cheeks. "This is nice, the lunch. Thanks, Jake. Should we—should we clean a little and then get back to the game?"

It snaps him back to reality, that Tank and Emily are here because they have to be, and they have a project to do. "Yeah, we played for most of the morning," Jake says. "Let's go through the kitchen since we're already here, and then we can play."

The kitchen is tougher than the first storage room, which had been books and knicknacks and files. The fridge thankfully is empty and unplugged, so no surprises there, but Jake can't believe how much stuff is in the cupboards. There are cobwebs and crusted-over pans from ages ago, and Emily gags at the smell of them when they dig them out. With gloves, they manage to dump all the unusable cookware into the trash, and finally get everything out of the pantry.

"Don't eat that!" Jake says in horror, grabbing a box of Twinkies out of Tank's hands.

Tank takes another bite out of the one he's already unwrapped. "It's still good."

"You're gonna get sick!" Jake flips the box over. "The expiration date on these was—oh. I guess they're still good . . . When did these get here?"

"There's so many preservatives in these, they're fine. I mean, it probably doesn't taste good. Only one way to test, though." Emily holds her hands open.

Tank reaches into the box in Jake's still-shocked hands and tosses one at Emily.

She bites into the cake and shrugs. "Not the best. Bet it would be great deep-fried. You wanna try?"

Jake shakes his head.

"Oh, come on." Emily grins at him. "You scared?"

"No way!" Jake takes a Twinkie out of the box and unwraps it. It looks like a normal Twinkie, unnaturally yellow, and bits of cream on the wrapper. He takes a tentative bite.

"Tastes like a Twinkie," he admits.

Tank brings the box with them back to the computer lab, where they get to work mining and gathering what they need for the Potions of Water Breathing. "I think we're all set," Tank says. "Got the sand, made the glass, plenty of glass bottles. You know what would be pretty? A greenhouse. I've made one before—I mean, you can't really grow crops in it, but they're real pretty with the glass walls."

"Sounds nice, Tank," Emily says. "So we have everything we need for the potions?"

"Nether wart," Jake says.

The three of them exchange nervous looks.

Emily is the first one to say it, her mouth hardened into a tough line. "We need to go to the Nether."

Jake's phone beeps.

Dad 5:32 P.M.
Still at community service? Made pesto linguini and chicken!

"I have to go," Jake says. "But yeah. Let's plan for the Nether tomorrow."

"Same time?" Emily powers down her computer and grins at him.

"Absolutely," Jake says.

Tank offers his hand to Jake for a fist bump, and he taps it with his own before pulling it back and miming an explosion. Tank mimics the gesture, shaking his head, but his eyes twinkle with amusement.

Tank offers his fist to Emily, which she gently taps while rolling her eyes. "I'll see you tomorrow. First thing: Nether. Be prepared."

"Tomorrow," Jake says, like a promise.

Tank clasps him on the shoulder before he leaves, and it dawns on Jake how strange this should be, playing videogames with the last two people he ever would have thought he'd have anything in common with. And yet it feels natural and right. Something warm blossoms inside him, deep in his gut, and the feeling is new and strange.

It feels like friendship.

CHAPTER NINETEEN

TANK

Tank doesn't want to admit he's nervous about going to the Nether, so he suggests working in the second storage room first. This room is filled with books and art supplies that they box carefully.

Emily blows the dust off a book decorated with cartoon mermaids.

"What's that?" Jake asks.

"Someone's old sketch pad. Or journal?" Emily gingerly turns the page, showing it to Tank. Crayon illustrations of mermaids holding tridents, and fish and dolphins swimming in the ocean fill the pages, each of them lettered carefully in childish handwriting.

"There once was a mermaid princess named Bella," Emily reads from the first page. "Kingdom of Kelp, that's original."

Tank chuckles as he points to the name scrawled on the inside of the front cover.

"Bella, age seven," Tank reads. The large letters and awkwardly formed E's and L's make him think of Viv's early drawings and things.

He feels a little guilty; he hasn't told her he's been playing Minecraft with Jake and Emily. Part of him wants to have something that's just his, but he knows—he knows Viv would love the mystery of the world. She'd probably be great at all the puzzles.

He flips the page. A group of mermaids drawn in crayon swim in front of a clumsily decorated underwater village. Scales meticulously drawn one by one decorate each mermaid's tail. On the next page, a massive sea monster with monstrous teeth crashes into a fortified wall as terrified mermaids swim away.

The whole morning has been spent deciding what to clean and keep, and what should be trashed, but no one asks the question "Trash or keep?" about this.

Tank stares at the hand-drawn book one more time before saying softly, "We can put it in the box with the photos and stuff."

Jake nods. "Good idea. Eventually Mrs. J will want this stuff."

Emily gingerly places Bella's storybook inside the box with the mementos, and Tank shuts the box.

Tank hangs back, watching Jake and Emily methodically sort through their inventory. There's no more putting it off, it's time to go.

"Are you sure we need to go to the Nether?" Tank asks. He's seen Viv with her friends—he's never gone himself, and Viv's never asked him to. She knows the music alone is enough to creep him out.

Tank doesn't like to admit to many things, but everything about the Nether—how you can die at any minute, whether from lava or the terrifying mobs of monsters and those things that shoot fire, and how it's an endless expanse of fire and that deep, dark red of his nightmares—terrifies him.

"Yeah. We need nether wart to brew the potions," Jake says.

"Torches, we'll need a ton of torches," Emily's muttering to herself. "How are our weapons? I'm going to go enchant more— which armor set are you bringing?"

"Diamond. I don't have enough for—do we have more diamonds?"

Jake and Emily are working away. Emily's already disappeared into the house, humming to herself, "Gonna go to the Ne-*ther* . . ."

Jake looks up from the crafting table. "Tank, do you want some more armor?"

"Do we have to go?" His voice sounds small and scared. Weak. Tank regrets saying it immediately because he's not, he's strong and tough and—

"Hey, are you okay?"

"I've just never gone to the Nether before."

"Yeah, it's scary. We're probably going to die. But in order to find the treasure, we gotta do it. The first time I went, I had no idea what I was doing and died immediately, but I've learned a lot. Emily's a super strong fighter, and we're gonna stick together."

Jake's words are so sure that Tank finds himself nodding. He's not ready, but he picks up the diamond armor Jake crafts for him and puts it on. His enchanted pickaxe glimmers in his hand, and he follows Jake inside the house where Emily's pacing back and forth in the library in front of the enchanting table.

"What are you doing?" Jake asks.

"C'mon, don't tell me you don't have a ritual," Emily retorts.

"It's random!"

"Don't question my process!" Emily groans. "Now I gotta start over. One, two, three—and enchant!"

Emily whoops. "Yes, Looting III and Breaking III!" She turns to Tank. "You got a bow?"

Tank hands over his bow.

"We gotta go, Em," Jake says.

"Lemme make sure Tank's got all the best equipment first," Emily says, continuing her pacing as she enchants the bow. "All right, now we're ready. Let's do this."

The portal is in one of Emily's mining shafts, and they get lost a few times but eventually find the level where she keeps it.

It looks just like an arch, albeit made of obsidian, but Tank swears he can feel the evil energy emanating from the blocks even though it's just a structure. He hangs back, watching Jake activate it with flint and steel. The purple portal blooms within the obsidian frame, churning with a dizzying speed.

Emily stands next to him. "You got this," she says. "We can do it."

"If any of us die—you have to get our stuff and get home," Jake says.

"Me?" Tank takes another look at his inventory. Even with the last-minute equipment and the new enchantments, he doesn't feel ready.

"Well, any of us, but I think you're most likely to survive." Jake stands in front of the portal and turns back to regard Tank. "You ready?"

Tank bites back the comment about how both Emily and Jake

are way stronger than he is, a pleased comfort settling in over his shoulders. It's steadying, his friends' confidence in him. It feels good, in an entirely new way. Shark and the guys have always been second-guessing him or offering ideas on what kind of shoes he needs, how his hair should be, what kind of jackets he needs to wear.

"Yeah, let's go," Tank says, surprising himself with his own boldness.

"YEAAAARGH!!!" Emily roars, charging into the portal. She disappears into the purple swirling void.

Jake pauses, like he's waiting for Tank to step through.

Tank takes a deep breath and approaches the portal. For a second, nothing happens, but then the whole world seems to spin, clouds of purple swirling forth.

Everything goes dark.

The world is red and fire. Lava streams down from tall, dark cliffs, the monoliths casting shadow over everything. Emily is already running ahead, disappearing over the dark horizon.

"Wait up!" Jake calls as he exits the portal. "We gotta stick together."

"We gotta find these warts is what we gotta do," Emily retorts. "Let's go!"

Tank wields his sword at the ready, nervous. "We're surrounded!" He yelps as he notices strange creatures advancing on them. He's never seen these mobs up close before—they're pig-headed people, covered in moss and heavily armed, and they're *everywhere*.

"No, no, don't attack!" Jake calls out suddenly. "The zombified piglin will leave us alone, but if you attack one then they're all going to go after us and we're goners."

Tank shudders but follows Jake's lead as they carefully pick their way through the lava and ruin to catch up to Emily.

She's hacking away at the ground. "Nether quartz. Get some if you see it, but let's keep moving. Maybe we'll find a fortress."

Tank can barely handle a stronghold in the Overworld. He takes a deep breath to calm his nerves. Time seems to pass by slower than normal, and the foreboding music rising all around them doesn't help, either.

They wander for what seems like forever, but according to the computer's clock, it has only been ten minutes. There's endless mottled dark red rock, some mushrooms that Tank starts to gather until Emily informs him that they should keep their inventory for essentials only, and they can find red and brown mushrooms any-where.

"Up there! Do you see it?"

Tank can't see anything. He tucks mushrooms into his inventory. Just in case.

"It does look like some sort of building with columns," Emily says, bouncing up and down.

Tank follows her gaze to the top of a tall, skinny rock outcrop. "How do we get up there?"

"Carefully," Jake says. "One fall and that's it." He picks at the outcrop, hacking stairs into the blocks, and slowly makes his way up. Tank follows with trepidation up the switchback stairs in the narrow one-block-wide hallway that appears, hanging back so Jake has enough room to keep working.

RoxXStarRedStone has made the achievement [A Terrible Fortress].
MCExplorerJake has made the achievement [A Terrible Fortress].

They must have made it inside already. Tank's still a few switchbacks behind, so he hurries ahead, trying to catch up.

"Okay, it looks like this bridge here leads inside—"

"AAAGH!"

Tank turns the corner and takes the last step up just in time to see a bright red-hot fireball careening right at his face.

TankFarms has made the achievement [A Terrible Fortress].

CHAPTER TWENTY

EMILY

Emily backs up, switching from her sword to her bow so she can put some distance between her and the blazes. There are three of them, clouds of smoke swirling around their fiery bodies. *Should have packed snowballs,* she thinks. *Should have prepared better.*

A blaze hurls a fireball directly at the staircase.

No.

No, not her friends!

Friends? A small voice inside her questions. When did she start thinking of them as friends?

"TANK!" Emily shouts. She shoots an arrow right at the blaze, ignoring the damage she's taking from another one to her left. "Go back down!"

Tank ducks just in time, disappearing back down the stairs until she can just see his head poking out. "What's going on?"

The bridge is too narrow and they can't afford to die, not here, not yet. Not until they've found what they need and one of them can make it back.

"Blazes!" Jake says, plunging his sword into the last fiery blaze. "That was close. Did we get them all?"

Emily sinks another arrow satisfactorily into the last blaze, and picks up the rod it drops. "Yeah. Come on, Tank."

She quickly eats a couple steaks; Jake next to her is doing the same with a noisy *cronch cronch cronch*.

"Are you all right?" Tank offers her a stack of bread.

"Yeah. There're going to be more. Are you ready?" Emily looks at Tank and Jake, who follow closely behind her, their weapons glimmering in the scant light from the lava below them.

"Let's stick together," Jake says.

"Thanks for handling that," Tank offers, his voice sounding small.

"Anytime," Emily says.

She leads the way into the fortress. There are more blazes inside, but the trio makes quick work of them, alternating between Jake's melee attacks and Tank's and Emily's arrows. They're a well-oiled machine.

"On your right!"

"I need more arrows!"

"I'll craft them. Cover me!" Tank scoots backward and sets a crafting table down.

Emily pulls her sword out and charges at the blaze.

"Emily!" Jake calls out.

"They have a cooldown period—wait until they shoot three

fireballs and then go!" The blazes look really funny when they're not on fire, a sickly green swirl of arms that disappear into a puff of smoke. She exhales with relief when the cavernous hallway is empty once again.

"More blaze rods, yes!" Jake hands her a few. "Are you holding them? How's your inventory?"

"I'm okay, still got space," Emily says.

"Can we build things with these blocks?" Tank asks curiously.

"Yeah, but let's keep moving. We're here for the wart. Don't get sidetracked. Tank, what are you—why are you still picking mushrooms?" Emily shakes her head as she sees Tank lingering behind them.

Tank shrugs. "Habit, I guess. I dunno. We can eat them if we run out of food."

"Yeah, I guess stew is helpful," Emily admits. "Nice job, Tank."

The great hallway intersects with another one; all of the mottled-red stone halls look the same. "Did we already go down this way?" Jake asks.

"Yeah. I left a torch there. See?" Tank gestures at the glimmering trail in the distance.

Emily looks at the other intersections—two out of three have torches. "Great idea. C'mon, let's get moving."

The hallway leads to a dark room with a small grate. "What is that? Treasure?" Jake asks.

"No—spawner! Run!"

They run away from the blazes, and Emily nearly crashes into Jake, who's stopped right in front of lava overflowing the hallway.

"This way's clear!" Tank shouts.

They turn back from the lava and go down a new hallway until they're back out in the open on a bridge to a floating chunk of netherrack.

"Nether wart! I see them!" Jake shouts.

The bridge is covered with a stream of lava, pulsing red hot as it flows down from the floating landmass. Emily darts forward, jumping up onto the raised edge of the bridge, speeding forward right after Jake. It doesn't make her nervous, going out for long stretches at a time like this, but the Nether is different—this mission is different. There are people counting on her.

Jake's almost to the other side of the bridge. "Good, there's a whole bunch of them, I'm gonna—"

MCExplorerJake tried to swim in lava

"Agggh! I was carrying so many blaze rods!"

"It's okay, it's okay." Emily slows down, picking her way carefully across the bridge now. Behind her, Tank is doing the same.

She picks as much nether wart as she can. Tank works quietly next to her until they've gathered all the plants. He peers off into the dark Nether horizon. Zombified piglins roam in circles, and Emily is out of arrows. Even her enchanted weapons are starting to wear down, and she doesn't think she can survive another fortress run.

"How many potions can we make with this?" Tank asks.

Emily doesn't know, but they've got bigger problems. Three blazes have just spotted them, rising up on the sides of the bridge.

"Tank, take the wart! I'll cover you! Run back to the portal!"

"Emily, I—"

Emily throws all the loot at him and brandishes her sword at the blazes. She can do this. They can't have come all the way here for nothing.

"Here. I have arrows," Tank says softly.

Emily turns back to grab the arrows lying at her feet. One blaze is already setting itself on fire, swirling and turning menacingly toward both of them.

"Go!"

Emily sinks an arrow into the blaze.

"You guys . . ."

Emily looks away from her screen for a split second. Jake is standing at the window of the computer lab, peering intently outside.

"Mrs. Jenkins is coming! She's walking this way from the courtyard!"

Emily's taking too much damage, but she finished one—now for the others—Tank, *move*—

Tank pales. "Can we disconnect?"

"We're under attack so no! Next time you log in we'll be right back here and probably die and lose everything! Try to get to a safe zone first!"

Tank darts backward, running back along the bridge and then toward the cliff edge and the first staircase they climbed to get into the fortress. A line of torches leads off over the disappearing horizon, toward their portal.

"Run, Tank!"

Emily shoots her last arrow and charges forward, taking down the last blaze headed for Tank.

"YEARRRGH!" she yells as she slashes at it. "You're going down with me!"

RoxXStarRedStone was slain by blaze

Emily pushes away from her computer, scooting back from her chair. To her relief, she can see Tank is still running. He's made it down and off of the staircase now and is following their trail of torches.

"Come on, you can do it!" Emily mutters.

"Hurry up! Quit the game! We're supposed to be working!" Jake calls from the window. "She's almost here!"

"My escape key is stuck!" Tank tries.

"Go for the portal. Jake, help Tank unstick his key so he can disconnect when he's safe at home." Emily readjusts her ponytail.

"Where are you going?" Jake asks.

"To make a distraction."

CHAPTER TWENTY-ONE

TANK

"Hello? Are you kids hungry? I made you all sandwiches."

Mrs. Jenkins's voice echoes from the lobby.

"Oh, that's so nice!" Emily chimes cheerfully. "We finished cleaning up the kitchen yesterday. We can eat in there. How *are* you, Mrs. J? Did you cut your hair?"

"Oh. No. I brushed it, though."

"It looks great!"

"The key isn't unsticking!" Tank fumbles for it. "I can't quit!" He freezes, alternating between running and trying to disconnect.

"I'm getting it, you just concentrate on getting out of the Nether!"

Jake tries to wedge his finger under the key, but the ancient keyboard doesn't budge. He looks around frantically toward the boxes they packed away.

"Come on!" Tank whispers.

"Pens, pens, pens—" Jake rifles loudly through the box of pens and random office supplies until he raises one in triumph. He bends the metal clip at the top of the pen deftly with his fingers, approaching Tank and the keyboard.

"I see the portal!" Ahead, the shimmering purple portal that he's always been afraid of is now his salvation. He runs, following the line of torches through the purple-red netherrack. He can't afford to die now. His friends are counting on him.

Outside, Emily and Mrs. Jenkins are still talking, but it sounds like the voices are coming closer.

Jake wedges the pen's clip under the escape key. "Come on, come on—aaah!"

The escape key pops right off the keyboard and clatters away. It would be almost funny if Tank wasn't desperately trying to log out of the computer.

He reaches the portal and everything dissolves around him. He's back in Emily's mine at their base. Tank exhales with relief. "I made it," he says, surprised at himself.

"Okay, you're safe—you can just minimize it." Jake presses the mute button just as the door opens and Mrs. Jenkins walks in.

Emily makes an apologetic face and mouths *I tried* as Mrs. Jenkins sets the sandwiches down.

"I thought I was a little harsh on you kids yesterday, and wanted to say I appreciated all of your hard work."

Tank can't tell what kind of sandwiches they are, but the smell of fresh baguette wafts toward him. His stomach growls in anticipation.

"Good work," she says, her voice gruff. "I thought you might be hungry. You know, you can take a break for lunch if you need to. You don't need to ask me. You can go home for an hour or go out or whatever. I trust you all to keep coming back and finish this. I'm not going to check on you, either. I don't really like being here. I think kids your age have the responsibility to manage yourselves, and I trust you'll be able to figure out a schedule that works for you. You have a key, work out when you want to be here, leave the finished boxes at my doorstep." She glances at the room and then back at the three of them, her eyes lingering on the computers and then the organized boxes of electronics in the corner. "It looks good so far."

"Thanks," Tank says, trying not to let his chest swell up with pride. The affirmations are comforting, and he likes knowing he's done a good job. He reaches for one of the sandwiches and bites into it. Bursts of flavor—savory and some sort of herb, like basil maybe? And a sharp tang. There's a soft, pillowy texture that contrasts well with the crunchy baguette roll. "Wow, this is good," he says, around a mouthful. "What's in this? Tomato? I've never had a tomato sandwich before." He thinks this white stuff is cheese. It's like, really moist and soft and good. Tank likes cheese on pizza but always thought cheese in sandwiches was terrible—the school made these awful dry ham-and-cheese things that stuck to the roof of your mouth, but this is a whole other world. He wants to keep eating this forever.

"Gross, close your mouth," Emily says. She wipes her hands delicately on the towel hanging from her shoulder before picking up her own sandwich, taking a small bite. "This is really nice, Mrs. Jenkins." She closes her eyes, humming happily. "Caprese, right?"

Jake's enjoying the sandwich, too, and Tank nods at him. This guy gets it.

"Yes, that's right. I grow these tomatoes and the basil on my patio. I used to—that whole lot out there used to be a community garden. Part of the center. We would have fruit and vegetables, and in the summer, there would be so many grapes. Grapes for days. You could eat them right off the vine."

Tank follows Mrs. Jenkins's gaze out the window, where trash lines the lot of dirt and weeds between the community center and the street. He never thought about the land outside the entrance to the building much, but knowing it was a real garden—it makes him sad.

"Well, there's no point in revisiting old ghosts. That garden is long dead, just like this place." Mrs. Jenkins sighs, standing up. "You know, I used to take chances on kids like you all the time. It's why I built the center in the first place. So kids would have a place to hang out, make friends."

"That's so cool!" Jake exclaims.

Mrs. Jenkins nods, her eyes sad. She looks back to the window, lost in some memory. It's clear that she doesn't want to talk anymore.

"Why did—" Jake starts.

Tank elbows him and shakes his head.

"Thank you for the sandwiches," Emily says softly.

"You're welcome." Mrs. Jenkins gives them a small smile. "I—I didn't mean to just walk out on you yesterday. This place— this place means a lot to me. And having memories like that hit you out of nowhere is hard for an old lady like me." Mrs. Jenkins looks down at her feet. "Well, enjoy. And don't get used to this. I'm not going to bring you lunch every day," she adds, returning to her stern tone, but her eyes are still smiling. "I'm going to check on the other rooms and your progress."

"Did you quit? Did Tank make it back with all our stuff?" Emily whispers as Mrs. Jenkins leaves the room.

Tank grins at her, adrenaline still pumping. The Nether, the quick escape, the thrill of avoiding detection—it was scary, but they made it. It's over. And it was actually fun. And these sandwiches are great.

Jake nods, reaching for another sandwich.

Tank's already had two. He kind of wants another one, though. "I wasn't able to quit—the escape key is broken. But I made it back to the base."

"It's fine, it's fine," Emily says. "If she says anything, we can say we were testing the computers—"

"Maybe we should just tell her that," Jake suggests.

"No, no, we'll look guilty! Come on, haven't you ever done this before?" Emily rolls her eyes at Jake.

Tank takes the empty plate and gives it a rinse in the kitchen. He wonders now if people used to cook here, if it was filled with laughter and people sharing a meal.

"I brought you back your plate, Mrs. Jenkins. I washed it and everything. Do you have more boxes? I think we used most of them for the stuff in the storage rooms and office." Tank pauses, realizing Mrs. Jenkins is sitting at his computer.

She's staring at the screen thoughtfully.

Well, Minecraft is minimized, so if she was looking at it, she probably just sees the desktop—

"We were checking to make sure those were working," Tank offers. "So, yeah, they work. So you don't have to recycle them. I mean, they're pretty old, I don't think they'd be worth selling, but you could keep them for the computer lab in the new center."

A number of expressions flash across Mrs. Jenkins's face—sadness, anger—most of all, pain. "I don't think the new owner is interested in restoring any of the original community amenities," she says. "All of this is going to be boutiques and restaurants. But—like I said, I appreciate all the work you're doing." Mrs. Jenkins glances at Tank. "It looks like you've finished this room. You can just box up everything to be donated, but don't worry about this one being a priority. I can schedule the electronic recycling pickup anytime." She smiles at him, a different one from the soft, apologetic one she'd had when she brought them the sandwiches. This one feels a little self-satisfied, like she knows something Tank doesn't, and it makes him nervous.

Did she see the open game?

Surely she would say something if she did, like scold them for not working.

Mrs. Jenkins nods at Tank and takes the plate. "Goodbye," she says to Emily and Jake behind him as she walks back out of the community center.

"What did she say? Did she see?"

"She just reminded us that we can do this room last," Tank says. "Not that there's much left to do."

Emily jiggles the mouse on each of the computers. "Mine looks fine. Jake, did you have this folder open?"

"Uh, I'm not sure. I think I was referencing it for the riddles." The folder full of screenshots of all the things Jake's discovered so far is indeed open, all the files laid out.

Tank's avatar is standing in the mineshaft right where he left him. He doesn't remember getting so far away from the portal, though. Maybe he did. "Looks okay."

Emily collapses on her chair. "That was close."

CHAPTER TWENTY-TWO

JAKE

"Let's play first and then close to lunchtime, start cleaning. Just in case she pops by again," Jake suggests.

"I brought Carmen's old keyboard to replace yours, Tank," Emily says, raising up a black keyboard covered in stickers of cartoon skulls. "Go ahead and laugh."

Tank takes the keyboard and raises his eyebrow, but he doesn't say anything.

Jake pokes one of the skull stickers. "Does your sister like . . . death?"

"And poetry. Don't ever mention poetry to her, she'll never stop." Emily shakes her head. "Let's go."

Jake feels an elated sense of accomplishment when they finish brewing the Potions of Water Breathing. With their new sets of diamond armor and enchanted weapons—they had just enough levels between them to get some basic buffs—he feels ready to take on the next clue.

He's so used to just talking out loud with Tank and Emily that it isn't until he copies and pastes coordinates that he sees the entire chat scroll.

The message right after the three of them logged in makes him pause.

TheCrestWizard has joined the game.

"Uh, guys? We aren't alone." Jake looks around nervously, expecting this Wizard character to show up at any moment, but nothing happens.

"What?"

"Look at the chat log."

"Who is the Wizard?" Emily frowns.

< MCExplorerJake > hello?

"Good idea," Tank says. "Totally forgot about that function because we always play in the same room."

Jake watches the screen for a few moments, but nothing happens.

"Wait, there's something over there—I think. Look to the east!"

Jake follows the gaze of Emily's bouncing avatar.

Movement on the side of the mountain catches Jake's eye, and at first he thinks it's just granite, maybe a rockfall or something, but that's impossible.

Maybe not in this world, Jake thinks. Mermaids and mysteries everywhere. Whoever modded this place could have changed anything, even the physics.

An avatar.

The Wizard?

Emily's already racing toward the mountainside, wading directly into the massive lake and swimming across it. The figure is still moving, a few bricks of gray going up the mountain, moving like—

"Emily! Where are you going?" Tank drops a boat into the lake before cruising after her.

"I've got an extra one, she keeps forgetting to pack it," Jake says, following suit. They catch up to Emily quickly, and Jake tosses the extra boat into the water for her.

"I know I saw something on that mountain," Emily mutters. "It's still there."

"It could be an alpaca or a chicken or something," Tank says.

"I don't think so. It's gray. You think of any mobs that color?" Jake looks at the unmoving gray figure at the top of the mountain. "Plus, it didn't move like an animal." Animal mobs drift slowly around. This moved like a person.

"A skeleton?" Tank asks.

"Why would a skeleton be just hanging out on the side of a mountain during the middle of the day? That would be impossible. It would have burnt up by now." Emily pushes forward with her boat. "Do you not want to see what it is?"

"Yeah, what if it's this other player?" Jake asks.

Tank gestures at the dusty computer lab. "Wouldn't it have to be someone in this computer lab?"

"It's a server," Emily says. "As long as they know the address they could connect to it."

Jake shakes his head. "Theoretically, yeah. The server is hosted on the local area network here. But I can't connect to it from my apartment without a password. Whoever made it already installed it on these computers so it works without one."

"So someone knows the password. Who else in the building plays Minecraft?" Tank asks.

Emily shrugs. "I mean, there're a lot of kids who live here."

Tank pauses. "Look, even if it's another player, we have our own things to do. Let's just ignore them. We have the map to the next clue, and we have all the potions. Come on, we spent all this time getting ready and we're going to get distracted?"

Emily turns her boat around. "You're right," she says after a moment's consideration. "We have our own plans. Isn't that right, Jake? You want to solve the mystery, let's do it. We don't know them and they don't know us. It's a big world. Leaving them alone is probably the best idea."

"Look, there's a river going east out of this lake. It'll be quicker to go by boat," Tank says.

They're already moving in that direction, away from the mysterious figure.

"I hate traveling by boat," Tank says conversationally. "I always get stuck when I try to turn." He drifts left and then goes in a circle before bumping into Jake, who deliberately pulls his boat to a stop in front of Tank.

"Look, you both said you wanted to solve the mystery," Jake says.

"Yeah. By getting the next clue," Tank says.

"The first clue I found was number seventeen. The underwater city, the mermaids, the treasure maps, the riddles—it's all a part of something, but we need to figure out what it is."

Tank shrugs. "Treasure is treasure, man."

"I think whatever is on that mountain—whoever is on that

mountain—is going to have answers." Jake starts making his way toward the mountain.

Emily hums in agreement. "I'm gonna say hi." She flexes her fingers before typing a few quick words into the server chat.

< RoxXStarRedStone > hi! We're having fun exploring this world. What do you know about it?

Jake watches the question sit in the chat log unanswered as he approaches the side of the mountain. There's still no response as he stashes his boat and starts to climb. It's difficult going, especially with the steep slope, but he doesn't want to risk losing the other avatar. He can see the gray blocky shadow ahead stop, like it's watching him. From here he can see the still-too-small white text on top of their head.

"It's definitely a person!" Jake calls out triumphantly.

He's aware of Emily and Tank following behind him, and as he gets closer he can see the avatar clamber over the top of the mountain ledge and disappear from sight.

"Maybe they just want to play by themselves," Tank says. "Look, if they wanna run away, we should let them go. We've got other stuff to do."

Jake reaches the top of the ledge and steps forward onto the plateau. Up here, snow covers everything and trees grow sparse amongst the forbidding rock. From across the rocky expanse, the other avatar stares directly down at Jake.

He approaches slowly, taking in the other person as he draws close. It's clear extensive mods were used to craft this avatar: They look like an old-timey wizard, complete with a white beard, pointy hat, and long gray robe. The robe is shimmering with the telltale look of enchanted armor, and the Wizard is carrying a long staff of some sort in his hand. The avatar's username reads *TheCrest-Wizard.*

It *is* the other person in the server.

"Whoa," Tank says, coming up on his left.

With Tank flanking him, Jake approaches the Wizard cautiously. The other avatar doesn't move, just watches them.

"You couldn't put ladders up or anything?" Emily says, joining them on the ledge. "What's up with this guy? He hasn't said hi back."

"Let me try," Tank says.

< TankFarms > do you live in pacific crest?

No answer.

< TankFarms > is this your world? Did you do all the mods?
< RoxXStarRedStone > they're pretty cool!
< MCExplorerJake > where do all these riddles go to?
Where does it start? Where does it end?

The three of them regard the Wizard in a strange standstill, and then finally new words appear.

< TheCrestWizard > This is MY world. You need to leave.

Jake balks at this. "No way, it's infinitely big, there's plenty of room for all of us to play."

"What's he gonna do, kick us out?" Tank laughs at this, jerking his head at Jake.

Jake, on the receiving end of Tank's head-nod-jerk thing, finds it . . . nice. That Tank sees him as an equal, a friend.

```
< MCExplorerJake > Hey, we haven't messed up any of your
stuff. It's really cool, the structures we've found. All
these riddles and maps and stuff, were you planning a
scavenger hunt or something for your friends?
< TheCrestWizard > This game isn't for you.
< RoxStarRedStone > Clearly whoever this was for, they
haven't played it. Whoever you're waiting for, they're long
gone.
< TheCrestWizard > This game isn't for you.
< MCExplorerJake > Look, I've seen a bunch of versions of
this world—you obviously have a backup file. You can
create another version of this if you want to so badly.
We've already started a really cool base and are having a
great time exploring.
```

Jake is in the middle of thinking of another way to explain, without being cheesy, that he has friends now, and he doesn't want to lose the one nice thing he has here. Maybe Emily and Tank are only hanging out with him because they have to do the community service hours, but as long as they're having fun, they can keep playing Minecraft, and he won't have to know if they're really his friends or not. He wants to express this to the Wizard somehow, why this particular server is so important to him, that he doesn't want to lose any of his progress he's made in the game—or with his new friends.

He's typing his thoughts when several things happen at once.

The Wizard charges at them. Glass clinks at their feet, and multiple potions cover them from head to toe.

"I can't move!" Tank shouts.

"Attack, attack! How is he so strong!" Emily dodges another potion, backing up and fumbling for her weapons.

Jake watches in shock as his health drops low—the Wizard is only armed with a stick, but all his arrows seem to have no effect on the Wizard at all. He tries to get out of range of the attacks, but he's still affected by the Potion of Slowness and the Potion of Harming was a heavy blow. He shoots arrow after arrow, but the Wizard just keeps approaching. The staff is replaced by a gleaming diamond sword, and Jake knows he's done for.

```
RoxXStarRedStone was slain by TheCrestWizard
TankFarms was slain by TheCrestWizard
MCExplorerJake was slain by TheCrestWizard
```

Jake leans back and looks at his friends in horror. "What just happened?"

CHAPTER TWENTY-THREE

EMILY

"We have to be better prepared if we see the Wizard again when we get our stuff," Emily says, pacing back and forth at the base. "Those were our best weapons *and* our Potions of Water Breathing!"

She can't believe that other player just *attacked* them like that. She's never had that happen to her in multiplayer, ever. The nerve!

"Let's brew some potions of our own so we're prepared for battle," Jake says.

"Did you get the coordinates for where we were last?" Tank asks.

"Right here."

Emily leads the way; she's gone from neutral and uncaring

about the Wizard to muttering and preparing like a fiend. She forges armor and weapons, cursing all the while.

The three of them pause to eat the tamales Emily brought from home, and then clean up while discussing what they still need to do to face the Wizard again. Emily notices that the community center is mostly organized now—there isn't really a need for them to do much else. They could technically just bring the rest of the boxes to Mrs. Jenkins and be done with it.

But she can't stop now, not when they have a score to settle.

Emily decides not to say anything about the completed cleaning project when they finish lunch and they get right back to their preparations.

"Stupid old man. How's that poison coming along?"

"I have no idea. Is this right—ahh!"

TankFarms died from poison

Tank grimaces. "I accidentally drank it."

Finally they finish preparations and, with a few more potions at the ready, set off for the coordinates where they last saw the Wizard.

Emily hacks her way up the mountain, grumbling.

"Should we announce ourselves?" Jake asks.

"Let's just attack," Emily grumbles.

There's a part of Emily that wants to ask what the Wizard knows. She doesn't want to admit it, but she also wants to know the secret of the mermaids, the underwater village in the mural, and why it all exists. The idea that there's a huge interlocking puzzle all across this world is an enormous mystery.

She also wants revenge.

At the top of the plateau is a ring of torches. In the center of the ring is a single chest.

"Watch out, it could be booby-trapped," Emily says. "That's what I would do."

They approach cautiously, throwing things to activate any hidden pressure plates, but nothing happens.

Finally Tank goes up to the chest. "There's nothing here but a piece of paper," he says. "It's a note."

```
If you want your things
They can be found
Where birds dare not sing
Far beneath the ground
Beyond the fiery mouth of the dragon's lair.
```

"Dragon?" Emily frowns. "What is he talking about? You mean he took our things to the End? It's going to take forever to get there. We barely went to the Nether for the first time."

"No, it's another riddle," Tank. "I mean, it could mean that, but I think the Wizard hid our stuff somewhere underneath what a 'dragon's lair' could look like."

Jake bounces up and down. "It's a hunt. He's starting us on a scavenger hunt. Let's do it!"

"I want to know where he is so I can give him a taste of his own medicine," Emily grunts.

Tank sighs. "See, this is why I said we should just focus on our own quest. I just want to work on our farm and do this adventure and find the treasure, but no, you both had to be like, 'let's go chase down that mysterious person in gray over there.'"

"You can farm anytime," Jake says, knocking shoulders with him playfully. "This is new and different."

Emily has to agree. It's a *challenge*. "All right, so dragon's lair. That sounds like a cave."

"I don't think it would be on the other side of the world. It should be within walking distance, at least, for this clue," Jake says. "Let's split up and look around."

Emily is the one who finds the lair.

The lava is flowing directly out of the cavern, falling in long rivulets down the cliffside before flowing into a large pool. From here it's unmistakable that the mountain's peak is formed into the shape of a dragon's head, with the lava flowing from its mouth, looking every inch the fire-breathing terror it is. The cave inside looks almost impossible to get through with all the lava.

"What should we do?" Jake asks. "Try to build up a bridge or something and plug it up so the lava flow stops?"

"Where birds dare not sing far beneath the ground," Emily muses.

"I don't think going into this cave is the answer," Tank says. "What if we start here at the base and just dig down?"

Emily's already got her pickaxe out, and Jake follows suit. They dig, getting into a rhythm of going downward and creating a stairway into the depths of the earth, just wide enough for a single person.

"Let's spread out until we find a cavern," Emily suggests.

They each pick a direction. Emily follows a vein of lapis lazuli ore, collecting the minerals along the way. She's got a pretty solid path going when she hears the *quip quip* of a spider nearby. "Hey, monsters in here!"

Emily slams her pickaxe into the rock again, and this time it gives way to an opening. She blasts her way through, and then too quickly the spiders descend upon her.

"Gah!" Emily manages to kill one but she's outnumbered by spiders, and they're rapidly gaining on her. "Third level, go right—help! Spiders! I've found the cavern but spiders!" She backs up into a corner, eating bread as quick as she can, and then she's nearly done for—

SPLAT.

Tank barrels through the spider about to chomp down on Emily, wielding his sword high. Jake is right behind him, shooting arrows. Spiders squelch out of existence, disappearing all around her.

"You okay?" Jake asks.

"Thanks," Emily says. It feels good, knowing they have her back.

"There are mine tracks over here," Tank says. "Should we follow them?"

Jake adds torches to the walls, lighting the way. "You think we're right underneath the fiery mouth of the dragon?"

Emily frowns. "Did anyone write down the coordinates? I sure didn't."

"Got them here. Looks like we need to go to negative two-ninety-eight."

She follows Tank, Jake close behind her. Finally at the coordinates of the dragon's mouth, they come upon a room with a single chest in the center.

"Our stuff!" Jake exclaims.

Emily rushes forward, but as soon as she takes a step, everything goes dark.

CHAPTER TWENTY-FOUR

JAKE

"What just happened? Did I die?" Emily cries out. "I just respawned somewhere weird—oh, hi. Did you both die, too?"

Jake frowns. "I didn't get a death message. I don't think we died."

"I just saw you two disappear, and the next thing I knew I was here," Tank says. "This isn't any spawn point I've ever set, though. Where are we?"

Where is *here*, exactly?

Jake takes it all in, walking around to get a sense of where they are. They've spawned into the center of what look like ruins. The stone structure is cracked, open to the elements. Piles of rubble are scattered across the floor, columns broken in half as if a great earthquake had split the ancient building and the jungle has since reclaimed it. Everything is covered in trailing vines, lines of green tracing the walls and creeping in from the dark outside. Above them, night and a dark forest rustle through the openings of the building.

Jake stares. It's clearly designed this way; there's no passage of time or erosion that takes place here, no earthquakes, no force of nature that could destroy a building like this. Whoever made this structure wanted it to feel ancient.

It does.

Music starts. Lilting, haunting, almost as if on cue.

"How did we get here?" Emily demands. She pauses, and then lets out a high, angry shriek. "Did either of you make it to the chest in time? My inventory is completely empty! Do you guys have *any* of your stuff?"

Jake's inventory is empty, too.

"Nooooo, I was carrying so many seeds." Tank groans.

"My Silk Touch axe! All my enchanted items! My diamond sword! Gah!" Emily punches at a pile of rubble, lashing out in anger.

Nothing happens.

"Whoa. Weird." Tank does the same to the stone wall next to him. "I can't break anything! What gives?"

Jake punches at the ground experimentally as well.

```
You can't break this here.
You have no effect here.
```

"How do we get out of here?" Tank runs toward the opening in the wall, but it's too high up. He jumps, his character bouncing comically as he tries to reach for the next jut of stone, but it's too far.

With no building materials and no way to affect their immediate surroundings, Jake is at a loss.

"The Wizard," Emily says. "He's the one who built this world, right? He's got the power to do anything. Including teleport players wherever he wants."

"Why would he bring us here? To mess with us?" Emily asks.

Jake freezes. He thinks about the riddles he's seen and the glimpse of a mural that promises *something*. Adventure. Mystery. Fun.

"I think . . . I think the Wizard just invited us to play." Jake paces the length of the room. "It's the beginning of the game. He's started us over from the beginning."

The more he thinks about it, the more it makes sense. Like finding their things was a test, and the Wizard decided that instead of blocking them or deleting the game, he wants to let them play. See how they do.

Jake's chest puffs up with pride. He knows they did well, solving the clue and making it to the hidden chest where their things were. He wonders if anyone else has done this challenge, if they've done better. Maybe the Wizard was just bored, and at first was upset but now sees this as an opportunity to try his might as a gamemaster.

He takes a closer look at the room and admires the work that went into this whole setting. This kind of artistry takes not only time but the eye of a master builder, someone who's had a lifetime to spend in this world.

A crescent moon shines above them, stars wafting slowly across the night sky. In the distance, there's the *tsk tsk* of spiders moving about nearby.

Jake shudders. The stone dais he's standing on is also as intricately built, even with its cracks. They're standing in the center of a crumbling monolith, built by some strange entity, covered in vines and dust.

Jake's played so many videogames, but he's always gone into it knowing what the objectives were, the premise, what he could expect. Here, he's completely out of his element. He has no idea what will happen next.

It's terrifying and unnerving, especially since this is the one game he can always rely on to have the same rules, the same construction elements.

But since he's started playing in this world, the mysteries that have been unfolding—he's been meeting each challenge and taking it in stride. And it's been fun, adapting to the new changes, learning more about the mystery as he goes. It's unexpected, the kind of joy he's found here in exploring this world with his friends.

The realization shocks him. That he likes change, the newness of it all.

Tank glances at him. "So what do we do now?"

"You're supposed to spawn here and figure out where to go. We have nothing because it's the start."

Emily jumps up and down in frustration. "Or *maybe* because he knows if I had all my weapons I would totally kick his butt!"

"My farm," Tank says sadly. "Do you think our base is still there?"

Jake brings up the coordinates and lets out a low whistle. "We're real far from home."

He can tell Emily's doing the same from the way she immediately starts yelling. "Like twenty thousand blocks away! You know how many in-game days it'll take to get there, and plus we have *nothing*! We're gonna have to fight our way through and camp along the way and—"

Jake's heart starts to pound with excitement.

"YEARGH!" Emily stomps again.

The raspy sound of heavy stone scraping echoes in the cavern.

Jake whirls around to see a long, dark hallway revealed in the wall. "You activated a pressure plate!"

"Great. Let's go down the dark hallway that the homicidal Wizard opened for us, after he took all our stuff and dropped us in the middle of nowhere." Tank stares up at the sky.

"You got a better plan?" Jake steps forward into the dark. Up close, he can see a bit of orange flickering in the distance: a torch. "Looks like there's a light at the end. Let's go!"

Jake walks down the hallway, letting the darkness envelop him. He's never ventured into the sheer unknown like this, unprotected, unarmed, with not even a torch to light the way.

"When I find that Wizard I'm going to completely obliterate him," Emily mutters. "I'm going to craft a new diamond sword and enchant it with everything I have and then ram—"

"Am I walking into you or something else? Jake, I can't tell."

Jake chuckles. Well, he's never had friends by his side to join him before. Even though he has nothing, he feels more prepared than ever before.

CHAPTER TWENTY-FIVE

TANK

Tank has never really been scared of the dark. First of all, it happens once a day, and you can always turn on your phone or something to light your way. At home, even without the lights it's easy to see; the complex is always lit, if not by the fluorescent lights in the buildings, then by the ambient spillover from the streets, headlights shining in as cars flock to where they're going. Even during the day the apartment is always shrouded in grays and shadows; the curtains are always shut so Ma doesn't have to strain her eyes. At night, when Tank's helping Mr. Mishra take out the trash or bring in deliveries from the dark alleyway around the corner, it doesn't bother him at all.

It also never really gets dark in Los Angeles; the faint orange glow of the city twinkling away, the red-and-white gleam of cars trapped on the freeway. Stars, if you can see them, blink through the muddle of the night sky, trying to glimmer through the haze of light pollution and smog. Sometimes he dreams of a star-filled night, clusters of galaxies so far away and larger than he can fathom.

Once, his class went to the California Science Center and watched this movie in a circular theater; the whole place lit up with stars, and the narrator explained how big everything was. It freaked out a lot of the other kids, but it made Tank feel good. Safe. That the universe was so big that it didn't matter what he did, it was going to keep on going. Nothing he did would change it or stop it or affect it; he was just a small speck. It was comforting, knowing that.

The whole presentation did have one part that unnerved him. It wasn't the stars or the planets or the way the universe was expanding, but that notion of the dark, what scientists didn't understand. It was deep and unforgiving, a darkness that could only exist beyond the realms of imagination, darkness that was so far away and impossible that he couldn't even begin to understand it.

He doesn't usually bother with caves and stuff in Minecraft because Viv tackles them, always lighting the way with torches or exploding things or charging headfirst into some danger. Tank prefers to stay above ground where he can always see what's in front of him.

He doesn't like this dark, this endless hallway with only a bit of flicker on the other end to show that there's even an end to it in the first place. It makes him nervous, this setting where he can't affect the environment, where he doesn't have anything to defend himself with. It reminds him of that endless darkness that he'd thought he'd forgotten about until he started walking down this hallway, thinking about the universe and all of its unknowns.

He doesn't like the anonymous Wizard person who stole all their stuff and took them on a wild goose chase in the first place.

But it was fun, a small part of him says. Figuring out the puzzle, spending time with Jake and Emily.

It's been weird, playing Minecraft with people who aren't Viv. Tank's come to appreciate Jake's steady and levelheaded logic, the practical way he stops to empty out his inventory and remind Tank to do the same before they head somewhere dangerous. Emily's no-holds-barred aggressive combat style unnerves him, but it works for their group dynamic. He feels like part of a real team.

"Come on," Emily says.

Tank takes a deep breath and keeps trudging forward. The few minutes in the dark seem to stretch out forever, but finally the flickering torch is in front of him. It's barely enough to light the small room the hallway opens out into. Unlike the ruins they were teleported into, this room is bare of detail and design. A simple cobblestone floor, surrounded by more cobblestone walls — wait, no. There are five doors embedded in the walls surrounding them, and the single torch flickers against a stone column with a chest sitting at the foot of it.

"Weird," Jake says. "I can't affect anything in this room, either."

"I bet these doors open to something interesting," Emily says, pacing in front of them. Above each of the doors, an item is framed on the stone wall: a bottle of green potion, a bucket of water, an apple, a sword, and a bucket of lava.

"Don't open any of them yet, we don't know what's behind them," Jake warns. "What if it's lava?"

Tank opens the chest. The creak echoes in the room, and then the foreboding music starts.

"What's in it?"

"A book," Tank says. He opens it to read the contents aloud, growing more and more confused with each line.

Riddle the First

I am both life and death. Feed me three things and I live.

Give me one drink and I will die.

You must defeat me to move forward.

"It's the first clue," Jake says, bouncing up and down. "I told you! We're at the start of the game."

"The answer must be one of these doors," Emily says. "So first, what is the thing? And what is the thing we need to kill it?"

Tank has no idea. He punches experimentally at the ground, but it doesn't budge. He tries the chest, which does give after a few punches, so he tucks it away in his inventory for later, watching Emily pace back and forth.

"That's poison," Jake says, pointing at the door with the painting of the green potion.

"Great! Poison will kill anything. Let's go!"

Emily opens the door.

For a second, nothing happens, and Tank can only see another hallway full of darkness—and then the darkness moves, moves right into their room, with eyes and legs and—

"SPIDER!" Tank yells, leaping backward instinctively and raising his weapon, but he's got nothing in his hands except the stupid chest—

Emily screams and starts punching at it. Jake is fighting, too, but there's another spider, and another—

Tank turns around and runs, even as he knows it's too late.

RoxXStarRedStone has died in battle

MCExplorerJake has died in battle

TankFarms has died in battle

They respawn back on the stone dais with nothing again.

"Okay, the answer clearly wasn't the poison," Jake says. "Come on, and don't open any of the other doors until we solve this."

"Process of elimination!" Emily protests.

"I hate spiders," Tank offers. "Let's not go through each door and keep dying."

"I mean, we could, four more times," Emily says.

"Let's just solve the riddle!" Jake triggers the pressure plate and opens up the hallway. This time, he opens the chest and reads the riddle again slowly. "You must defeat me to move forward."

"What if behind each door is a different monster that we have to defeat?" Tank asks.

"No way, we have no weapons. It would be a stupid game if the Wizard wanted us to fight something like that right away," Emily mutters.

Tank wouldn't put it past the Wizard, who seems like someone who would find that funny.

"We have to pick the item that will defeat the thing in the riddle," Jake says. "The sword seems the obvious choice, or the poison, but we know it's not poison . . ."

Tank takes the chest again, and tries to grab the torch for good measure. He's pleased to see it does work, even if he can't affect the stone column behind it.

"Hey! Tank, put that back! I can't see anything," Emily says.

Tank holds the torch aloft. "Better?"

"Feed me three things and I will live," Jake mutters. "I feel like the answer is staring me in the face, and it's going to be really obvious or something."

Tank follows behind Emily with the torch so they can see each of the paintings in clear detail.

"Well, the most obvious answer would be the fire," he offers. "I mean, since the torch was in the middle of the room."

Emily stares at him. "Three things—that's it! Oxygen, heat, and fuel. The riddle is about fire!"

"So—" Jake pauses at the door marked with the bucket of water.

Tank opens the door. Behind it is dark, but it's not the suffocating finality of the hallway—it's the open rustle of the night and the wilderness.

"Yes! We did it!" Emily cries out exuberantly. She runs to the nearest tree. "Yes! I can punch things again!"

"Awesome," Jake says, clapping Tank on the shoulder.

Tank blinks, and everything comes into focus: the three of them sitting in this dingy computer lab, Emily whooping as her avatar punches a tree, Jake grinning excitedly at him.

"Thanks," Tank says, and means it.

"Oh, it's four! I have to go," Emily says. "My mom wants me to go grocery shopping with her." She shakes her head and sighs, disconnecting from the server. "It's like ever since I've been grounded she's been bringing me everywhere with her on errands and stuff, like it makes up for not having any apps on my phone." She makes a face. "She made Carmen change the password to all of my accounts, so I can't even access them. It's really annoying."

"That sucks," Jake says, following suit. "We can pick this back up tomorrow."

"Sounds good," Tank says. He guesses if he leaves now he'll get to Mr. Mishra's early. He hadn't realized they'd stayed this late already.

Tank waves at Jake, watching him leave as well. The afternoon light softly filters through the windows, dust motes swirling in the air. Tank shakes his head; it's still the same old computer lab, but now there's something to it. He turns off the computers one by one, running his hand along the monitors and letting the warmth seep into his fingers. He wonders what's going to happen at the end of the service project, when they don't have to be here anymore. Emily and Jake—they're here because they have to be, like him. They're just passing the time with this game, like he is.

It doesn't mean anything.

CHAPTER TWENTY-SIX

EMILY

Emily sees it first, the irregular shape at the top of the plateau. It could be just a rock formation, but it's a little too regular, edges too uniform. Too small to be a structure, but definitely not a natural part of the mountain. In fact, it looks almost like the signs she used to make to differentiate between caves or areas she's explored. She went through a phase where she'd give places fanciful names plucked out of storybooks, though she stopped doing that a while ago. If she still did it, though, she'd name this place Mystery World.

And Emily can't leave a good mystery alone.

She climbs the mountain face, looking for an easier route and finding none; it's too steep to find a regular rhythm, and she has to carve steps into the rock and throw down blocks of dirt and cobblestone to make the way easier. Emily pushes forward, getting closer and closer to the top.

From here she takes a moment to admire the view: the deep valley and the river pulsing through it, leading toward the faded horizon and what she knows to be the sea just beyond. To the west, the torches on the edge of their base are just visible. Movement in the east—that must be Tank and Jake, herding sheep back to the new base they started today.

"How's it going?"

"They move so slow," Jake complains.

"Be patient. If you go too fast you'll get out of range and they can't find you and your wheat," Tank says, whistling. A quick glance at his screen next to Emily's shows Jake running off after his sheep as Tank's own three sheep wait idly at his feet.

"I found something," Emily says. "A sign. I think it's a clue." She looks through their basic new inventory and sighs. "Come on. It's not too far from here."

She leads them away from the plains where they've settled and up the mountain face to their immediate north. Sign are stuck into the center of the plateau.

Riddle the Second

My soul is empty until you begin to walk. I'll show you a vision of forests with no trees, oceans with no waves, mountains without rocks, and the place of your next clue to the greatest treasure of this world.
Bear northeast a thousand paces and find me below the thicket with no roots.

"The greatest treasure of this world," Emily repeats with interest.

"What does it mean, an ocean with no waves? Mountains without rocks? These things don't exist," Tank says.

"It's a riddle. We just have to figure it out," Emily says. She gives the boys the coordinates and paces back and forth, thinking. Obviously the builder is pointing them toward something that will start this adventure and lead them to the next clue. "Below the thicket with no roots," Emily repeats.

"I think we just have to walk northeast from the sign a thousand paces and then just go down." Tank shows up behind her, switching out his pickaxe for a shovel. "I made us all shovels in case it's really deep."

Jake reads the sign again. "A thicket is just a bunch of bushes, right?"

"It could be trees, too," Emily muses. "But no roots. Plants don't have roots in Minecraft anyways, so it could be anything!"

"I don't think we need to know what we're looking for just yet," Tank says. "Just that it's exactly northeast from here."

"All right, let's go, and be careful down the mountain, it's st—"

Tank tumbles off the cliffside and groans. "Great. Fall damage already."

"I've got some food, here, Tank—"

Emily keeps a careful eye on her coordinates and tries to make sure they're going directly northeast. They push through the forest, getting distracted when Tank pauses to collect different flower types they don't have at the base yet. Emily shakes her head but waits for him. She even spots those azure bluets he's been looking for and adds them to her inventory.

They get back on track, following the coordinates until they reach the sparkling sea.

"Um," Tank says. "We've still got a hundred blocks to go."

"Right into the water? Do you think we'll have to dig underground?" Emily shakes her head, thinking of how long it takes to break blocks underwater. They're going to need to keep coming back up for air, or get all the ingredients to make Potions of Water Breathing again.

"It's a map," Jake breathes. "A treasure map."

"What?"

"Oh, like on another shipwreck? Didn't you find that already?"

"Look, the final treasure is all about this underwater city, right? But suppose the Wizard already knows what we know—that we solved riddles seventeen and eighteen, and found the mural, and were working toward riddle nineteen. What if he started the game over, and changed it?"

"What about the bits about mountains without rocks?"

"Yeah, on a map you can't see the individual details, just the big picture," Emily realizes.

Jake throws a boat into the water and starts sailing out toward the horizon. "Come on!"

Ugh, boats. Emily crafts her own, forgetting how much wood she needs, and fumbles until she catches up. Jake's already ahead, his boat speeding off. Tank watches her, spinning around in circles as he waits.

"What kind of flowers do you need this time?" Emily teases.

"Very funny," Tank says. "I was just waiting for you. Ready?"

They catch up with Jake and then leap out of their boats, diving into the deep.

Emily keeps an eye on her health as it starts to drop as the water gets darker and darker the farther they go. They swim past clouds of green kelp, drifting in the waves—oh. The thicket without roots.

Below them, a shadowy shape on a rock outcrop comes into full focus.

A shipwreck.

Emily's seen shipwrecks before, and the first ship Jake showed them to prove he saw mermaids. But now that they've met the Wizard and are in the throes of the game . . . well, it's not just a story anymore. This is part of the riddle, part of a game that they've been invited to play.

They're really here.

Lilting music starts, and Emily swims forward. Eerie green-blue light from underwater torches swathes the shipwreck in a ghostly aura, and shadows dance all around them.

Mermaids.

They're covered in shimmering scales of blue and green and red and gold, swimming and laughing as they beckon the group forward.

"Don't follow," Emily says to Tank, who's already swimming after one. "Haven't you heard the stories about sirens? We're here for the riddle and the map to the next clue. Stay focused."

"Trapdoor here!" Jake announces.

Below the deck is a stately captain's quarters, with bookcases surrounding an enchanting table. With everything underwater, the familiar glow of the miasma floating from the open book in the center takes on a sinister, otherworldly light.

They take their time investigating what they can in between bouts of returning to the surface for more air. Chests creak open as they look for the map in the riddle's clue; Emily pockets gold ore and gems and precious items that mean little when there's a map to the next riddle to be found.

"Did you find anything?" she asks.

They've searched everywhere. Emily's running out of air again, and maybe it would be better to come back when they have the Potions of Water Breathing to —

Wait a minute.

Item frames decorate the walls, like paintings of food, and Emily remembers something she saw in one of PacificViv's videos, about where you could put hidden rooms—

She charges headfirst at each painting, hitting the wall until finally she runs right through the painting of a seashell.

"Emily? Where'd you go?"

"The seashell painting—it's a hidden door!" Inside the plain room is a single chest containing a map. "I got it!" Emily says triumphantly, grinning with the thrill of adventure.

CHAPTER TWENTY-SEVEN

JAKE

There's no way of measuring distance on the map when the pointer is lingering in the margins; the most they can do is just head in that general direction until the pointer actually appears on the map.

"This could take forever," Emily groans as Tank puts the finishing touches on their quick shelter.

"You know, we could always go back for our stuff first before we go solve this clue," Jake says.

"Do you think our stuff is still there? I mean, the Wizard could have just destroyed everything," Tank says.

"I think so," Jake says optimistically. "I mean, there's no harm in looking."

"Days and days of walking sounds harmful," Emily says.

"We're going to be spending forever getting to the next clue

228 C. B. LEE

anyways," Jake says. "I think going and getting our stuff now would be better than wanting it later and not having it."

"That's true," Tank says.

"What about the stuff we had on us before the Wizard killed us?" Emily asks.

Jake shrugs. "It's just armor and weapons. We can make more. It's the nether wart that took forever to get, and we still have those potions back at the base. I'm sure we're going to need them."

He also doesn't want all that planning and hard work to go to waste.

Emily and Tank agree to the detour, and when the sun rises they head toward their new goal.

It's strange how easily they settle into a routine; showing up at the community center, playing for a while and then taking a break to clean. Most of the things are organized now, and every day they bring a box of stuff over to Mrs. Jenkins's door. Jake's nervous as the pile grows smaller and smaller. What will happen when they officially finish the service project? They'll have to give back the gate key and the construction crews would come back and they won't be able to work on the puzzle anymore. Without the mystery of the riddles, would Emily and Tank still want to play Minecraft with him?

They made it back to the base in record time; luckily enough, it looked untouched, right down to Tank's intricate flower spirals decorating the crop fields and Emily's torch-lit paths to her mines.

There was also a chest in front of the western entrance containing all of their missing items and a book inscribed with the following:

Seeing as you've discovered this unfinished world and
started working on the riddles halfway through

I have devised a completely new challenge for you.

There are seven riddles total to find the treasure—
you've solved two.

Good luck,
The Crest Wizard

"Whoa," Jake said when they first arrived back at the base.
"Look at this."

Emily had been surprised, scoffing as she read the book.
"Whatever happened to 'this world is not for you'?"

"I would be mad, too, if someone just started messing around
with my world," Tank said.

"I think the Wizard was impressed with how we solved the
riddle," Jake said. "That's when he teleported us to the beginning,
and then we solved the first two riddles. I mean, it must be awfully
lonely to make a game and have no one play it, right? That's why
he made a special challenge for us."

Jake feels good about this, like winning a soccer game. He
feels like they made an impression. The Wizard saw how well
they did without any resources, saw their potential, and recognized all the hard work they put into getting this far, too, so he
gave them their things back. Since then they've been rotating between tasks like building up the base, enchanting weapons, and
brewing potions to get ready for the next clue. Once they've found
enough nether wart for the potions they want, traveling through
the Nether is easier without having to navigate the challenges of
a fortress. Even Tank feels confident, venturing out toward the

map's location and building shortcuts back to their base through the Nether as they make progress.

The past few days have been busy, preparing for the challenges to come. Jake isn't sure what to expect, but after trial and error with brewing potions and a lengthy attempt at a turtle farm to try to make helmets, they've finally come up with a system. They've created enchanted helmets, a bunch of Potions of Water Breathing for backup, and prepared stacks of ladders that can create pockets of air underwater. He feels ready for anything now— another shipwreck, ocean monuments, elder guardians, anything the Wizard can throw at them. Each day they've been getting closer and closer, exploring more of the world and new biomes, badlands and plains and snow-covered mountains, and more.

Tank appears through a Nether portal. "Okay, the portal shortcut back is officially set up. I was really close to the spot marked on the treasure map, guys. I think this will be it. Once we come back here it would be within a day's walk."

"Thanks," Jake says. "You ready?"

"If we see the Wizard and he attacks us again, I'm going to be so prepared," Emily says, laughing maniacally as she brandishes a brand-new enchanted sword in the hallway of the main room in their base. Her diamond armor glimmers, and she bounces up and down in excitement. "Can't wait to see what the next riddle is! Do you think it's going to be another set of coordinates?"

"Maybe. I don't know. I think these are some that the Wizard tailored especially for us. I have no idea what to expect."

Jake follows Tank through the portal. The Nether looks as forbidding and dangerous as usual with its glowing red sky, but this area has been warded off with torches, and marked signs point the way to other portals. He smiles proudly at the way they've settled into this world and the various biomes for harvesting resources.

The new portal leads them to open, grassy plains. The map from the second clue shows their destination in clear view. When they log in tomorrow, they should be able to find the next riddle easily.

"Same time tomorrow?" Emily powers down the computer and grins at him.

"Absolutely," Jake says.

Tank offers his hand to him for a first bump, and Jake taps it with his own before pulling it back and mimicking an explosion. Tank holds his gaze, mischief dancing in his eyes as they both take a step back, the narrow computer lab aisle barely big enough to do this but they make it work. Jake raises his arms and then brings them both down like he's swinging a pickaxe, and Tank makes *clink clink* noises and sways back and forth like he's digging, and then both of them jump up and high five.

"Nerds," Emily says, with a soft, fond smile.

Jake smiles back at her. Next to him, Tank offers his fist to Emily for a tap of her own, which she gently returns, and to Jake's utter surprise, they both pull their fists back and open their hands, warbling their fingers as they pull back.

"It's a jellyfish," Tank explains.

Emily rolls her eyes. "I'll see you tomorrow." She waves cheerfully at the two of them before sweeping out of the computer lab.

"Tomorrow," Jake says, like a promise.

The corner of Tank's mouth curves up like he's fighting a smile. He claps Jake on the shoulder, and they walk through the courtyard together before setting off for their own towers.

Jake waves back at Tank as he disappears into the West Tower's stairwell.

The summer afternoon light is warm and golden, and it makes their little run-down apartment center seem almost dreamlike.

The glass doors glitter as the sun dips low behind the distant downtown. Inside the chain-link fence surrounding the community center and the empty lot that once held a garden, construction equipment has piled up. Bags and bags of concrete, impossibly large rolls of plaster, steel beams all stacked together.

It feels startlingly real, and Jake is in shock at how the clock is running out.

But maybe . . .

After today, Jake feels like maybe Tank and Emily would spend time with him after the project is over. They've settled into this pattern of hanging out during lunch, one of them bringing food or going out after it.

Jake's been waiting this whole time for Dad to get ready to leave, but it's halfway through the summer and he hasn't done any of his restless pattern of hiring new people to take over and looking for the next job.

Maybe they are going to stay here. Maybe Jake can have friends.

Something dangerous, like hope, settles in Jake's chest as he, for the first time, starts to think of Pacific Crest Apartments as home.

CHAPTER TWENTY-EIGHT

TANK

Tank flattens the last cardboard box and tosses it into the recycling bin. He hums to himself the lilting notes of the melody he's come to associate with the underwater city and the mermaids, and thinks about how close they are to solving the mystery.

"You haven't been answering your phone."

Tank whirls around. Shark approaches him. AJ and Gus follow from the path from the courtyard. Gus kicks a stray soda can, watching it clatter to the ground.

"I told you, I was grounded. I'm busy with the community service." Tank doesn't know how to say that hanging out with these guys hasn't always been fun. Sure, Fortress Park is cool, but only when you have money to spend on tickets and games. They usually end up wandering around the mini golf course, and so much of what Shark likes to do is talk about all the great stuff he's going to do, the money he's making with his brother, and how to scare the kids in the neighborhood.

"I dunno," Shark says thoughtfully. "Saw you over by Taco National with some kids, including that guy from this building. Thought we agreed, Tank. They're losers."

Shut up, they're my friends is the first thing that leaps to Tank's mind, surprising himself. They *are* his friends; they've never laughed at him for the way he likes to play the game, or how he likes to collect flowers and build his mazes and farms. It was Emily's idea for him to help make the shortcuts back through the Nether, and Jake had gone through with him several times, showing him how to avoid the zombified piglins until Tank felt comfortable going on his own.

"I—" Tank doesn't know how to answer. He was annoyed, at first, at having to clean every day, but he's come to enjoy spending time with Jake and Emily. He doesn't have to pretend to be someone they think he should be. He can just be himself.

"Look, you can see them when you're doing your service thing," Shark says. "But you should remember that without us, without me to watch your back, you'd be nothing. A nobody." Shark's teeth glint menacingly in the morning light. "You want to go back to kids laughing at you and calling you Frankenstein?"

"No," Tank admits quietly.

"Then remember who you are. You're one of us, and we don't hang out with losers," Shark says. "Next time I say we're hanging out, you're gonna be there. Okay?"

A curl of dread starts in Tank's stomach, and he nods.

"Are you sure we're in the right place?" Emily asks.

Tank was sure that his last portal would result in just a short walk to the next clue, but he might have done the math wrong to get coordinates from the Nether to the Overworld. They're standing in a grassy field, approaching what looks like a massive, thick growth of forest.

Tank refers to the map in his hand. Sure enough, the red X is ahead of them, and they're walking right toward it. "I think so," he says.

"I thought this would be another underwater clue," Jake says. "We spent all that time preparing. I just see green."

As they approach, it comes into focus: a massive, thick growth of forest expands as far as the eye can see. It's clearly unnatural — a uniform wall like this would have to have been built deliberately, stacking leaves from trees cut with a Silk Touch axe.

Tank is standing where the X is. On the map, his marker is right on top of it. Sure enough, there's an opening in the wall here — almost invisible with the way the other green wall behind it blends in.

The green hedge walls extend up so high Tank can barely see the sliver of blue sky above.

"What is this?" Jake asks. "Where do we go now?"

There's no sign, no instructions, but it feels incredibly clear to Tank.

He steps inside.

"It's a maze," Tank says confidently. "I think to find the next clue we have to go through it."

"A maze?" Emily says, glancing around nervously. "Just of leaves?" She takes out an axe and slams it directly into the hedge wall.

Nothing happens.

"Same mod as in the beginning," Jake notes. "We can't break this."

"We'll have to go through. This is the riddle," Tank says. "Solve the maze."

Emily sighs. "Great. Just great." She stands at the ready with her sword. "Let's get this over with, then."

Tank blinks. "I don't think this challenge is about fighting anything."

"Wait, let's set a spawn point here just in case," Jake says, throwing a bed on the ground.

"Good idea." Emily follows suit.

Tank shrugs and does the same, even though he's sure this will be an easy challenge. After the Wizard attacked them, he was worried that this whole game was going to be player-versus-player style, but solving those first two riddles was actually pretty fun.

Music starts—a different motif from the haunting melody from the shipwreck. This one is playful but has a twisted air to it, a quick staccato of movement.

Something inside Tank rises up; he may not be the best fighter or know how to build any complicated things with redstone, but he knows that to solve a puzzle like this all you need is patience.

He's always seen it as something to hide away, something people would make fun of, because it's not normal, to sit down with a tangle of wire and lights and come out with a single strand, but Tank loves the steady quiet of a single task like this.

"I've built a ton of these," Tank says, surprising himself by speaking. "I love mazes. They only seem complicated, but we can go through it. The easiest way to solve a maze is to make a map." Tank pulls out a notepad and plops it down next to his keyboard. He starts drawing an outline so he can keep track of which paths they've taken.

The first step is to fill in the blank page.

Tank makes a quick decision and heads left, following the path until it meets an intersection. He adds the route to the map he's creating, drawing each dead end and open route he finds.

"I am so lost," Jake mutters.

"We're not lost at all," Tank says. "Look, being lost means you don't know where you're coming from and you don't know where you're going. Where you have nothing to refer to and no way to make a plan. But we are not lost. We know exactly which path leads back out, and one of these is going to lead to the end. And hopefully the next clue."

The first outer walls are all made of different leaf materials, variations of oak and birch leaves; as they move inward the hedges burst into a riot of color with lilacs and rose bushes lining the paths. Tank takes a minute to admire the design as he adds a dead end to his map. It's a little more difficult now that the walls are shorter—he can somewhat see to the other side and where he has to go, but it's frustrating still trying to figure out the paths.

Clink.

"What was that?" Jake asks.

Emily takes out her sword.

"It sounds like a skeleton shooting at us," Tank says. "But that would be impossible because it's daytime—"

Tank's suddenly hit by an arrow.

"We're under attack!" Jake shrieks. "They must have been modded. Bows, quickly!"

"I—hate—these—stupid—bushes!" Emily says, shooting frantically at the skeletons.

"Let's hurry up and get out of here!" Jake calls out. "Come on, Tank! Which way do we go?"

Tank breaks into a run, darting down a new pathway, only to

come face-to-face with a group of skeletons. These are different from any kind he's seen before, covered in moss with flowers growing in the crevices of the bones.

He backs up frantically, his heart in his throat.

"We got you," Jake says. "You can do this!"

Tank takes a deep breath and concentrates on his map. This corridor of lilacs had three paths—they've already tried one. He quickly calculates that based on what they've already explored, the one on the left has nowhere to go.

"Right!" Tank says, running quickly as he crunches on a loaf of bread.

Tank takes the lead.

He ignores the skeletons firing at him and concentrates on what he does best: being patient. He writes down every new path he discovers, doubles back to his last known solid point, and keeps going. Left. Right. Turn. Mark down this intersection. Wait, no, they've seen that lilac–rose–azure bluet formation before. Turn around. Go back in order to go forward.

He keeps moving.

The next turn, Tank comes face-to-face with a spider. He doesn't think about it, just slashes at it with his sword, plowing forward.

More spiders scuttle down the path, and this time, Tank is sure. He's sure of his map and how the mobs are positioned here—they're to scare off the adventurers, make them second-guess where they are in the maze. But he knows exactly what he's doing.

"This way!" Tank calls out.

With Emily and Jake at his side, Tank feels like he's capable of anything.

An open archway beckons them. Dandelions and peonies

grow in soft yellow and pink blooms, and beyond it, an open stretch of sand and the sparkle of water.

They climb up the sandy knoll. Ahead of them, the ocean glimmers. A single chest stands at the center of the sandy beach.

Emily opens it and reads the coordinates aloud. "These are super far," she groans. "Even if we go through the Nether."

"We can figure that out," Jake says. "But first, good job, man. We made it!" Jake exhales in relief.

"Yeah! We did it! We finished the maze," Tank announces, his triumphant heart pounding in his veins.

"You did it," Emily says, grinning at him. "We couldn't have done this without you."

Tank looks back at the maze. Now it's just a sheer mass of green again, hiding the complicated tangle of hedges and flowers inside. It was more complex than anything Tank's ever built. And he solved it. He got them through it.

Jake claps him on the back, and Emily throws her hands up in the air, delighted, and Tank can't help but smile back. He's not used to this at all, the unabashed way they're proud of him, celebrating their accomplishments together, but mostly celebrating *him*.

Maybe he isn't a nobody after all.

CHAPTER TWENTY-NINE

EMILY

Emily takes a selfie of the outfit she's put together—a blue dress that makes her think of diamond armor shimmering protectively with enchantments. She plays with ideas for captions, wondering if she could make that Minecraft reference before remembering that she's still grounded and she doesn't have access to her social media accounts anymore, and phone calls and texts are only for family right now.

She ties her hair up in a ponytail and hums to herself. It's still early; Jake and Tank usually get to the center by ten, but she can get some mining done while waiting for them.

Papa looks up at her from the dining table, sipping a cup of coffee and smiling at her. "You know, it's been nice to see you take this community service seriously."

Emily shrugs. It *has* been nice, having something to focus on.

And while she misses hanging out with Pattie and Nita, she's also been really enjoying just spending time with the boys, playing Minecraft and solving the riddles.

"I ran into Mrs. Jenkins yesterday, and she mentioned how smoothly the cleanup has been coming along. I thought since you've been doing well, we figured you would be responsible enough to have your social media things back."

Emily blinks. "Really?"

He smiles at her and ruffles her hair. "Carmen said she changed the passwords to your things back to your original ones yesterday, so you can use them again. And here is the new Wi-Fi password as well for you. Consider yourself ungrounded. You're still helping out at the center until the project is completed, of course—"

"Are you serious?" Emily squeals in excitement. "Thank you, thank you, thank you! And of course I'm still going to help, I don't start things I can't finish, duh." She gives him a tight hug before bouncing off back to her room.

Emily wastes no time reinstalling all her favorite apps, logging in to all her accounts and immediately changing her passwords. She texts Pattie and Nita to let them know the good news, and then speeds through all her notifications, responding in a flurry. There's Pattie and Nita in the group chat, responding to likes and comments on her posts, oh and Viv has been messaging her through YouTube, wondering where she's been—

Emily's phone chimes with a flurry of texts, and suddenly her heart races with indecision.

Pattie 9:46 a.m.: Mall today? Omg orange julius for lunch? To celebrate the end of an era?

Nita 9:47 a.m.: Yeah! I've missed hanging out with you

Emily 9:49 a.m.: Can't. I still have community service

Pattie 9:49 a.m.: Oh no! I thought you said you were ungrounded, free now!

Emily 9:50 a.m.: I just got my Insta back. Can't go out yet!

Pattie 9:50 a.m.: Oh, step one, gotcha. Don't worry, we'll be here! And step one is great!!! Omg what do you think of this outfit?

Emily types out a quick response; she's missed this, too, the clever way colors and patterns can come together. Part of her feels guilty about the lie—she probably could go out, if she asked her parents, but today they have big plans in the server, and she doesn't quite want to explain to Pattie that she's just busy instead.

The courtyard's faded shrubberies look kind of nice today, Emily thinks, swinging her feet on the old bench. There are some small blooms struggling to sprout through the dirt. Have there always been flowers here? She never noticed this place much in front of the community center; she just thought it was an empty lot of trash. She thinks of the photos they boxed away, and the way this place used to shine with care, plants and flowers growing in abundance.

"Hello there," a voice says from behind her.

Emily sits up a little taller when she spots Mrs. Jenkins walking through the double doors of the community center out to the courtyard. "Oh hey," she says, looking up from her phone. "We were just taking a lunch break."

Even though Mrs. Jenkins hasn't been enforcing a set start and finish time, they've just ended up meeting at ten every morning, cleaning until lunch, and then playing Minecraft until late afternoon. Sometimes they'll bring leftovers from home and share, sometimes they'll wander down the block and get tacos together.

Today Emily's been catching up with her friends after being away for so long; the boys are supposed to be on their way back with lunch.

"That's good," Mrs. Jenkins says with a smile. "The cleanup looks like it's been going well."

"Thanks!" Emily smiles. "You look nice today," she adds.

Mrs. Jenkins is wearing jeans and a T-shirt that reads PACIFIC CREST COMMUNITY CENTER BEACH CLEANUP DAY instead of her usual pajamas and bathrobe combo, and her salt-and-pepper hair is combed back into a loose bun.

"Thank you," Mrs. Jenkins says. "It's been nice to get out of the house."

Jake and Tank cross the street and join them in the courtyard, setting down greasy paper bags on the bench. "Oh, hi, Mrs. Jenkins," Jake says.

"You can call me Ellen," Mrs. Jenkins—Ellen—says, her eyes twinkling. "Emily was just telling me about your progress before your lunch break. You know, you don't have to worry about bothering me when you bring the boxes over to my apartment, you can just leave them at my door. I just wanted to stop by and say you're doing a great job."

"Thanks," Tank says, looking from Emily to Mrs. Jenkins, blinking slowly as if to ask *Are we in trouble?*

Emily shrugs at him. It doesn't seem like it.

"Well, that was all! Enjoy your lunch," Ellen says, getting up from the courtyard bench and going back inside the community center.

"That was weird," Jake says.

"Probably just checking up on us. Good thing we *have* been cleaning every day," Emily says. She jerks her head at the paper bags. "Did you get peppers?"

Jake grins as he rips open the paper bag and pulls out Styrofoam boxes, handing them out. "Fish for you, carnitas for Tank, one of each for me," he hums. "Oh, peppers."

"I got them," Tank says, placing out little takeout cups of peppers, limes, and various salsas.

"This place is amazing," Jake says, biting into a taco. "I told my dad about it and he's been getting a burrito there every day for lunch."

Tank places a whole pepper into his mouth, crunching noisily, his eyes crinkled up in amusement as Jake takes a tiny bite of his and winces.

Emily squeezes lime onto her tacos and takes a bite, trying not to laugh as Jake says something incomprehensible with his mouth full, a string of onion dangling from his lip as he chews.

"I said, do you need to get that? It's been ringing for forever."

"What?"

Jake jerks his head toward her phone. It's buzzing on the bench next to them, Pattie's face smirking from it.

Emily blinks up at them, not even realizing she'd been getting a call. She'd been so caught up with eating and hanging out with Jake and Tank.

"That's Pattie, from school, right?" Tank asks, even though Emily's sure he knows who she is.

Emily wipes her hands hastily on a napkin and declines the call. She texts Pattie quickly, *Sorry, family stuff! Ttyl* before grabbing her second taco. It's not that she doesn't want to see Pattie, but right now she'd rather be having tacos with the boys. Pattie knows she's busy today anyway.

"I'll call her later," Emily says.

"Your phone is just going wild," Jake says, peering at her screen. "Oh, what! You have a YouTube channel?" He grins at her. "Sorry, didn't mean to be nosy. The notifications just kept popping up."

Emily finishes her taco and wipes her hands again before taking her phone. Sure enough, it's another few likes on an old haul video.

Pattie 12:42 p.m.

No worries!!! Just wanted to share I shouted out your vid in my newest Makeup Monday Tips! Can't wait to hang out with you soon!

"Yeah, it's like for clothes and makeup and stuff." Emily sighs. "I mean, I love all of that, I just don't really like making videos about it." She pauses, thinking about her Minecraft channel. She's never shown it to anyone, but maybe Jake and Tank would like it. "I also have a channel for some of my builds."

Emily offers her phone to the guys, her heart pounding nervously in her chest.

"Oh whoa, this is so cool!" Jake says immediately. From the music it sounds like he's watching one of her first videos where she made a simple vending machine tutorial.

"The graphics look amazing. Which shaders did you add?" Tank says, awed.

"The water looks so real!"

"You really like it?" Emily asks, fiddling with a piece of her hair. "You don't think it's dumb?"

Tank gives her a nod. "It's great. It really shows, like, a lot of different ways to build cool things. I'll have to watch some of these later."

Jake hands her phone back and Emily takes it with a relieved laugh. They like her Minecraft videos. They like this side of her.

"Oh, now that you can text people and stuff let me add you so we can have an actual group chat finally. Tank barely texts me back."

"We see each other all the time. Stop sending me those weird cat photos."

"But they're funny, right? You laughed?"

Tank rolls his eyes, but he's smiling throughout it.

Emily suddenly feels strange, realizing that when summer ends and school starts again, she won't be able to hang out like this anymore. It'll be back to who she used to be, or, well, just a part of who she was. It's not like she can talk about videogames with Pattie and Nita. But she wishes she didn't have to have only one group of friends.

They connect to the server, the world coming into focus around them where they left off at the end of the maze.

Jake's already talking about going back to the base and preparing more before they set out for the new coordinates, but the sight of something new in the distance stops them all short.

Floating on an outstretch of sand in the water, directly across from where they're standing, is the purple shimmer of a Nether portal.

"Was that there before?" Tank asks.

"I don't think so," Emily says.

"You think the Wizard built it?" Jake swims out toward the portal. Emily follows, Tank right behind her.

The Nether portal leads them to a platform of purple-red

netherrack. Red clouds lurk above ominously, but the ground is even and uniform. Unlike the portals they've set up, carefully laying out torches across the uneven and unforgiving landscape, this is clear of mobs or lava or any natural obstacles of the Nether. Emily realizes they're up in the air, and that she's seen this before: shortcuts built high above the dangers of the mobs lurking on the ground below. The mottled blocks stretch out in a long path lined with a short cobblestone wall lit with torches as far as the eye can see.

They follow the torch-lit path; in the distance Emily can see dozens more of the purple portals marked by signs. "I wonder where all of those go," she says aloud.

"Must be how the Wizard was setting up this whole world," Jake muses.

"But why show us this?" Jake asks.

Emily thinks about the note the Wizard left for them at their base. "It must be a shortcut. The original riddles and everything are still here, but the Wizard must have made this recently."

Tank takes the lead, rushing ahead. It's been nice to see him grow more and more confident since they've begun to play. "The Wizard said we had to solve seven riddles to find the ultimate treasure, but who knows how many the original game had."

"I bet he picked out the most challenging tasks for us to solve," Jake says. "Or the ones that have been perfected. I mean, he spent so much time making this, he's got to have some that are favorites. Or he made new ones. This must be so we're skipping to the next challenge he wants us to focus on."

Emily grins, charging full speed ahead. "I can't wait to see what's next."

She's curious to see where all these other portals go, but she stays focused and follows Tank down the path the Wizard laid out for them until they reach a portal sitting behind an elaborate polished stone archway.

The portal spits them out in a badlands biome, cliffs of oranges and reds and golds rising up in tall crags. Scraggly dead bushes and cacti are scattered across the terracotta plateau, and ahead of them in the cliffside Emily can see an open cavern and a few broken pieces of minecart tracks. "A mineshaft?" she asks.

"The portal did lead us directly here," Jake says. "This must be where the Wizard placed the next clue. If the hedge maze was the third challenge, this must be the fourth."

Emily draws her sword. "Who's up for a little mining?" she says, grinning with excitement.

The cavern is filled with mobs, and Emily leads the way, charging through the creatures ruthlessly. She keeps cutting down spiders and destroying skeletons, but it doesn't seem to make any difference, as more mobs spawn from the depths of the cavern.

"What is this?" Emily scowls.

"There're too many of them!" Jake says frantically.

"Aaaah!" Tank yells, running in a different direction. "I'm getting away!"

"Must have been modded to keep spawning," Emily says. "What kind of challenge is this!"

"Maybe the point isn't clearing out the cavern, because it's impossible," Tank says. "There are more here, too! No way!"

Emily switches from her sword to her bow and aims at the skeletons shooting at Tank. "Like an endurance test? But for what?"

"I see a chest all the way over there by you, Tank! Make a run for it!" Jake calls out.

A chest! That must have the next clue.

Emily ignores the damage she's taking from the spiders closest to her and barrels right through them so she can have a better shot. Across the cavern, she sees Jake rushing to Tank's side to fend off the skeletons approaching.

"I got the book!" Tank shouts.

"Let's get out of here!" Emily calls out. "Come on!" She tosses an instant health potion at Tank and Jake as she fights off the rapidly multiplying mobs. She gulps one down herself, hoping it will be enough to make it out. Together, they fight their way through the twisting turns of the mineshaft caverns until they're outside in the bright sunshine again.

Emily exhales, catching her breath. "That was fun," she says.

"That was terrifying," Tank says.

"Is it a clue?" Jake asks.

"Yeah. There're coordinates and another riddle." Tank reads the contents of the book aloud:

RIDDLE THE FIFTH

This challenge will surely test your mettle
Cross the bridge of fiery doom
By managing how a conduit settles.
The path to the next challenge courage will show
By going high to go low.

The coordinates lead them to a plain rocky plateau. It looks like this area of the world is barren, just rock stretching out for forever.

Something glints in the distance; it's almost far enough for it to look like it's floating above a hazy, impossible sea, but Emily knows better. She used to think everything in the distance was ocean until you get closer and realize it's just too far away to see.

"That must be it. There isn't anything else around here," Tank mutters.

"It looks like a castle on top of a mountain," Jake says with awe.

"A castle we're totally going to own! Let's get this party started." Emily charges forward, excited to take on whatever monsters may lurk within. Those skeletons in the maze had been fun, but she's itching for a good fight.

Shining obsidian takes the form of towers and spires, menacing in the distance. As they race ahead, a deep chasm comes into focus. The only clear way to the castle is a thin obsidian bridge one block wide, leading straight to the front door. The bridge looms at them menacingly as it juts out from the castle. Angry red lava flows in the chasm below, marking a swift and efficient death for anyone who missteps while crossing the bridge.

There's some sort of wall blocking the way to the bridge—a thick wall of cobblestone directly in front of the entrance at the cliff's edge. Emily pulls out her diamond pickaxe and charges forward.

"Take that!" she screams, slamming it into the wall.

Her diamond pickaxe shatters with a dissonant *clank*.

Emily huffs.

"I knew it couldn't be that easy," Jake says. "The challenge must be getting inside."

"Could have told me that before I ruined my pickaxe," Emily mutters. Looking closer, she can see some sort of glimmer of pink enchantment on the stone.

"We'll have to try another way," Tank says. "It'll be fine."

———

It is not fine.

At first, the wall seems impenetrable. But a closer look at the riddle makes Emily think there's more to it than just breaking down the wall. While Jake and Tank attempt to build another bridge on the edge of the cliff with no success, she paces back and forth, studying it.

"Test your mettle . . . conduit settle," Emily mutters to herself. What if it's not a wall? What if it's a door? Conduits are operated by redstone, so there must be . . .

Emily pauses. "What if we just can't see it?" She crafts a wooden shovel quickly and digs directly down in front of the wall. Emily takes a wide swath, uncovering block by block carefully—if there is a controlled system here, she has to be careful not to break it.

"Aha!"

A line of redstone.

Emily digs to the block next to it, careful not to dig any deeper now. For a few moments there's only the sound of her shovel crunching into the dirt as she reveals an intricate system of redstone circuitry. It's way more complex than anything she's built before. It's definitely not a simple button to push or a pressure plate to step on. There's some serious programming going on here.

"Whoa, what'd you find?" Jake says.

"This is what the riddle meant," Emily says. "We have to use redstone to open the door."

Tank and Jake help her carefully excavate the entire area in front of the wall.

"There's a chest here!" Jake exclaims, holding up a shovel. "Redstone dust, redstone torches, concrete . . . are we going to have to build something?"

Tank peers closer. "I don't know how to do any of this stuff."

Emily examines the lines of redstone, studying how they connect. She sighs. "I'm going to try."

She gets to work, building repeaters and attempting to figure out what exactly this setup is missing to make the door work. Emily tries attempt after attempt, and she rips pieces up and can't remember what the original configuration was, and she tries to repair it, and it keeps not working. She feels like they've been at it forever, and Jake and Tank are at a loss.

"Maybe it's like a red herring. Like a distraction, and the real way to solve it is something else," Jake suggests after Emily's fifth attempt.

Tank and Jake have been trying everything to get through the wall every other way while Emily has been working on the redstone.

All tools and weapons shatter upon trying to break through the block. Building a new bridge is impossible. The Wizard thought of everything: They can't place any new blocks anywhere on the cliff edge or alter the cliff itself in any way.

"There must be a way to remove that wall," Jake says, pacing back and forth.

"I really think we're going to have to open it by figuring this out, but I—" Emily groans. "I'm such a fake. I'm not a rock star at redstone construction at all. I really wanted to be, but I can't— figure this out."

"It's okay to ask for help," Tank says. "That's what my mom always says."

Jake nods in agreement. "You are a rock star! You made that automated sorter with the hoppers for all of our inventory back at the base!"

"Yeah!" Tank says. "That was awesome. You worked really

hard on that. You're great at redstone. But like you said, this is complicated stuff. Just because you can't figure out this one problem doesn't mean you can't be good at it."

Emily takes a deep breath and smiles. "Thanks." She looks back at the unsolved problem, the pieces out in front of her. *PacificViv would love this*, she thinks.

"I think I actually know someone who could help," Emily says. "Only problem is, she could be on the other side of the world." She's never asked Viv where she or any of those people on her server was—didn't they come from all over? Different time zones and stuff? "I think the easiest thing to do would be to get her in here to look at it, but since this server is only on this LAN, we'll just have to take lots of screenshots."

Emily backs up, trying to get a good view of the whole thing; she'll need to build a platform or something to stand on.

"Do you think she would do it?" Tank asks.

"I mean, we haven't talked in forever because I was grounded, but I can ask. She's a YouTuber, her channel is full of problems and stuff like this. I bet she'd love it." Emily takes a few shots at different angles, trying to get as much as possible in. "Her name's PacificViv, you can look her up. She does stuff like this all the time."

Emily disconnects from the game, saving the shots. Jake's pulled up her channel on his computer, trying to load a video on creating an intruder alarm with the very slow Internet. Emily's gonna have to catch up—Viv's posted a lot since she's been grounded.

Tank stares over Jake's shoulder and sighs.

"What? You know someone better?"

"Getting her in here to look at it won't be a problem," Tank says. "That's my little sister."

CHAPTER THIRTY

TANK

This is it. Tank knows the minute he introduces Viv to Jake and Emily that they're going to like her better than him. She's smart and actually good at Minecraft; Tank is just slow and quiet. Days like this, eating companionably at lunch, are gonna be over. He's been looking forward to spending time with his friends every day; it's been nice to have people that actually seem to want him around. Shark's certainly never brought food for him before.

Tank's come to like having a normal schedule—he dusts and organizes stuff for a bit with Emily and Jake in the morning, and then they play a whole bunch of Minecraft before he goes home. It's a nice way of spending the summer; he'd thought he'd be working the whole time, helping make extra money for Ma to pay for those repairs, get Viv some new books and maybe those sneakers as a treat for himself. But Ma had said not to worry about it, that everything was okay, whatever that means.

Ma still doesn't know he got into trouble, and Tank's planning to keep it that way. The less she has to worry about, the better. She's usually sleeping during the day, and he can still make sure she eats before she heads out to work. Mr. Mishra was really understanding when Tank said he couldn't work as much, and it all worked out, since he didn't have much for Tank to do in the first place now that he hired someone for real. It's been weeks now and Tank kept making excuses not to tell Viv about the server; he knows she would love it but . . . he's just a boring farm-and-flowers guy, and Viv is a redstone genius. After they meet her, it'll be obvious they'd rather play with her.

A large part of him doesn't want to admit that he likes having something that's just for himself, that he doesn't have to share. That he's been looking forward to sitting in that dusty computer lab, laughing at Jake's terrible jokes and Emily eating hot Cheetos with chopsticks.

"It's so I don't get the orange dust on my fingers," she once said, rolling her eyes at him the first time he saw her do it. It's actually super smart, and a good way to keep snacking without worrying about messing up the keyboard.

And now instead of the three of them, it's going to be Emily and Jake and Vivian, and Tank hopelessly plodding along after, trying to keep up. Viv is going to be the one they'll want to solve the puzzle with.

But if they're close to solving the puzzle, if Viv is the one who can get them there, and all of this is going to end soon, then Tank might as well go for it and bring them all together. He might lose Emily and Jake as friends, but he was going to lose them anyway.

Emily and Jake are still staring at him; the computer lab has gone silent except for the soft electronic whir of the old computers. An unnatural stillness wraps around them until Tank finds it in himself to muster again, "PacificViv is my little sister."

"Wait, really?" Emily asks, her mouth falling open in awe.

"Vivian, yeah. She's really smart and loves programming and redstone stuff."

"Perfect. Let's ask her." Jake stands up decisively after turning off his computer.

Tank does the same and then shuffles into the lobby, noticing how *much* construction equipment has been stacked here while they've been working. He knows Grant has been here at nights, and they've been making deliveries in the early morning, but it's been easy to forget this whole place is going to disappear while they've been all wrapped up in another world.

He turns around to wave goodbye, but Emily and Jake have followed him into the courtyard.

"You're in the West Tower, right?" Emily asks curiously. "Figure we can say hi to your sister and ask if she wants to come back with us. My parents and the twins are at Carmen's poetry reading tonight; they won't notice if I'm back late."

"Yeah, my dad is looking at some materials for work and he'll be a while," Jake says. "We can definitely bring her back here if she's free."

"Oh," Tank says, looking toward the community center. "I could just go get her."

"I don't mind," Emily says cheerfully. "Yours is the only place we haven't gone to."

Tank realizes she's right; they've lunched at Jake's before, hung out at Emily's. He's the only one who hasn't shared this aspect of himself.

They look at him expectantly, and Tank can't think of a good enough reason why they shouldn't come to his place. He winces as he leads the way up the stairs, thinking about Jake's clean home and the laughter and warm smells of cooking in Emily's. "It might be just Viv and my dad at home. My mom works nights so she'd probably be asleep," he says awkwardly. He hopes Ba is out. He doesn't want Ba being weird to his friends.

Tank's never had to think about this before. He's never had friends who wanted to see where he lived.

"This is it," he says, turning the key. He squeaks the door open and jerks his head inside. "Uh—shoes."

Emily's already toeing off her shoes and kicking them to join the pairs lined up inside the door. Jake follows suit, his eyes taking in the messy living room.

Tank sees it all laid out: the shabby couch, the decades-old television propped up on milk crates that he brought from the convenience store. This morning when he left Ba was asleep in the lounge chair wearing a stained white T-shirt and pants with holes down the knee. But he's not here now. Maybe he went out.

"This is it," Tank says.

"Cool," Jake says.

Emily grins as she points to the cookie tin on the side table. "Heh, you have the same cookie tin—"

"Those are sewing supplies," Tank says.

Emily laughs. "They're always sewing supplies."

"Viv's room is over here—"

Ba steps out of the hallway, adjusting an orange polo shirt. "Oh, hey!"

Huh. What is he wearing? "Ba, these are my friends," Tank says. "Emily and Jake."

"So nice to meet you! Are you going to stay for dinner? I'll bring groceries back after work." Ba smiles at Emily and Jake.

"I thought your shift at the mechanics was in the morning," Tank says, confused.

"I'm also working at the convenience store now!" Ba says cheerfully. "Sanjay appreciates me being such a good handyman."

"Mr. Mishra . . . hired you."

"I've already fixed his vending machine. And he shares my appreciation for invention. We had a great conversation about tools the other day. Did you know he has his own workshop where he builds robots?"

"That's great, Ba," Tank says, surprised and pleased. He's glad Ba has somewhere he can be creative instead of looking for ways to be useful.

"I'll see you later!" Ba waves at them as he exits the apartment.

"So that was my dad," Tank says.

"He seems nice," Jake says.

Tank blinks. "Yeah. Um. Viv is over here." He gestures for Emily and Jake to follow him to her room. Vivian's at her computer, headphones on; she's in her server again, talking to her friends and shouting rapid-fire instructions.

Tank taps her on the shoulder.

"Hey, Thanh-anh," she says in singsong.

Emily giggles. "Is that like a nickname?"

"Tank is a nickname," he says. Shark gave it to him. He'd felt honored at first, being one of the guys with a cool name. A tough one, one that carried weight. He thinks about it now and wonders if maybe it was because Shark couldn't pronounce Thanh. It's too late, anyway; even teachers call him Tank. "Thanh is my name."

Jake glances at Emily. "Do you want us to call you Thanh instead, or . . . ?"

Tank shrugs, but something inside of him feels warm and pleased. "If you want to. I like both. I like being Tank. I like being Thanh. They're both me."

"Anh means big brother," Viv says. "Are you the detention friends?" She waggles her eyebrows at Tank, who ducks his head sheepishly.

"Community service," Tank corrects. "She thinks it's funnier to say detention. Yeah. This is Jake and this is Emily. We've been playing Minecraft together at the community center."

"That's awesome!" Viv claps her hands together in delight and squeals, "I'm Vivian! I play Minecraft, too."

"Hey, nice to meet you," Emily says, suddenly shy. "I'm—I'm RoxXStarRedStone. I was gonna ask you about this thing—"

Viv jumps out of her chair, bouncing up and down. "Ahhh, I was wondering why you hadn't responded in forever!"

"Yeah, I was grounded with no social media or games so I haven't been able to play at home or message you on YouTube or anything. No way, is that Mina's new house?"

"You two already play Minecraft together?" Tank asks in disbelief. It's already starting. Emily and Viv are already friends.

Emily shrugs. "We started talking at the beginning of the summer and I played in Viv's server once—oh wow, you've done a lot!" She peers over Viv's shoulder as Viv excitedly starts showing her around.

"Have you told her about the server?" Jake asks from Tank's right.

"Viv, hey. I wanted to ask you a redstone thing."

"Really? Why? You never wanted to learn before." Viv's eyes widen in interest.

"So in the community center, you know how you've played

Minecraft there—have you ever logged in to one of the servers on the LAN?" Tank asks.

"Eh, no. Figured they were somebody's pet project. Why?"

Tank hedges, trying to figure out how to explain what they've been doing for the past few weeks, but Jake beats him to it.

"One of them is set up like an epic game, and we've been playing it. Look."

Jake pulls up a screenshot on his phone from the first shipwreck; the mermaid is as clear as day, tail, scales, and all. Tank remembers that moment vividly: It was the start of something new, a change from the reluctant dynamic of a way to pass the time to really playing together, going into the game to uncover the truth of the mystery.

Viv takes the phone and tilts her head. "A mermaid mod for your avatar?"

"No. We saw them around this shipwreck." Jake flips to another shot of the first shipwreck, and then to the mural of the underwater city.

The story comes out in bits and pieces, how Jake had found the seventeenth riddle and they were playing around and working on figuring out the next clue until the Wizard appeared and forced them back to the start.

Vivian is buzzing with questions, about the mermaids and the riddles themselves, the strange structures all over the world. "The mermaids act like a neutral mob? Where did they spawn? Are there more?"

"We've only seen them near shipwrecks, and yeah, they've mostly just swam around and then disappeared somewhere," Jake says.

"I think that the clues that we've been finding, they're all leading toward this treasure in a completely hidden underwater city."

Tank shows the mural again. "This is where we're going. The treasure is in here."

"Atlantis," Viv exhales with wonder.

"Something like that," Emily says. "But the treasure, really."

"I've never heard of anything like this. Who made this and modded the server?"

Jake and Emily share a knowing look. "We only know the player as TheCrestWizard."

"Yeah, he's a real grumpy jerk," Tank says. "He's really strong and aggressive and attacked us the first time he saw us. He wanted us to leave at first, but he's been kind of helpful since."

"Yeah, he gave us back all our stuff," Emily says. "And made us a shortcut."

"I think we are impressing him," Jake says. "If he didn't want us in the game, he could have deleted the world, or made it private or banned us or something. He hasn't done anything except start us at the beginning, and he picked out seven riddles for us to solve."

"So far we've done four. So we're about halfway there," Tank says.

"I think you might be able to solve this next clue," Emily says. "Want to help?"

Vivian stands up and flexes her fingers together. "Do I *ever*."

The energy inside the community center is charged with a frenetic excitement as Tank leads the way back to the computer lab. Jake is trying to catch Vivian up on everything they've done, with Emily's colorful commentary, telling her the story of the creepy temple they first found themselves in and all their adventures in the Nether along the way. Tank boots up the three computers and sits Viv in the center. A feeling of dread rises in his stomach as Vivian laughs and accepts Jake's high five. Emily squeals as Viv joins them with Tank's avatar in front of the bridge.

It's happening. The first friends he's had who like him for who he is are going to like hanging out with Viv more, and then they'll forget all about him and he'll just fade into the background.

"Show her the clue, Jake," Tank says, jerking his head impatiently.

"Sure," Jake says. "Oh man, we should show you the base and all the other cool stuff we found sometime."

"I bet Thanh has a farm, huh!" She giggles. "Has he found all the different flower biomes yet in this world?"

"Shush," Tank says.

"Aw yeah, he loves decorating. Our base looks amazing. Check out this hedge maze and flower field," Emily says proudly, her lips quirking up in a smile.

"Our last clue Tank totally solved in no time," Jake said.

"Aw, nice. It's good to see you having fun in a server with friends, Tank." Viv beams at him.

Tank folds his arms together, embarrassed but pleased. He jerks his head back toward the screen to remind them to stay on track.

"This is pretty intense." She looks at the screenshots of the clues they've solved so far. "So each clue leads you to the next?"

"Yeah. There have been different challenges, like solving a riddle or finding the next clue in a shipwreck or a book hidden inside a cavern filled with mobs. It's like the Wizard wanted the game to take you all over the world, chasing down this impossible treasure. None of the clues are the same. Sometimes the riddle is a poem, or it points you toward specific coordinates." Jake flips through his phone, showing her each of the clues.

"All right, so where are you stuck?"

Tank hangs back behind Vivian's chair. Emily walks her to the edge of the cliff. The obsidian bridge stretches out behind the impossible barrier, the redstone circuitry in front of the door laid bare in the dirt.

"Whoa." Viv paces back and forth in front of the exposed circuitry as Emily walks with her, pointing it out.

"Here, look at this," Emily says. "All I've been able to figure out is that when it works, standing on the pressure plate here should open a hidden door in that wall to the bridge, but I can't figure out how."

"There's redstone dust and a bunch of supplies in the chest here," Tank says, pointing at Viv's screen. "Do you need anything else? Crafting table is here."

"No, no, I just want to see." Vivian examines the circuitry, Tank's avatar zipping all over the area so quickly it makes Tank dizzy. It's disorienting, watching three different screens from behind with too many perspectives looking at the same thing. He tries to concentrate on Viv's, but she's going too fast, so he settles on watching Jake's screen and focusing on the bridge and the landscape behind them. Emily and Jake at least aren't moving as erratically as they're talking, and he can barely follow that conversation as it is.

Emily and Viv are hunched over the lines of redstone and repeaters in the ground. "Okay, so this repeater here—"

"Tried that. What about this over here?"

"That doesn't go to anything, it's a decoy. Let's see. The whole thing is wired to this pressure plate somehow—Jake, can you stand over there and be ready to hop on it for the test when I say go?"

"Yeah." Jake follows her direction, bouncing over to the pressure plate.

Tank taps the back of Viv's chair, watching her do her magic. Her face is scrunched up in concentration as she studies the wire work, walking back and forth and checking in with Emily about the placement, what she's tried and hasn't tried. Emily follows her to the crafting table as she deftly builds another one alongside it.

"Can you make me—three repeaters? And five bits of wire— no, I got three here."

"Two bits of wire, done!" Emily says quickly.

"Do you get redstone at all?" Tank nudges Jake.

"Tried to build a trapdoor once, seemed more trouble than it was worth," Jake says. "I just like building in general." He grins at Tank, patting the empty seat beside him. "What do you think, Tank? See anything with your eagle eyes?"

"My what?" Tank sits down next to Jake.

"You know, since you've got the bird's eye view." Jake tilts his head, watching Emily and Viv laugh as they try another solution. "Your sister is pretty cool."

"I know," Tank says, accepting what's about to come. "You know, if you want to do the rest of the puzzle and stuff with her, I don't mind."

"What do you mean? You don't want to play with us anymore?" Jake blinks at him in confusion.

"No, I mean, if you'd rather play with Viv. You know, instead of me," Tank says quietly.

Emily turns around. "We started this together, Tank. We're gonna finish this together."

"I—" Tank doesn't know what to say.

"I mean, if you really don't want to play anymore, you don't have to. But is that true?"

Jake nods. "There isn't a limited inventory for people, you know. We don't have only so many spots for friends."

Emily looks quickly at Jake and then back at her feet.

"You're so weird, Thanh-anh," Viv says, rolling her eyes. "I like meeting new people, but you know I have no patience for riddles or RPGs. Even if I did, this is your thing, not mine." She smiles up at him, as if it's so simple.

"Oh." Maybe it is. Maybe Tank's been making this complicated all along.

Emily and Jake both nod in understanding.

"I also have my own server filled with friends. I'm glad you found this crew, though, they seem awesome." She cracks her knuckles together. "Anyway, I think I figured this out!" She stands on the pressure plate, and then a set of hidden double doors in the center of the wall slide open, revealing the bridge. "There you go!"

Jake whoops in celebration. "Thank you so much!"

Viv scoots back on her chair, stands, and gives Tank a jaunty little salute. "It was nice to meet you two. Have fun storming the castle!"

Tank sits down in the chair between his two friends and looks forward at the open pathway between them. He feels Jake clap him on the shoulder before turning back to his own computer.

They're ready.

CHAPTER THIRTY-ONE

JAKE

There's nothing standing between them and the castle now. Jake reevaluates his inventory, but with the looming spires and towers ahead, he has no idea what to be prepared for. He thought of all the time they spent on the base, gathering the supplies they'd need for breathing underwater, and he wonders if they're even going to need it. If there's going to be something new he hadn't thought of. It definitely feels like they've been tested, thrown all over the world into deserts and plains, and now, this castle of dark volcanic glass oozing with lava and red-hot intent. The mountaintop they're all on is so tall there's no way they can see what's beyond it. This clue could be anything from defeating all the monsters inside the castle and getting past it to finding a new set of coordinates.

"Okay, it's a narrow bridge, so be careful, you should set a spawn point here just in case." Jake sets down his bed on a spot, leaving room for Tank and Emily to do the same. "We should do this again on the other side—"

"YEEEARRRRGH!" Emily shouts, running full speed ahead across the bridge.

Tank laughs as he follows, keeping up a quick pace. "Come on, Jake."

"It would suck to die here—there would be no way to get our stuff back! Come on, you should be more careful!" Jake picks up his bed and sighs. He follows them across the bridge, moving slowly and taking care to stay on the path. Lava bubbles far beneath him, and the bridge seems to stretch out for hundreds of blocks.

"It would suck to grow old waiting for you to get here!" Emily laughs, her avatar bouncing up and down on the other side.

"Whatever," Jake grumbles.

He finally joins them in front of a massive obsidian door, glinting ominously, reaching up toward the sky. The castle is all points: spires and towers and smoky dark glass revealing nothing of the contents.

"I hope there isn't another puzzle for this door," Jake says.

"Say things like that and there will be," Tank mutters. "That's how it usually works, right?"

"Nope. It opens automatically. Pretty cool setup, actually. Double doors. Watch this." Emily steps toward the door. It creaks open with a heavy clunk, revealing a set of polished blackstone doors that swivel and disappear into the walls. Jake walks into the cavernous hallway with his friends, getting more and more nervous. Is there a sleeping dragon? What sort of riddle is this?

All the doors shut behind them with a heavy finality.

Jake pulls out his sword. It appears that they are alone in a grand hall, although Jake has his suspicions. After the mobs that attacked them in the hedge maze, he has to be ready for anything.

Their footsteps echo on the blackstone floor as they step inside. High above, lanterns flicker with bright blue soul fire, casting a soft light. A secondary faint blue light is emanating from somewhere else, but Jake can't figure out its origin.

"All right. What's next? Clearly getting into the castle was part of the riddle." Emily slaps a torch on the wall. The fire looks strange and unnatural in this cold and dark stone place.

"Somewhere in this castle is the next clue," Tank says. "Do you think it's another maze? I don't see any corridors, just this room. What do you think 'go high to go low' means?"

"It could be literal; it could be a metaphor. Let's explore," Jake says. "Remember the hidden painting before? Let's check all the walls and the floors, just in case."

Jake nods at them to split up; they take a few moments to search the large room. The walls and floors are unbreakable, as Jake suspected, but they seem to be just that: walls and floors. No pressure plates, no hidden passages, just the endless dark blackstone stretching onward.

No, there's something more here.

Jake approaches the other end of the room, where a raised stone dais has been built. A single throne stands proudly in the center, a column of blue glass rising up in the wall behind it.

Wait, that's not a solid block —

It's water. Behind glass panes. Jake can see a faint drift of bubbles moving downward. But going where?

He looks up. The column of water stretches toward the ceiling, but it seems to stop about halfway up the wall.

"Couldn't find anything," Emily says. "No monsters, either."

"Nothing on the other end," Tank says.

"Look at this water column. You think it leads to a passageway?" Jake tries to see if there's another floor high above them, but he can see only darkness looming ahead.

"Ooh, maybe," Emily says. "From the outside, this place just looked super tall. There might be a huge basement or something we haven't explored under. And we have no idea what's behind the castle, too. It could be anything."

"What if this is it?" Jake asks. "We go high so we can go low to wherever the water is going."

Jake jumps and throws a block of dirt underneath him, moving higher and higher, the rest of the throne room falling out of focus as he inches up alongside the water column. Emily's already ahead of him, her own column of dirt rapidly growing as she rises up.

"There's an opening here!" There isn't any light, but where the water column ends is a single clear block amidst the stone, and it looks wide enough to squeeze into.

Emily takes a flying leap from her dirt column, landing squarely in the space. She places a torch on the wall, and now Jake can see it clearly: a small alcove in the castle wall, with a single block of water leading into the unknown.

"Nice work, Jake. I don't think I would have seen this, it just looked like more of the wall to me," Tank says. "Did you run out of dirt?" He stacks a block from Jake's dirt tower into the air, building a clear path to the alcove.

"Thanks." The three of them stare at the water; there's no way of knowing what awaits them on the other side. Jake takes a deep breath. "All right, let's go."

The roar of rushing water surrounds him as he plummets head-first into the column. They speed down, down, down, past the glass wall that peeks out to the throne room, a brief blip of blue light, and then it's just darkness.

"How far down are we going?" Jake wonders.

Tank hums next to him. "It could be anywhere. I mean, we could be going toward another one of the Wizard's Nether portals—"

"The Nether portal at the end of the maze clue was a short-cut," Emily says. "I'm sure of it."

"This water tunnel here is part of the riddle," Jake says. "We solved it, see? We went high and now we're going low. Just sit tight and let's see where this leads."

"Doesn't water move super fast? We must be almost hitting the bedrock—"

FLOMP.

There must have been a hole for the water to splash into, but wherever they are is dry. And dark.

"There's a wall here," Tank says.

Emily laughs. "Over here, this is open—whoa!"

Jake sets a torch on the nearest surface, and their surroundings come flickering into view: They're standing in a cave of some sort, mossy stone lining the walls, sand beneath them, with the water elevator spilling in from above. There's only a sliver of sand, the rest of the irregularly shaped cave is filled with water.

"Guess the only way out is under. Think this leads out to the ocean?" Emily lets out an impressed whistle. "Must have taken forever to terraform that mountain so we couldn't see the ocean behind it." She starts swimming, disappearing into the dark.

Jake tosses a potion at Tank, grateful that the time spent planning and brewing potions is going to pay off. "Night Vision, we're probably going to need it. Emily! Wait up!"

Jake gulps down the potion and wades into the water after her, Tank by his side. They swim away from the shoreline, Jake's heart pounding as he goes.

With the Night Vision, the watery depths suddenly become clear as day. Jake can see drifting forests of kelp and in the distance, the shadow of a pyramid in the water.

"Watch out for the guardians," Emily says, swimming directly toward it. "They're the worst."

"I wish we knew we were going to an ocean monument for this clue," Jake grumbles.

"Come on," Emily says. "We've got great armor and those extra Respiration enchantments on our helmets, and you brought the Night Vision potions."

Jake's never taken on an ocean monument without extensive preparation. Emily's confidence impresses him, but he wishes he had even more potions or a different set of armor. He has boots with Depth Strider and an even better helmet with Respiration enchantments, but he supposes what he has on him now will have to do. If they die they'll respawn in front of the castle, so he guesses they could go back to the base and prepare more if they need to.

"There's usually like three of them around these ocean monuments—there! Aack! Laser beams!"

A shot of energy blasts through the water right toward them.

"AAAH!" Tank careens out of the way, but knocks right into Jake as another blast fires directly at him.

Jake takes immediate damage and groans, backing up. No, no, no. He wishes he had his best bow with infinite arrows right now, this is the worst!

The guardians move with a threatening purpose. One darts forward, its gaping open maw groaning with an endless hunger. Its single eye stares relentlessly, and the beast's scales are the same faint green-blue color of the monument below.

Jake fires his bow at it and watches his arrow barely creep forward, unflinchingly slow in the water before it drops to the ocean floor, useless.

"Quick! In here!" Tank swims down to the bottom of the monument, disappearing behind pillars stretching out to the sands.

"Take that! And that!" Emily shrieks. "Yes, give me all the loot! Come at me!"

"This place is so cool," Tank says, rounding a corner. "Aren't these prismarine blocks pretty? I'd love to take some home—"

"Not now, Tank!" Jake whispers, even though he knows the guardians can't hear them. "Great, great, we're running out of air and I can't remember the last place I set a spawn point; if I die it's gonna take forever to get back here—"

"No worries," Tank says, slapping something on the wall. It's not a torch, which would have been useless underwater anyway, but a ladder.

Jake watches as a pocket of air forms around the ladder and Tank ducks in and out of it quickly. "Viv always brought ladders with her, but I didn't realize why," Tank says, chuckling a little. "This was a good idea, building all of these beforehand," Tank says.

"Yeah, it's great. Now we can take our time and defeat all these monsters."

"I've got a whole stack of these. We can keep placing them as we explore. I'll just keep them on the left so we know what areas we've gone through already."

"Good thing you brought them, too," Jake says, glad to be with Tank.

"I got two of the guardians outside," Emily announces. "The last one is probably gonna be the boss one. Are you all inside?"

"Bottom floor," Tank says. "Let's search all around."

The inside of the monument is filled with empty chambers built with the ancient blue-green prismarine. Pillars and columns and watery halls open up to more rooms, stone standing strong as water drifts around the support columns of the monument. Jake and Tank swim between the rooms, collecting sponges and looking for—Jake isn't quite sure what they're looking for. Inscriptions on the walls? Another clue? The clues have gotten so drastically different that he isn't sure anymore.

There's one room filled with tiles that play haunting, musical notes that fill the air if you press them. Another room is filled with murals of merfolk wielding tridents, and another has chests filled with emeralds and gold.

Emily joins them on the second floor, taking a grateful breath in one of Tank's air pockets. "What are we looking for? I don't see anything so far that could be a clue. This could just be another pretty place to explore."

"What, like a false start?" Tank considers. "I don't know. I think the riddle definitely pointed us here. We crossed the bridge to the castle, found the entrance to the water elevator."

"Yeah, but . . ." Emily trails off. "What if we messed up on the first step? I broke the circuitry and programming when I was trying to figure it out, so Viv was looking at what I made and the whole castle could have been . . ."

"No, I'm sure you and Viv solved that right. We were meant to go into the castle and find that elevator and go down here. This isn't like a regular ocean monument. That music room had to be designed by the Wizard, and there were murals of mermaids. This feels right," Jake says. "Look, this whole time we've been looking for this underwater city, right? We're here, and I know the next clue is part of this monument. Come on guys, trust me." Jake turns back toward the inside of the chambers. "We haven't explored the next floor yet and the castle definitely led us here. This is where the next clue is."

Emily sighs. "Jake, I think you come up with great plans—we couldn't have done these challenges without you, and going back to the base and preparing was super helpful. But think about this: This whole world, the Wizard has been working on it for ages. And then when he saw we were playing, he picked out the most challenging riddles for us, and he said there were seven, right?"

Tank slowly starts counting off the challenges they've done. "Getting out of the first temple, finding the map, the hedge maze, the mineshaft with the never-ending mobs, the redstone door to the castle . . . There would only be two left."

"Right? And that elevator, being spit out here into the ocean and finding this monument close by, of course we're going to think it's the right direction because it's underwater. But I think we should go back and rethink the castle. I just think maybe the redstone part of the riddle wasn't right, and maybe it should have opened up a different secret passageway or something."

Emily swims away like she's going to go back to shore. Jake darts in front of her, blocking her path.

"Look, you're a great player and fighter—you always dive headfirst into danger, and it's awesome. And you *are* a rock star at redstone stuff," Jake says.

"Yeah. You're just second-guessing yourself," Tank says. "I think we're exactly where we need to be."

"Right now, we need to stick together. We can't afford to lose anyone, especially if what Tank says about where we are in solving the puzzle is right." Jake doesn't say that they're almost at the end, but it lingers over them in the heavy silence, words unspoken.

"There's one more floor here, and we can go check out whatever's there. It won't hurt to look, and if there's nothing, we can go back to the castle and look at the redstone to see if there's another door or something. But I think that part is solved." Tank swims back inside the hallway, toward the last opening to the top floor.

Emily looks at Tank and then back at Jake. "You're right. I trust you and your plan," she says. "And—thanks." She gives him a soft smile. "I think the both of you are great players, too. I've never had this much fun in Minecraft before."

It feels bittersweet, and Jake doesn't want this to end, but it's going to very, very soon, and he doesn't know what he's going to do when it's over.

The three of them go through each and every room, and every time Jake finds nothing his disappointment grows, like a heavy stone weighing him down. Emily doesn't say *I told you so* like he expects, though, just keeps pushing forward.

"This is it. This is the treasure chamber," Emily says. "Gold, usually, in there—" She breaks out a pickaxe and starts hacking at the dark prismarine.

Jake double-checks the hallway to see if there are any more doors or rooms they've missed, and this is it. It's the last one.

He rounds the corner and comes face-to-face with an elder guardian.

CHAPTER THIRTY-TWO

EMILY

Underneath the dark prismarine, gold gleams and Emily grins. Treasure is treasure—it's not a clue, but it's certainly nice to have.

"Jake! No!"

She whirls around to see Tank frantically trying to fight off an elder guardian that's blasting a powerful laser at Jake. This must be the boss—she's found these one-eyed blobs of doom incredibly annoying and potent, but they're no match for her. Emily switches her pickaxe for her diamond sword, charging at the guardian. The blasts are powerful, and she sees that Tank and Jake keep hanging back so they can eat and regain health or duck into an air pocket, but Emily has no such fears. She hacks and hacks at the elder guardian, cornering it into a wall and it's got nowhere to go except to succumb to her power. Finally it's destroyed, and she hears the familiar ping of experience and picks up the loot.

"Emily, watch out, your air!" Tank calls out, making an air bubble right next to her.

"Thanks," Emily breathes.

Jake hacks away relentlessly at the dark prismarine. "Why isn't it working? You were mining it just a second ago! Do you think the Wizard is watching us somehow? Figured to make it harder by making everything unbreakable here, too?"

"The elder guardians," Emily says, eyeing the debuff on her screen now that she's been in close range of the guardian. "They have this fatigue effect. It's going to last a while."

"Ugh, I forgot about that," Jake says.

"At least now that we've cleared out all the guardians we can just keep looking super closely to see if there's anything we missed, room by room—ahh!"

"Tank! Are you okay?" Jake calls out.

"Yeah, I thought it was another player at first, but it's like a statue or something. Come check it out!"

Emily swims into the next room. She'd gone through this one earlier and didn't think much about it as there wasn't any treasure, just columns of light and dark prismarine. Tank's in the corner, staring at what she thought was a column earlier, but now with her Night Vision potion activated, she can see it more clearly in detail: a sculpture of a mermaid wielding a trident.

"Whoa, that is neat," Jake says, swimming up to it.

The prismarine statue looks as if it's guarding something, and it is clearly too elaborate to be anything but someone's personal design embedded in the game.

Jake was right. It has to be a clue.

Emily interacts with the statue as if it's a door and is rewarded by the sound of stones heaving and churning apart. The entire wall of the chamber slides open in a complicated motion, stacking and restacking as the wall unfolds to reveal a long hallway leading off to new, unknown depths. The hallway is lined with green and blue glass, glowing faintly with the soft blue light of sea lanterns.

"Wow. It's almost the same decorations as that village," Jake says in awe.

Emily's only seen the images of the seaside village Jake found. But being in the here and now and seeing all of this is exhilarating. Where has the Wizard been leading them all this time?

"Let's go," Tank says decisively.

They swim out away from the monument, following the blue glow of the lanterns in the dark prismarine hallway. The hallway seems to stretch out to eternity, and in this single path, it's unclear where they're going or what they're passing through outside the narrow corridor, or even how far they've come. There is only forward, and Emily presses on.

They set up ladders as stopping points when they run low on air, taking quick breaks to rest before heading down the long, watery hallway again. Who knows what lies ahead?

The light changes, and ahead the sea lanterns disappear.

"Huh. Windows," Jake says.

Blue- and green-glass windows now line the hallway, scant light filtering through the watery path, beckoning them on. Outside, the ocean depths await.

"And more statues," Emily adds.

As they make their way forward, they pass by statues of mermaids alternating with the windows. Emily is sure her eyes are playing tricks on her, since you can't really see subtle expressions in Minecraft, but she thinks they look wary, each of them gripping their tridents, ready to attack at any moment. An unearthly melody plays as they follow the path, and outside in the deep, shadows move a little too deliberately to be fish.

The pathway disappears into darkness, and not just because it's beyond the realm of focus. The sea lanterns sporadically lighting the way have disappeared. Emily's Night Vision is wearing off, throwing everything into shades of dark blue and gray. She can barely see the mermaid statues flanking the pathway, and it's starting to look like they're moving.

Wait.

Are they moving?

"What's that?" Tank gestures at a shadow outside rushing them in the water, speeding from the monument and heading toward wherever the pathway leads.

The shape moves in the distance, coming closer and closer until it's in focus: a mermaid, covered in scales. She doesn't seem to notice them as she swims forward with her trident.

"A mermaid! That's what I'm talking about!" Jake exclaims. "See, we are going in the right direction."

The mermaid overtakes them, swimming ahead, and another one follows. The music quickens, as if these two mermaids were trying to catch up, late to something.

"Oh no," Tank groans. "Are they gonna attack us?"

"Get ready," Emily says, drawing her sword.

"No, no, wait." Jake swims forward after another breath at one of their ladder stopping points. "They're all swimming toward something over there. Can you see it?"

Emily tries to peer out the window, but the angle makes it difficult to see anything except the kelp forest and the occasional fish directly outside their walkway. She readies her pickaxe and prepares to be disappointed if this is also unbreakable.

"Wait, look ahead!" Tank says.

Sea lanterns illuminate a set of double doors at the end of the pathway.

Emily swims forward. She braces herself, switching between weapons, ready for anything. When Jake and Tank catch up to her, she pushes through the doors.

The open ocean beckons them, dark and filled with shifting shadows. Something looms in the distance, some sort of structure.

"Another monument?" Jake asks.

"Looks like a wall," Emily says. "There's stuff behind it, too."

Emily drinks another Night Vision potion and the ocean floor becomes as clear as day. Beyond a stretch of sand dotted with rocks and seagrass, kelp drifts slowly as fish swim in calm circles. Mermaids swim erratically, but as they approach, Emily can see many of them carrying blocks of prismarine and stacking them carefully like a wall. The mermaids with tridents swim back and forth, a nervous energy surrounding them, as if they're waiting for something.

And just beyond the wall, Emily can see it, a vision in sparkling blues and greens and golds, flickering in the soft glitter of secondhand sunlight: the city from the mural. Lights sparkle from blue lanterns hanging outside a myriad of buildings, some small and cozy, some decorated with flags and colors like shops.

Merpeople covered in scales of every color swim through archways between the buildings, flitting in and out, everyone with their own destination and purpose. Temples and monuments loom above the smaller buildings, rising up in tiers around them. Coral and sponges decorate the city, growing in lush multitudes all around them.

It should feel tranquil, but the energy of the merpeople building the wall and those with weapons swimming back and forth make Emily nervous.

"Wow, that's amazing," Tank says. "It's like a whole kingdom of these merpeople just living and doing their own thing. I wonder if they're like villagers with jobs and we can trade with them."

"Probably," Jake says thoughtfully. "But why are they building a wall?"

"Why would anyone build a perimeter wall?" Emily mutters. It feels too easy, just swimming toward the city they've been trying to find the whole game. *Finding* it surely isn't the challenge. Every riddle has had a challenge: a puzzle of logic, mobs to defeat, a maze to solve. If the ocean monument was the sixth challenge . . . then there's still one more. There's something more just lurking beneath the surface here, and if these merpeople are building something—they're trying to keep something out.

As they cross the wide expanse of sand between where the pathway ends and the wall surrounding the city begins, something rumbles in the distance.

The sound gets louder, and then a deep, earth-wrenching *BOOM* reverberates from almost directly underneath them.

"Whoa, what's going on?" Tank asks.

All the merpeople stop what they're doing, those stacking stones carefully on the wall now gripping their tridents with fear.

Emily can see the wall more clearly. The massive hole in the center, the cracks in it, the blocks scattered all across the sand.

She rifles quickly through her inventory to see what she has. What would work best? A bow with Piercing? A sword with Unbreaking? Extra Sharpness? What?

Another rumble, louder this time.

Jake and Tank also draw swords. Emily swivels around, trying to locate the source of the sound, but there's just ocean and the prismarine pathway behind them, and the terrified merpeople trying to protect their kingdom in front of them.

A thunderous cracking noise seems to echo across the ocean floor. It's coming from below them.

"Get ready!" Emily calls out, brandishing her sword. Whatever happens next is going to be excruciatingly difficult, she can tell.

In the sandy field, a massive trench opens up in the deep to reveal glowing molten magma and streams of lava pulsing from below, turning into obsidian all around the trench. Columns of bubbles rise frantically from the magma, and then something *else* starts to push through the blocks of obsidian and magma, breaking them as easily as if they were nothing but sand.

The beast emerges and roars. It frees itself from the magma depths and swims forward, and Emily can see it clearly in all its terrifying glory: a massive creature covered in mottled dark green scales, with long fins billowing out behind it like the sails of a sunken ship. It opens its giant gaping maw and a blast of power shoots out, like an elder guardian magnified a thousand times.

The merfolk scatter just like villagers do when attacked, the builders shrieking in terror, their panicked voices rising higher and higher.

Emily's heart races as the merfolk attack the beast with their tridents, throwing them in swift and decisive arcs. It seems not to matter to the beast, the projectiles nothing more than mere annoyances.

Emily charges forward, because her instinct is calling her to fight, to protect these people, in a story that she never expected to find herself in. "This is it! Let's go!"

Jake and Tank rise up with her, and they swim headfirst toward the massive creature, the three of them so small against the looming monster.

It's Jake who shoots the arrow. It moves impossibly slowly and deals practically no damage, but it draws the attention of the beast, which roars at them. The blast is like a shock wave, pulsing through the water with an intensity that immediately drains all of Emily's health to zero.

```
RoxXStarRedStone was slain by Leviathan
TankFarms was slain by Leviathan
MCExplorerJake was slain by Leviathan
```

CHAPTER THIRTY-THREE

TANK

The Leviathan is the worst.

"There's no way we can defeat this boss," Tank groans. He's tired of Jake's cheerful *One more time?* It's all they've done the past couple of days, and he's sick of it. The first time they went back, they felt so ready. They had trekked all the way from the castle to the base to get more supplies and back, and then set up a spawn point in the cave under the castle. But then the Leviathan killed them instantly with its powerful blasts, and they regrouped and tried again. And again.

He's tired of going through the motions of waking up on the sandy beach, swimming to the ocean monument, the long walk to the mermaid kingdom, and then getting killed by the Leviathan over and over. The sequence where the Leviathan rises out of the deep doesn't stop being terrifying, especially when there seems to be no way to defeat it. They've tried everything, from throwing Potions of Poison to using TNT to fighting the Leviathan with ranged attacks to charging directly at it with swords.

It's the most powerful boss Tank has ever encountered, and he's starting to think that it's hopeless. Nothing they have done has ever made any impact on the monster's health, and it's impossible to get close enough to deal damage anyway with those deadly power blasts. This used to be an adventure, part of an epic quest of discovering new things and solving riddles, but being stuck in a loop of getting killed, losing all their items, going back to the base and crafting more, and doing it again is not fun at all.

Jake's already come up with another plan. "What if we enchanted the arrows—"

"Tridents," Emily says. "They're the most effective underwater weapon."

"There's no way to craft a trident," Jake groans. "We have to find some drowned that have them, and that's random! Let's just stick to what we have!" He glares at Emily. "If you actually stuck to the plan, I'm sure we could take it! Okay, let's go over it again. Once we cross the field, that prompts the Leviathan's entrance. Now, if we split up and get in position—"

"The plan *sucks*!" Emily throws her hands up in the air.

Tank has to agree. Jake tends to overprepare, and it takes forever to get the enchantments they keep having to replace. Emily had to engineer a skeleton farm for them to level up quickly, but everything about this week has been tedious, frustrating, or boring.

The community center is also the cleanest it's ever been. They've stopped pretending that it's why they're here, because the rooms are all neat and tidy, all their contents carefully organized, labeled, and boxed away. All of them have been brought to Ellen's doorstep, all of them except one empty box for the last three computers. There's no need to be here anymore, aside from finishing this game. Tank supposes they could just pack up the last of it and bring the gate key back to Mrs. Jenkins, but once that's done, they won't be able to come back.

"It wouldn't suck if you stopped charging in headfirst and then dying! Look, we've got it timed: as soon as you walk down the pathway you have three minutes before the Leviathan wakes and comes up from the trench. As long as we are far enough away, we can avoid the blasts!"

"There's no way to avoid the blasts, they go forever! We don't need to plan out every single detail, Jake!"

"We do have to plan in order to figure out how to defeat this Leviathan! We've got to be missing something."

Tank sighs. "Hey."

The two of them ignore him, their voices getting louder and louder as they argue about melee versus ranged weapons.

"All we have to do is coordinate the attack so we do enough damage over the long run!" Jake throws his hands up in the air.

Emily shakes her head, spinning in the computer chair. "I still think we're missing something. I feel like the Leviathan can't be taken down using any of our normal weapons."

Scratch that, *this* is the worst. Tank never thought his friends would treat him like this, like what he has to say doesn't matter.

"Hey!" Tank stands up, pushing the chair back. He towers over the two of them, and he folds his arms together.

"Do you have a better idea, Tank?" Emily scowls. "Wanna build a maze so the Leviathan gets stuck in it?"

The jab hurts far more than Tank expects, and he bristles. "Look, who says we have to finish *this* game?" He gestures at the clean computer room around them. Everything aside from the three computers they've been using has been stacked against the wall, and the room is bare. "We're done with the service project." They don't have to solve the mystery just because it's here, tied to the server. They can start their own world or even continue playing this one and build new things. There are endless possibilities. That's the fun of Minecraft.

Emily blinks. Hurt and confusion flash across her face for a moment before they disappear. She stands up a little straighter and sniffs.

"You're right, Tank," she says, flipping her hair behind her with a certain finality. "We *are* done. We don't have to finish this, and I can't believe I wasted so much time with you two anyways." She disconnects and then stands up without looking at them. She smooths her dress and flounces out of the room.

Jake casts one horrified look at Tank before running after her. "Why'd you say that, man!?"

"I didn't mean—"

Jake's already out the door.

Tank groans and follows him.

The empty lobby echoes with his footsteps. The furniture has already been taken away, the floor bare and the windows scrubbed clean. It's strange how Tank has come to think of this place as something he's looked forward to, this lobby a portal on his way to adventure with Emily and Jake in Minecraft or hours spent laughing and enjoying lunch together.

Emily pushes open the glass doors and walks through the construction site to the fence separating them from the courtyard.

Jake has his arms spread out, blocking Emily from the gate.

"Get out of the way, Jake. I'm going home."

"You can't leave! You're the one who said we started this together and we're going to finish it together!" Jake's voice is pitched high with desperation. "Emily, please! Come on! I know the Leviathan is hard, but it's the very last boss and we can win this together!"

Emily taps her foot on the ground, her shoes clicking impatiently with a staccato rhythm. "What do you think is going to happen when we finish the game in the server, Jake?"

"I—" Jake looks at Tank like he has the answer.

We can start our own world, Tank has on the tip of his tongue, but before he can say anything, Emily jumps right back in.

"You think when high school starts that I can hang out with the two of you?" Emily laughs and shakes her head in disbelief. "That's not the way it works, okay." She pushes past Jake into the courtyard.

The words sink like a heavy stone. Tank's been dreading this the whole summer.

He knows she's right. It's going to be just like middle school, but worse. Everything he's heard about high school is that it's rough, that all it takes is one misstep and you're the one being made fun of in the hallways.

Jake follows her and gestures at Tank to come with.

He steps through the gate, his shoulders slumping with defeat. No matter what Jake says now, Emily's already made her decision.

"Oh my *gosh*, Emily! It's been forever!"

Tank pauses at the excited squeal coming from the courtyard. A girl is waving excitedly at them—no, at Emily—and another girl is pushing her way through the south entrance gate. The two of them practically run across the courtyard, flinging their arms around Emily, whose eyes widen in shock. Tank recognizes the two of them from school—Pattie and Nita, part of that popular crowd he's learned to avoid, kids who spend lunchtime holding court in the cafeteria and making fun of guys like Tank.

Emily's eyes widen in shock. "Pattie, what are you doing here?"

Pattie toys with a stray curl that's fallen out of her bun. "My mom called your mom to see if she wanted to be in the PTA and there's gonna be a welcome-back-to-school bake night, and I was so surprised because I thought you were still grounded, but your mom said no of course we could come over anytime! And then funnily enough when I got your address it was different, did you move?"

She's speaking so fast that Tank has to wonder how she's even breathing.

Pattie's eyes flick from Tank awkwardly hovering in front of the construction site to Jake standing stiffly behind Emily, and she wrinkles her nose like she's smelled something sour. "What's going on? Who are these guys?"

Emily's eyes meet Tank's, and he doesn't see the funny, courageous girl he's come to know. There's a wall she's thrown up between them, and she's a million miles away.

"No one," Emily says. "Just some guys I was doing my community service with." She laughs, throwing her arm around Pattie's shoulders, and walks directly past Jake.

"Whatever! It's not like I wanted to be friends with you anyway," Jake says, his lip wobbling. "I had a much better time playing on my own anyhow. I don't need to be babysitting a reckless fighter with no impulse control or a guy who just wants to build pretty mazes."

"I thought you . . ." Tank takes a step back. He thought Jake said he didn't care that was what he liked, making pretty things. He thought they would never make fun of him for what he liked to do.

Apparently he was wrong.

It seems like Emily heard Jake, too, her shoulders stiffening as she quickens her pace and disappears across the courtyard and into her tower without another look back.

Jake seems to return from whatever embarrassed dimension he was transported to, and he looks at Tank and then back at his feet. "I—"

"Okay. Yeah. You're right," Tank says, feeling defeated. "We just played Minecraft together. It's not like we could be friends. And we couldn't even do that well. Some team we were." The past couple of days they've just been going in circles, trying and failing to defeat the Leviathan. Maybe it's better this way. The service project is over, and the community center is going to get torn down. The server was just something interesting they were doing to pass the time, and now that time is over.

His phone buzzes in his pocket.

Shark 11:21 A.M.
We're hanging out Friday. Remember what I said. I'll see you at your place.

Tank looks up at Jake. He's spent this whole summer avoiding the reality of who he is, who people see him as. It would be pointless to pretend he could be anything else.

Tank shakes his head. "Emily's right, you know. People like us—we all have a specific place where we belong. This wouldn't—" Tank clears his throat. "It wouldn't have worked. We're all too different, and yeah, hanging out while working on the community center was fine, but now that's over."

Jake's mouth falls open, and then he closes it, his eyes glittering.

Tank gives Jake one more look before he heads home. "When school starts, it'll be better that we pretend we just don't know each other." He looks down at his phone and walks away from Jake, from the community center, from everything he was pretending he could have.

Tank taps out a simple *Yes*.

CHAPTER THIRTY-FOUR

JAKE

Jake can't believe this. He keeps turning over the morning's events in his head, lying down in his bed. It feels like it happened so fast, the way Emily and Tank just left. Jake had felt the blood rushing to his head and he found himself knocking on Ellen's door. She'd answered with a smile that Jake couldn't return.

"We're done," Jake said, the words heavy and final and awful. He hands her the key. "There's uh, three computers still, and a box for them. And that table. I can—I can get it for you."

"Oh, don't worry about that. The recycling crew is just gonna come by my place anyway, they can go get that stuff directly from there." She smiles at him kindly, looking like the grandmother Jake thought she was when they first met. "So you're all done, huh? Did you have fun?"

"Yeah." Jake's voice sounds even more hollow than he feels.

"Oh?" Ellen says. "That's great—I baked cookies, if you and your friends—"

Jake wanted to throw up, and all he could manage was a brief shake before he found himself running all the way home.

It feels weird to be home during the day, weird to be here and not in the community center. He sits in his bedroom, opening his laptop. He has Wi-Fi. The cable company connected it a while ago, but it didn't seem important when the best game he's ever played is on a rinky-dink server in a building about to be torn down.

He buries his head in his pillow and groans.

"Hey, are you okay?"

Jake looks up. Dad hesitates in the doorway of his bedroom, holding his clipboard and a thick sheaf of folders.

"I heard from Ellen that you're done with the community service project. That's great!"

"Yup. We're done," Jake says with finality.

Dad steps inside, sitting on the bed beside him. "You know, I'm really proud of you. You dealt with the consequences of breaking the rules, and you went above and beyond in helping a senior citizen."

Jake doesn't look up from his pillow. He wants to just disappear and pretend nothing else exists outside of the soft cotton dinosaur-print sheets.

Wait, he can disappear. "Dad, are you done with Pacific Crest? The project? We can move now, right?"

Dad shakes his head and smiles. "I told you, I'm staying put for you, buddy. I want you to be able to finish high school without worrying about making new friends every year."

"But—"

"I'm keeping my promises." Dad sighs. "I know I haven't always been here for you, but this has been a good summer, right? We've had a good time, and you know, those baseball games happen every year, and you've been telling me all about your new friends. I think that's great." He smiles, looking around Jake's room. "This place looks good, Jake."

Jake glances around his bedroom. His desk is cluttered with notepads and scribblings, drawings of the Leviathan and the underwater kingdom, pages with coordinates scattered across them, a Polaroid Emily gave him of the three of them having lunch in the courtyard. His clothes are in the drawers because he kept getting tired of rooting through his suitcase, and the bookshelf is full because it was easier than going through the boxes every time he and Tank exchanged comics. Somehow without realizing it, he's settled in here.

But it doesn't matter anymore. It's over. Tank and Emily are just going to ignore him when he starts school, and he's going to just be the new kid again.

Or maybe it'll be worse. Worse now knowing that they had a good time together, that every time he sees them he'll just remember the way Emily looked at him when she walked off, like he was no one, the way Tank shrank away from him when he said those awful things. He regrets it now, of course. It's annoying playing with them sometimes, but it was good. They were a good team.

"Hey. I know what might cheer you up. You always wanted to swing a sledgehammer at a wall if it needed to come down, right? I bet when we do the renovation I can bring you on the site and you can take a few swings, eh? How about that? Isabella told me they're starting on Monday! Isn't that exciting?"

Right. The renovation. They came so close to solving the mystery. They found the city. Jake thinks about the poor mermaids in their underwater kingdom, cursed to be besieged by an awful monster every day with no one to help them.

Now no one ever will.

After Dad goes back to work, Jake plods around the apartment listlessly, staring at the TV, flipping channels idly, attempting to watch a movie, and not enjoying any of it. He opens his phone to text Danny to see if he wants to play Minecraft in their server, but he realizes that Danny never responded to his last message from two weeks ago. Jake sighs. He's been worried they've been drifting apart for years now, but it's one thing to suspect it and another thing to see it confirmed. Jake boots up Minecraft and opens his old worlds, going back to them for the first time in a long time.

It's not the same.

Every single achievement he's made, the cool worlds he's built, he just wants to show them to his friends. He misses going on their adventures, he misses the way Emily yells when she recklessly charges right into a mob of monsters, and Tank's blunt comments that are just so weirdly funny.

Apparently the renovation is starting Monday and it'll all be over.

Maybe there's something Jake missed. Maybe there's a way to defeat the Leviathan.

He makes his way toward the community center. Now that their service project is officially complete, technically he shouldn't be in there, but he hasn't seen the construction crews back yet and Grant usually doesn't start until ten P.M., so Jake's got time. He can slip between that crack in the fence.

The weeds in the courtyard rustle as Jake pushes through the overgrown mess, and he pauses as an annoyed voice rings through the air.

"I'm not hungry, and you can't keep doing this, Mom. You can't keep showing up where I work."

"I didn't show up, I live here, too, and I manage this building! Where else would I be?" That's Mrs. Jenkins's—Ellen's—voice. It's weird, calling adults by their first name, but she's not as scary as she thinks she is. And she brought them lunch that time, which was nice.

She's walking with another woman—her daughter? Jake ducks behind a shrubbery.

Heeled shoes tap against the pavement with sharp clacks as they walk past Jake's shrubbery. He recognizes the woman in the sleek business suit walking away from Ellen, holding a clipboard. Isabella Reyes, the new owner of the building.

Wait. *Mom?* She's Ellen's daughter?

"Come on, you have to eat. You said it yourself, you're really busy all the time, and I've already made the food, you don't have to—"

"Look, I see what you're trying to do here, and I don't want it." Isabella grips the clipboard to herself like a shield. "It's too late, okay? I don't need you to nag me about dinner or anything. I've got my own life and my own business—"

"I know, I know, you're really successful. I'm real proud of you, you know—"

"You don't get to be proud of me," Isabella hisses. "You had nothing to do with this. Just leave me alone."

She stomps off, the sound of her heels fading away into the distance.

Ellen watches her go, her chin wobbling. She wipes hastily at her face, and Jake scoots back, trying to slink into the shadows. Something behind him topples over and clangs against the pavement—an empty soda can.

Ellen whirls around and spots Jake in the shrubbery.

He gulps. He wishes he had an Invisibility potion or some easy way to disappear, but there's nothing he can do except run.

CHAPTER THIRTY-FIVE

EMILY

"Your room is *so cute*! I can't believe we've never been here!" Pattie's voice is a high trill as she flounces into Emily's bedroom. She reaches for Emily, a wide smile on her face.

Pattie wraps both her arms around Emily and pulls her close, giggling. "It's so good to see you!"

"Good to see you, too," Emily says, smiling in spite of herself.

Nita joins the hug, pulling them both close with a soft smile. "It's been way too long," she says. "We gotta post a reunion pic!" She extends her arm and it's like no time has passed, the three of them smiling for the camera.

Nita giggles as she snaps a few of them and then busies herself with filters and shows Emily and Pattie a few options before Pattie approves the final.

Emily realizes that she's missed this, how nice it is spending time with Pattie and Nita. She's missed Pattie's endless stream of ideas and Nita's ridiculous puns, Pattie's charming confidence and Nita's constant affirmations, how they always had a way to turn a boring afternoon into one filled with excitement and joy. And they are friends, even with all the doubts and insecurities and games in this relationship.

It's just like before with the three of them, except they're here now in Emily's space.

Pattie and Nita haven't said anything about the run-down apartment complex yet.

The two girls are sitting on Emily's floral bedspread, looking all around her room. A room that they've never been in, despite the many times they've hung out together. Emily shifts nervously as they take in the details: the fairy lights strung up above her bed, the messy closet, the desk cluttered with Polaroids and her camera sitting proudly on top.

Emily realizes with a start that amongst the mix of photos of nature and architectural elements she's been snapping all summer there are also a bunch of random pictures of Jake and Tank: Tank wearing a weird hat they'd found and Jake laughing in the background; Jake dancing with a mop; Tank holding up a bouquet of daisies he'd picked on one of their walks, grinning and pointing at the flowers; and one of the three of them wearing the matching masks Jake brought, their eyes shining with the smiles hidden behind the fabric.

Guilt seeps into her when she thinks about the way Jake's lip wobbled as she walked away. Looking at the photos, Emily feels a pang of sadness. Sure, sometimes they were annoying, and trying over and over to defeat the Leviathan absolutely sucked, but spending time with the boys, playing Minecraft with them . . . it was nice, not having to hide that part of herself.

She sweeps the photos into an open drawer, quickly hiding them from view. It was nice, but it's back to reality now. It's all for the best, anyway. Her heart feels like it's shattering into a million pieces, but it's better like this, to hurt now rather than spend more time pretending that she can have it all.

With Pattie and Nita back, she knows it would have been only a matter of time before they found her out, and it's not like she could have led a double life.

"Sorry it's such a mess," Emily says.

"Oh no, I love your setup!" Nita squeals.

Pattie nods her approval. "We should film here. The lighting is so perfect, and this background with the curtains you have would be so, so gorgeous." She glances at Emily quickly before scrolling through her phone, but she doesn't say anything about the apartment after Emily didn't respond to her question about moving.

It's a test. It has to be. She has to know Emily was lying the whole time about where she lived. But Pattie doesn't say anything else about it.

Emily shrugs. "Oh, it's just that your house is so beautiful, I always thought it was the best setup for filming your videos," she says casually. "And you have that classic minimalist decor, it really goes well with all the haul videos, and this is just so cluttered."

Pattie laughs. "Well, we can do other types of videos here!" She squeals in delight. "Em, we have so much to catch up on! First, I have so many ideas for your channel."

Emily's heart sinks as they dive right back into plans for You-Tube. She can't even enjoy that Pattie wants to actually feature her because she realizes that while she loves planning outfits with her friends, she'd really rather just hang out than pretend to be into working on a YouTube channel.

"Aw, this is adorable! Did your little sister draw this?" Nita flips through a colorful book on Emily's bedside table.

Emily takes the book Nita offers her—oh. It's the mermaid book that kid from the center drew a while ago. She'd taken it because she thought the twins would enjoy looking at the pictures, and Mama was asking for more picture books to read to them, but she'd forgotten about it.

"It's something one of the kids in the community center drew back when it was a thing," Emily says. "I thought it was cute . . ." She trails off, her fingers lingering on the page.

In green and black crayon, clearly outlined, is the Leviathan.

Emily rereads the story, her heart racing.

"Sorry, I forgot I have to do this thing," Emily says. "Can we hang out another time?"

CHAPTER THIRTY-SIX

JAKE

"**D**id you know that Isabella is Mrs. Jenkins's daughter?" Jake asks Dad over dinner.

He'd gone right back home after she caught him watching her from the bushes, her sharp eyes following like a hawk. There was no way he could go back to the center with her watching him like that, especially after they were supposed to be done.

"Huh? Oh, yeah. It's been a major pain for this whole project, since she doesn't want anything to do with her mom," Dad says.

"Why?"

Dad sighs and looks at his plate. "Something to do with Ellen not really being around when she was a kid."

Jake pokes at his food, twirling spaghetti onto his fork until he can't get any more wrapped around the utensil. "The community center and these apartments—did Isabella grow up here? Why would she want to change everything?"

Dad shrugs. "Bad memories, I guess. She wants to turn it into something new, something better."

Jake thinks about the photo of the girl in the pictures, looking up at her parents, and wonders what could have happened.

"Did you know the community center used to have all these programs and stuff? I found lots of old photos and articles while cleaning it out," Jake says. "There were, like, beach cleanups and camping trips and kids were there all the time."

Dad nods. "Yeah, it sounds like it was great back in its heyday. Back in Seattle, when Isabella first hired me as the project manager for this complex, we talked a bit about the designs and she asked me for any input given my experience. One of the first designs I submitted had a place for a center like that, but Isabella hated it immediately. I think she resented the fact that her mother spent more time with those other kids than she did with her, but I don't know the full story." He gives his spaghetti bolognese a sadder look than it deserves. "Look, you know that I'm trying my best, right?"

"I know, Dad." Jake looks down at his plate.

"You know, at the beginning of the summer I said a lot of things, about spending time together and everything. I know we weren't able to go to that Dodgers game like I said, or go to the beach, but I've been really busy. I know that it probably just sounds like excuses to you, but I'm serious. I know after your mom passed away, I wasn't . . . I wasn't great." Dad gulps, his chin wobbling. "I was just running away, you know? Anytime it would feel too close to what we used to have, it would scare me."

Jake's always thought Dad was larger than life, maybe because he hung out with all these tough people who built things and worked hard making cool stuff. He's always been in charge, an intimidating man who gets his way, one who always has an answer.

Now he looks nervous and small the way he hunches his shoulders and looks up at Jake.

"I get it," Jake says. "I think I was like that, too. New schools, new people. I'd always start out wanting to talk to people and trying to make friends but didn't bother keeping it up because I knew we would move again. I didn't want to get attached to anyone, so I didn't really give anyone a chance."

"I'm so proud of you," Dad says. "The way you jumped into this service project, and making friends with Emily and Tank—they're good kids. Like you're a good kid."

Jake doesn't feel like a good kid. He feels terrible. It was his fault Emily and Tank left; they didn't like the plans, he shouldn't have been so pushy about them, and now the center is going to be destroyed and they're never going to be able to finish the game.

His eyes blur with what definitely aren't hot tears. Jake jabs at his plate with his fork and twirls a gigantic mass of noodles before shoving them into his mouth. The spaghetti sticks to the roof of his mouth, and Jake thinks about how Dad used to just order takeout for him or leave him money to fend for himself. But tonight he watched a dozen YouTube videos to figure out how to make the sauce from scratch, and then asked Jake to make the noodles with him. It had been fun and totally new and different and Jake doesn't know what to do with this Dad who tries. Now they're going to *stay* in this place and Jake's ruined it, ruined it all with his friends.

He takes another bite and just chews and nods so he doesn't have to talk.

"You know you can talk to me anytime, okay? Doesn't matter. I know I might not understand everything, but I sure am gonna try."

Jake swallows. "Dad, I think I messed up." The story tumbles out in bits and pieces: finding the server, playing with Emily and Tank, becoming friends—or so Jake had thought—and then their fight that morning. Jake's voice wobbles.

"You can ground me. I know that the service project was supposed to be a punishment, and instead we've just been playing this game."

Dad chuckles. "I think you're not giving yourself enough credit—it sounds like you and your friends got all the work done to organize things for Ellen, and you also discovered a great game."

"Right." Jake sighs. "But now there's no point. Everyone hates me, and there's no way we can save the mermaid kingdom before the whole place vanishes completely."

"Sometimes people say things they don't mean," Dad says. "I think your friends will understand. Just apologize to them and be honest and tell them exactly what you told me."

It can't just be that simple.

Can it?

Jake knocks on Tank's door, his heart pounding nervously. He paces back and forth, the apology thick in the back of his throat.

The door opens and Vivian looks curiously up at him. Jake looks at the ground, dragging his shoe awkwardly. "Hey. Um, is Tank home?"

Viv shakes her head. "Hanging out with Shark, I think."

"Oh."

"Want me to tell him you stopped by?"

"I'll text him, I'll—" Jake doesn't know what to do. He doesn't want to apologize over text message. "I'll just come back later."

He leaves the West Tower and cuts through the courtyard to the North Tower, bounding up the stairwell and down the hallway toward Emily's apartment. He knocks and waits, wondering if she's spending time with her other friends, too. *Everyone has someone they'd rather be with than you*, he thinks glumly.

The door opens, and Emily's older sister Carmen looks down at him with a bored glance. "Hello? Oh, it's you," she says. "Emily isn't home."

"Do you know when she'll be back?" Jake asks nervously. He could text her, but he feels like this is important to do in person.

"No idea. Bye." She rolls her eyes and shuts the door, leaving Jake to his thoughts.

He walks toward the stairwell when a light on in the community center catches his eye.

Jake races downstairs and runs across the courtyard, his heart skipping as he slips between the crack in the chain-link fence and ducks under the caution tape. He throws open the door to the computer lab.

It's empty, but one of the computers is on. Jake frowns, looking around. "Hello? Is anyone here? Emily? Tank?"

He sits down. The Minecraft window is open, like someone had been playing recently.

Jake eagerly logs in when he sees the notification on the loading screen that one player is already in the world. Maybe Emily and Tank weren't ready to let this go. The fact that they came back here must mean something, right?

He spawns on the strip of sand inside the cavern underneath

the castle. He looks at the other two beds with a pang of sadness, thinking about his friends and how much they've gone through together to solve this. There's no one around the little area, but they could be somewhere else in the world.

The recent chat log doesn't have anything except the last time the three of them logged out together . . . except for one new line that makes Jake's heart skip.

TheCrestWizard has joined the game.

Jake looks around. The Wizard hasn't shown up since that first time he attacked them, but they've been playing this game, following his clues. Why appear now?

< MCExplorerJake > hello? wizard?

< MCExplorerJake > we've been fighting the leviathan. Is there any way to defeat it?

< TheCrestWizard > Of course there is.

< MCExplorerJake > is there one riddle we're missing? What do we need to do?

There's no answer.

Jake dives down toward the ocean monument and follows the pathway. He has to see the Leviathan one more time, to see if there's any clue he's missed. If the Wizard is here, surely it's to help them.

< MCExplorerJake > you built that shortcut through the Nether, you've helped us before. Is that why you're here now?

Jake opens the door at the end of the pathway. Outside, standing just before the stretch of sandy field, is the Wizard, staring out toward the mermaid kingdom.

< MCExplorerJake > hey! are you here to play with us? Let me get my friends!

< TheCrestWizard > There is no point. I made this game so many years ago, but I don't remember how to defeat this creature I created.

< MCExplorerJake > you don't have notes or anything?

< TheCrestWizard > I have gotten rid of so many things that reminded me of the past. I'm sorry.

Jake stares at the avatar; it's just a collection of pixels, but the Wizard seems to be lost in thought, staring off into the distance.

< MCExplorerJake > but you've helped us before!

< TheCrestWizard > Do you want to see the end? I can just bring you there.

Just teleport into the kingdom? That's no victory. Jake wants to be a part of the story, to save the merfolk from this monster.

< MCExplorerJake > no way! that would just defeat the purpose of playing the game

< MCExplorerJake > I just feel like we're missing something!

< TheCrestWizard > I don't remember where it is or how to get it. I could just look through the code, but that would take ages. And the renovation is beginning tomorrow, and they're ripping out the land lines. There's no point.

The Wizard steps forward, and the sequence happens exactly how Jake has seen it happen so many times before: The crack opens and the Leviathan rises. A single blast of power emits from its mouth, catching the Wizard before an attack can even be made.

`TheCrestWizard was slain by Leviathan`

Jake stares. He wasn't sure what he'd expected, but that certainly wasn't it. Is the Wizard just giving up?

`TheCrestWizard has joined the game.`

`< TheCrestWizard > Thank you for the adventure.`

`TheCrestWizard has left the game.`

The Leviathan lunges at him, eyes glowing bright red. Jake disconnects before it reaches him, and then sits back against his chair in a defeated slump.

The Minecraft opening screen lingers, waiting for his choices on how he wants to play. The evocative music seems to mock him now.

The door flies open.

"There you are!" Emily says, wide-eyed and gasping for breath, holding a notebook in her hands. "Why weren't you home?"

"You went to my apartment? I went to *your* apartment!" Jake blinks at her. "Your sister said you weren't home."

Emily approaches him, her eyes lit up with excitement as she waves the book in the air. "I found something—I—" She falters, hesitating as she stops a few steps away.

They look at each other for a long moment, and Jake takes a deep breath. His dad's words echo in his head, and he thinks about Ellen and her daughter and how they can't even talk to each other. He doesn't want to have regrets like that, he doesn't want to miss out on having friends.

"I'm sorry," Jake says.

"I'm sorry!" Emily blurts out at the same time.

They take a second to laugh, and then laugh again when they both make gestures for the other to continue. It's a little awkward, but Jake's glad to see her smile a little.

"I didn't mean what I said, you know," Jake says. "I think your gamer style is awesome, Emily. It's way different than what I'm used to, but it works for you."

"I think your style is cool, too," Emily says. She looks at her feet nervously and then back at Jake. "I really like hanging out with you and Tank, but Pattie showed up and I was so frustrated with the Leviathan and the game ending . . ."

Jake nods. "I get it. And I know I'm a loser . . . you don't have to hang out with me at school if you don't want to."

Emily shakes her head. "You know what? I'm going to figure this out. Like you said, it's not like there's a limited number of slots for friends, right?"

"Right," Jake says. "Friends?" He puts his hand out to Emily for a fist bump, and she knocks knuckles with him, smiling.

He grins back, thinking about the first time all three of them had played together. They fit together like clockwork, solving the riddles, each of them bringing a different strength. Emily's fighting skills, Tank's patient problem-solving—

"I gotta talk to Tank," Jake says. "He probably hates me."

"Let's go find him," Emily says. "Especially since I think we can solve the puzzle." She flips open the notebook she's holding—

the crayon drawings of the mermaid story they'd found a while ago. "This look familiar?" Emily flips open to a page featuring the Leviathan. A single mermaid stands in front of it, holding a gleaming golden trident.

Jake gasps.

"That's it! The secret weapon!" Jake can't help jumping up and down with excitement. Hope rises up in his chest, and he feels recharged. They can still do this.

CHAPTER THIRTY-SEVEN

TANK

Tank has been dreading Friday all week, but when it arrives he's almost relieved. Shark is already there when Tank shows up in the alleyway by the recycling bins. The boy is pacing back and forth, kicking a stray soda can. It clatters against the wall of the North Tower, bouncing with an aluminum *clang* and coming to rest at Tank's feet.

"Hey," Tank says, announcing himself.

Shark grins at him, the metal on his teeth glinting unnaturally in the yellow lights drifting in from the courtyard. "I got a treat for you."

"Yeah?" Tank folds his arms together, not expecting much. Shark's last present was hair gel because he wanted all the guys to have the same slicked-back look.

"You know those sneakers you've wanted for forever? And that I said I could get them for you for cheap?"

"I don't have all the money yet," Tank says. He's been saving his money slowly, but he hasn't been putting in any shifts since Mr. Mishra hired Ba for real to fix up things around his shop. The shoes seem like a distant memory. Sure, they'd be cool, but he doesn't need to have them now. Plus it's been nice, with Ba having something to focus on other than their apartment. They even had a weird conversation this morning. Tank's still trying to process it.

For as long as he can remember, Ba has always tried to be fun and cool and do his own thing. It had annoyed Tank to no end, especially since he was the one having to fix Ba's messes. But that morning, Ba had made him breakfast and sat down across from him and handed him an envelope with some cash. "You don't have to work so hard, Thanh," Ba had said. "I'm sorry if you thought you had to be a grown-up. That's my job."

"Oh," Tank said.

"I got Vivian some of those programming books she was interested in. You don't—you don't need to have an after-school job, okay? Your Ma and me, we can take care of you. You're a good kid, Thanh. I'm happy you're so responsible. But you deserve to be a kid."

Tank is still thinking about it now, thinking about getting to be a kid and what he wants. Maybe he does want those sneakers. But he doesn't need them now. He can wait.

Shark laughs and shakes his head. "Good news. Turns out, my brother needs a little help on his"—Shark smiles, slow and wide—"shopping run. If you come help, I'm sure he can throw in those shoes for you. Size eleven, right?"

Tank blinks slowly at him. "What do you mean, 'shopping run'? I thought your brother worked at Shoes N' More and you said he just needs to use his employee discount."

"Nah. He got fired, so he's gonna just take what he can tonight." Shark jerks his head at the car lingering in the street. A guy with Shark's wide forehead is leaning out the window. He gives Shark and Tank a little wave. "He needs real muscle to come help."

"What about AJ and Gus?"

"Those guys would be useless. I need *you*, man." Shark grabs Tank's arm and pretends to flex his bicep for him. "You're big and scary and anyone would think twice if they saw you with us."

Tank flinches, jerking away from Shark's grimy hands. He hates that his size is what everybody sees. It's the only reason Shark wanted to be his friend in the first place.

And when has Shark ever taken into account what Tank's wanted? He doesn't care about slicking back his hair, he doesn't care about intimidating other kids at Fortress Park so they can have game tickets, and he doesn't like it when people are afraid of him.

Tank thinks about how Mr. Mishra is always working so hard, how long it takes Tank to make enough money to help with the groceries and the rent, about his parents and how much time they spend working to make sure the family keeps going. He thinks about how long it takes to build an intricate hedge maze and the satisfaction of putting in the work to complete a design.

Tank's always been a follower.

But he doesn't have to be.

"No," he says, planting his feet. The concrete feels firm against his shoes. This feels steady, good, solid.

"It's just moving some boxes from the store to Chris's car. Come on."

Tank crosses his arms. "No way. I'm not helping him steal stuff."

Shark's eyes flash in anger. "Are you serious? After all I've done for you?"

"You haven't done anything for me."

"You know what everyone at school used to call you? Frankenstein. Yeah. Like the monster. Because of that stupid sweater you wore in seventh grade." Shark folds his arms, looking up at Tank with a cold glare. "Because that's what you look like. Me? I saw opportunity. I turned your name into something cool."

The word *opportunity* bites through the air. This is the only reason why Shark bothers to hang out with him—because he's big and tough-looking, and he makes Shark look cool. Shark doesn't actually care about Tank at all.

"I don't want to go," Tank says.

"Think you're too good for us, then? You're nobody, Tank. You're nothing but a loser. You're gonna regret this. I'm gonna make you feel so sorry you ever said no to me." Shark gestures at Chris in the car, and steps forward with a menacing grin. "And you know what? I was the one who started the Frankenstein name in the first place. And I can definitely bring it back."

Tank takes a step back instinctively. For all people assume about him, he's never actually been in a fight before. He gulps, watching Shark's brother get out of the car and start walking toward him. His back is to the recycling bins, and Shark is blocking the only exit to the courtyard or to the street.

He doesn't want to hurt anyone. He doesn't want to get hurt, either.

Shark makes a fist, punching his open palm with a grin. "That's right."

Tank backs up into the bins, throwing his hands up. This is it. He's done for. Shark and his brother are going to beat him up, and then everyone at school is going to laugh at him forever—

The loud blare of police sirens cuts suddenly through the air, shrill whoops that pierce the alleyway.

"What the—" Shark stumbles backward.

A voice crackles, as if over a loudspeaker. "Be on the lookout for suspicious activity, we are looking for a former employee of Shoes N' More, brunette—"

Chris grabs Shark roughly by the shoulder. "Let's get out of here!"

Tank watches them rush to the car and speed off into the night. He blinks, looking for a police car, but doesn't see anything.

"Up here!"

Jake and Emily peer over the open stairwell ledge and wave at him.

"You know, it's amazing what you can do with a voice filter," Emily says proudly. "You okay?"

"Yeah," Tank says in amazement.

From the floor above, a stairwell door clangs shut, and a few moments later, Jake and Emily bound out of the side door into the alleyway.

"Hey," Jake says. "I wanted to say I'm sorry. I didn't mean what I said this morning. I think you're a great player, and it's really cool that you like to decorate, and the flowers look great. Your farms are super efficient and amazing." He takes a deep breath. "I really like hanging out with you, Tank."

"Me too," Emily adds. "I'm sorry. What I said in the center— I didn't mean that we weren't friends, and that spending time with you this summer was a waste or anything. It's actually been really awesome. Like, the best. I got caught up in my friends from school, but you two are my friends, too. If you still want to be."

"Yeah? Friends?" Tank asks with a small smile. He looks off into the distance, a slow pleased happiness growing in his belly. His friends came back for him. Because they cared.

"Of course," Jake says.

Emily nods quickly as well.

"I don't think I'm going to be hanging out with Shark and those guys anymore," Tank says decisively. "I don't even think he liked me at all. He just wanted me around because I was tough-looking and made him look cooler."

Emily laughs. "Come on, Tank. We know that you're the coolest."

Tank chuckles. He does feel pretty cool with Emily and Jake by his side, the three of them having adventures together, making jokes in the community center, going on long walks, and hanging out. He's glad they feel the same way.

"Oh, you know when I said we didn't have to finish the game, I didn't mean I wanted to stop playing with you guys," Tank says. "I meant like, we don't have to defeat the Leviathan. We can start a new world, or just keep exploring, or just build fun things together. We can do anything."

Emily pushes a notebook at him. "What if we *can* defeat the Leviathan?"

CHAPTER THIRTY-EIGHT

JAKE

"The king and queen gave her a magic spell so she could journey to the world above and find the one weapon that could destroy the monster and save the kingdom," Jake reads aloud. Some of the words are written in a neat, rounded hand, and some are in the clumsy child's scrawl. The story fills out about half the notebook, a few words on each page, the majority of the space dedicated to the clumsy crayon illustrations—the merfolk in their peaceful kingdom, the Leviathan, the mermaid princess transforming into a human and adventuring through the Minecraft world and then returning with the trident.

"Let me see it again," Tank says. He frowns, a wrinkle starting between his eyebrows. "I forgot we found this. It's great, but it doesn't exactly show us how to defeat the Leviathan." He looks out the window. "And with construction starting tomorrow, I don't think we have the time."

Jake flips through the pages again. "You're right. This book just proves that the Wizard had based it on this story, but there's a lot more that we don't know. Like all the riddles we solved, they're not all in here."

Emily sighs. "But there *is* a solution. We just have to find this magical trident. All we have to do is solve the entire game for real, without the Wizard's shortcuts—"

"We need more time," Tank says.

Jake takes a deep breath. "You know, it won't hurt to ask. Isabella Reyes, the new owner of the building? She's the one doing all the renovations. Remember we found all those photos about how cool the community center used to be? What if we show her how important it was, and how cool it would be again?" He tries to remember how Dad always talked about pitching projects. "And we can talk about our own personal experience, and why it's important to us. Why having a space like this is important to make friends."

Emily and Tank glance at each other. "I think it's a long shot."

"If we don't try, then we'll never know," Jake says.

Tank nods. "Let's go for it. How do we find her?"

"Shh!" Jake whispers as he gestures for Tank and Emily to head inside his apartment. He sneaks in, padding softly across the carpet. A soft *thump* sounds next to him, and Jake whirls around to see Tank stumbling over a footstool.

Sorry, he mouths, setting it back upright.

The door to Dad's office is open, and Jake can hear him clicking away. The *tap-tap-tap* of the keyboard stops for a moment. "Jake? Is that you?"

"Yeah, Dad!" Jake calls out.

"What were you doing out so late?"

"Oh, um, I went over to Tank's!"

"That's great, son. Did it go well? Did you talk to Emily, too?"

Jake flushes with embarrassment. He does not want to talk about wanting to apologize to Emily and Tank when they're right here.

He hurriedly ushers Tank and Emily through the nearest open door—the bathroom. "I'm gonna distract him, you look in his office for a business card or something for Isabella's office information. It should be on his desk or all over his plans! He also has an address book planner thing—it's purple!" He shuts the door, hoping they understand.

Dad squints at him. "Are you just hanging out in the hallway?"

"Oh yeah, I was waiting for you!" Jake says brightly. "Hey, you know how you were showing me to break in the new glove you got me? I'm not sure if I'm doing it right."

Something clunks from the bathroom and Dad looks for the noise.

"Oh, do *not* go in there," Jake says, making a face.

Dad laughs. "You know we have a fan, you can turn it on if you have to drop a bomb."

"So the glove! Yeah!" Jake gestures toward his room and finds where he plopped the glove under his mattress like Dad suggested.

The door creaks slightly as it opens, but Jake coughs to cover the sound. He spots Emily and Tank tiptoeing past his room carefully toward the office.

"Oh, buddy, you can't just stick it under your bed. Rubber

bands and shaving cream, that's the trick." Dad clucks his tongue as he takes the glove.

Tank pauses to watch.

Jake gestures frantically for his friends to go, exhaling a sigh of relief as they disappear into the office and the door shuts behind them right as Dad heads for the bathroom.

He comes back with the shaving cream and waggles it at Jake. "All right, let me show you how to do this."

"Great, Dad," Jake says, watching the office door creak open again.

Emily grins and points at a card in her other hand. Tank gives him a big thumbs up as they disappear down the hallway.

Jake keeps Dad's attention on him as he asks way too many questions about why shaving cream is necessary and if any other creams can be used. Dad's laughing about whipped cream when the front door shuts, and Jake exhales in relief.

His phone chimes with a text.

Emily 7:32 P.M.
Got it! Her office opens at 8 a.m.
It doesn't look like it's on any bus routes.
I can ask my sister to drive us!

Jake taps out a quick response. "I'm gonna hang out with Emily and Tank tomorrow morning, is that cool?"

Dad smiles at him. "Yeah, of course. I'm so glad you three made up."

"Thanks, Dad," Jake says. "Your advice was the best."

Dad chuckles. "Yeah, well, you can't just give up on something that's worth fighting for," he says.

"Absolutely."

"This is really weird," Carmen says, glancing at Jake and Tank in the rearview mirror as they pull away from the parking lot.

"You're really weird," Emily says.

"What even is this address? It's, like, almost downtown."

"Part of our community service project," Emily says. "It's a surprise. For Mrs. Jenkins."

Carmen sighs. "Fine. But only because you promised me your share of your allowance for clothes this month, and I need more eyeliner."

The freeway is crowded this morning, and Jake watches the landscape speed by as the strip malls and residential neighborhoods give way to industrial buildings and warehouses. Downtown sparkles in the distance, and they pull into the wide lot of a cheerfully painted modern building with a sign that reads REYES ARCHITECTURE AND DESIGN.

"Wait right here! We'll be back!" Emily says.

"But for how long?" Carmen drawls.

"It won't be long," Jake says, patting the car door as he shuts it. He follows Tank and Emily as they enter the building. They've got a little time; according to his dad's calendar, the official teardown won't start until noon. Isabella isn't even scheduled to be there, so he hopes that she's in her office.

It's all bright sunshine streaming in through glass walls, posters of completed designs scattered everywhere, a light blue motif running along the walls. There's a front desk with a smartly dressed woman typing away behind it, and several offices labeled with names.

Jake gestures and they drop down to crouch below the eye

level of the receptionist and sneak toward the office labeled ISA-
BELLA REYES.

Emily reaches up and cracks open the door.

Isabella is sitting at her desk, poring over a set of blueprints;
she looks up, raising her eyebrow at the three of them.

"Oh, hello," she says, looking at them with some confusion.
"Jess, did I have a school tour booked here today?" she calls out in
a louder tone.

The woman from the front desk leaps up and looks at the three
of them sheepishly. "No, there's nothing on the schedule except
for the Pacific Crest construction today," Jess says. "I'll see these
three out."

"No, wait, please!" Tank says, stepping closer to Jake and
Emily.

"We're actually here about Pacific Crest," Jake says, stepping
forward. "Please don't tear down the community center."

Isabella tilts her head. "You're Jake, Nigel's son, right?" she
asks. "Did your father say something?"

Jake shakes his head. "I'm here because I think it was a good
place for kids. And it could be a good place again."

Isabella looks at him and then waves her hand at Jess. "Give
me a few minutes with these kids."

Jess gives Jake a suspicious look before ducking out of the office and closing the door.

Jake takes a deep breath.

Isabella leans forward and steeples her fingers together. "Now,
what's this about the community center? Last I heard that nonprofit hasn't been active for about eighteen years."

"You grew up in Pacific Crest, right?" Jake asks.

Isabella smiles. "Sure did. Your dad tell you that?"

Tank gently places the folder they saved of all the news articles on the desk. On the top is the photo of Isabella and her parents standing proudly in front of the community center.

Isabella picks up the photo gingerly. "Look, I appreciate you kids standing up for what you believe in. It's great. It really is. There are so many nonprofits and clubs and programs for kids to do in L.A. Wouldn't it be cool if there were restaurants and shops right outside the complex?"

Emily shakes her head. "Look, we're so close to the mall and all this other stuff. We don't need more shops and restaurants. This place has been empty—"

"Right. An eyesore. A waste of space," Isabella agrees.

Jake fans out the photos and newspaper clippings. "But it was so important to so many people," he says.

"I wouldn't have met Jake and Emily if it wasn't for the center," Tank says. "We wouldn't have gotten to know one another or become friends."

Emily nods. "What if instead of just putting something new in there, you can remake the center? Fix it up and bring it back? There would be so many possibilities, like you could hold classes or workshops, kids could hang out and play games or learn to code!"

Isabella laughs. "Look, the nonprofit my mother ran was very ambitious. She was always spending time there, organizing trips or busy at work." She shakes her head. "Why am I telling you this? It doesn't matter. She lost interest in the center at some point after I went to college." She plays with a paperweight on her desk, a haunted expression on her face. She looks like Ellen, Jake realizes; the same eyes, the same nose, and the same soft sadness.

She picks up the stack of paperwork on her desk and straightens it neatly before putting the papers away in a drawer, and then leans back to look at them. Her gaze settles on Jake's. It's not exactly the easy dismissal Jake was expecting.

He stumbles forward, trying to remember the speech he prepared. Maybe it would have been easier if Isabella had come at him with a counterargument already, one he's planned for. But she just looks tired, like she's had a long day and it's not going to be over for a long while.

"You know, it's not too late to reach out," Jake offers. "I think she misses you, too. Why else would she want so badly to talk to you every time you're at the building?"

Isabella sighs. "It's too late."

"Look, can we just have a little more time?" Emily asks, her eyes alight. "I totally get wanting to run your business the way you want to, but this center is important to us. While we were working there this summer, we found this game."

Tank nods. "It's on a server on the LAN in the community center, and we haven't solved it yet, and we're so close."

Isabella lifts her eyebrows, tapping her fingers impatiently on the desk. "I really appreciate you coming all the way down here to my office, and I certainly applaud your determination, but this project has already been approved by the city. I've worked too hard on this to let your attachment to this videogame delay hundreds of people's hard work—"

"It's not just a videogame!" Emily snaps. "Someone created this mystery, and it's all tied to the server in the community center. If you get rid of it, it'll be gone forever, and we'll never know the answer!"

"Please. It's important to us. To me. I know it's just a game, but this Minecraft server is special, and I really can't—" Jake takes a deep breath.

Emily puts her hand on his shoulder and squeezes it.

On his other side, Tank nods empathetically. "It's a good game, Miss."

Isabella pauses, looking at the three of them. "Hm. What makes this server so special?"

Tank pulls up a photo on his phone: the mermaid kingdom glimmers in the light, merfolk swimming amongst the monuments and towers.

"Haven't you ever wanted to finish a game?" Jake asks.

Isabella shrugs. "Like get to the End and defeat the ender dragon? Sure."

Tank flips to the next photo, showing the castle surrounded by lava and the precarious bridge. "So you know Minecraft already! This is something new, something exciting, and it's *still* changing."

Emily nods. "The Wizard kept adding things and making things challenging. We're almost at the end, and there's this whole underwater kingdom that's in danger. That's all we want to do: solve the mystery and help this lost city."

"The server is hosted on a LAN in the community center. If you tear it down, it'll all be gone."

Isabella stares at the images on Tank's phone and gets up, smoothing her suit jacket. "All right. I'll have a look. But just a look, and only because I happen to like Minecraft and I don't have any other meetings today. But I'm not promising anything."

CHAPTER THIRTY-NINE

EMILY

Emily's not quite sure what to make of Isabella. First of all, her outfit is super cute. Professional and powerful. She walks with a commanding presence, the kind that even Mama would appreciate and be intimidated by. She's an award-winning architect, according to the multiple seals and certificates in her office, having designed tons of beautiful buildings and complexes. She's got great taste in shoes, and Emily's sure the Patties and Nitas of her world would certainly respect her.

Jake whoops from the back seat. "We've got a shot! I can't believe it!"

"How did you know talking about the game would work?" Tank asks.

"I didn't," Emily says simply. "I just had a hunch." There were little nods in Isabella's office that made her think she'd appreciate the mystery of a game: the pixelated swords hanging on the wall, the figurines on her desk, the giant twenty-sided die paperweight.

Isabella arrives at Pacific Crest Apartments before them and is already waiting outside, clacking her heel impatiently, when Carmen pulls into the lot.

"You all have weird hobbies," Carmen says, rolling her eyes.

"Thanks." Emily laughs. "I'll see you at home."

Isabella lifts up the caution tape and strides into the fenced-off construction site like she owns the place. Which she does. But still. The presence.

Jake pulls out a chair for her and lets her sit at the center computer. Emily's come to think of it as Tank's, even as the one on the right is hers, the way it's right next to the plug where she charges her phone, and the left one is Jake's, right next to the aisle so he can keep getting up to go to the water fountain once in a while like he does. Emily isn't sure when she started thinking of the lab as theirs. Now that there's someone else in it, she feels protective of it.

Isabella sits gingerly at the computer, touching the stickers on the monitor. Emily used to wonder about those; she thought they were just left over from some kid and Ellen would junk the computer like everything else in the building. She wonders now if this used to be Isabella's computer, if those were her seashell stickers.

"So these are riddles we've solved so far," Tank says. He pulls up the folder where they've been saving the screenshots. Emily's saved other grabs there, too, and she realizes as she looks at the sheer number of images that they aren't just of the riddles and clues that they said this folder was for in the first place. There are shots of the impossibly gorgeous mountain that is shaped like a wolf, a beautiful setting sun. Tank's detailed farm. Jake's intricately decorated library and organized chests, his avatar standing proudly in front of them. Her own collection of swords. Jake's and Tank's avatars trapped on top of a tree. The zombie that got stuck in their sheep pen. The automated inventory sorter Emily built. A million little in-jokes and moments from the time they've spent here.

Emily at first feels embarrassed at how many pictures she's saved, but her images aren't the only ones. There's her avatar, too, bedecked in diamond armor, that first time she got the full set and ran around the base all excited and thrilled. Jake had laughed at her, but she had no idea he was saving this. And then there's a shot of her diving headfirst into the cave filled with spiders, Tank right behind her.

"It looks like the three of you have had a lot of fun in this game," Isabella says slowly.

"We didn't build all this," Emily says, gesturing to the images. "Look, redstone is one thing, and I'm decent at it, but *this* is advanced computer programming!"

"I think it's sweet that you kids are really attached to this game. I get it, I really do. I used to play Minecraft, too, and of course you don't want to lose your progress—"

"Did you play with your mom?" Jake asks.

"Yeah, a little. She got really busy, though, with work." Isabella sighs. "I shouldn't have come here, it was a mistake to think . . ."

She trails off, staring at the screen.

Tank has an image of the shipwreck open, and he's zooming in slowly on the side of the ship. Emily's not quite sure what he's doing with the blurry image—it's not a great shot to begin with. Jake was trying to catch the mermaids swimming around in it, and he doesn't quite have Tank's eye for framing and aesthetic.

Emily likes Tank's photos best, the way he can capture the right amount of drama and beauty in one shot. Jake tends to just shoot whatever he's looking at.

Tank stops, gesturing at the screen.

On the side of the ship are letters, barely visible in the zoomed-in frame, but there.

BELLA.

Emily hadn't even noticed it had been named in the first place.

Isabella goes still.

"How long has this server been here?" she asks after a long moment.

Jake shrugs. "I dunno. I mean, years, probably. From the amount of work that went into them, and how many versions there are. There's tons."

"Show me." Isabella takes a set of wire-rimmed glasses out of her purse and puts them on. She ties her hair back and watches as Jake brings up the multiplayer screen. "This is all just on the LAN?"

"Yeah. That's why we can't connect to it from anywhere else. And if you get rid of the community center, it will all be gone."

Isabella scans the list of the server names, her mouth pressing into a severe line. She looks back at Tank's computer, her face unreadable as she flicks through the images: the mermaids swimming around the shipwreck, the ocean monument looming amidst the depths, the stone pathway leading to the underwater kingdom, the Leviathan rising up from the ocean floor.

"Do you want to play?" Emily asks suddenly. She recognizes the look: Isabella's fingers twitching, the way she's taking in all the images.

"Yes, I do," Isabella says, her voice suddenly small. Emily can see the hints of the little girl who put seashell stickers on her computer.

Emily logs in for her. The world loads, glittering and full of promise.

CHAPTER FORTY

TANK

"I can show you where we are," Tank says. He logs in and appears right next to Emily's avatar. He looks at the three beds surrounded by torches on the bare strip of shore, where they kept coming back to every time they were defeated. The last time they were all there they had given up on the game, on ever seeing one another again.

Tank reaches out and touches Jake on the shoulder. Jake turns and gives him a reassuring smile. From the other computer, Emily makes a silly wavey gesture with her hand, and Tank chuckles: the jellyfish handshake he taught her. She remembered.

They've been through so much together, have traveled this whole world the Wizard created, solved all the riddles the Wizard gave them except this one.

"Come on," Tank says, bouncing as he dives into the water. The ocean monument is still, all its guardians defeated.

Isabella's voice shakes as she opens the door at the end of the long prismarine hallway, the kingdom glittering just a short distance away. "I don't believe this," she says, her voice trembling with awe.

"It's cool, isn't it?" Emily hums.

Tank smiles at Jake and Emily. Isabella looks mesmerized by the sight of the merfolk building their wall, the warriors swimming back and forth in anticipation.

"The Leviathan wakes up as soon as you try to cross to the kingdom," Jake says. He nods at Tank, who takes a step forward. The ground rumbles and the massive monster rises up, smashing through the wall, shooting powerful blasts of energy and taking them all out in a single blow.

They respawn back on the beach.

Emily places the storybook on the table. "We figured out that the Wizard was basing the story in the game on this," she says.

Isabella reaches for the book. Her fingers brush gently over the crayon drawings of the mermaid kingdom, the Leviathan. "I drew this," she says softly. "I can't believe she kept it."

"It was here in the community center," Jake says. "We found it in all the stuff that Ellen couldn't bear to throw away."

Isabella shakes her head. "It's too much to believe. The details . . . I thought she never paid attention to me and my stories, and all of this?" She clutches the book to her chest, her eyes brimming with tears. "She's the only one who could have created this world with my story."

"Your mother is the Wizard?" Tank's mouth falls open in shock. He thinks about all the times Ellen had come to check in on them, and it falls into place. After all, the Wizard hadn't noticed they were in the game until that time Ellen saw them in the lab.

Isabella nods. "She's a programmer. When I was a kid, she was always working, either at the community center or at her company, and she'd always promise to spend time with me, but it never happened. After my father died, she threw herself into work and I hated it. We got into this huge fight when I was a little older than you all—I left and never looked back."

She flips through the book slowly and looks back at the game. "I thought she didn't care."

"It sounds like she did," Tank says. "She just didn't know how to say so."

Isabella wipes at her eyes. "The kingdom, the mermaids, the quest to get the trident . . . it was an ongoing story that I made up. My parents and I—we used to hang out in the pool all the time, and I would act it out with my toys." She laughs. "I had this old dinosaur figure that was the Leviathan, and all my stuffed animals would hang out by the side of the pool in their kingdom. The pathway—that was the walkway that separated the shallow from the deep end." She turns and smiles at them. "I haven't thought about that game in forever."

"How does the story end?" Jake asks. "How do you find the trident to defeat the Leviathan?"

"We've tried everything: bows, swords, enchanted weapons. It's like trying to defeat the ender dragon but with every disadvantage," Emily says.

Isabella pauses on one of the pages. "I believe the trident was hidden in an underwater temple very close to the kingdom. I thought it was funny, coming up with a story where the princess spent the whole adventure going all over the world only to come back and realize that at the end of her quest, all of the riddles had brought her right back home."

"The monument! I knew we hadn't looked everywhere," Jake says.

Isabella leads the way, Emily's character diving back down toward the monument. Tank and Jake walk her through each floor, showing her the different rooms, the treasure chamber with the statue that activated the pathway. Isabella pauses, swimming into the room filled with note blocks.

"I thought this was just for ambiance," Emily says. "You know, to add to the mystery."

The room is expansive, the floor decorated with a number of note blocks that each play a musical note when stood on. They echo through the water, resonating with a deep bass.

Isabella touches a stone, a high note pinging in the air. She taps on all of them experimentally, trying out the notes. "No way," she says.

"What?"

"There's a song that I used to hum all the time, it was just this silly melody I made up," Isabella says. She presses three notes, the beginning of a familiar song—Tank realizes it's the music that's been specially programmed into this server, that same light and playful melody that has followed them throughout the game.

Isabella finishes out the song with one ringing note, and then pistons clank and clatter, revealing a hidden compartment in the prismarine wall. The golden trident is floating inside it, and Emily picks it up.

Isabella pushes back from the computer, standing up. "I can't—this is too much. Here, you go ahead."

"Are you sure?" Jake asks.

Isabella nods, folding her arms around herself. "I want to see how it ends. Go on."

Tank, Emily, and Jake follow the stone pathway out to the kingdom like they have so many times before. This time, though, he can feel the energy radiating off Isabella as she watches the scene unfold intently.

The Leviathan rises.

The merfolk scatter.

Emily raises the trident, and it shoots out a beam of golden energy right at the Leviathan.

It roars in pain, and Tank realizes with satisfaction that it's actually done a significant amount of damage.

"It's gonna blast us, it's making the face!" Jake calls out. "Evasive maneuvers, come on!"

Tank remembers the plan — he scatters to the left just as Emily dodges to the right and Jake dives into a stand of nearby coral. They barely escape the blast, and Tank's health dips, but he's still alive. He drinks an Instant Health potion, watching Emily dart to the base of the wall, readying the trident again, but the Leviathan is already preparing to send a blast at her.

It attacks what's in its line of sight, Tank remembers.

Tank fires at the Leviathan with his bow to distract the beast, and it roars and turns to him, aiming another blast just as it takes a hit from one of Jake's arrows. He and Jake alternate their strikes as Emily gets another shot in. The sluggish speed of the arrows underwater used to mean they could barely cause any damage before it destroyed them with its blasts, even with the three of them drawing its attention. But now all Jake and Tank have to do is distract it long enough for Emily to attack, and they're actually still here, still fighting even after this long.

"Throw it!" Isabella says. "That's how tridents are most effective!"

The Leviathan roars, charging right for Emily as she throws the trident. It arcs in the air, gleaming, and spears the Leviathan in the eye.

For a brief second, nothing seems to happen, but then a crack of golden light begins to form from the wound, expanding as the whole beast splinters into pieces of light. Small items rain down onto the ocean floor and as Tank swims closer he realizes they're all pieces of kelp and seaweed.

Jake takes a deep breath next to him. "Did we do it?"

A great cheer comes up from the merfolk from the wall. They gather around the three of them, their happy voices overlapping.

"I think we did," Tank says. "Let's go see the kingdom."

They swim forward past the no-longer-necessary wall into the kingdom. Sea lanterns flicker and sparkle as they wander through the graceful towers and monuments decked out in greens and golds. Celebratory music sounds out all around them, and merfolk pirouette past them in a joyous flurry.

All the tension and nervous energy they've seen every time they've glimpsed the kingdom before is gone. Now, swimming through the prismarine archways, Tank can see in detail the way the buildings are stacked one upon another, columns stretching out from the ocean floor. Banners and lanterns wave in the ocean current, wrapping around delicate towers built of colored glass. Sponges dot the landscape, and outcrops of colorful coral flourish, and, in the distance, a grand sparkling palace awaits.

Tank's never had the patience for long-term goals before, isn't even sure if he's ever completed one. Maybe now he can try, knowing he's done it before.

CHAPTER FORTY-ONE

EMILY

Emily exhales, grinning at Jake and Tank, who both still seem stunned that they've made it here. She turns around to see Isabella watching them with a soft smile on her face. "Thank you," she says. They couldn't have solved this without her—the whole last riddle was all a reference to her specific childhood, a song she used to sing.

"You've been playing this for weeks?" Isabella asks.

Emily nods.

Isabella takes a deep breath. "I'm going to go talk to my mother. Thank you for showing me this."

She smiles at the three of them and wipes carefully at her face before leaving them. The door shuts, and then they're alone in the computer lab.

"What now?" Tank asks. "We beat the game."

Jake is still mesmerized by the movement of the merfolk swimming around him, wandering through the village. "This place seems super cool. I mean, I bet each of these mermaid villagers have like, a job or role! I wonder what we could trade with them?"

"We solved the mystery, though," Emily says. "This whole time we've been wondering: Why is this game here? Who built all this stuff? And it's been Ellen, this whole time, trying to connect with her daughter."

Jake leans back on his chair, tilting precariously. "Yeah. It's pretty cool. I think that's pretty amazing."

"What do you think is going to happen to the community center?" Tank asks.

"I think that's up to Isabella," Emily says. "But whatever happens, it's going to be okay. You know, we can always start a new world."

Jake brightens. "Oh yeah!" He falters, tapping his fingers nervously on the keyboard. "Would you—would you still want to play with me?"

Tank nods. "Of course." He looks at Emily, as if he's still unsure.

"I said a lot of things," Emily says. "I didn't mean it, that we weren't real friends. I was just scared of losing my old friends."

"Do you feel like you can be yourself around them?" Tank asks. "I realized, like, Shark and those guys, they'd always laugh at me for the kind of stuff I like."

"I hope you know I just like spending time with you," Jake says. "We could be cleaning and joking around and it's still a good time."

"Me too," Emily says. "I feel like I don't have to pretend to like anything I don't like. I can just like the stuff I like." She elbows

Tank playfully. "Like just building pretty things. There's nothing wrong with that."

Tank brightens up, his face breaking into a smile that completely transforms him. Emily feels protective of this boy twice her size; he's got such a good heart and he cares so deeply, but people struggle to look past his size. "Thanks. This has been the best, you know. I'm kinda glad I was stuck here cleaning with you guys."

Jake laughs. "Well, now that we've finished this, we can just hang out! Play Minecraft, go get tacos, anything!" He reaches out for a high five.

Emily slaps his open palm, shaking her head. She used to think Jake's earnestness was annoying, that he was naïve, but she appreciates his positive attitude, the way he can get so excited about anything. It makes her excited about things, too.

"Do you guys like action movies?" Tank asks. "Or like" — he frowns, like he's trying to remember the word — "go-karts? At Fortress Park?"

Emily laughs. "That sounds fun. You know when school starts, if you want, we can eat lunch together sometimes."

"I'd like that," Tank says.

Emily disconnects and turns off her computer. One by one, the machines power down, and the three of them exit into the empty lobby. She knows whatever comes next for this place, it won't matter. The magical thing that happened here, how they were able to connect and become friends, that's beyond a building now. She loops her arms with Jake's and Tank's, walking side by side with them into the courtyard.

Outside, Isabella is pacing back and forth in front of the apartment next door to the community center. She sees the three of them and pauses.

Emily gives her a thumbs up.

Isabella smiles, fixes her hair one more time, and knocks on the door.

She hesitates, looking down at her feet, tapping her heel nervously, and then the door opens.

Emily feels like she'd tried on half of her closet before she found the right outfit to face Pattie. She isn't sure what she expects from this meeting, but she wants to feel strong and capable and ready, like putting on armor.

She's still not sure how she feels about Pattie knowing where she lives, and she doesn't know what to do about the fact that the sight of Pattie still makes her smile, that she still remembers all the good times hanging out, how Pattie always knows which ice cream she likes and always sends her cool new videos on photography techniques or sends her photos she might like.

Pattie smiles at her from outside the side entrance as Emily unlatches the gate and lets her in. Mrs. Anderson is parked across the street and waves at them both, watching Pattie slip inside.

Emily wonders if Pattie asked her mom to wait because this would only take a minute, if she knew what was coming. Emily was pretty vague in her text, just a simple *Do you want to hang out?*

"Sorry for all the mess, it's been a construction zone here forever," Emily says. "They're taking their time on the renovation plans for this front building."

"Oh, no worries," Pattie says breezily. She pauses to study the projected model of the new complex and the simple printed sign that reads REDESIGN COMING SOON.

"Come on, this way." Emily leads Pattie down the alleyway into the center of the complex.

Pattie prances into the courtyard after her, the skirt of her dress fluttering prettily as she sweeps in.

Today Pattie is wearing a sleeveless floral-print sundress with boots, set off with chunky jewelry. At a glance Emily knows that the dress was from last summer, the attempt to update the look with the necklace doesn't quite work, and the boots are definitely an autumn look and overcomplicate the silhouette. Emily would have suggested strappy sandals and a simpler necklace. The overall affect is a bit rushed, and Pattie's lipgloss is smudged. She also looks kind of cold, shivering in the early evening air.

Maybe a few months ago Emily would have deliberated over and over in her head the perfect way to compliment Pattie while at the same time pointing out the flaws in her look, playing into the endless back-and-forth for approval that she'd worried was the core of their relationship. Because in Emily's mind, that doubt, that insecurity, those little games of power and dominance they played were always simmering in the background.

And she's tired. She's tired of wondering if her friends like her for who she is, and she's ready to talk about it. No matter what happens, even if she loses her spot in Pattie's inner circle.

Emily turns around, wondering if she should just dive in and explain and get it over with, and is pulled into a close hug.

Pattie giggles, drawing her close. "It's so good to see you! I'm so glad you had time to hang out today! I've missed you!"

Pattie grasps both of her hands and jumps up and down, and her excitement is infectious, and Emily lets out a laugh.

"I've missed you, too," Emily says. "Hey, I'm sorry about last time. I was being weird about, like, you finding out where I lived. I didn't mean to hide it from you. I was just embarrassed." Emily kicks her heel awkwardly against the tile, looking very carefully past Pattie and not meeting her eyes.

Pattie raises one manicured eyebrow and pulls back a little to place her hands steadily on Emily's shoulders. "You think I care where you live? Seriously?"

Emily had been playing a game for so long that Pattie's abrupt statement takes her by surprise. Emily used to replay every interaction, think about every move, every comment, every single possible hidden meaning. But now, thinking about it, Emily wonders if she did that because she thought she had to, and if there was ever any hidden meaning at all. Maybe Pattie just says what she thinks, and she's been Emily's friend all along.

Emily blinks.

"Really?" She's has been avoiding this moment for so long—Pattie at her apartment complex, her real apartment complex, in all its glory, faded paint and ripped chain-link fence. It feels oddly anticlimactic, talking about it for the first time. Pattie's just looking at her and shrugging it off like it's nothing.

"I care more about the fact that you thought you had to walk somewhere else! Come on, you could ruin your shoes. Seriously, it's way easier to pick you up from here." Pattie huffs. "So. There's a double feature at the Annex. Nita can't drink a Slurpee without getting brain freeze, and there's no way I can finish one on my own. I wasn't sure what you wanted to do, if you wanted just me-and-you time, which we can do here or we could go out to a movie, whatever. Just let me know, and my mom can either drive us, or I can tell her to go home."

"I—" Emily doesn't know what to say; she's completely bewildered. She'd been prepared to have to explain even more about why, that Pattie would say they couldn't be friends anymore, but there's only this, an awkward sidestep around the whole issue. And . . . an invitation? Pattie still wants to hang out with her?

Pattie smiles at her and maybe for the first time Emily isn't looking for the thorn under the rose, for a hidden meaning or backhanded compliment. It's a real smile, stretching from ear to ear. Pattie doesn't want to prove anything. She's just really happy to be here.

"The movie starts at four. If we leave now we have time to get ice cream at that place you like."

"Hey, um—"

Pattie pauses, looking back at her.

"Look, when we hang out—I used to freak out, all the time. Worry if I was good enough, you know? And it's fun helping you with your channel and stuff, but I don't really care about having my own."

Pattie gives her a long look that could possibly stretch to infinity. Emily can feel her palms start to sweat, and she feels suddenly nervous, starting to babble. "It's not that I don't like the haul videos and putting together cute outfits and stuff like that for you—I just—I don't like it as much as you do. I'd rather just hang out and, like, go explore and go to the mall and stuff with you. I like finding cute stuff but it's not, like, the same for me as it is for you. I actually don't care about being a YouTuber at all, really."

The admission hangs in the air, and for a moment Emily thinks it's all over, that Pattie will scoff and tell her they can't be friends anymore, that they never were friends, really. She takes a deep breath and tells herself it's okay, that she's done all she could, and saying this—spending her time the way she wants to—is more important than what Pattie thinks of her.

"Oh! That's great. Glad you figured that out. You know I went through three different versions of my channel before I figured out what I wanted to focus on?"

Emily shakes her head, relief flooding through her.

"Was that it? You were afraid of hanging out with me because you don't like something I like?"

It feels silly now that she says it aloud, but Emily nods.

"Friends don't have to like all the same things, you know. And come on, I don't care about any of the Final Fortress movies, but Nita loves them. And it's been weird without you, you know?"

Emily throws her arm around Pattie's shoulder and lets herself relax. It's as if a huge weight has been lifted off her. She thought she had to choose—that she could only be that girl who was friends with Pattie and Nita and liked finding cute dresses and makeup and loved putting together cute outfits, or the girl who liked to charge headfirst into danger in Minecraft and find all the hidden pieces of treasure.

"All right, let's go."

"So what have you been doing aside from your community service stuff? Bet you've been bored out of your mind without us."

"Yeah, yeah. I've actually been playing a lot of Minecraft."

"Oh, that game with the blocks?"

"It's really fun, you can build things, or go on adventures . . . Wanna try it sometime?"

Pattie smiles. "Sure. As long as you won't laugh if I'm bad at it."

"Aw, never. And it's not like there's a point system or anything. It's not a competition at all. I've actually been playing with some new friends—Jake and Tank. They're really cool. If you want to ever hang out with everyone. It could be fun."

"Sounds good." Pattie grins, leading the way. "Let's go, my mom is waiting! Do you wanna call Nita?"

Emily grins as she follows her friend out to a new adventure. She thought she could only have one kind of friend. Turns out, she's got plenty of space for all of them.

CHAPTER FORTY-TWO

JAKE

Jake groans as he picks up the ball from the ground and tosses it back to his dad. "Come on, what are you aiming at, my feet?"

"You have to be flexible!" Dad laughs. "You never know where a ball's going to be, all you can do is prepare for it."

The next toss is a high arch that Jake has to back up to catch, and he tumbles back, back, back through a bunch of shrubberies and grabs the ball just before it sails through a window.

"Nice catch," Ellen says from behind the open screen, taking a sip of tea from inside her apartment.

"Thanks," Jake says. "Oh, Dad wanted to know if you wanted to join us for dinner?"

"I'd love to. Isabella is also coming over. Can she come, too?"

she asks. She slowly approaches the door, opening it and stepping outside, watching the sun setting over the distant city.

"The more the merrier! I'm going to go get started," Dad says, ruffling Jake's hair. "I'll see you two later!"

"How are you doing?" Jake asks. It's been a week since they solved the last puzzle in the game. He hasn't seen any construction work start on the site, and Dad hasn't said anything about it, either.

"Good," Ellen says, holding her tea gingerly. She smiles at Jake, her eyes dancing and full of life. "You know, when you kids first found the server, I hadn't thought about the world I created in so long. I was rather upset, just like when you all found those photos. I hadn't wanted to think about my life, my failures."

Jake tosses the ball a little into the air and catches it. "You did attack us and steal all our stuff," he says, teasing.

"I gave it back," Ellen says, chuckling a bit. "I realized you three were serious about playing. Of course, the whole world was meant for Bella, but she never even knew about it. We hadn't spoken for years, not since the fight we had when she left for college. She already wanted nothing to do with me by then."

"You were busy with the community center?"

"That was always Christopher's forte. He loved it, and then his cancer was rough on all of us. But I helped out a lot, and the three of us—we had so much fun." She sighs. "And then I had to keep working, keep everything afloat, and . . . I lost perspective."

Jake reaches out to touch Ellen tentatively on the shoulder. He'd spent so much time thinking she was mean when she was sad and lonely the whole time, missing her daughter. "I know it's hard. My Dad couldn't . . . we never talked about it, either."

"You two look pretty happy now," Ellen remarks.

Jake shrugs. "We're working on it. He used to work all the time, too, and he still does, but we're both talking about it."

"That's all any of us can do," Ellen says. "Thank you, for showing her the game. I don't know if I ever would have had the courage. I know I just gave up there. But seeing the three of you play, how much fun you had solving the riddles, seeing what you'd built together, reminds me of why I made it in the first place."

Jake throws himself forward into a hug, wrapping his arms around her. "Thank you," he says, muffled into her bathrobe.

Ellen stiffens like she's surprised, and then pats him gently on the back, accepting it. "You're welcome," she says. "I'm glad you found the server and enjoyed the game. Makes me feel young again." She laughs, wiping at her eyes. "Thank you for the adventure."

Jake smiles at her before he makes his way back home. He passes by Tank and Viv in the courtyard and waves to them.

"Science experiment," Tank explains. "Go ahead, drop it in."

Viv pours white powder from a measuring cup into a bottle filled with clear liquid on the ground, squeals and runs away just as it bubbles up and over Jake's shoes. He skips backward, shaking his feet.

"Sorry, man. It's just vinegar and baking soda, should come out easy. Your shoes okay?"

"Oh, yeah," Jake says, and then does a double take. Tank is wearing brand-new stylish sneakers. "Great shoes!"

Tank grins. "Thanks. My dad got these for me as a back-to-school gift." He glances at Viv, who is taking pictures of the now inert bottle and the aftermath. "Hey, we still on for tomorrow?"

"Yeah, for sure! Hey, have you ever built a beacon before? Emily really wants to have one in our new base."

"Never. But I'm excited to try," Tank says. "I'll see you tomorrow."

"I'll see you tomorrow!" Jake calls out.

The apartment is filled with the scent of freshly baked bread and in the living room is something new, covered in plastic. "Oh, check it out! It was delivered earlier. I wanted to wait until you were home to unwrap it."

Jake approaches the bulky object and grabs the sheet of plastic. Dad takes the other side and together they reveal a soft-looking couch, with big fluffy pillows. It looks quirky, with a weird, offbeat stripe pattern of blues and greens that reminds Jake of running water.

"I went with the color you said looked good," Dad says. "What do you think?"

"Looks great!"

Dad flops down onto the couch and says, "You nervous about school starting next week?"

Jake shakes his head and smiles. "Not at all." He settles onto the couch next to Dad, thinking of all the adventures waiting for him and his friends.

"Everything feels just right," Jake says.

It feels like home.

ACKNOWLEDGMENTS

This story could not exist without so many incredible people, and I'm thankful to everyone who has been a part of my universe, whether in this particular world or the next.

I'd like to thank my incredible agent, Thao Le. Thank you for believing in all the possibilities, for helping me grow as a writer and a person. Every day I am so lucky to be on this adventure with you, and I can't wait for the stories to come.

To Sarah Peed, for seeing the story that could come from the seed of an idea. Without you it could not grow into the flourishing tree I'm proud of. Thank you for your steadfast wisdom and support and being the best editor and fellow adventurer on this journey.

Thank you to Mojang for creating a world so many people have gotten to be endlessly creative in and build not only dreams but connections, and for letting me be a part of it.

To the Tomodachi Cuties and the Pleading Mantou crew, thank you for the late-night voicechat camaderie, to giant sheep and parkour and talking circles, to endless adventures and builds, adei0s, BlerpityBlorp, ZhangMayi, artze, _vagues, missemperor, feyuca, kyuoko-tan, you all are the best. To Michael, for your patience and sense of humor, the quests, and the worldbuilding, thank you for the initiative to create. To Daniel, for combing the ends of the earth for coral to help me decorate my underwater pavilion and general terra-cotta shenanigans and laughter and support. To Katie, for the bees and joy and to hatching (and protecting!) turtles together under constant attack. To Mason, for your constant kindness and patience and occasional dry snark and construction inspiration. To Kevin, for the farms and all the UWU times. To Jeremy, for being the first to survive a first night in Minecraft with me, thank you for being my friend from the very beginning. I would go to the End and back with all of you, thank you.

To the wonderful team at Interlude Press—Annie, Candy, and Choi—for believing in me and taking a chance on my selkie story once upon a time. I would not be the writer I am today without you.

My dear friends, Lisa and TingTing, thank you for the joy and support, the companionship, the spontaneous adventures in hotpot nights and crab carnage and desert night stargazing, I couldn't ask for a better TLC household. To Michelle, Katrina, and Kate, thank you for being there for the good times and the rough times, for the memes and the jokes and the cry sessions. My writing partners and friends, Amy, Nilah, Jayden, Jackie, and Nina, may we one day meet in a coffeeshop and write together again. To Keely, Cass, Angela, Jessie, and Sylvia—thank you for being there and making the time go by with joy and laughter.

Thank you to all the irreplaceable and wonderful folks in the Procrastination Zone, the Yellow Gardens, and Inkwell, to the endless group chats and channels and gifsets and joy. Thank you for all your love and support, to my friends, named and unnamed, thank you for being there for me, for sharing your time and energy.

And finally, and perhaps most importantly—I'd like to thank you, the reader, for being here and taking a part in this adventure.

ABOUT THE AUTHOR

C. B. LEE is an author of young adult science fiction and fantasy and a Lambda Literary fellow. Her works include the critically acclaimed Sidekick Squad series (Duet Books), and *Ben 10* graphic novels (Boom! Studios). Lee's work has been nominated for a Lambda Literary Award and also featured on NPR, and in *Teen Vogue*, *Wired*, *Hypable*, Tor's Best of Fantasy and Sci Fi, and the American Library Association's Rainbow List.

cb-lee.com
Twitter: @cblee_cblee
Instagram: @cblee_cblee

ABOUT THE TYPE

This book was set in Electra, a typeface designed for Linotype by renowned type designer W. A. Dwiggins (1880–1956). Electra is a fluid typeface, avoiding the contrasts of thick and thin strokes that are prevalent in most modern typefaces.

JOURNEY INTO THE WORLD OF
MINECRAFT™

For younger readers:

Learn about the latest Minecraft books at **ReadMinecraft.com**